*Three men have one passionate
mission—to be a...*

Hero in Her Bed

Three exciting and pulse-racing romances from
three top Mills & Boon authors!

Hero in Her Bed

CATHERINE MANN

AMY J FETZER

LYN STONE

MILLS & BOON

First published in Great Britain 2010
Harlequin Mills & Boon Limited,
Eton House, 18-24 Paradise Road, Richmond, Surrey TW9 1SR

HERO IN HER BED © by Harlequin Enterprises II B.V./S.à.r.l 2010

Joint Forces, Out of Uniform and *Down to the Wire* were first published in Great Britain by Harlequin Mills & Boon Limited in separate, single volumes.

Joint Forces © Catherine Mann 2004
Out of Uniform © Amy J Fetzer 2005
Down to the Wire © Lyn Stone 2004

ISBN: 978 0 263 88051 9

05-1210

Printed and bound in Spain
by Litografia Rosés S.A., Barcelona

JOINT FORCES

BY
CATHERINE MANN

Catherine Mann began her career writing romance at twelve and recently uncovered that first effort while cleaning out her grandmother's garage. After working for a small-town newspaper, teaching at the university level and serving as a theatre school director, she has returned to her original dream of writing romance. Now an award-winning author, Catherine is especially pleased to add a nomination for the prestigious Maggie Award to her contest credits. Following her air force aviator husband around the United States with four children and a beagle in tow gives Catherine a wealth of experiences from which to draw her plots. Catherine invites you to learn more about her work by visiting her website: http://catherinemann.com

Prologue

"We've been hit!"

The aircraft commander's words popped like bullets through Senior Master Sergeant J. T. "Tag" Price's headset. Ricocheted around in his brain. Settled with molten-lead heat as J.T. sat in his solitary loadmaster perch beneath the cockpit in the cargo plane.

Not that he even needed the aircraft commander's announcement. The teeth-jarring thump still shuddered through the C-17. Yet up to that last second, he hadn't given up hope of a minor malfunction.

Minor? The wash of warning lights blazing across his control panel told him otherwise. "Details," he quizzed, quick. Brief. Never one to waste words even on a good day.

This sure as hell wasn't a good day.

Aerodynamics went to crap. The craft already rattled, strained.

"Missile hit," the aircraft commander, Captain Carson "Scorch" Hunt, answered from the cockpit above. "Probably a man-portable, fired from a boat, I think."

The plane bucked. Shuddered. His checklist vibrated off the console. "Are we gonna have to put down somewhere bad or can we make it to Europe?"

"We're not going to make it to Europe."

Silence echoed for two seconds, cut only by the rumble of engines taking on a progressive tenor of pain.

Crap.

J.T. pivoted toward the cavernous cargo hold containing a pallet full of top-secret surveillance equipment. The technology could not fall into another government's hands. Beyond that, the stored intelligence from monitoring terrorist cell-phone traffic would give away field agent identities. "Plan of action?"

"We'll have to circle back and haul ass toward the coast to land in Rubistan."

Definitely bad. But not as bad as it could be. Relations with the country were strained, yet not outright hostile. Still, the equipment on that pallet made for a serious time bomb if they didn't offload it before reaching land. "How much longer 'til feet dry?"

"Ten minutes until we make the coastline."

Tight, but workable. Scooping his small black binder off the floor, he flipped through to the destruction checklists. "All right, then. Stretch it if you can while I destroy as much of this crap back here as possible before ditching it in the ocean."

Then pray like hell they didn't end up ditching the plane, too.

"Make it quick, Tag. I can buy you one, maybe two extra minutes over the water, but hydraulics and electrical are going all to hell."

"Roger, Scorch." J.T. unstrapped from his seat. "Beginning destruction checklists. Get the back ramp open."

He pivoted toward the man strapped into a seat two steps away. Spike—Max Keagan—also an OSI agent undercover as a second loadmaster on the flight, another potential land mine if the Rubistanians discovered the man's real job. "Stay out of the way 'til I'm through, then get ready to start pushing."

Spike flashed him a thumbs-up while keeping clear, laser-sharp eyes processing from his agent's perspective. He raked his hand over his head, normally spiked hair now in a buzz cut for his undercover military role.

Feet steady on the swaying deck thanks to twenty-four years in the Air Force and five thousand flying hours, J.T. charged toward the pallet. He flipped red guard switches, started hard drives erasing data about terrorists financing operations by trafficking opium out of Rubistan. And somewhere on their own base in Charleston was a leak. Thus the involvement of the Air Force's Office of Special Investigation.

As he destroyed data, J.T. tried not to think about all the government time and money wasted on the trafficking investigation. He hooked his fingers in the metal rings, pulled while also pushing a small plunger. Foam filled the motherboards, seeping out.

The load ramp yawned open. Wind and light swept the metal tunnel. The coughing drone of wounded engines swelled.

Now to finish the last of the destruction the old-fashioned way. He yanked the crash ax off the wall. Hefted back. Swung.

Hack.

What a helluva way to miss an appointment with his wife at the divorce attorney's office. *Sorry I can't make it, babe, but I'm a guest of a foreign government right now.*

Or worse.

He jerked the ax free of the cracked metal, swung again. God, he'd worried more times than he could count about leaving Rena a war widow, knew she had prepared herself for it, as well. But how the hell did anyone prep for a peacetime front-door visit from the commander, nurse and chaplain?

He'd already caused her enough grief over the years, and now to end it this way. Damn it. She deserved better.

But then she'd always deserved better than him.

J.T. hefted, arced the ax over, repeated, again, endlessly. Sweat sheeted down him, plastered his flight suit to his back. Air roared and swirled through the open hatch. Still, perspiration stung his pores, his eyes.

The aircraft's tail end swayed more by the second. His muscles flexed, released, burned until the surveillance computer equipment lay scattered, split into a pile of metal and wires.

"Destruction checklist complete," he reported, then nodded to Spike. "You ready?"

"Roger." The undercover agent charged forward to push, no help forthcoming from the screwed electrical system.

They tucked side by side behind the pallet. Air and ocean waited to swallow the equipment.

J.T. shoved, grunted. Rammed harder. Toward the gaping open hatch yawning out over the gulf. Boots planted. Muscles knotted, strained, until…

The pallet gave way, hooked, caught, lumbered down the tracks lining the belly of the plane, rattling, rolling, tipping.

Gone.

Swiping a sleeve over his forehead, J.T. backed from the closing ramp, avoiding the friction-hot rollers along the tracks. "Quickest you'll ever throw away a billion dollars. Now get your ass strapped in upstairs."

"Roger that." Spike clapped him on the back on his way toward the front.

J.T. jogged past his loadmaster perch, up the steep stairwell to the cockpit. For a crash landing, the higher up, the better. Two seats waited behind the pilot and copilot. J.T. darted right, Spike left, and buckled into the five-point harness.

The clear windscreen displayed coastline and desert meeting, sunrise cresting. He plugged in his headset again, reconnecting to the voices of the two men in front of him. Their hands flew over the throttle, stick, instrument panel as they battled the hulking craft.

Scorch, their aircraft commander, filled the left seat, a fairheaded guy who looked more like some mythological Greek god from the book in J.T.'s flight-suit pocket, a book he'd packed in anticipation of the quiet time out over the Atlantic. Hell. Scorch would need to tap into some godlike powers to get them out of this one.

Bo, the copilot, sat directly in front of J.T. The dark-haired kid must be all of maybe twenty-five or -six. Not much older than his two kids, for God's sake. Nikki was just finishing up her junior year at UNC. Chris was still in high school.

Regret seared. Damn but he wanted to see his daughter graduate, the first member of his family to get a college education. Of course, he'd attended Rena's graduation a couple of years ago, been proud as hell of her honors grades and quick landing of a job as a civilian counselor employed by the Charleston Air Force Base hospital.

But educational successes were expected for her since all her siblings had already sported a few diplomas triple matted on the wall when he'd met her. Hers had been delayed because of marrying him so young.

His head thunked back against the seat. Images of Rena scrolled through his mind on high speed as if to jam forty years more living into the next four minutes in case he never saw her again.

Never made love to her again.

Hell, right now he'd even settle for fighting with her, something they did as well and frequently as making love, which was mighty damn often. *I'm sorry, Rena.* For so many things.

Scorch thumbed the interphone button. ''We're not going to make it to an airstrip. We'll have to put her down in the desert. Strap in tight. This one's going to smack so hard your children will be born dizzy.''

J.T. braced his boots. And if they survived the landing? The Rubistanian government would detain them. Question them. It wouldn't be pleasant by a long shot, but they would make it home.

As long as the tribal warlords didn't get them first.

Chapter 1

May: North Charleston, S.C.

The doorbell echoed through the house.

Rena Price resisted the urge to duck and run upstairs to keep from answering. Instead, she kept her feet planted to the floor for a steadying second while she tipped the watering can into a potted begonia by the sofa.

Yeah, that sure would make a dignified image, a forty-year-old woman cowering under her bedroom quilt. And all because she was scared spitless she wouldn't be able to resist jumping the man standing on the other side of her oak door. But then her emotions had never been easy to contain. Especially around J.T.

Water gushed Niagara Falls style over the sides of the porcelain pot.

''Damn it.'' Rena dropped the watering can and scooped up a burgundy throw pillow from the sofa to blot the water off the floor. She'd just wash the pillow later.

Sheesh. She wasn't the same eighteen-year-old at an air show all gaga-eyed and drooling over a hot airman in his flight suit. She was a mature woman.

The bell pealed again.

A mature woman who needed to answer her door so her soon-to-be ex-husband could start his weekend visitation with their teenage son.

She Frisbee-tossed the soggy pillow across the room and out of sight into the hall. Flipped her long hair over her shoulder. Whew. Composed? Ha. Not inside. But enough to pass muster outwardly for at least five minutes.

Rena tucked around and past the ficus tree beside the overstuffed armchair. "Hold on. I'm coming. Just, uh—" her eyes fell on the telephone "—finishing up a call."

Liar. Liar. Her heels chanted with each click along hardwood floors, then muffled on a braid rug as she made her way toward the broad-shouldered shadow darkening the stained-glass inset.

Regret pinched, not for the first time. How sad that she'd come to a point in her life where her husband had to ring the bell at his own house. He deserved so much better than this.

Better from her.

They'd sure as hell tried for years until she'd booted him out six months ago. Taken him back once he returned from Rubistan and whatever horrors he'd endured after being captured. Only to have him walk out on her a few days later.

She slowed in front of the door, pressed her hand to the glass magnolia pattern, her cluster of silver bracelets jingling and settling up toward her elbow. He wouldn't think anything of the gesture if he saw her on the other side since she was unbolting the lock with her free hand. But she let her fingers linger on the colored window for a second longer over the place where his body shadowed the pane.

After twenty-two years of sleeping with this man, her body instinctively hungered for the comfort and pleasure she could find in his arms. Her mind, however, reminded her of the heartache.

Her hand fell away from the glass.

She opened the door. "Hi, J.T."

Whew. She got that much out without stuttering or panting over his hard-muscled body in a flight suit. Still, she couldn't stop herself from soaking up the image of him to reassure herself that yes, he had survived the ordeal overseas. New threads of silver flecked his dark hair beneath his hat, adding to his appeal, shouting maturity. Experience.

Stress.

"Hello, Rena," rumbled her husband of few words.

She sidled outside with the company of passing cars, safer than inside alone, and commandeered a spot by a potted topiary reaching shoulder high. "Chris should be home any minute now. His shift ended an hour ago and he knows he has an algebra test tomorrow. He's looking forward to your weekend together."

"Me, too. We'll be camping, but I'll have my cell phone on me if you need to call."

Camping. A shared sleeping bag with J.T. under the stars while their children snoozed inside the tiny tent. So many memories she'd made with this man.

"Great. Just make sure he packs extra bug spray. West Nile virus and all that, you know." Closing the door and hopefully sealing away at least a few more of those tempting memories made in a bed upstairs, she couldn't stop babbling about everything her son should pack. At least she wasn't throwing herself at J.T. as she'd done the last time they'd been alone together.

How flipping unfair that he should look better at forty-two than at twenty. And he'd looked mighty fine at twenty with those brooding eyes focused intently on her while she gobbled up the vision of shoulders stretching his uniform to the limit. Fine enough back then to entice her out of her clothes and virginity in less than two months.

Of course, when he'd returned from Rubistan, it had taken him less than two *minutes* to talk her out of her clothes.

Rubistan. Her heart clenched tight.

J.T. was alive, she reminded herself. Much more than that she didn't know because this man wouldn't talk to her. He never talked to her. Never had, not about anything that mattered, just let her keep babbling on to fill the silences in their marriage.

And just that fast, her words dried up.

J.T. blinked slowly, gray eyes as shuttered as ever. "I didn't expect to see you here. Your car's not out front."

Good or bad? Did he want to see her? After so many years together she still couldn't read him except in bed. There, she knew his every want, desire. And God, was he ever a man of endless desire.

She shivered in spite of the ninety-five-degree spring day. Rena wrapped her arms around herself and strode past him.

"I left work early and had a friend drive me over to pick up Chris's car from the garage." She stopped at the porch railing, reached to the hanging fern to snap off a dead frond. Her marriage might have withered, but at least she knew how to keep her plants alive. A skill she'd developed in their early days together, an attempt to fill an empty apartment.

"A friend?"

Her fingers stopped midsnap. Jealousy? From J.T.? No way. Even considering it started a slow spiral of hope that would lead nowhere. Besides, she wouldn't play those kinds of games.

Shifting to face him, she crumpled dead leaves in her fist. "Julia Dawson took me. Then we had a late lunch."

Rena searched for relief in his eyes even as she told herself it shouldn't matter. She waited. Wanted... What? She didn't know anymore around this man. Although being able to hold on to her pride would make a nice start.

Heavy boots thundered across the planked porch until he stood beside her.

She swallowed.

He hooked a boot on the low rung. "The new paint job on Chris's car looks nice, don't you think?"

Paint job? So much for jealousy. Argh! Couldn't the man even acknowledge a normal emotion and throw her a bone here?

She wanted to scream. Stomp her foot. Even smack him. But that was one line neither of them had ever crossed, no matter how heated their arguments became and how many plates she pitched. Never once had their fights turned physical.

Well, except for the very physical release of sex that inevitably followed.

O-kay. No arguing today. Paint talk sounded good after all.

The story of their marriage, talking about things that didn't matter when so many more important things loomed. Divorce papers to sign. Children to bring up in a split home.

Whatever hell he'd endured during his nine-day detainment in Rubistan.

The capture had left bruises on his body, broken bones on another crew member. Heaven only knew what bruises and breaks on J.T.'s soul accompanied those new strands of gray. Part of her longed to hold his big solid body, while another part of her raged over him shutting her out—again.

He gestured toward the blue Cavalier. "The body shop did well sanding down the rust spot. Can't even see it. Just keep on Chris not to park so near the beach at work."

"He's doing well with his job at the restaurant. He's picking up some waiter duties as well as his regular busboy job. Better tips." She pivoted, rested back against the railing, late-afternoon breeze sweeping her hair over her shoulders. "And his grades are holding steady. He's keeping it together in spite of everything that's going on with us."

"He's a great kid."

Side by side, they looked into each other's eyes. Memories leapfrogged back and forth between them as tangibly as her loose dark curls floating on the breeze. Memories of Chris's birth. J.T.'s pride in his son. J.T.'s stoic features softened by a smile when he'd held their daughter, their firstborn.

And in that special moment twenty-one years ago with his daughter, Rena had thought maybe, just maybe everything would work out after all. Even if he'd married a woman he didn't love—a spoiled rich teenager who didn't know how to cook and clean, much less balance a checkbook or clip coupons.

She brushed the windblown hair from her face, tossing the long strands back over her shoulder, J.T.'s eyes watching her every move. Lingering on her hair.

More memories filled the air between them while countless cars cruised past. Images of her hair draped over his bare chest, of J.T. twining a long curl around his finger, tugging her closer. Closer still.

She swayed. "We did a good job with Chris. And Nikki, too. We got that much right, didn't we?"

So much for keeping things light.

Magnolia-scented gusts whispered around them while the hammock squeaked a taunting song from behind J.T. She thought for a minute he might dodge answering a question that delved into deeper waters. She wasn't sure why she even bothered pushing him anymore, pushing herself as well, because deep waters were dangerous for them, both with so many secrets unshared.

"Yeah, Rena. We did." His broad hand fell to rest beside hers on the white railing, not touching. But still she remembered well the pleasure of his calluses rasping against her bare skin.

She knew better now than to ask him what went wrong. If she did, he would sigh, dig in his boot heels to weather the storm while she did all the talking. Or yelling. She didn't like what she was becoming around him.

And she didn't want him to step away yet.

Oh God, she was so weak around this man when simply exchanging body heat across air turned her on. Rena backed toward the steps. "I really need to go. Chris has my car. I was hoping he'd come home sooner so we could trade, but I'm supposed to be at the base hospital in a half hour to head the support group meeting." Babbling again, damn it. "I'll just take Chris's car."

Then she wouldn't have to go inside with J.T. where no doubt they would end up naked on the floor in under two *seconds*. Maybe she needed to learn to be away from the house when J.T. picked up their son for weekend visits. Every meeting put her heart, her sanity, at risk.

"Rena?" He stopped her with a hand on her upper arm just below the sleeve of her peasant blouse. Skin to skin. Her bracelets tinkled in time with wind chimes to ride the magnolia-scented air in a sensuous serenade of more want, and God yes, she could see the desire smoking through his gray eyes, as well.

It wasn't enough. Not anymore.

Had he ever loved her? Somehow she thought maybe she could handle his leaving better if, for at least part of their time together, he'd loved her. If she'd been more to him than the woman he felt honor-bound to marry because the condom broke.

Yes, J.T. was all about honor, which made him even more admirable in her eyes after her father's "imports" business dealings. A cover for laundering Mob money, not that the feds could ever nail him.

J.T. was a man of honor to trust, and trust had been rare for her growing up.

"Rena?" he said again, his grip tightening.

"Oh, uh…" She startled and stared up at him, a long look even in her heels. "What did you say?"

"Is it okay with you if I wait inside? The temp's cranking up out here."

Just as when he'd rung the bell to the home he'd helped restore, this request to enter their house tore at her. They would need to talk soon, but now wasn't the time, when their son could walk in at any minute.

And not when she was seconds away from losing it. "Of course. Make yourself at—" *Home.* She swallowed down the word like lemonade without sugar.

A flicker of anger snapped in his eyes, a rare display of emotion from J.T., therefore even more potent. Well, damn him, he could get mad all he wanted. At least he would be talking.

The storm clouds in his eyes dispersed, distance reestablished. "Thanks."

"There's tea in the fridge." She inched away. From him. From herself, too, for that matter. From wanting him, hating him, even loving him still a little, which made her resent him all the more. "I need to head back to base. I'll pick up Chris on Sunday."

"I'll bring him back by tomorrow to swap cars."

"Thank you." No arguing. They would be civil about their offspring.

Nodding, J.T. turned away, twisted the doorknob, left her.

Her shoulders sagged with her sigh. Rena blinked back tears blurring the setting sun and J.T.'s broad shoulders. She'd already cried countless tears over this man—many of them bathing his bruised body after his return from Rubistan. Yet still he'd rejected her offer of reconciliation. Zipping up his flight suit on the way out of their bed and her life, he'd made his position clear.

They really were over.

She'd spent three months trying to get through to him, to make him talk about something more meaningful than painting a car, if not for a reconciliation, at least to assure herself he was okay. Now, life had left her no choice but to move ahead and make plans for her children.

No question, they would have to talk soon, when Chris wasn't due home and her eyes weren't threatening to overflow. And when the time came for that talk, she would be stronger than the teenage version of herself.

Head held high, she sprinted down the steps on legs more wobbly than her purple high heels.

Punching numbers on the cordless phone, J.T. watched his wife through the lace curtains covering the living-room window. Wind whipped at her white blouse and long purple patchwork skirt, plastering fabric to her gentle curves. Rena's wild dark curls sailed behind her as she unlocked the driver's-side door.

She couldn't get away from him fast enough.

Yeah, that bit. More than it should. He wanted to bury his face in her hair, his body even deeper in hers. And she was running like hell.

He pressed the phone to his ear. It rang once, twice. Ended.

"Flight scheduling. Lieutenant Rokowsky."

Bo? J.T.'s brain stuttered for a second until he remembered the lieutenant had just started working in scheduling to mark time until he recovered from his injuries sustained in Rubistan.

J.T.'s hand gravitated up to his ribs, rubbed over bruises long faded. Bruises bathed by his wife's tears when he'd come home. So much damn emotion, too much to process then or now. He'd only known that no way in hell did he want to put his wife through that again. Since they'd already split, leaving seemed the obvious answer.

"Hi, Bo. Tag here," he said while watching Rena slide behind the wheel of Chris's two-door Cavalier. "I didn't get a chance to check the schedule since we landed late and I needed to pick up my son. What's on the boards for me next week?"

"You're on a training flight. Monday. Showtime 0600."

"Uh, okay. Got it. Thanks." J.T. peered through the sheer lace and still the car didn't leave. He moved closer until he could discern... Rena slumped over the steering wheel. Her forehead rested on her hands.

He forced himself to stay inside when every muscle inside of him screamed for action. "How long's the flight?"

"You're scheduled for five hours local area, instructing Airman Brad Gilmore."

J.T. winced. "Good God, not Gabby. That guy talks more than a four-year-old overdosing on Mountain Dew and Pixie Stix."

Bo's chuckles turned downright wicked. "What'll you give me not to stop by the flight kitchen and sweet-talk someone there into adding extra caffeine and cookies to his lunch?"

"Listen up, ladies' man." J.T. settled a hip against the window ledge, batting aside a flowering something-or-other hanging from the ceiling. Waiting for Rena to go. Hoping it would be soon before he ended up outside. "You go any-where near that flight kitchen and I'll tell the nurses over at the hospital what your call sign really stands for. We've been letting you get away with that 'Bo stands for Beau, want me to be yours' crap long enough. Hmm, just think if I tell them you're really—"

"Okay!" The squadron Casanova rushed to interrupt. "No need to say it out loud and risk somebody overhearing. These are government lines, dude, with people listening."

J.T. let a much-needed laugh roll free. "All right, then.

You're safe for now. But I'll be double-checking that flight lunch of his for contraband Pixie Stix.''

Why wasn't Rena leaving? His boots started twitching on the hardwood floor. Maybe he would just—

She sat up, started the car. J.T. exhaled a breath he hadn't realized he was holding. The car backed to the edge of the driveway while a steady stream of after-work traffic flowed past.

''No Pixie Stix,'' Bo promised. ''Wish I was going with you Monday. I'd shut Gabby up.''

Hell yeah, they all wished Bo was flying, instead of indefinitely grounded until docs determined if his left hand would be worth a crap in the airplane once it healed. Flying. They all needed it, actively doing something to discover who had sold out their flight plan that day in Rubistan.

Although having Bo sit his butt in scheduling wasn't a half-bad plan for keeping an ear to the ground. God, the thought of one of their own turning traitor... J.T.'s fist numbed around the phone.

Not gonna think about that day. Keep it level before the weekend with Chris. ''Looking forward to flying with you again soon.''

''Yeah, me, too.''

Quiet echoed again, the lines occasionally smattered with the background sounds of another phone ringing, conversations off to the corner. But J.T. was hooked in that experience—linked with Bo and the young officer's fears over never flying again.

J.T. scratched along the neck of his flight suit. Even after twenty-four years in the Air Force, he couldn't imagine hanging up his helmet. Flying also offered an escape and release since his personal life had landed in the crapper. He'd be screwed right now if he couldn't fly out his frustration.

Yeah, Rokowsky must be in his own personal hell.

Age and officer/enlisted realities might separate them, but

the shared prisoner experience transcended all for a more casual relationship. A bond. J.T. searched for something to keep the guy on the line a while longer, until the edge eased from the kid's voice.

The parenting role came easy, and he figured Bo didn't get much of that since the guy didn't have any family. "What are you doing working the late shift?"

"Easier to call the flight attendant I'm seeing. She's in Japan this week."

"I thought you were dating a research tech from the medical university. Hannah something."

"Hell, man, that was last Thanksgiving. I've had my heart broken at least three times since then."

Bachelor days. J.T. shuddered as Bo rambled on about all the ways Hannah had ripped his heart out before trouncing on it a few extra times.

J.T. sank to the arm of the overstuffed sofa, his gaze never leaving the front yard. Jesus, he was too damn old for that crap. Although the thought of indefinite abstinence pinched. Hard. And having Rena in sight—even out of reach in the driveway still waiting to leave—didn't help with all those images of the two of them tangled on the hardwood floor.

A van turned the corner. After that, finally a break in the stream of cars. Soon, she would be on her way.

The van roared, picking up speed.

Irritation nipped. Damn it, this was a residential neighborhood. J.T. reached for a pad to nab the license number on the front while Bo reminisced about heart-stomping Hannah. The van eased over the center line.

What the—

Into the wrong lane.

"No!" J.T. shouted even though Rena wouldn't be able to hear him. Or move out of the way. He couldn't be seeing—

The van surged. Forward. Faster. Rena jerked to look just as—

The van rammed her passenger door.

Chapter 2

Grinding metal echoed.

He'd expected his marriage to end, but please God, not this way.

J.T. spared critical seconds to bark instructions at Rokowsky. "Call 911 and have them send EMS. I'm at the house. Car wreck. Rena. No time to talk."

He jammed the Off button. Tore open the door. Sprinted down the steps, vaulted the hedge. The car pinwheeled across the road. Rena slumped against her seat belt. The van recovered, righted.

Roared away.

Professional instincts? Calm in a crisis? Damn near impossible at the moment. But he scrounged, pulled them to the fore, logged as many details about the van as he could while his boots pounded grass closer to Rena.

Rage pumped through him with every step. The Cavalier slammed against a telephone pole. His wife's fragile body jerked inside like a rag doll. The crash thundered through the ground. Through him. The car bounced off, skidded side-ways, tires squealing.

Stopped. Silence echoed, broken only by the hiss of the engine and a late day bird squawking its way out of a magnolia tree.

Glass glinted on the pavement. Jagged edges rimmed the door. Hand steady, his insides not so very, J.T. reached into the car.

"Rena? Damn it, Rena, wake up."

He pressed two fingers against her neck to check her pulse as his other hand yanked at the handle. The door held firm.

Her pulse pounded under his touch. Okay. One good thing to focus on instead of the bruise purpling her forehead. And at least no blood spurted that he could see.

J.T. sprinted to the other side of the car. Mangled. Dented. He gripped, hefted. Nothing budged. He could bench-press his body weight, but couldn't move the crunched metal.

Even adrenaline wasn't going to work this free.

He dashed back to the driver's side, pried the jagged edges of glass off, tucked his head inside, skimmed his hands over her face, shoulders, arms, checking for injuries and chanting, "Hang on. Just hang on and the paramedics will be here soon, but they're gonna need to talk to you. Come on and wake up for me."

Her head lolled toward him. Relief pressed like weights against his chest. "That's right, babe. Wake up."

"Baby?" she mumbled, dark lashes flickering.

Ah, hell. He shouldn't have slipped and called her that. But twenty-two years of marriage and intimacy were hard to shrug off just because his brain told him they'd reached the end.

"Are you okay, Rena?" He forced himself to speak carefully, say her name. Just her name.

Color drained from her face, leaving her deep brown eyes

all the wider, darker. Her hand fell to her stomach. She swallowed hard. "I think so."

Her voice shook. Her teeth chattered. All unusual reactions from his normally feisty wife. Nothing brought her low. She never complained or faltered if illness or life kicked her. She just kicked right back.

Not now.

For her to be this rattled, afraid even, scared the hell out of him. "You'll be free soon. I can't get the doors open. You were hit on the passenger side, and this side bounced off a telephone pole. I can't risk moving you until the paramedics check you out."

She frowned, fidgeted, bit back a moan. "My foot's stuck. I don't think I could crawl out anyhow."

His eyes fell to the floorboards. Blood trickled down her foot onto the plastic mat.

Damn it, where was EMS? Still no sirens. Only birds, wind rustling the trees, traffic on other roads cut the silence, the working-class neighborhood homes mostly empty at the moment. "Just hold still. Help will be here soon. They've already been called."

She blinked slowly. "I should tell you."

"What?"

Her hand drifted over her woozy eyes. "Um, oh God, I can't think and I need the words to come out right."

"You're hurt, and a little shaken up. Nothing more. No need for gut-spilling." He hoped. "This isn't a good time for soul-searching."

What would she tell him anyway? He'd backed from emotional outpourings nearly three months ago when he'd returned from Rubistan. He damn well couldn't handle it now.

"You're right, of course." Her hand fell away from her forehead. "Maybe you should step away. What if the car blows?"

"It's not going to blow up."

"You should step away anyhow. Just in case."

"Like hell."

"Somehow I knew you'd say that." She stroked his face with a limp and so soft, cool hand.

He stilled under her touch, hadn't felt it willingly come his way in months. What a damn inconvenient time to want her. But then adrenaline could screw with a man's better intentions, as he'd found out three months ago when he returned from Rubistan.

Her hand fell away, landing on her thigh. Her eyes flickered to the slowing cars driving past, to the handful of gawkers watching from sidewalks and windows, then back to the car. "Well, there goes the new paint job."

He smiled because she wanted him to. He'd do anything she asked just to keep her awake, talking.

Alive.

"Babe, there goes the whole car." Babe? Damn. "Insurance should take care of it, though."

And by God, he'd wrap his family in a helluva lot more metal and air bags next go-round, no matter how deep it slashed his currently hemorrhaging budget. Maintaining two households with a kid in college while they were still paying off Rena's college debt...

Not the time to think about money, he could almost hear Rena saying.

"J.T.?"

He landed back in the moment. "Yeah, Rena."

"Would you please call the base clinic and let them know I don't think I'm going to make it in tonight?"

"They can wait. Dedication to your job only goes so far." He clamped his mouth shut. End of discussion.

He held his tone level, tougher by the second. "I'm not leaving this car until they have you out, so stop wasting energy trying to maneuver me away."

"I don't want people waiting around for me. Parents arranged sitters so they could attend this particular meeting. We have a guest speaker.''

''Damn it, Rena, the guest speaker can start without you. Or they can just wait and eat cookies for a few extra minutes.''

Hell. Great way to calm her, by fighting. He mentally thumped himself.

She laughed.

Laughed? Which stunned the fight right out of him.

Soft, breathless, her laughs tripped out with a huskiness that would have been sexy any other time but was too weak for his comfort level.

''Damn, J.T. We even fight about who's going to take care of whom.''

She had him there.

Eyelids blinking slowly, holding closed longer every time, she stared back at him. He reached to take her hand from her thigh. Her bracelets slid, chimed, two sliding from her limp wrist to *tink, tink* on the floor of the car.

''Come on, Rena, stay awake.''

Sirens wailed in the distance. About damned time.

She squeezed his hand without speaking, but her eyes stayed open longer at a stretch as she fought unconsciousness. He stared back, held her hand and willed her awake, sirens growing louder, closer. Pain glinted in her eyes, radiated from her tightening grip around his hand. His fingers went numb, but no way would he tell her, instead kept holding while praying the sirens would move faster.

Her gaze fell to their linked hands. Her grip slackened. ''Oh God, J.T., I'm sorry. I didn't mean to cut off your circulation like that.''

''No problem.'' He needed to keep her distracted, talking. ''Reminds me of when you were in labor with Chris and transition hit you so hard and fast during the drive to the hospital. I was trying to recall all the coaching stuff I should be doing. Except I was scared as hell I'd be delivering the kid on the side of the road. Remember that?''

"Yeah, I do." Her grip firmed again. Not painfully this time, but holding on in a way she hadn't done in a long time.

Emergency vehicles squealed to a stop beside them. Doors flung open. He didn't want to let go. God, he'd missed her needing him. What a damn selfish thought.

She frowned. "J.T., I really have to tell you—"

A paramedic jogged toward them. "Hold the thought, ma'am. Sir, please move so we can get her out faster."

J.T. backed away. "We'll talk later." He would promise her anything, even one of those conversations she craved. "Hang on and we'll talk all you want soon."

The paramedic chanted a litany of encouragement to Rena while crawling through the passenger window to sit beside her. He placed a C-shaped collar to stabilize her neck, draped her with a protective blanket.

Then noise ensued, grinding and groaning of metal as the Jaws of Life pried her free. His wife's every wince sliced through him during the endless extraction.

Of course, he already knew just how difficult it was to cut Rena out of anywhere. Hell, he'd been trying to cut her out of his life for months without a lick of luck.

Christos Price hated whatever dorky unlucky star he'd been born under. It totally sucked being doomed to a life of geekdom.

Elbow hooked out the open window of his mother's car, Chris finished clearing the gate guard's station leading into Charleston Air Force Base housing. At least with his friends Shelby Dawson and John Murdoch he could be himself without worrying about being cool.

And he was anything but cool.

Chris accelerated past the never-ending pines and oaks lining the street. He could wear double his regular wardrobe of baggy cargo shorts, open button-down shirt over a T-shirt, and the extra layers still wouldn't be enough to pad his bony body.

What guy wanted to be the "spitting image" of his short, scrawny mama? Geez. Scrawny wasn't a problem for girls, but it really blew monkey chunks for guys. Especially when all the other dudes in high school were so freaking big.

He was tired of hearing that five foot eight was a respectable height for a sixteen-year-old and that he would hit a growth spurt soon. Easy enough for his dad to say from three inches over six feet tall with more muscles than a linebacker.

Then his dad would ask him to work out together. Like wrapping a few muscles around his spindly arms would help. Can't make something out of nothing. And that's exactly what he was.

Nothing.

Clicking the turn signal, Chris rounded the corner toward Shelby's house. At least he wasn't getting pounded at school anymore. His friend John Murdoch kept the bigger guys off him, the ones who called him a marching-band wimp just because he played the trumpet. Murdoch played the saxophone and nobody called him a geek. Of course he was tall, a senior, tall, a wrestler, tall and had a girlfriend.

Shelby.

God, she was so hot. Nice. Totally hung up on Murdoch.

And, hey, had he mentioned the guy was tall?

Except Murdoch was also a friend, which meant staying away from his girl. Not that she would have noticed a dweeb like him that way.

But man, he noticed her.

Her corner lot came closer. Shelby sat cross-legged on a quilt in the side yard playing with her little brother while Murdoch sprawled asleep. She didn't see him yet, and Murdoch was out for the count, so Chris allowed himself the rare moment to just look at her.

Her silky black hair swished over her shoulder in a ponytail. And—oh yeah—her bikini bathing-suit top with jean shorts showcased her belly-button ring. Suh-weet.

He pulled into her driveway. Wanted to pull her right to him and kiss her. Of course, he was more likely to grow ten inches by the end of the day.

"Hey, Chris!" Her greeting floated through the open window. "We're gonna order pizza in a minute. Can you stay?"

Even her voice was hot.

"Yeah, sure. Let me dig out my CDs first." And will away the evidence of exactly how hot he found her. Layered clothes weren't helping him much today on a number of counts.

Teenage hormones totally sucked.

But he couldn't go home, not yet. He needed to give his parents time alone. Maybe then his mom would finally tell his old man why she'd been puking her guts up every morning for the past couple of months. Her stomach was already poking out a little and still she didn't say a thing to anybody about being pregnant.

She must think he was a clueless bonehead like his dad.

Chris turned off his cell phone so his parents couldn't razz him about coming home and snagged his CD case. He would hang with Shelby and Murdoch for a while, and pretend everything was okay. Pretend that his parents weren't splitting. That he didn't love a girl who belonged to his best friend.

And most of all, pretend he wasn't hiding from a threat in his life that even tall John Murdoch couldn't warn away.

"Don't move, please, ma'am," the paramedic warned.

Pain jabbed from her ankle up her thigh. Rena gripped the edges of the gurney, taking mental inventory of her body as much as her muddled brain would let her while she stared up at the entrancing sway of oak branches overhead.

An air splint immobilized her foot. Her teeth cut deeper

into her lip to bite back the need to cry out. She couldn't have pain meds anyway because of the baby. Besides, she welcomed the ache that kept her conscious and reminded her she didn't hurt anywhere else, like her stomach.

Her baby.

Rena gripped the gurney tighter. Love and protectiveness for this new little life surged through her until the pain faded. She'd barely allowed herself to think about this baby she and J.T. had made the night he'd returned from Rubistan.

She had to tell the paramedics about her pregnancy soon, but her mind was so woozy. She would explain once J.T. was safely off to the side, rather than risk springing it on him without warning.

Why hadn't she told him sooner? It wasn't as if she was waiting for a miraculous reunion first. She would have to tell him, today, but later in her hospital room, away from the others, when he wasn't about to crack a crown from clenching his teeth.

If only he would step away, but J.T. always did his duty, and being by his wife's side right now would rank right up there as a responsibility.

A car door slammed. She couldn't turn her head to see.

"Tag!"

A voice. Who? Her muddled mind sorted through… Bo Rokowsky, a member of her husband's squadron.

Bo would make the perfect distraction to keep J.T. occupied at the moment.

She patted his arm. "Go talk to Bo. I'm fine."

J.T.'s scowling eyes flicked from the uniformed workers back to her before he finally nodded. "Okay. But I'll only be a few yards away if you need anything."

"I know. Thanks." She tracked his towering body retreating as best she could without moving her head until he disappeared.

She opened her mouth to tell the paramedic about the baby—

"Ow!" Her foot jerked in the paramedic's grasp.

J.T. landed right back in her line of sight. "What's going on? Is it broken?"

"We won't know for sure until we get X rays, sir," the paramedic answered.

X rays? Not while she was pregnant. And especially not during her first trimester. Pain flashed through her foot again. A whimper slipped free.

The paramedic called to his partner, "Seventy-five milligrams, Demerol."

"What?" Rena struggled to understand through her pounding head.

"Just something to help you with the pain, ma'am." The uniformed man swung toward her with a syringe.

"No!" she shouted involuntarily.

J.T. stepped closer. "Yes. Do whatever she needs. Rena, you don't have to grit through this."

Oh, hell. She needed to spit this out fast and quiet to the paramedic. "I can't take any medications."

"Ma'am, really, this will help settle you." The syringe hovered closer to her arm.

Damn. Damn. Damn. No more time for quiet, reasonable explanations.

Rena inhaled a deep breath that stretched achy ribs. "I'm not agitated. Just pregnant."

He'd already taken one missile strike this year. Didn't seem fair a man should get blindsided twice in a few short months.

Boots rooted to the ground, J.T. watched Rena being loaded into the EMS transport. She stared back at him apologetically without speaking. There wasn't time or privacy to talk anyway since the paramedics had moved even faster after her surprise announcement. A whole new set of medical concerns piled on now that they knew she was pregnant.

Pregnant.

The lone word knocked around inside his brain along with anger at Rena for her secrecy—and an undeniable surge of protectiveness for this new child. J.T. braced a hand against the oak-tree trunk, forced his breaths to stay even.

Rena was pregnant. Again. Well, they'd sure celebrated one hell of a reunion after his return from Rubistan. One with apparently lasting results.

More of that protectiveness chugged through him. Five minutes ago, he hadn't known this kid existed. Now he did and that changed everything.

He understood Rena well after twenty-two years, and she was too proud to let him back in the house because of the baby. The woman carried around enough pride to break the average human being.

The EMS truck lights cranked on. He pushed away from the roughened oak, tossed a quick farewell and thanks to Bo before stalking toward his truck.

J.T. slid inside and slammed the door. Shifting into drive, he steered off the curb to follow the fire department's EMS down the tree-lined street.

He would have to tread warily with his wife. Because damn it, he wasn't walking away from her now any more than he would have twenty-two years ago when she'd been pregnant with their daughter. He may not have planned on this kid, but already it lined itself right up there equally with Nikki and Chris in importance.

And what about his feelings for Rena? The gut-shredding fear he'd felt when the van started toward her?

The pine-scented air freshener dangled from his rearview mirror, swayed hypnotically while images of the wreck pounded through his brain.

He couldn't think of that. Not with so much at stake and

convincing her likely to be a hellacious battle. Safer to focus on the work ahead of him.

Priorities in order, he fixed his mind on a dual mission as unwavering as his path behind the emergency vehicle. He had a family to patch together. And a niggling question to solve.

Why had the van swerved deliberately toward Rena's car, rather than away?

Chapter 3

Tucked into her hospital bed, Rena extended her arm for the nurse's routine blood pressure check, antiseptic air making her long for the scents of home and the comfort of her own bed to gather her thoughts. Her foot throbbed from the sprain and four stitches, but her baby was okay and that's all that really mattered.

And J.T.?

She would face the fallout with him soon enough, once everyone left. Doctors, crewdogs, their spouses. There hadn't been a minute to talk between all the visitors and giving police statements during what was turning into the longest evening of her life.

Longest?

Well, except for when she'd waited to hear if her husband had been located after his emergency landing in Rubistan. Since J.T. was the only married crew member, the squadron commander had come to her house along with another flier's wife to tell her...

The plane had gone missing. Shot down. A special ops reconnaissance helicopter had been deployed. Hours had felt like years.

Okay, so this was the second longest evening in her life.

Tap. Tap.

Rena looked toward the door, adjusted her hospital gown. "Come in."

The door creaked open, a blond head peeking around— Julia Dawson, the wife of the previous squadron commander, an approachable down-to-earth woman in spite of their husbands' differing ranks. "Hey, there. Is it okay to visit now?"

The nurse patted Rena's arm. "Everything looks good. I'll come back later for the rest so you can visit with your friend." She circled round the empty bed in the semiprivate room on her way to the door. "Buzz if you need anything."

"Thank you." She definitely could use a friend today more than anything the hospital offered.

Canvas bag swinging from her shoulder, Julia rushed inside and swooped over for a quick hug, already lighting toward the closest chair before Rena could blink.

The leggy blond plopped into a seat beside the bed, one foot tucked under her, casually, just like her unassuming jean overalls. "Are you okay? Really? It scared me to death when I got to the support group meeting and heard what happened. I mean, God, just hours ago we were picking up Chris's car at the shop, talking about the guest speaker for tonight's meeting."

"I'm fine. Really. Just achy and shaken, but okay. I hope the meeting went ahead without me."

Julia waggled her hand. "The speaker talked, but who could listen? We were worried."

A regular at the base support group meetings for parents of special-needs children, Julia attended because her son had been born with Down syndrome. The weekly gatherings had forged a friendship with Julia that went beyond their husbands' shared profession.

The friendship between the two women had deepened into an unbreakable bond the evening Julia waited with Rena for news about J.T. Heaven only knew what it had cost the woman to stay that night, since Julia had lost her first husband to a crash.

Rena's fingers clenched around the sterile white blanket. She could never repay the gift of her comforting presence. Of course, Julia insisted friendship was priceless.

"Oh, before I forget." Julia leaned to scoop her oversize canvas bag from the floor and rummaged inside. She pulled out a lemon-yellow gift bag. "Present for you."

"You didn't need to do this. But thank you."

Julia's blue eyes twinkled as she thrust the bag forward. "Open it."

Rena grasped the top. The bag clanked and she tucked a cradling palm underneath before she peeked inside to find... "Nail polish?" Lots of it. In a rainbow assortment of colors. "How fun!"

And unusual, but then Julia Dawson was one of the most refreshingly unconventional people she'd been blessed with knowing.

"Soon you won't be able to see your toes." Julia wriggled her toes in her Birkenstocks, blue sparkly nails glinting. "So you might as well enjoy them now."

The bag clanked to Rena's lap. "Word got around about my pregnancy that fast?"

"Bo's a walking megaphone. Half the squadron's out there checking up on you and congratulating Tag."

Great. Just what she needed, more tension heaped on him before their discussion. "How thoughtful."

"Are you sure nothing's wrong?" Julia straightened, her sandaled foot swinging from under her to the floor. "Should I call the nurse?"

"No need. I'm fine. Just worried about J.T."

"He's holding up well. Although he's worried about you, too, and driving the police crazy with his push for more man-power checking out the accident. They're convinced it was probably a drunk driver."

"Hmm." That explained why J.T. hadn't been in to see her yet. His absence hurt more than she wanted to admit when she should be grateful for the temporary reprieve.

"I hadn't told him about the baby yet," Rena blurted. Why had she spilled that? At least Julia could be trusted not to gossip.

"Oh no."

"Oh yes."

"Men don't like secrets."

Rena knotted her fingers tighter in the blanket. "Nope."

Julia looked down and away, fidgeted with an arrangement of daisies and carnations by the bed. "I thought since you were pregnant that meant you two had reconciled."

"Brief reunion when he returned from Rubistan. And well—" shrug "—here I am. A knocked-up forty-year-old."

Julia abandoned the flowers and leaned in for another hug, held tight for an extra minute. "Ah, sweetie, I'm so sorry things aren't happier for you right now."

Rena fought the sting of tears that couldn't be totally at-tributed to hormones. "He's going to want to come home because of this."

Julia eased back. "And you don't want that?"

"Things were bad before. How will they magically get better when I know he's only there because I'm pregnant?"

"Raising a kid alone is tough." Julia and her current hus-band had in fact married for their children from previous marriages, both finding single parenthood overwhelming. And somehow they'd discovered love. Except they'd been friends first, with common dreams and hopes.

Rena's marriage of convenience had started with no such foundation.

Still, the woman's words dinged Rena's resolve. So many years had passed since she'd brought a baby into the world. Did she even have the energy to chase a toddler around the house again? And late-night feedings for a newborn. It had all been hard enough even with J.T.'s help.

She couldn't actually be considering…

Of course, her emotions weren't clear-cut. Being ready to sign divorce papers didn't erase twenty-two years of history with the man. He was the father of her children. She'd once loved him.

Now she didn't know what she felt for him anymore. Their marriage had crumbled slowly over twenty-two years from the stress of job separations, financial strains followed by his dogged determination not to touch her income.

She'd been on the fence when she tossed him out six months ago. But when he'd left her at a time they should have clung to each other more than ever, she'd known. They didn't have what it took for the long haul. The children had been their only common link.

Well, that and hot sex.

"J.T. and I *are* getting a divorce. Of course, we'll have to redo the divorce papers anyway to include the new baby."

"You don't have to do anything but take care of yourself. It's been a nightmarish few months for you two. Give yourself time to let it all settle out. Nothing has to be decided today or even tomorrow. Paint your nails to pretty up that injured foot. Let us pamper you." Julia waved the air over Rena's toes peeking free from the Ace bandage wrap. "It's not like you can get around much anyway."

Sit still with nothing to do but count her failures? Ugh. She'd spent years busy bringing up her children, trying to build a marriage, hoping if she filled enough hours of the day she wouldn't see everything that was missing in her life.

In her marriage.

Sitting still with nothing to do but think about all the things she'd worked to ignore was a daunting proposition.

Almost as daunting as the impending showdown with her husband.

J.T. turned the page, reading with a lone corner light while Rena slept. The hospital halls outside stayed silent in the early night but for the occasional rattle of a passing cart.

He couldn't bring himself to wake her yet for the talk. Like he could have roused her anyway. Pregnant women slept like the dead.

Dead.

Pregnant.

Baby.

Breathe, damn it. Forcing breaths in and out, he loosened his grip on the bending paperback. Escape through the words.

Who can control his fate?

J.T. reread the line from Shakespeare's *Othello,* let it roll around in his head for an extra second. He liked the old Bard's take on life. Human nature stayed the same. Warriors such as Macbeth and Othello and Mark Anthony faced universal issues still relevant in modern day.

The horrors of war.

Getting screwed over by a woman.

Which brought him right back to Rena. No escape through reading tonight. J.T. let himself look at her, something he used to do for hours on end while she slept. Not so easy to do now that he parked his ass in an apartment at the end of the workday.

Her dark curls splayed over the stark white pillowcase. Odd how he still forgot how short she was until she slept and he realized what a small portion of the bed she occupied. A few more curves than when he'd first met her, but the softness from bearing their children only made him want to lose himself inside her all the more. She was a striking woman.

Age had been kinder to her than he had over the years. He'd taken much and given little back.

Well, he sure as hell wouldn't let her down when it came to her safety. Again, he studied the even rise and fall of the hospital blanket, reassured himself she'd come through the day alive. Albeit, still pale under her normally bronzed Greek complexion inherited from her family.

Her family…

Damn but they'd been furious that he'd knocked up their little princess Irena. But the minute he'd seen her—so full of energy and fire—he'd felt as if somebody flicked on a light switch. Colors splashed over a world that had been a monochromatic routine of work, eat, sleep, start over again.

For one time in his life, he'd ignored the practical choice and he'd gone after her. Full force. No holds barred, he had to have her.

He braced his boot on the end of her bed. He still wanted her, even when he was so damn pissed the top of his head felt ready to pop off.

Which pissed him off all the more.

Yanking his eyes away from temptation, he opened his pocket-paperback Shakespeare again. Wouldn't the crewdogs have a field day with that? Yeah, he liked Shakespeare, the classics, even poetry sometimes. He enjoyed the rhythm of how the words went together.

Reading did for him what meditation likely did for other folks. Relaxed him. But he balked at the point of the whole woo-hoo yoga idea. Not to mention the loss of control.

No need for yoga. Iambic pentameter would get the job done for him tonight.

He'd started reading more when Rena went back to college and he thumbed through a few of her books, paused, enjoyed. When others were around, he still kept to more pop fiction selections, like a Tom Clancy novel. The Bard, however, he saved for moments alone when he needed to quiet the roaring frustration in his head.

After the crash in Rubistan and his final split with Rena, he'd worked his way through Shakespeare's whole damn historical canon.

Footsteps sounded outside the door seconds before a soft tap, followed by the door creaking open. A slice of light slanted across the room before Chris tucked his head inside. ''Dad?''

J.T. snapped his book shut and held one finger to his mouth. ''Your mom's sleeping,'' he whispered, shoving the book into the thigh pocket of his flight suit. ''Come on in, but keep it quiet.''

An almost comical request given how deeply Rena slept.

''Oh, sure,'' Chris whispered in response, shuffling inside, untied laces on his gym shoes dragging as he squeaked across sterile tile.

The door shooshed closed. Ball cap backward over his dark curls, his son slouched against the wall between the rolling tray and window. His clothes hung off his wiry body, which wouldn't in and of itself be annoying except for the fact the boy wore his cargo shorts so low it was a miracle the things stayed up.

And being angry about his teenager's clothes made him wonder how the hell he would handle it all over again sixteen years from now. ''Hey, pal. Where've you been? Were you working overtime at the restaurant?''

''Nope. Just hanging out with Shelby and Murdoch. Listening to tunes. Eating pizza.'' His guilty gaze skated to the hospital bed. ''Sorry I wasn't around sooner, but Mom's okay, right? Mrs. Dawson wasn't holding anything back when she came home and told me, was she?''

''Your mother's going to be fine. Only a sprain and some stitches. She'll be on bed rest for a couple of weeks, but no long-term problems.'' Relief still pounded through him, fears giving way and making room for questions. ''Why didn't you have your cell phone on?''

''I dunno. Battery ran down, I guess.'' He swept his ball cap off, adjusted the fit and tugged it on again. ''That's probably good for her, huh? Resting.''

''Yes.''

''So everything's okay? With *everything,* I mean.''

Suspicion nipped. ''Everything what?''

''Uh, you know, the baby. Uh…'' He rushed to add a little too quickly, ''Mrs. Dawson told me.''

He scuffed a gym shoe again just as he'd done at nine years old when lying about dumping his sister's makeup into the sewer system. *Squeak. Squeak.*

J.T. pinned him with a parental stare and knowledge. ''You knew already.''

Chris stuffed his hands in his pockets. ''Geez, Dad, and Nikki calls *me* a bonehead. How could you not notice Mom's getting fat?''

''Good God, son. Shh!'' J.T. shot a quick glance at Rena to make sure she was still sleeping. ''Don't let her hear you say the f word.''

''Sorry.'' Shuffle. Squeak. ''I figured it wasn't my place to mention anything and Mom didn't need to be upset in her, you know, condition. Guess this means you're coming home.''

He intended to, but no need to raise Chris's hopes. ''Your mother and I need to talk first.''

Chris slouched, muttering something that sounded like a surly ''About damn time.''

J.T. bit back the urge for a reprimand on a day already full of enough tension. ''Son, I'm sorry to say your car's totaled. The van that hit it wiped it out.''

Chris paled under the bronzed complexion he'd inherited

from his mother along with the head of dark curls. "Totaled?"

"Afraid so. Insurance will cover everything after the de-
ductible, but it may take a while for the check to come
through. There isn't money for a replacement until we get
the settlement." And didn't that bite a chunk out of his pride,
not being able to provide for his family.

"Sure. I understand. It's just good Mom and the baby
weren't hurt."

The accident kicked right back to the forefront of his memory. He couldn't let the emotions shake his focus. The cops
hadn't been much help and wouldn't be unless he could give
them something more to go on. Figuring out what the odd
black-and-red emblem on the bumper represented would be
a good start.

Once he got his family settled.

J.T. stood, leaned against the opposite side of the window
frame as his son. "Are you all right?"

"Yeah. Sure. Why wouldn't I be?"

Chris's tone and chalky face sent parental antennae on high
alert. With deployments keeping him away so much, time
with his son lately was scarce. What might he have missed?
"Is there any reason someone would come after you? A gang
from school?"

Meeting his father's gaze dead on, no shuffling, Chris answered, "I'm not mixed up in a gang at school."

Slowly, J.T. nodded, believed. "Okay, then." Still, he
wasn't taking any chances on leaving Chris alone yet. "Bo's
been waiting at the house in case we didn't find you first to
tell you about your mom's accident. He's going to crash there
on the sofa for the night so I can stay up here."

Chris straightened away from the wall. Anger snapped
from his eyes, his temper another inherited legacy from his
mother. "Geez, Dad, I'm sixteen. I can stay overnight on my

own. It's not like I'm gonna throw some drug-flowing orgy while you're gone or anything.''

God forbid.

''Bo will crash on the sofa,'' J.T. restated, unbending. Arguing never solved anything.

His son slouched back again, layers of clothes rippling over his lean body. ''Okay, okay, stupid me thinking anybody could have an opinion.''

While he sure as hell didn't intend to justify himself to a teenager, he needed to remember his son wasn't a kid anymore. Some explanation might go a long way for easing tension. ''Chris.''

''Yeah, what?'' He stared at his shoes.

''It's been a crappy day, son. Cut me some slack.''

''Sorry,'' he mumbled without meeting his father's eyes.

No, his son wasn't a kid anymore.

The teen years hadn't seemed as difficult with easygoing Nikki. But there hadn't been a marriage breakup in the works.

Since he'd be around more helping out while Rena recovered, he also needed to make use of the extra time with Chris. ''What do you say when I bring your mom home from the hospital, we take a couple of hours and lift some weights?''

Not a bad suggestion and the only thing he could remember doing with his old man in between double-shift-work hours.

''Lift weights?'' Chris shrugged. ''Yeah, sure. Whatever.''

J.T. fished in his flight-suit pocket and pulled out a ten-dollar bill. ''Here, get something to eat on the way home.''

''Thanks. See ya.'' Chris took the money and shuffled across the room, gym shoes squeaking long after the door closed behind him.

Dropping back into the recliner, J.T. snagged his book again, not that he expected to get much reading done, just pass time while he prepped for battle. As much as Rena might prefer full-out confrontations, he knew gaining ground back into their house would call for a more covert operation.

Rena grappled through layers of sleepy fog, blinked until her eyes adjusted to the sparse light in the narrow room that was private only because no other patient occupied the bed beside her. The antiseptic smell churned her stomach, but she welcomed the reminder of a healthy pregnancy.

A pregnancy now out in the open.

Her gaze skipped to J.T. sprawled in the corner chair, reading lamp on, paperback gripped in his broad hands. She couldn't make out the cover, but imagined it was whatever military-action bestseller hit the shelves recently.

J.T. filled her eyes as completely as he filled the chair. Such a large man shouldn't be able to move so silently, yet he did. Always. Magnetically. Until her world narrowed to dark hair, muscles and slow-blinking brooding eyes.

As tempting as it was to stare at his rugged handsomeness instead of dealing with real-life worries, she was through repeating past mistakes. She couldn't hide from the truth any longer. There wouldn't be a more private time than now for their discussion. "Hi, J.T. Good book?"

He glanced up, studied her without speaking for four clicks of the second hand on the institutional black-and-white wall clock. Closing his book, he righted the recliner. Both boots thudded on the tile floor. "I hope I didn't disturb you with the light."

"Not at all." She'd slept beside him in bed while he read many a night.

Gulp.

Where was some crushed ice and a water pitcher when a woman needed them? "How long have I been out?"

J.T. flipped his wrist to check his watch, a gift from their daughter, complete with stopwatch and listings of multiple time zones for his flights. "Just an hour and forty minutes.

Doc says to wake you up every couple of hours through the night. The nurse will check in, too.''

Which gave them twenty more uninterrupted minutes to talk in the quiet intimacy of a bedroom that wasn't packed with memories. The hospital at least made for comforting neutral ground for their discussion. Might as well confront things straight up. "I'm sorry for not telling you about the baby sooner.''

Guarded eyes almost hid nearly banked anger. He shifted, slow, silent, tucking the book in the thigh pocket of his flight suit. "Why didn't you?''

Why?

The truth blindsided her while her defenses were laid low from the accident. Because she'd wanted J.T. to come home on his own. For her. Something that, for the first time, she completely accepted would never happen.

The last of her dreams, hope, love died. There was nothing left for her now but to strengthen her resolve to protect her children and her heart. "I was still reeling from hearing you'd been shot down and whatever happened to you in Rubistan, trying to sort through what happened to us afterward. Pretty difficult to do with so little information from your end.''

Rena's words sucker punched him. Leave it to his outspoken wife never to pull punches. She stared back at him defiantly, daring him to talk about Rubistan.

He didn't need to think about it, much less talk it out. He'd lived it. Dealt with what happened, and wanted to move on, not bring everything up again until the top of his head blew off. He'd walked away before rather than—

Ah, she was pushing him to walk now.

Not gonna happen. "I'm assuming the baby was conceived after my return then. You don't look far enough along to have gotten pregnant before we split.''

Although, good God, Chris was right. She did have a slight bulge under the white sheet. How could he have missed it?

She would be three months along. While carrying Chris, she'd been unable to button her pants by that stage.

Damn. He *was* a bonehead not to have noticed or even considered the possibility.

"Yes, it was that night. I missed a pill while you were gone. I was…upset. Days jumbled in my head."

Her pain from then radiated just as powerfully now. Pain he'd caused.

He needed to regroup. Now. He turned his back, reached for the water pitcher, pouring a cup for himself, another for Rena.

"J.T.? It was an accident."

"Of course it was." He jerked around to face her, passed her a water glass. "I never thought otherwise."

Did she really think so little of him that she expected recriminations? Jesus. He might have hurt her, but never like that.

Brown eyes wary, she took the cup from him without touching. "You are *not* moving home because of the baby. Let's get that straight right now. Our reasons for splitting still stand."

He leaned back against the wall, crossing one booted foot over the other. "What were those reasons again?"

"Don't be an ass."

"Ah, reason number one." He drank half the cup of water in one swallow, icy cold along heated anger.

She'd called him a major ass during their fight six months ago about the number-two strain on their marriage. Money.

"I'm sorry." Rena's voice softened. She rolled the cup between her palms. "My temper is right up there on the reason list. I drive you crazy. I know that."

"Oh yeah, babe—" a slow smile crept over his face "—you've definitely always driven me crazy."

Well, hell. So much for smart strategies. But the unstoppable spark between them always had messed with their minds. Apparently still did.

"J.T., damn it." She slammed her cup down on the end table beside a basket of flowers. "That's what got us into this mess before. And again now."

His smile faded. "Don't worry. I'm not planning to pressure you about getting back together." No pressure about it. Slow and steady won the day with his wife.

"You're not?"

"No." Think strategy, not how much easier it would be to kiss her quiet. Not about how tight the knot twisted in his stomach over the thought that even if he made it home, they weren't any better off than before. "You made yourself clear when you pitched my barbells and books out on the lawn six months ago."

And the reason for that final fight? They'd argued over the flipping family Christmas vacation, for God's sake. She'd insisted his lengthy deployments were taking a toll, making growing apart too easy. His fault. He knew it.

So he'd offered to take leave. Not good enough. She'd wanted to rent a cabin in the mountains, something she insisted they could afford now that she was working.

Hell. As if he needed it thrown in his face that he couldn't provide for his family on his own. As if he needed reminding of all the things she'd had growing up. Things he couldn't come close to giving her.

A fact that had been stewing in his gut for twenty-two years.

"Well, J.T., tossing those possessions on the lawn was just the start of venting problems years in the making. Three months ago proved that." She gripped the length of her hair in her hands and began twisting it into a knot on the back of her head. "We'll just draw up a new set of divorce papers."

His eyes tracked the moves of her hands against her glossy curls. He'd always wondered how the hell she did that trick with her hair, had watched her hundreds of times, the memory of those strands gliding through his fingers never failing to make him hard.

He finished his water, pitched his cup in the trash. "Not until you're up and moving again. The doc said you need to stay off your feet for at least two weeks."

She paused midtwist. "What happened to doctor-patient confidentiality?"

"We're married." For better or worse, they'd vowed. Vows that were about to be broken if he didn't ignore the chemistry and put a stop to this. "I already logged in a call to my commander for a lighter schedule while you recover."

"J.T.," she warned, arms reaching up as she finished securing her hair. "Remember that *you* left the last time. I'm not the only one who said we don't have a chance."

And that's what he got for talking. All the more reason to guard his words, so she couldn't throw them back in his face later.

He plowed ahead. "I can't be away from the squadron totally now." The drug surveillance flights with the feds were too sensitive to pass off to anyone else. Since he was already in the loop from the overseas mission, he'd been tapped for the flights. Bringing another loadmaster up to speed this late would cost valuable days anyway.

What a helluva time to have a family crisis. "But all my flights will be at night, when Chris is around."

He ignored the burn in his gut that told him those flights would only bring more stress to his wife if she knew the truth about the mission. But there were so many things he could never share about his job.

However, since C-17 night flights were common around Charleston, his wife wouldn't question late takeoffs any more than anyone else in Charleston. All of which made the craft the logical choice to cart the DEA's surveillance equipment— much the same as used during the fateful flight in Rubistan.

With a little luck—okay, a lot of luck—the high-tech equipment loaded down on those pallets would eventually cough up the crucial link to who the hell in the States had sold them out overseas.

And more importantly, how.

J.T. tamped down the twitch of conscience over keeping it from her. After all, he'd had twenty-two years' practice. "I'll be asleep during the day, so you don't have to worry about me being underfoot. But I'll still be on call for whatever you need. Simple. Reasonable."

"I'll manage just fine."

"How do you plan to take care of yourself while Chris is in school? Nikki's exams start next week, so she can't help."

J.T. searched for signs of Rena weakening but she was too preoccupied playing with her hair and driving him crazy. Low-blow time. "You need to be careful for the baby."

Rena sagged back into her pillow. He'd won. "God, J.T., you don't fight back often, but when you do, you sure fight dirty."

"I save it for the battles worth winning." His victory felt hollow as he inventoried the worry, fears, in his proud wife's gaze.

"Fine." Her hands fell back to her lap, a lone curl sneaking free to bob against her chin. "Whatever. You're right and you know it. Thank you for the help."

Where had her fight gone? Seeing Rena deflated, defeated, worried him more than the purpling bruise on her forehead. But he couldn't afford to back down, as dangerous as pressing ahead too hard and fast. "I'll take some stuff back over to the house in the morning."

"Why not now?"

"Because I'm staying here."

Starch inched back up her spine. "But Chris—"

"Bo's staying over." He dropped into the chair beside her bed. "I'm not budging on this one."

Fire heated her brown eyes and J.T. rushed to forestall her argument. "You owe me right now for not telling me about the baby sooner." A truth that seared his gut. Canting forward, elbows on the edge of her mattress, he continued, "Now go to sleep and I'll read my book. It's not like I haven't watched you sleep before."

Her breath caressed his face.

Her face only inches away.

The familiar scent of her favorite peppermint mouthwash and flowery perfume washed through his senses along with images of sharing a bed. And somehow it didn't matter that they were in a hospital, or that divorce papers had already been drawn up.

He wanted her. She wanted him. With an inevitable intensity that had almost incinerated them both three months ago.

Tears sheened her brown eyes. From hormones? Or another reason?

Something cracked inside him and he didn't want to examine the fissure too closely to see what lay beneath. But he couldn't stop the urge to take her in his arms, not for passion, just to hold her—

She flinched away.

And he hadn't even moved yet. Apparently she'd read his intent in his eyes and didn't want his comfort. Fine. Okay. No surprise. His hands fisted against the mattress.

She blinked away moist emotions. "Just so we're clear. It's two weeks. And during that time you won't be watching me sleep."

"Roger." He read her loud and clear. Not that he'd expected to park his boots under her bed—yet—but it still smacked being reminded of the fact.

Emphatically.

Leaning back in the hospital chair, he fished his book from his pocket, the weight of her eyes on him a heavy reminder of all their unfinished business.

He resisted the urge to look back up, which would only instigate a conversation he sure as hell didn't want. Strategy. Too much was at stake here with only fourteen days to persuade her to give things another try. Again. He'd soothed her temper in less than that often enough before. Problem was, the determined glint returning to her eyes made it totally clear.

He wouldn't be able to get naked with Rena to win her over this time.

Chapter 4

Two weeks alone with J.T.? Gulp. Surely, given all that was at stake now, she could hold strong against the temptation to ditch her clothes every time those long legs of his lumbered into the room.

Still, the upcoming fourteen days of intimacy scrolled through Rena's mind as endlessly as the winding roads through her tree-packed subdivision on her way home from the hospital. Brick and wooden tract houses whipped past her passenger window, a much safer view than staring at her hot husband driving. Even peripheral glimpses of him rocked her thoughts like hanging ferns at the mercy of a Charleston tropical storm.

Nope. She wasn't looking at him. Just staring at his reflection in the passenger window.

J.T.'s window open, gusts puffed inside to flap his unbuttoned, loose Hawaiian shirt over a white T-shirt. Unlike Chris's baggy style, J.T. kept his T-shirt tucked into his khaki shorts, neatly leaving his trim waist and flat abs right there for her to admire even in profile reflection.

She pulled her gaze away, down, found no relief there, either. Thickly muscled legs worked the clutch, brake, gas—shorts putting plenty of tanned skin on display. Her fingers curled at the memory of exploring the bulging cut of tendons, the masculine texture of bristly hair.

Rounding a corner slowly, careful as he cruised past an overgrown magnolia, J.T. draped his wrist over the old Ford's steering wheel, a truck he'd rebuilt himself as he'd done with their fixer-upper home. This talented man could repair anything through sheer determination, ingenuity and sweat equity.

If only relationships were as easy to maintain.

Their two-story white wood house eased into view. Vehicles packed their driveway—her sedan, Julia Dawson's minivan, Bo's Jeep, Nikki's compact car. Welcome buffers against the tension so she would spend less time alone with J.T.

Good, right?

And how could she not be touched by Nikki's visit? Her eldest had come home to check on her. So sweet, her easygoing daughter with an oversize heart. The breakup had hurt her most, even though she showed it least. "Nikki's here?"

J.T. eased off the gas pedal, cruising to a stop on the narrow street. "She drove in this morning for the day. She's heading out after supper for an all-night study session. I didn't have a chance to tell you with all the out-processing at the hospital. You ready to go in?"

She nodded, conversation time apparently over for her husband. Looking back, she wondered now if they'd been doomed from the start to a life of miscommunication followed by quiet distance—Tag's family full of stoicism and silence, hers reverberating with chatter but so much of it lies and anger. Even if she knew better now, with her newfound counselor perspective she could see what a shaky foundation they'd built from the start.

For this baby, for her other two children, she would hold strong. She would model healthy relationships in hopes of helping them build ones of their own.

J.T. ambled around the hood of the truck to her side, opened the door, filled her eyes. He extended his arms, Hawaiian shirt flapping in the breeze, crisp white cotton stretching across an endless chest she could lose herself against.

He couldn't really expect to carry her? He waited, arms out. Unmoving.

She knew he could do it, just wasn't sure she could bear the heartbreaking reminder of other passionate trips in his arms that ended oh so differently than this one would. "Would you pass me the crutches from the back, please? I can make it up there on my own."

"Damn it, Rena." His eyes snapped along with his voice. "Is it really that distasteful to have me touch you?"

His arms dropped, hands hooked on his hips, narrow hips, his fingers pointing a direct arrow to—

Her eyes jerked up. Heat delivered a double whammy to her cheeks, then pooled lower. Hotter. "What?"

"I know you can maneuver around on crutches. And I realize the doctor said everything looks okay with the pregnancy. But you know as well as I do that I can carry you inside. The strain will be less than your trying to maneuver with crutches. Why exert yourself? Unless my touching you is so damned awful."

"Oh."

"Yeah. Oh." He hooked a hand on the open doorway, just over her head. "I'm sorry if my touching you is a problem."

"It's not a problem." Not how he meant, anyway.

"Good. We've always put the kids first. This baby shouldn't be any different."

Rena swung her legs to the side and out, waiting. Bracing herself for the feel of his hands on her body, the unyielding wall of his muscled chest against the give of her own softer flesh.

Broad palms slid under her, one arm around her back, the other under her knees. By instinct, her arm glided up and around his neck. Her fingers found the bristly shortness of the hair along the nape of his neck. Only a soft grunt from him indicated any reaction.

And the reaction wasn't from exertion.

Even with the few extra pregnancy pounds she'd packed on, carrying her posed no hardship for her honed husband. He kept in tip-top shape for the physical aspects of his job that even more mechanized cargo holds couldn't completely eradicate.

So many times she'd stood in the doorway leading to the garage and watched him lift weights, his muscles straining and shifting under sweat-sheened skin. Determination and focus. Strength.

She drew in a shaky breath and found the scent of him, fuller, stronger. How could she have forgotten the familiar potency of his smell—pine soap and musky man? Clean. Arousing.

Pure J.T.

What the hell was with the immutable, near-insane physical attraction she felt for this man? Would she spend the rest of her life starving for his touch?

A daunting thought.

His gym shoes thudded along the flagstone path and up the wooden porch steps. Already voices drifted through the door along with someone playing show tunes on the piano. The lace curtains rippled with the movement of bodies inside.

Only a few seconds more in J.T.'s arms. A few seconds more for the memories to tempt her. Unstoppable images so she didn't have to waste energy trying to tamp them down.

Yes, she and J.T. had hurt each other, done so many things wrong, but some things right. And at the moment, all those beautiful, special, right things about her marriage blossomed through her mind. Did he remember them, too? She couldn't change the past, but she had control over the present, and she intended to make sure J.T. carried something positive with him from their years together.

Her hand fell to stop his on the doorknob. "J.T.?"

He peered down at her. "Problem?"

She squeezed his hand, let her fingers linger in spite of his stunned eyes widening. "No doubt we're wrong for each other in a hundred different ways. But never, never have I found your touch distasteful. Far from it."

His fingers twitched against her, tightened, the only sign he'd heard her as his face stayed stoic. Unemotional. Handsome ruggedness carved in granite.

Still, he'd heard her, and her words meant something to him. Her defenses slipped, and she didn't have the heart to recall them, instead allowed the need building during their ride home to bloom.

She brought her hand up to rest on his neck again. "I thought you already knew that, except now I'm realizing maybe with everything else going on, you somehow forgot. Or wondered. And even though we both realize it's not enough, I just wanted you to know that we did share something mutual."

A smile dented a dimple in his face, so incongruous, and therefore all the more enticing. "Thanks, babe."

Her eyes fell to his mouth, lingered on the sensual fullness of his lower lip. She waited, wanted, even as pride wouldn't let her make the move forward. But if he leaned? She definitely wouldn't move away.

J.T. struggled to control the heat surging through him over something as simple as holding his wife. Damn it, he was not going to kiss her, no matter how good her soft hands and softer body felt against him.

He steeled his resolve. Steel? More like tinfoil, which meant he'd better haul ass inside. Pronto.

He twisted the doorknob. Disappointment flickered through her Godiva-rich eyes. Resolve shredded into foil confetti.

The door jerked open beneath his hand, snapping the mood. Thank you, Lord.

Chris lounged in the open portal with a bag of Cheetos clutched in his hand, fingertips deep orange from munching. "What took you so long? I'm starving and folks brought food that I can't eat until you get here."

J.T. looked away, up. "In a minute, son. How about unload your mother's things from the truck first."

"Sure," he answered through a fresh mouthful of cheese curls.

J.T. angled sideways, guiding Rena's trim legs over the threshold first. Over the threshold. Just as he'd done when they were young, nervous, full of plans.

Ready to break in the new mattress in their efficiency apartment.

Her fingers twisted in his cotton shirt, her touch as hot now as it had been then. Except today, she could hardly stand to look at him. She focused on the hanging ivy that, damn it all, he'd forgotten to water.

He stopped in the middle of their overflowing living room. Bo shared the piano bench with Nikki, playing the right hand from the open score sheet while Nikki plucked out the left. Well, if Nikki's plunkings could be called playing, his tomboy daughter always preferring running track to running scales.

And if Bo didn't move his ass a little farther down that bench—

"Mom!" Nikki bolted up with an athletic grace gained from hours on the university soccer field. Thank God for soccer scholarships, even partials. "Ohmigod, are you okay? Dad didn't call me until this morning or I would have come sooner. Probably why he didn't call me. Geez, like I couldn't drive after dark.''

"I'm fine, hon," Rena rushed to interrupt. "The crutches are just awkward right now."

"Okay, good, that's what Bo said when he filled me in on the latest, but I thought maybe he was soft-soaping things so I wouldn't worry."

J.T.'s scowl deepened. Bo? She'd been talking with Bo?

So what if Nikki was already older than Rena had been when they married? He wanted his daughter to have a chance to be young. And while he liked Bo in the workplace, no way was Nikki getting near that squadron player renowned for wooing women with his guitar and singing. And apparently the piano now, too.

"J.T., you can put me down now. J.T.?" Rena tapped his chest lightly.

"Where?" he asked.

"Chair."

"Ottoman?"

"Yes, please."

As he lowered her carefully into the overstuffed floral chair, he couldn't help but notice how easily they'd fallen back into marital shorthand conversation.

Footsteps sounded from the kitchen, down the hall, soft padding steps, seconds before Julia Dawson strode into the living room, carrying a blond-haired toddler on her hip. "Hey there, sweetie. I've plugged in a Crock-Pot full of chili. There's also a platter of buffalo wings."

While the two women exchanged greetings and food-reheating instructions, he tried like hell to ignore the warmth of Rena's calf as he arranged a pillow under her foot.

"Don't thank me," Julia insisted. "Thank my multi-talented husband. Zach made it all before he headed in to work for a couple of hours. I'm only the delivery person. A good thing, huh?'' said the lady carpenter, more comfortable with a hammer than a spatula.

Rena inhaled, bringing her breasts closer to J.T.'s face. ''Everything smells great. You really know how to rev those pregnancy cravings into overdrive.''

He finished adjusting the pillow under her foot, his fingers lingering above her ankle. Oh yeah, he remembered those pregnancy cravings of hers well. All of them, especially how her sensual appetites increased, too.

Julia hitched her son higher on her hip. ''Well, I need to hit the road. Patrick's about ready for his afternoon nap.''

Bo swung his legs around the piano bench, rising. ''Little fella looks like he's getting heavy. How about I buckle him into the car seat for you, ma'am?''

A ploy to impress Nikki? Or was he just being a nice guy? Bo certainly seemed at ease with the baby—and with flaunting that ''talent'' right under Nikki's nose with a smile and wink.

Down, Lieutenant.

J.T. followed Julia and Bo out the door as Chris jogged past inside with a small suitcase and basket of flowers in his hands, Cheetos bag in his teeth. J.T. plowed ahead. He might not be able to do much about his wife, but he could make damn well sure a certain lieutenant kept his musical ''talents'' zipped up tight.

Rena watched her husband stride out the door after Bo and Julia, J.T.'s mercurial moods unsettling to say the least. One minute he seemed ready to kiss her. The next he was Sergeant Scowl. Then Mr. Sensitive with the footstool. Then back to Sergeant Scowl.

And she was definitely Counselor Cranky. Knowing her irritability came from pure sexual frustration didn't help.

Nikki plopped down on the ottoman, long legs folded to the side. ''Do you need anything? A glass of water?''

"I'm fine for now, hon." Rena reached to tuck a stray strand of her daughter's chin-length bob behind her ears. If this sleek, earthy changeling didn't look so much like her father, Rena might wonder what rainbow Nikki had slid down into the hospital bassinet marked Baby Girl Price. "Thanks for coming home to check on me with exams starting."

"We don't all get much time to hang out together in the same house anymore," she said, her tone light, her clear gray eyes piercing. "Sorry I have to go back after supper. But where would I sleep, anyway, with Dad's stuff piled up in my old room?"

Easygoing kid? Not always. Nikki landed her sly digs in with the best of them. "Then let's enjoy this afternoon and the chili before you go. Your father's home to help until I'm on my feet since you and Chris have school. Nothing more and you know that. I'm sorry, hon, but that's the way it is."

"Like you helped him through after he got back from Rubistan." She nodded her bob into a steady swing. "Right. Got it. Lots of helping going on for two people who say they don't want to be married anymore."

Rena folded her arms over her increasing waistline. "Back off, kiddo. I'm the mom. You're not. Boundaries. Respect them."

"Sure thing." She reached to put her hand over her mother's crossed arms. "Hey, cool news about the baby."

"Thank you, hon." Nikki might be pissed, hurt even, but she never held a grudge. Rena envied her daughter the ability to let concerns slide off her. "You're okay with this? Not all embarrassed by your old pregnant mom?"

"Old? You've gotta be kidding me." She patted her mother's tiny bulge again. "And of course I'm okay with the kid. If you're happy about the baby, then I'm happy."

Rena placed her hand over her daughter's and let herself enjoy the momentary peace of simply celebrating the new life in their world. She blinked back tears.

"Oh Geez, Mom. Hormones, huh?" Chuckling, Nikki drew her hand away. "Have cravings kicked in yet?"

"God, yes." She swiped the back of her wrist over her watery eyes. "With a vengeance. I can smell those chicken wings from here."

Nikki's gray eyes flecked with sparks of mischief. "Be nice to me and *maybe* I'll fix you a plate once they're done heating."

"Brat."

"That's me. Always in trouble." Always in motion, too, Nikki scooped three granola-bar wrappers—starving Chris's, no doubt—off the coffee table, wadded them into a ball before lobbing them into a wicker trash basket. "How far along are you?"

What a loaded question since it would reveal the full extent of J.T.'s homecoming. Like her adult daughter wouldn't have guessed anyhow.

"Three months," Rena announced, then waited for the smart-ass comeback. Grown-up kids didn't accept quite as blindly as the little ones.

A knowing smile dimpled her cheek, inherited from her father. "A baby in time for Christmas. Cool."

Rena exhaled. Off the hook for now. Nikki pushed to her feet, starting a long-legged strut out of the room. Rena shifted in the overstuffed chair, adjusted her throbbing ankle on the pillow. She just wanted to get through this bizarre family reunion without an argument. One peaceful gathering. Bone-weary, heartsore and more than a little rattled by the wreck and a short ride in her husband's arms, she didn't have the energy for confrontations before a serious nap.

They could all bolt back buffalo wings and chili and pretend everything was fine. Easy enough to do after twenty-two years' practice.

Nikki paused in the archway leading from the dining area back into the hall. She glanced over her shoulder, patting her own not-pregnant belly. "Oh, and Mom? Way to go, keeping those boundaries in place with Dad three months ago."

Winking, she spun away, glossy hair swinging against her ears with each cocky strut out of sight.

Rena wanted to call her daughter on that statement. Call herself, for that matter. But the brat had a point.

Thumping the minivan roof, J.T. stepped back from Julia Dawson's Windstar. She eased into the street and straightened, clearing the way for Bo's blocked Jeep to leave.

Which the young copilot would do as soon as J.T. addressed one pressing matter.

J.T. jammed his hands in his pockets, dodging strategically planted clumps of flowers in Rena's tropical jungle that would put professional tour gardens to shame. He stopped beside the black Jeep. "Thanks for the help, man."

"No problem." Bo secured the canvas roof for an open-air ride. "Glad I could be here for you."

"You were more than just here for me. I won't forget." True. And he would do anything for this fellow crew member. Except give over his daughter. He wanted easier for his kid than the worries of military life.

A big part of the reason he'd left Rena, and now he had to figure out how to resolve all of that.

"Family's about more than blood relations, you know." Bo stared down at his wrist cast, flexed his scarred fingers poking out. Slowly. No wince. Not that showed anyway. His arm fell to his side heavily. "I owe you."

Spring sun baked J.T.'s head with reminders of a February desert sun in another country. "You don't owe me a thing."

God, he didn't want to talk about that time. Especially not now when he needed his defenses up in full force to work his way past his prickly wife.

"Whatever." Bo's fingers continued to stretch, crook, stretch, crook until the strain lines erased from around the corners of his mouth. The old Bo slid back into place as smoothly as his smile. "Nikki sure has grown—"

"Watch it, *sir*," J.T. growled. "That's my daughter you're talking about."

Bo swallowed his laugh. "Damn, but the old master sergeants know how to make 'sir' sound like an insult."

"Then I guess we're even for the *old* comment."

"Guess so."

Tension eased from his spine. "If you're thinking you owe me something, pay me back by keeping away from my daughter."

"You can relax. Just yanking your chain. Jesus, man, you've got hot buttons so big, it's tough not to push 'em sometimes. No worries, though. I want to keep my other hand out of a cast for a while anyhow, only just got the damn thing off. As fun as it was having those nurses feed me, give me sponge baths…" His baby blues twinkled with devilish intent. "Well, eventually I gotta act, and two casts can get in the way."

"Just so you're not acting with my daughter. She's still a kid in a lot of ways. I want her to have the chance to stay that way a while longer."

"Life has a way of throwing curves fast enough."

J.T. sure as hell agreed, but hadn't expected a heavy comment from the carefree lieutenant. Bo Rokowsky had a rep around the squadron. Never serious. Edgy. Great set of flying hands, but reckless.

As much as J.T. respected restraint, a part of him grieved to see that free spirit stomped out of the young man. Only four or five years older than Nikki in years, but so damn much more in experience now. All the more reason for the copilot to keep his distance. "It's nothing personal. I just don't want any crewdogs sniffing after my baby girl."

Baby girl. What about the new baby? Boy or girl? God willing, healthy.

"Message received about Nikki. I really was just razzing you. Lighten up. I'm totally hung up on my flight attendant."

"This week."

Bo thumped his chest with a fist. "But with my whole heart, dude."

Lightness reestablished. Comfort zone reclaimed. "Well, then, get your sorry ass out of my yard and go call her or something."

"Will do." Bo gripped the steering wheel, fingers poking from the cast while he downshifted gears with his good hand.

He was smiling again, but the new partial cast gleamed white in the afternoon sun. A reminder that hell no, J.T. didn't want his daughter marrying a crewdog like Bo, like himself, just going through the motions since coming home. Both still stuck overseas in their minds…

J.T. flung aside the seat-belt harnesses strapping him into the downed C-17. Through the windscreen, desert, scrubs, jagged peaks, dunes sprawled ahead, offering minimal options for hiding after an emergency landing in potentially hostile territory.

But no sign of rebels or troops yet, either.

Tearing off his headset, he looked to the copilot, Bo, for the prepared evasion plan. Different stages of the mission called for different contingencies to escape until pickup by rescue forces. Forces hopefully already en route.

Bo cinched his survival vest tighter. "We'll run to the right, north, toward the outcropping. Haul ass until we drop. Put distance between us and the plane."

Then they would set up a rescue signal. And pray. "Roger." The affirmation echoed in triplicate from the other crew members.

Scorch, the aircraft commander, cleared his seat and headed out first, followed by Spike—the faux-loadmaster, their undercover OSI special agent and personal time bomb.

J.T. tucked into the narrow stairwell behind Spike, down

into the belly of the craft, popped the side hatch. Critical seconds ticked away. His heartbeat ticked faster, louder. His boots pounded down the metal steps. Still no sign of anybody.

One after the other, four pairs of boots landed on hard-packed desert, already sprinting, each man taking only what he carried in the survival vest. A knife. A pistol. Piss-poor protection against the elements and the enemy.

Fear pounded through him as hard as his heart and running steps. Only an idiot wouldn't be scared. And only a bigger idiot would let it immobilize him.

Sun baked his back, his head, his brain. Rays reflected off sand, even February hot as hell during the day here. If they could only buy enough time for a U.S. rescue chopper to locate them…

Grounding in training, he reviewed the facts on his ISOPREP card—isolated personnel report on file. The ISOPREP gave answers to questions a rescue crew would ask over the radio to positively ID them, to confirm the chopper wasn't being led into a trap.

Questions.

The street from his childhood home.

His mother's maiden name.

Rena's first car. A sleek silver blue BMW, where they'd made out. Made a baby.

Damn it. He spit curses out with sand. He couldn't think about her. About being with her.

Run. Harder. Focus on the three most important elements of survival.

Maintain life.

Maintain honor.

Return.

His feet drummed a steady beat across the desert floor in time with everyone's huffing breaths exhaling more grit-filled curses. Each man's favorite cussword chanted, powered feet faster. His own favorite of the moment spilled free—just like when baby Chris had parroted it back at him from his high chair, Rena behind their son, her hand clamped over her mouth to subdue laughter.

Her face, her smile, even her voice so incredible, exotic, different from the monochromatic world he'd grown up in.

Eyes sparkling, she'd brought more of that light of hers to their tiny apartment filled with babies and plants. She'd subdued her smile then into a parental reprimand and skirted around to the front of the high chair to tell their son, ''Truck. Your daddy said tr-uck.''

Well, he sure as hell was truck, truck, truck on his way as far as he could get across this desert.

God, how long had they been running? Years? Minutes? He didn't dare spare the energy for a look over the shoulder.

Spike slowed as they neared a clump of brush, a slight swell of dune. Damn pathetic coverage. The OSI agent stopped, braced his hands on his knees while the others drew up, halted as well. ''Don't think,'' Spike said between panting exhales, ''it's going to get any better than this, guys.''

Scorch, as senior-ranking crew member, could disagree. But Spike's counterintelligence experience, his days deeply undercover during his CIA stint prior to joining the Air Force as a civilian employee of the OSI, offered weight to his opinion.

And the set of his face told them well this seasoned agent thought their odds sucked no matter where they hid their asses. But that wouldn't stop them from trying to buy time for the good guys to get as close as possible.

J.T. dropped to his knees on the desert floor along with the others, scooping out sand, fashioning a trench behind brush. He dropped flat on his belly beside his crewmates. Sweat soaked his flight suit, caking sand to his skin.

Silence.

His heart tried to slow to a regular beat, exertion complete. Adrenaline kept him revved. How long would they wait?

"Damn," Spike whispered. "I'd kill for a ghillie suit right now." Camouflage made of strips of either desert-colored fabric or jungle hues, the ghillie suit was nearly undetectable to the eye.

Instead, they lay with only the scant cammo of desert tan flight suits, better than their regular green, at least. The Rubistan government, American troops and local warlords would all have picked up their landing. Who would arrive first?

The answer came quickly, rumbling from the hazy horizon. Clouds of sand puffed a toxic premonition before the vehicles cleared into sight.

Vehicles. Not an aircraft. Not Americans.

He swallowed more gritty air. Okay. Rubistan's military? Police? Or local warlord rebels?

The sand swirl parted to reveal…a caravan of crappy jeeps, trucks, RVs. Nothing organized about their approach to indicate military training. Damn.

J.T. slipped his emergency beacon off his survival vest, dug a hole in the sand. Tossed it inside. Pitched brush over it. If they were taken, at least rescue troops would have some point of reference and tracks to follow.

"Keep your head down," Spike instructed. "Don't move. Don't even look at them. With some luck they'll drive right by us."

Bo whispered out of the side of his mouth, "Unless they have dogs."

"Zip it, sunshine," Scorch interjected. "We can do without the gloom and doom."

The drone of engines increased with the cloud of sand spitting behind the vehicles, drawing closer, eating up the miles, becoming clearer as they broke through the rippling heat waves. A half-dozen vehicles, as best he could tell by sneaking peeks through peripheral vision. He couldn't risk looking at them directly, but God, it felt as if they were right on top of them. Still driving though.

J.T. quit breathing. His heart slammed his ribs until it seemed ready to explode out his ears.

The vehicles jerked to a stop, one after the other. The pounding in his ears stopped as well. Everything stopped inside him. Stilled.

Maintain life. Maintain honor. Return. Only that mattered. Survival. Returning home.

Voices shouted in Arabic. Movement flickered to the right. At least twenty or so men.

Honor. Life. Return.

Boots appeared in his line of sight. Paused. Stayed. They'd been found. Spit dried inside his mouth.

A shout sounded from above him. J.T. allowed himself to view through peripheral vision. No direct eye contact. No sudden movements or aggressive action to provoke.

The men looming over them weren't wearing uniforms. Mismatched weapons confirmed his fears. Russian-made AK-47 assault rifles. M-16s. Uzis. All weaponry of the very sorts of people they'd been sent to gather intelligence about. Underworld types dealing in opium trade to funnel money to terrorist camps.

J.T. knew. He was in a crapload of trouble.

His fingers jabbed into the sand as if to anchor himself for what would come next. Their captors would establish dominance and control from the start, pummel them to obtain information ASAP to maximize its utility.

He just needed to hold on, stay alive until rescue could come. He stayed on his stomach beside his three crewmates. Flattened his palms by his head, in the sand.

Keep calm.

Out of the corner of his eyes, he saw it. The betraying twitch from Bo, just seconds before—ah hell, don't do it, kid—the young copilot looked up.

Like making eye contact with the stalking lion.

The man over him shouted, stepped on Bo's right hand. Crunching.

J.T. swallowed down bile. Grit his teeth. Struggled for restraint.

Before Bo's echoing curse faded, the rebel raised his AK-47 above his head. Brought the butt down, fast, hard.

On Bo's other hand.

A strangled scream ripped along the roaring wind. Bo rolled to his side, cradled his mangled fingers, distorted wrist to his chest with his other abused hand. His face screwed up in agony even as defiance blazed from his too-young eyes.

Inviting the worst.

The crunch of breaking bones reverberated in J.T.'s brain, breaking something inside him, as well. He didn't remember making a decision to move, act, intercept. Just flung himself sideways while those cracking-bone sounds rattled around in his head.

Stupid. Reckless. Useless. But already the rifle was raised to come down on Bo again and J.T. couldn't stop the man. But he could control the damage.

J.T. shielded his copilot. His comrade in arms. Launched his body between the young soldier and the shouting rebel. Took a rifle butt to the shoulder. Caught a boot in the ribs.

Focused on the big three. Life. Honor. Returning home…

From the comfort of his porch, J.T. watched Bo's Jeep inch down the street, hesitate at the stop sign for opposing traffic. The white cast gleamed in the sun, stark, but not as harsh as the metal rods that had poked from his skin during the early days of reconstructive surgery after their release.

J.T. held tighter to the wooden railing until splinters cut into his fingers with grounding reminders that he existed in the present. In the States. At home.

Easier said than done.

God, he needed to get his head out of the desert. He told

himself Shakespeare had it right again in *Othello* by asking, "What wound did ever heal but by degrees?"

But he wanted this hell over now. Instead, his brain and his soul were still stuck in that time. Which left him less than half here when more than ever he needed his head on straight to fix his life. Salvage whatever was left of his marriage.

Bo's Jeep, his cast, if not the memories, disappeared around the corner. They'd maintained life throughout their capture. They'd maintained honor until their rescue.

Who'd have thought the toughest part would be figuring out how to return?

Chapter 5

Rena propped her foot on an extra dining-room chair and peered across the sturdy oak table at her family. Everyone was together for the first time since the weekend of J.T.'s return from Rubistan. Even if J.T. was in major brood-mode since he'd come in from seeing Bo off, her heart hungered to hold on to the moment more than her pregnant body craved chicken wings.

And that was mighty damned much.

She'd been so grateful to have him home and alive that nothing else seemed to matter. Not even their split.

She'd met him at the base with their children, never discussing where he would go afterward. Both knew and accepted he would come home instead of returning to the studio apartment he'd leased after she tossed him out.

All through that family dinner months ago, they'd sat together amid balloons and banners and favorite foods. And once the dishes were scraped clean of lamb chops, again there'd been no question but that he would follow her into her room. Their room.

Their bed. Two minutes later, they'd been naked.

Now her eyes met his over the Crock-Pot of chili, the platter of chicken wings and—oh yeah—her husband remembered, too, the night they'd made this baby nestled inside her.

J.T. shot to his feet, grabbed his empty plate and glass before hotfooting it to the kitchen, leaving her at the mercy of more memories.

Then when there'd been another night after his first night home, she'd thought maybe, just maybe they had enough to keep them together after all. She'd married him because of his strength, his honor, the reassurance that never would J.T. Price expose his family to men with concealed guns and shifty eyes. The "Price" last name would never show up in the news with reports about questionable acquittals and hung juries.

Once she'd entered J.T.'s world, people stopped whispering behind her back. Good, honest people no longer kept their families away from her.

Growing up, the promise of security had been everything to her, and she'd found security for herself and for her children. For years she'd thought it greedy to expect more. Finally, she'd learned to respect herself enough to demand everything.

But the cost was so much higher than she'd expected.

Chris scraped his chair back from the table, gathering his plate. "Gotta run. My shift starts in an hour. I'm closing up tonight, so I'll be late."

Nikki shoved back from the table, too, passing her plate to her brother on his way past. "Hold on a second before you go, runt, so I can say goodbye. I need to hit the highway soon to make it back up to Chapel Hill for the study session. Just need to talk to Mom for one more sec."

As Nikki rounded to her mother, Rena took her daughter's hand and squeezed. "Thanks for coming down, hon."

Crouching down beside the chair, Nikki leaned in with a

wide-open hug as exuberant as those childhood embraces, even though she now topped her mother by at least six inches. Rena let herself enjoy just holding on to her daughter and savoring those baby-shampoo and gummy-smile memories of her firstborn.

Finally, Nikki pulled away, rocking back on her haunches. "Boundaries are all well and good, Mom. But it doesn't hurt to push them sometimes."

Her free-spirited daughter would think so. And Rena was proud to have brought her daughter up in an environment where she could feel free to explore life, secure in knowing her parents loved her. That even if her father might be over-protective at times, he would always keep her safe.

Nikki would make a great teacher, with her love of children—an open, honest woman. Rena just hoped no one would take advantage of that.

"Well, hon, I want you to enjoy your time at college and exploring all those boundaries. Don't worry about me. I'm fine."

"I'm glad Dad's here, but I'm still going to drop in when I can." She held up her hand. "And no playing martyr-mom. My teammates are already asking when the next squadron picnic is."

"So they can check out the flyboys."

"Do ya' think?" Nikki almost kept a straight face.

Chris loped out of the kitchen, baggy clothes rippling with every step. "Which dude did you pick out for yourself? Used to be you begged off every picnic that you could. Hmm, I wonder who—"

Nikki smacked him on the back of the head. "Enough, motormouth. I'm just enjoying the scenery there."

"Ow, love you, too, bonehead."

While J.T. lumbered out to see their children off, Rena sagged back in her chair, affectionate sibling insults a welcome ritual in the middle of an upside-down day. J.T. stood in the open doorway until the last car faded, then turned to her.

Who would have thought silence could be so loud?

They were alone. Completely alone for the first time in months. No kids. No guests.

No interruptions.

Kicking the door closed, he ambled toward the table, hands in pockets, slow, deliberate, sexy. "Does she really have a thing for one of the guys in the squadron?"

Rena's brain stuttered as she tried to follow his conversational shift. Then it hit her. They always talked about their children to disperse tension and avoid deeper discussions.

A wise course of action tonight with plenty of tension snapping along the air between them.

"Nikki has been coming home more often since we roped her into helping out with the games at the squadron children's Christmas party. And of course she spent as much time as possible home right after..." Rena swallowed, forced herself not to sidestep the hard topics. "After you were released from Rubistan. But she's never mentioned any particular man to me."

"Good."

"Why so?" Had she soured his thoughts on marriage that much? "Don't you want to see your daughter settled? Have grandkids someday?"

"Someday. Not now." He jerked a spindle chair around, straddled it backward. "And not with a crewdog."

J.T.'s words shocked her silly. What an odd statement from him, a man so devoted to the Air Force. "No question, this isn't always an easy way of life. But I would think the load would be lighter for a couple meant to be together, in sync with each other."

She watched for a reaction from him, some sign that maybe this new perception of his might bode well for them on some level in dealing with their future, even if that future didn't involve them as a couple. A thought that still stung.

But she found no softening from him, just his regular closed expression, dark eyes with full-strength defenses in place. It was almost as if the man wasn't even with her. His body was at her table going through the motions, doing what was right, but his mind was somewhere else.

Definitely not with her.

Major sting.

She speared another buffalo wing off the platter, twisted the bones apart. *Crack. Crack.*

J.T. shot up from his chair.

Rena lowered her hands back to her plate. "Something wrong?"

He stared at the broken chicken bones in her fingers. "Are you ready to go upstairs?"

Did he have to sound so ready to get rid of her? "I'm still eating, but if you want to go up, I can maneuver a few steps. You don't have to stay."

He dropped onto the vacant chair beside her. "I'll wait."

His heels were dug in deep. She sighed her surrender, tossed aside the last wing and wiped her fingers. "Okay, fine. I'm ready. Thank you."

He stood, slid his arms under her, lifted her in a smooth sweep. Their faces were inches apart, and this time no one would open a door or interrupt.

J.T. cradled her against his chest and started down the hall. He turned sideways to angle up the stair, his gym shoes padding quietly on the wooden steps. Framed school photos and family portraits lined the walls, up, faces growing younger and happier with every step.

He cleared the top stair. "Do you, uh, need help getting into the shower or anything?"

"I took a shower at the hospital. I'm okay for now. And

I really can use the crutches with no problem most of the time.''

''No shower then.''

Was he disappointed? She couldn't tell by the rigid set of his square jaw. More frightening, was *she* disappointed?

Their bed sprawled big and inviting and lonely ahead of her with four large oak posts, wedding ring quilt, fluffy pillows in matching shams.

So many memories.

He lowered her to the giving softness as he'd done often before, except this time easing away. ''Shout if you need anything. I'll be right back with your crutches, and then right across the hall.''

In Nikki's old room, no parking his boots under their bed.

''J.T.?'' she called, not sure what she would say, just certain she wasn't ready to see those broad shoulders leave through her doorway yet.

For a reckless moment she wanted to blame on tumultuous hormones, she wondered what it would be like to loosen those boundaries, be sex buddies with J.T. for a few days and take the edge off so much tension.

But she was weak when it came to this man. Even if he agreed, she wasn't sure she could punt him out of her bed a second time.

''Rena? Do you need something?''

A kiss. His solid body on his side of the bed again. A way to erase the image of him walking out the door the last time she'd swallowed her pride and invited him home. ''Thank you for staying here with me. I know this has to be uncomfortable for you, too. But in two weeks, we'll have everything settled out, and you'll be able to return to your place. I'm a fast healer.''

Liar. But she was learning.

''Wounds need to heal by degrees. Just take care of yourself and rest up. The new kid will have you running soon enough.'' He backed into the hall. '''Night, Rena.''

Once his footsteps faded, she flopped into the fluff of pillows.

The baby. The reason he'd returned.

Funny, but apparently her heart didn't heal as fast as the rest of her.

Chris's stomach clenched as tight as the rag twisted in his grip while he washed dishes over the restaurant's industrial-size sink. An ocean breeze rolled in through the open back door. Not that it did much good sweeping out the fish stink. Heat popped salty sweat down his face, into his shirt.

Great for the acne. Not.

If zits were his only worry.

Chris glanced over his shoulder, checked, found the kitchen empty. He resumed dragging dishes under the spraying water to rinse away fried seafood and hush puppies before stacking each plate in the dishwasher.

Hell no, he wasn't a wuss. He could work out his problems. Face them like a man. He might not look like his dad, but he would be like him when it counted. He would finish up his shift at the restaurant. No big deal. And under no circumstances would he make any more deliveries.

He just wished he'd never answered the ad in the base paper about this job. But his mom and dad were always fighting about money. He'd taken the job to help out as much as to get away from the arguing.

The double doors from the dining area swished open. Sweat iced, then itched along his back. He snapped around to find…the busboy who'd recommended he take this lame job. The fellow military brat dropped off his tub of plates and left.

At least it wasn't *her*. But the swinging door still offered sporadic glimpses of *her* anyway. The hostess, Miranda Casale, smiling her million-dollar smile for the final departing customers. Miranda sure knew how to flash that smile along with a view down her silk shirts to get guys to do anything she wanted.

Even now he went dry-mouthed at the thought of her honey-golden skin with a charm necklace between two perfect breasts.

He tried to swallow. Failed.

Damn, damn, damn! He loved Shelby, so why was he drooling over someone he didn't even like? Teenage hormones so sucked.

One look down Miranda's dress two weeks ago and before he knew it, he'd been on his way out the door to run an errand for her. Just a food delivery for a special client—even though they didn't normally deliver squat.

Sucker.

He didn't know why Miranda had sent along so much money with the food delivery, but the fluky look he'd gotten at a stack of hundreds left him with zero doubts.

The reason couldn't be good.

He'd reported it to his boss, only to be told he must have misunderstood. Or maybe it was all innocent, but thanks anyhow, kid, and he would definitely talk to her. And, oh by the way, if rumors started, damaging business, Chris and his family would be sued and he sure would hate for that to happen and were they on the same page here now, pal?

God. Chris chunked another plate into the dishwasher. He'd clammed up faster than his father that day.

His parents would totally wig out if they knew. His dad was rigid on the honesty thing, and Mom went ballistic if he got so much as a detention for being tardy twice in a semester. Geez. Sometimes he wondered if it might be easier to forget about meeting their expectations.

But his mom was pregnant. And his dad was a freaking zombie since Rubistan.

So he would hang tough. Not be a wuss. And try like crazy to tell himself his mom's hit-and-run accident in *his* car was totally a coincidence.

Chris stacked the last of the dishes and flung aside the rag. Only a few more minutes and then home free for one more day. Maybe Miranda would transfer to another college and take her flashing boobs and smile somewhere else.

At least he knew better than to let himself be sucked in by her again. Jesus, like a nineteen-year-old hot chick would really be interested in him anyhow. But those raging hormones zapped IQ points.

The doors swished again. No Miranda—thank God. No busboy, either. This time his boss raced in, loosening his tie, a laid-back dude in his thirties with only two employee mottos: Don't make waves, and treat his wife and little girl like royalty.

The boss man, Kurt Haugen, definitely always sided with the chicks. "I have to leave now before I'm any later getting home. Don't forget to lock up behind you."

"I won't, Mr. Haugen."

"Thanks, kid, and make sure Miranda and the other waitresses get in their cars safe and sound. Okay? Wouldn't want anything to happen to them."

Chris stood taller. Okay, so the guy pampered women. Bet he wouldn't get a baby-sitter Bo to stay overnight when a guy was already sixteen. "Sure. No problem, Mr. Haugen."

Of course, now he had to wait around for Miranda, but he could just sit in the car and watch until she left. Yeah. That would work. Doors locked. Eyes on her face, which was more respectful anyhow. Not to mention safer.

"I really need to haul ass, pal. I missed my daughter's gymnastics competition this afternoon. Engine went out on the shrimp trawler, which had me on the phone all day tracking down repair parts. And damn but I hated missing the little princess turn her back flips. Wife's probably pissed, too. Hey, how about pass me one of those chocolate pecan pies. Maybe if I walk into the room leading with that, it'll soften her up. And a candy bar for the princess. What do you think, pal?''

Swinging open the refrigerator, Chris stretched to get the pie off the top rack. ''I think chicks dig chocolate.''

Mr. Haugen winked, lifting the pie from Chris's hand. ''You'll go far with the ladies, my man.''

''Sure.'' Adults could be so lame.

Mr. Haugen snagged two candy bars from the cooking station, Heath Bars for the specialty pies. He tucked one in his sports jacket and tossed the other to Chris. ''Chocolate. For the special chick in your life.''

Chris snagged the candy bar midair and tucked it into his droopy shirt pocket. ''Yeah, whatever. I'll make sure everyone gets out of here fine.''

A half hour later, he stood in the front parking lot, locking the door, taking his time until Miranda revved her engine, the last of the crowd to go.

Finally, Miranda spewed gravel on her way out of the lot. He exhaled long. Off the hook. Alone, just him and waves pounding the dock, sailboat lines snapping and pinging.

He rounded the corner to where he'd parked—away from the shoreline and saltwater so his dad wouldn't blow a gasket about rust.

And pulled up short. A lone street lamp backlit a person sitting on the trunk of his mother's car. *Shelby.*

She perched cross-legged, flip-flops off and beside her as if she'd gotten comfortable for a long wait. She hugged her knees to her chest, her jet-black hair lifting in the wind.

Damn. How could he have ever even looked at Miranda?

He tried not to think about the chocolate bar in his pocket. ''You shouldn't be out here alone. It's not safe.''

She turned at his voice, then rested her chin on her knees without answering. Did chicks practice this silent-treatment stuff to confuse guys? He didn't have much practice on how to handle it since the women in his family weren't ever afraid to speak their minds.

He strode closer, faster, until he could see her clearly. Ah man, her eyes stared back, all red and swollen, puffy from crying. He tried to think of something to say and only came up with, "Want a Heath Bar? Mom says chocolate cures everything."

Her bottom lip quivered.

Way to go, hotshot. "Okay, no chocolate."

Foot on the bumper, he propelled himself up to sit on the trunk beside her. Maybe quiet was good after all, kinda like his dad did. When his dad clammed up, Mom usually spilled her guts. Then a guy didn't have to guess what was going on and risk botching it by actually getting involved in the discussion.

Besides, sitting with Shelby, the ocean breeze puffing by, he could smell her. Be close to her. Why rush ending that? He stared up at the inky sky dotted with stars and just breathed salty air and Shelby.

She shifted beside him, slid her flip-flops back on. "You probably need to get home."

"Nah, my folks know I'm working." He would take the ass-ripping from his dad for being late. Time alone with Shelby was rare since Shelby and Murdoch were so tight.

Or were they?

Another tear glistened in the corner of her eye. From a breakup? He couldn't stop the hope.

Which made him feel like a disloyal scumbag. "Where's Murdoch?"

"Away for the weekend." She sniffled, blinked fast. "Some family-reunion thing."

Okay, not breaking up. "Bummer. Tough luck him being gone right now. You don't have too many weekends left before the moving truck pulls out. Then college."

"Uh-huh."

She chewed off her glitter lip gloss while more waves crashed. He waited and reminded himself he was her friend. Murdoch's friend. And friends didn't take advantage. He was cool with them as a couple.

"I think I'm pregnant."

Her simple sentence hung there and man it hurt. Bad. He wasn't okay with crap.

He'd known in his head that Shelby and Murdoch were probably doing it. They'd been dating for about two years, after all. But it wasn't something he let himself think about too much because it would drive him kinda crazy.

Not much choice but to think about it now. "Are you sure?"

"No." She swiped hair from her face. "Just, uh, late. Scared. I needed to talk to somebody before I totally lost it in front of my folks."

Honor forced him to say, "Shouldn't you be talking to Murdoch about this instead of me?"

She didn't answer, just kept brushing hair out of her face while wind streaked it right back again.

"It is, uh, his, right?"

She jerked toward him, shock, anger, hurt all glittering in her eye like the sparkles in her lip gloss. "God, yes. What kind of person do you think I am?" She started inching down the hood. "I shouldn't have even come here. This isn't your problem, anyway."

"Hold on." He gripped her arm to stop her from sliding off to leave. "Chill. It's just weird that you're talking to me first. But I'm totally cool with it."

The fight crumpled out of her spine. Tears flooded, dripped over. What kind of guy would he be if he didn't comfort her? No big deal. A friend thing. He patted her back. Safe. Still friend stuff.

A really soft curvy friend.

He clenched his jaw tight. Ditch the thoughts, dude. Remember the mess with Miranda. Shelby's current mess. Hell, his parents' mess.

Couldn't anybody besides him keep their pants zipped?

Shelby sniffed, pressed the heels of her hands to her eyes. "It's not like we were stupid or anything. We were always careful, used condoms."

That was so much more information than he needed. "Uh-huh."

"But no kind of birth control is a hundred percent, you know?"

Not really. But now didn't seem to be the time to mention his virgin status. "Says so on the box."

"We haven't even been doing it all that long."

So she'd held out against John Murdoch. Marginal balm for an aching ego. "Oh, um…"

"John wanted me to be sure."

Hell. Now he couldn't even hate the guy. "You must be really important to him."

A small smile broke through for the first time. "That's what he says." Her smile drooped. "But he's already pissed at me because I won't go to the same college as him, and now he's going to use this to make me do things his way. I'm just a senior in high school. I don't want to get married yet."

Married? "Whoa. Hold on. Why worry until you know for sure? No need to get all fired up and mad at him." Way to go, sap. Help the guy. Except in this case, helping Murdoch meant helping Shelby. "Why don't you get one of those home tests?"

"They're not a hundred percent for sure."

"It's a place to start."

"Maybe I don't want to know for sure." She snapped a hair band on her wrist, then again and again. "God, my dad's going to be so disappointed in me. I don't know how I'm going to face him."

"What about your mom? Can you go to her place for the weekend, talk to her first?"

Shelby snorted, yanking the band off her wrist and twisting her hair back. "She'll either totally freak out and just call my dad to handle it, or pretend everything's fine and offer to take me shopping at the mall."

"Maybe you could go to your stepmom."

"Julia's cool," Shelby conceded, giving her hair a final twist in the band. "But she'll tell Dad, because that's the way they are together. Tight, you know?"

"Hmm," he grunted, because he didn't know. His parents weren't that way, never had been, and it pissed him off that no amount of extra "alone time" together seemed to make any difference. "What do you want to do?"

"I want to scream. I want to cry." Her hands dropped from her silky black hair into her lap. "I want somebody to hug me and tell me it's gonna be okay."

"Well, I can help you out with half of that."

Chris wrapped his arms around her, tucked her under his chin and let her cry. Finally, he was holding Shelby Dawson against his chest—and he couldn't do a damn thing but comfort her while she crushed his Heath Bar.

J.T. creaked back in the office chair in his den, rubbed his hand along his stiff neck, stared at his computer screen offering nada, zip, zilch in the way of info. Damn it, that bumper sticker on the back of the hit-and-run van had to mean something, red circle with a black triangle inside. If only he could identify the damn thing and trace it.

The walls of the small paneled room started to close in on him. He needed progress. Action. Anything to shake the freaking inactivity.

He thumbed along the pages of the discarded book beside the computer. Even the Bard couldn't quiet the storm in him tonight.

Dinner with his wife and kids had been near perfect, so close to what he'd planned for himself during his teen years. Nice house. Plenty of food. The conversation was a bonus he hadn't known he was missing until Rena came into his life. Sure he didn't join in much, but he listened. Enjoyed. Like tonight.

And then she'd started cracking those chicken wing bones. Bo's breaking hand had echoed in his head. And…

It was all too much. Too much emotion, noise. Storm.

He'd retreated. Except his quiet office, books, computer weren't offering him much in the way of relief.

A noise broke the silence.

He glanced up at the clock again, pendulum swinging. Rena was asleep—he'd checked. That one look at her soft body curved into her pillow was the source of most of his current frustration.

Chris was due home over an hour ago, but the office window showcased an empty parking spot.

Floorboards groaned. Old house-settling noises? Or something else.

Unease cranked along with his heart rate. He slid the key into the bottom drawer of his desk, opened, pulled out his M9 Beretta pistol.

The sounds could be nothing. The hit-and-run could be nothing. Or it could all be something, and no way would any of it get near his family.

Another squeak of boards and a rustle spurred him to action.

He edged out into the hall, following the sounds. Quiet, stealthy sounds. Should he have called the cops first? His hand fell to his cell phone in his back pocket, pulled it free and ready as he followed.

His footsteps led him to the kitchen. He slipped around the corner, socks silent on ceramic tile until he found…

His hungry intruder head deep in the refrigerator, a mighty fine and familiar ass pertly in view, clothed in a red satin nightshirt he'd given Rena two Christmases ago.

Chapter 6

J.T. lowered the gun to his side and feasted on the luscious sight of his wife's incredible ass while she feasted on whatever held her attention in the refrigerator.

Adrenaline surged through him alongside relief. Lust raged at Mach speed, leaving him totally at the mercy of memories from last summer when he'd returned home from TDY—temporary duty. He'd been on the road so much over the past few years with Afghanistan, Iraq, and regular TDYs to supply troops all around the world, he'd spent little time in his wife's bed. In his wife's arms.

In his wife's body.

He'd eased into the kitchen last summer after his return from Guam, dropped his helmet bag softly to the floor. She'd heard, her spine straightening as she stood on a ladder stenciling an ivy border along the walls.

A smile had tipped her profile, but she hadn't moved, just waited for him to cross to her. He'd stopped behind her, so damn grateful for his son's band camp because—oh yeah—

now Rena was alone in the house and he could wrap his arms around his wife to lift her off the ladder. Slide her back along his front as he lowered her to the ground.

He'd taken the green-soaked paintbrush from her, cupped the gentle weight of her breasts in his hands as she pressed her bottom against the already straining length of his erection.

Seconds later she'd been gripping the edge of the counter, her dress had been up, his zipper open, her thong snapped.

An awesome memory. No chance of repeating it anytime soon, though. He needed to stay his course. No risking sex until he convinced her he should stay.

He crossed, placed his gun on top of the refrigerator.

Rena jumped, glanced over her shoulder. "God, J.T.! You scared a year off my life." She blushed, thrusting the bowl forward like a peace offering. "Want some chili?"

Peace would be nice. Except he couldn't get past the temptation of her unrestrained breasts against the satin nightshirt. Who turned the air conditioner on so cold? "Heard a noise, and since you shouldn't be up at all it never crossed my mind it might be you. What the hell are you doing up, anyway?"

"No chili? Okay, then. More for me." She popped open the lid on the Tupperware bowl, snagged a spoon and started shoveling. She shouldn't have appeared graceful in the midst of a feeding frenzy. But she did. "You seemed so intent on what you were doing in the study, I didn't want to bother you. Can you reach down there for the grated cheese, please?"

She'd been watching him, too? Adrenaline surged hotter, faster, throbbing low and south fast. Kneeling in front of her to find the bag of cheese didn't help. He was at the perfect level to hitch up that satin and—

"Thanks." She snatched the cheese from his hand and sprinkled some on top of her chili. "I woke up to, uh, go to the bathroom. God, I'd forgotten the seven thousand bathroom runs a night that come with being pregnant. And then

I realized I was starving. In the morning I can't eat without being sick, and then I spend the whole rest of the day unable to eat enough. Crazy, huh?''

Crazy? He stood. Yeah, he was definitely going nuts talking about puking when all he could think about was pressing her against the counter and hiking up her nightshirt. Reenacting that memory of a better time before their world exploded. He'd known the split was coming, always expected the end. Considered every day with her another dodged bullet. Nope, he hadn't been in the least surprised when his hand weights sailed out the window and bounced off his book onto the lawn.

However, he hadn't expected another chance three months ago, a chance he'd blown. A mistake he wouldn't repeat. Which meant no jumping Rena in the kitchen.

Her eyes flashed with inspiration. She snatched a pudding pack from the refrigerator door. ''Cravings.''

''Like before.''

''Textbook.'' She limped to the minuscule kitchenette table. Sighing, she sagged into a seat, swinging her injured foot up onto one of the other chairs. ''Hope you don't want any pudding, because this is the last one, so you'll have to pry it out of my hormonally tight grip.''

J.T. kicked the refrigerator shut. He dropped into a chair across from her and watched her savor alternating bites of chili and chocolate pudding. She licked the spoon clean every time. Rapture spread across her face.

His knuckles itched to glide across her high cheekbones as a prelude to kissing away the chocolate on the corner of her mouth. Damn, she was beautiful. ''I can't believe I missed it.''

''Missed what?''

He shook his head at his own blindness the past few months. ''That you're pregnant.''

He let himself reach, touch just his thumb to the corner of her lush lips.

Ducking his touch, she grabbed for a napkin. "Because I'm eating like a pig? Thanks. I'm now totally reassured you don't want to come back home or you would have never made that comment."

Her hands fell to her stomach. His hungry eyes followed her gesture to the slight swell. He could almost feel the taut skin over the growing proof of their child. Had in fact felt it in days past when she'd carried their other children.

Would he be allowed to feel the roll of their baby under his hand this time? "Lower the hackles. I wasn't commenting on the food."

"Oh, uh, well, you probably didn't notice because I wore loose clothes."

If ever he'd needed the Bard's way with words, it was now. He'd just have to settle for simple honesty. "That still isn't what I meant." He angled closer, elbows on the table. "You know I'm not much of a guy for woo-hoo stuff. But that pregnancy-glow thing—there must be something scientific to it. I mean, hell, Rena, you've been in a wreck. Suffered a concussion. Damn near broke your foot, and you're still glowing so bright I could read by it."

Not an intimate touch to her tummy, but he could see his words warmed her nearly as much. Victory chugged through him.

A slow smile lit that glow to blinding levels. "I think there's a compliment in there somewhere."

"I guess so. Wish I'd actually thought to give it. But honestly, I'm just amazed that I could have been so clueless."

"We see what we want to see."

"Putting that psych degree to work?"

"Maybe. Or maybe just one of those side benefits to getting older."

Older. Odd how he could feel so old some days but she still seemed the same woman he'd married.

Only with better curves.

He reached for her hand. "Are you scared?"

Well, hell, that was downright sensitive, and damned if she didn't let him hold her hand. Maybe the Bard was rubbing off on him after all.

"Does it bother me having a baby this late in life? A little. With my job, I know the increased risks with age."

"And that worries you."

"I probably worry less than I did at eighteen. Maybe because I feel more…at peace about motherhood."

"So your fears are…?"

Being alone. He read it all over her face. He worked his thumb over her wrist. Who'd have thought he'd get such a rush out of holding his wife's hand and neither of them was even naked.

"I'm just being emotional. Hormones and all that. The timing's not the best, but I'm going to have a baby."

"We're going to have a baby." He squeezed her hand. "*We.* This is my child, too, so we're in this for another eighteen. At least. Remember that."

He tried to read her again and found…more of that fear. Of him? He deserved a lot of things, but not that.

The back door rattled with a key. Rena jerked her hand away, momentary connection snapped. Chris swung the door open.

Frustration brewed in him. "Where have you been?"

"Talking with a friend." Chris snagged the bowl of chili from the table, found a fresh spoon and started shoveling. "Time kinda slipped away. Sorry."

Rena's hand fell to her son's arm to stop him midbite. "We worry. Call next time."

"Sure," he answered evasively before dropping the bowl

in the sink. Fishing a candy bar out of his pocket, he tore open the wrapper and tossed broken pieces into his mouth.

Warning bells clanged like an alert klaxon. The kid had plenty to be edgy about, but was there more?

He had two weeks to find out. Two weeks of nonstop one-on-one time with his wary wife, where he would be helping her with her every intimate need while refraining from giving her the most intimate of touches.

If J.T. didn't touch her, really touch her soon, she would burst into flames. Or scream. Or do something equally embarrassing that would leave her husband frowning pensively, then helping while giving her a wide berth as he'd done for the past week and a half.

True to his word, he'd been around whenever she needed him, all his flights conveniently scheduled at night after she fell asleep and Chris was already home. But even though J.T. slept part of the day, his presence still filled the house, reminding her of the good times, until she feared coming down with a convenient case of amnesia when it came to remembering all that drove them apart.

At least they were out of their too-close quarters, their home having become a sauna of need. Instead, spring heat baked the roof of the truck, lunch-hour traffic spewing exhaust on the highway leading toward the base. Nausea tickled, but at least it distracted her from her achy foot. Achy, but no longer throbbing and *sans* stitches.

A cargo plane roared low overhead on its approach for landing. She fidgeted along the bench seat, anxious to finish up the drive, get back to work, even for an hour or two. J.T. wasn't happy about it, but she couldn't juggle this particular patient to another counselor. And the afternoon would also offer J.T. the chance to fit in a training class at the squadron while he waited.

Could he tempt her from clear across base? Seeing him so hot and hunky in his flight suit didn't help.

He'd been doing a mighty fine job of tempting her the past few days even in his favorite Hawaiian shirts and jean shorts. So attentive. So blasted perfect. He carried her up the stairs. Down the stairs. To the shower. Sat beside her on the sofa, shared popcorn, watched chick flicks with her, brought tissues when she cried over the endings because her own life sucked so bad. And never, never once did he make a move on her.

Who the hell was this man and what had he done with her husband?

"We need to talk."

And now he wanted discussion?

The world was totally screwed up. Maybe his trip into base would mark a shift from all those night flights to day flights so he wouldn't be around to entice her during waking hours. "About what?"

He slowed onto the exit ramp off the highway at the base exit during lunch rush hour. "Do you think everything's okay with Chris?"

That sounded more like her husband, focusing on the kids. Safe territory.

She considered his question through an entire traffic light. She'd traveled this familiar parental route with her husband often in the past. He would ask her how he should approach one of the kids. She would give him advice that he always followed. She felt needed.

But he would be parenting alone during his weekends and vacations with Chris. Even though she was close now to help, what if he was transferred? He couldn't pick up the phone every time he had a question about what to say to their son.

He was a loving father, worked hard at being there for his kids. But only now did she realize how he always acquiesced to her way when it came to parenting.

She'd *let* him rely on her. Had she wanted him to need her

on at least some level? A painful notion because then she would have done her children a disservice.

Damn it, she'd tried her best to balance everything. He was gone so often, most of the daily parenting fell to her. They couldn't afford a slew of phone calls. The Internet and e-mails helped with keeping him in touch with his kids, but that hadn't been a major-player option until they were older.

She circled her jumble of bracelets round and round her wrist. No use beating herself or him up about the past. Just do the best she could with their present and future.

Concentrate on the present, improving the right now. Instead of giving advice, she would ask his opinion. "What makes you think there might be something wrong with Chris?"

"He was late coming home the day of your accident, then again the night you were released from the hospital. Sure he mouths off sometimes like any teenager, but he keeps close to home."

"Have you asked him what's wrong?"

"He's had plenty of chances to talk and no dice. I know I haven't been around much, but I sure as hell tried this week, worked out with him, jogged. I even showed him how to fix stuff around the house."

So Chris could repair things after his father left again? "Did you ask him what he's feeling?"

His jaw tightened in familiar defensiveness as he downshifted along the pine-lined entry road leading up to the base. "Men aren't into all that touchy-feely emotional crap."

"Lovely."

He rubbed a hand along his neck. "Back down, babe. I respect what you do. God knows, anyone who'd drag her wounded self up there to work is obviously devoted."

Sure he respected her job. Just didn't believe in it and wouldn't touch a penny of her paycheck for so much as a family vacation to blow off steam created by his job. "Some clients could wait a couple of weeks without setting back progress. With others, it's not so simple.''

"Tough one?"

Not nearly as tough as getting through to her own husband, but then he wasn't a patient, and she couldn't heal her family. She knew that. But accepting it? Not so easy.

J.T. flashed his military ID at the security gate and the guard waved him forward. "I'm not looking for you to break confidentiality. Just expressing interest in your world.''

"Thank you.'' She twisted sideways toward him. "You know that's borderline touchy-feely.''

"Touch?'' He echoed the word that had been plaguing her all day—for days, actually. Was he a mind reader now, too? "We probably need to stay away from that subject if we're going to lay some new groundwork for taking care of this little one.''

Of course he was right. She totally agreed. So why was she cranky? She'd won, after all.

J.T. turned off toward her office, red brick building sprawling in front of her, while he hunted for an empty spot in the jammed lot. She was confident in her job, but still her own screwed-up home life made her question her judgment. And, oh, this man did so have a way of jumbling her mind. "Just as well Chris interrupted last week. We're too old for the over-the-kitchen-counter quickies.''

"We weren't too old for it three months ago. And you sure as hell weren't too old for the table, the stairs, the shower—''

"Sex was never our problem, J.T.''

Steam filled the truck's cab. He shifted the truck into park. The packed parking lot of empty cars offered a pseudo sense of solitude in spite of the public locale, blue minivan on her left, an RV on the right, even a Humvee in front of them. Still, he didn't reach for her.

But his hands shook from the restraint.

Rena launched into his arms. Couldn't help herself. No surprise.

Did he meet her halfway? She didn't know, and with his lips and hands finally on her, she couldn't think or reason. Only feel. Savor. His touch licking fire through her veins.

He palmed her back, molded her against his solid body, soft breasts yielding against hard chest.

And taste, oh, the taste of him as she explored the warmth of his mouth. Talk about cravings. One apparently he suffered from, as well, his tongue delving deeper, sweeping, heating. She could almost forget they were in a public lot.

Rena inched closer, her calf-length skirt tangling around her legs, scrunchy fabric rasping against skin suddenly over-sensitive to the least sensation. How incredible it would be to park somewhere private and toss away inhibitions, pretend they were both twenty-two years younger.

Strong hands gripped her shoulders. Eased her back, broke their kiss, but not the touching. His forehead rested on hers. "God, babe, I've missed you."

Her eyes stung and she knew full well it had nothing to do with pregnancy hormones. "I've missed you, too."

She started to slide her arms around him again. Surely they could hug without getting arrested for a public display. She reached, her bracelets jangling to her elbow. He pulled away.

What?

He opened the door. Where the hell was he going? For the first time in months there was a hint of real emotion and he decided they should head on into work.

She longed for one of his books to throw.

Breathe. Think. Don't let the angry, passionate—pained—emotions clamoring through her reign.

Rena clamped a hand around his arm. "Hold on a minute. Jesus, J.T., you throw that land mine in my lap, clam up and then wonder why I explode."

Tension rippled under her fingers. "I'm not going to fight with you today."

"I don't want to fight." She really, really didn't want to fight at the moment. But a public parking lot wasn't the place for what her body demanded. "We were talking. That's good. Why do we have to stop?"

His smoky gray eyes brushed her lips as surely as his kiss, lingered, finally fell away. A long exhale cut the silence before he swung his feet back into the truck. "Okay, fine. We'll talk. We never did come up with anything concrete about Chris, anyway."

Her hands clenched. She didn't want to talk about their children. She wanted to hear more about how much he'd missed her. And why. Silly, frivolous words, considering her age and how long they'd been married.

All the more reason they were better off talking about their children. Safer for them. Safer for her heart.

J.T. slammed the truck door. "I'm not sure what's up with the boy anymore. I *have* tried to talk to him. Guys just approach things…differently."

"Guess that's why men have more heart attacks than women."

He draped his wrist over the steering wheel. "I'll try to talk to Chris. If you have any ideas for conversation starters, I'm not adverse to listening." His gray eyes lit. "Then I can translate them into manspeak."

"Manspeak?"

"Sure. You've seen those lists that float around on the Internet. Guy says 'uh-huh' and it means—"

"It means, 'I'll agree to anything if you'll quit blocking my view of the football game.'"

"Busted." He grinned.

"So if I asked Chris if he's upset and does he need to share what's bothering, you would ask…?"

"Something pissing you off?"

"Or if he's suffering from any anxiety about his parents splitting?"

"You okay about everything?"

Ah. Understanding hummed through her as clearly as the airplane's drone overhead. "Your question is a third as long as mine. And vague. What if he misses the point because of that vagueness?"

"What if *I'm* missing the point and he tells me something I never expected?"

Surprise at his insight stunned her quiet. What else might he have offered up if she'd asked his input on the parenting more often? "Valid thought."

"Yeah, I just made it up."

A laugh snorted free. His dry wit always snuck up on her like that. "But women need those extra words. Otherwise how are we supposed to know when you're in pain?"

"There's your logic flaw. A man's never in pain."

"That he'll admit."

"Bingo."

What else could she pry out of her reticent husband with a few more questions? "So how does a woman know when a man needs something?"

A slow smile dimpled his rugged handsomeness seconds before his smoky gray eyes steamed over her. "Oh, babe, trust me, you'll know."

The truck cab fogged all over again, heavier this time since it sparked the barely banked heat of their kiss moments prior. She wanted so much from him, and she was right in demanding he pony up more in their relationship.

But she'd hit a wall so many times with her clam-up husband. Regardless of whether they stayed together, they would be together in many ways because of their children. She needed to understand J.T.'s hidden emotions if she ever expected to survive without combusting into flames—from both anger and passion. "What does it mean when a guy stumbles on his wife in the kitchen and when she offers to share her precious chili, he says, 'What the hell are you doing up?'''

He stared outside at the red brick building for so long, she thought he wouldn't answer her. No surprise. However, she *was* mega-surprised by how much she wanted that answer.

Finally, he turned, resigned, like a man heading to the gallows, scouring guilt over her for having sent him there. "You want more words, Rena? Here they are. In this case, the snapping then and now means a guy is horny as hell since he hasn't been with a woman except for one weekend in six months. It means he misses coming home from work to his wife, being able to slip up behind her, wrap his arms around her, fill his hands with her breasts. Fill her body with his."

The steam came straight off her overheated flesh this time. He missed her, missed what they had together. And even as she knew they needed so much more to hold it together, it felt so good to know he'd found some comfort, happiness, something in their life together.

He cupped her chin, his touch not quite gentle, but then the emotions stinging through her were anything but gentle. "It means he's damn tired of life being so complicated. But it is. And he's got to deal with it the best way he knows how, which means keeping things uncomplicated."

His fingers threaded up into her hair. "And we both know, babe, sex between the two of us is never uncomplicated." He drew his hand back, gentle, insistent, tugging against tangling curls, long, slow. "Sex for us is intense and messy and mind-blowing."

Her breaths came in heavy bursts of need, nerves along her scalp tingling with awareness. If he leaned forward, she would kiss him again. Let him kiss her, maybe more, because his words touched her as firmly as his hands.

But he didn't kiss her. "And we both need a clear mind now more than ever."

He pulled away. Left her again. A few months ago she would have cried. Or raged. A part of her wanted to now.

Except as she watched him retrieve her crutches from the back of the truck, she couldn't help but wonder what two-thirds he'd left unsaid. And was she really ready to hear what else she might learn from deciphering his "manspeak" when they climbed back into the truck again?

Chapter 7

Who would have thought he'd prefer a chemical-warfare class to making out with his wife in a parking lot?

Saluting a passing officer, J.T. strode up the walkway toward the brick and brown building, late-afternoon sun beating down on his shoulders. Damn it, but Rena had wriggled under his skin and made him say more than he wanted. His trump card in their relationship had always been keeping his cool. Weathering the storm.

Somehow he'd managed to walk away a few minutes ago without giving in to the predictable urge to distract her with sex. Even with that out-of-control kiss of hers, he knew she would do a ninety-degree about-face once they took the edge off their frustrations.

She would start asking more of those chick questions. If he stayed quiet, he pissed her off. If he answered, somehow he came up short of what she wanted.

So he would go slow, soften her up since, no doubt, his prideful wife wouldn't easily get over his leaving. And with a cargo hold full of luck, they wouldn't die from hormonal overload.

He pushed through the glass door into the building, the full blast of air-conditioning catching him in the face. The soft echo of his boots on the industrial carpet echoed along with the low-pitched rumble of voices, ringing telephones, computer chimes.

From one of the rooms stepped Spike, his spiked hair longer than his previous buzz now that he wasn't undercover. In keeping with his regular OSI position, he'd exchanged the flight suit for khakis, a sports coat, and a palm tree-patterned tie that never stayed tight enough. Not exactly the normal look for an OSI agent, but Max "Spike" Keagan got the job done. His way. "Hey, dude. Are you on the schedule for chem-warfare update?"

"Heading that way now."

"Me, too. Thought I'd listen in." Spike slipped into pace alongside him. An easy man to hang with, the guy was as comfortable with silence as J.T.

They'd worked well together during the weeks training the OSI agent to pose as a loadmaster for the infiltration into the American base in Rubistan. Regs kept Spike from holding the crew position solo, but he knew enough to look credible when flying along with another loadmaster. No doubt Spike had picked up some additional tips from his pilot fiancée.

J.T. cleared the door into the room packed with aviators, tables in front of them littered with gas masks. Two more tables lined the front of the room with stacks of training carbon filters, a couple of training chemical suits. A mannequin stood propped in the corner, outfitted in the full gear.

C-17 squadrons didn't fly with set crews except during wartime or special operations, but allegiances gelled all the same, as could be seen by the seating choices. J.T. found his boots carrying him back to the corner with Scorch, Bronco, Crusty, Joker, Cobra...

And, God help him, motormouth Gabby, a six-foot-two-inch wiry guy in constant motion like a kid on sugar overload. Apparently Gabby had raided a Pixie Stix factory today.

"Hey there, sir, glad you could make it. How's your wife? Her foot doing any better? Sorry to hear about your totaled car, but good thing nobody was hurt bad, sir."

Swinging his gas mask up onto the table, J.T. averted his gaze from Scorch—smothering a laugh with his hand over his mustache. For some reason Gabby insisted on calling him sir no matter how many times he reminded the kid he wasn't an officer. Sarge would be fine. Or his call sign, Tag. Call signs were a universal leveler in the air to build a more cohesive team while flying. "My wife's doing better, thanks. She had to pull some office time, so I figured I'd work in the class, after all. Saves me having to make it up later."

Scorch leaned back in his chair, the Ivy League creases in his appearance and flight suit not the least diminished by his casual sprawl. "So she's getting around okay?"

"On crutches, yes sir."

"Glad you've been able to stay on the schedule with night flights." Scorch nodded. "We need you around here."

"I can pitch in extra," Gabby interrupted, "anytime you need time off or whatever. I'm always looking to log more flight time."

"Thanks." J.T. didn't bother arguing because it was a non-issue since the kid didn't have anywhere close to the security clearance needed to fly these missions.

Gabby reached for his Mountain Dew. "Where's Bo?"

Scorch shot over his shoulder. "Had some other appointment."

"Hmm." Gabby's combat boot twitched nonstop against the leg of the table while he banged back a gulp from his soda. "Wonder if his flight attendant's in town?"

J.T. hoped so since it would keep the squadron player occupied if Nikki came home for the weekend.

Cobra, the squadron's previous player but now happily married to one of the flight surgeons, hooked a boot on his knee. "If his girlfriend's not back soon, she'd better hurry. Word from my wife has it that the nurses flocked to the clinic yesterday when he got his cast sawed off."

Scorch swung his gas mask from the floor to the table. "About time he pulled his weight around here again."

They needed all the flying hands up and running. World deployments already taxed manpower, and the current surveillance flights added an extra load. But stopping the terrorist drug activity would put a serious dent in cash flow for the bad guys. Their dirty money bought things like shoulder-held missile launchers off the black market.

Already, their squadron had lost two planes in just that manner. His, shot down by the Gomer in a boat nearly four months ago. Another plane piloted by Cobra later was nailed during an operation to rescue American hostages being held overseas. Cobra's Gomer had camped his ass out in a field three freaking miles away from the runway for the fateful pop.

Gabby whistled low. "Damn, but Bo's got the good life. Women crawling over him. Guess we old married guys have to live vicariously through him, huh?"

Old? Gabby was what? All of twenty? But he certainly was married—to a nineteen-year-old wife who worked checkout at the base commissary to help make ends meet.

J.T. remembered those days well. If life wasn't so crazy he'd have the talkative kid and his wife over for a few meals and mentor him. Except Gabby and his wife would probably run screaming for divorce court with him as a model.

Cobra ducked to the side, lifted a brown grocery sack from under the table and passed it to J.T. "Oh, hey, Tag, when we heard you were coming today, we decided to throw you an impromptu baby shower like we did for Crusty a few months ago when his little half brothers came to live with him. We all chipped in and got you a few things.''

Ah hell. If Gabby's goofy-ass grin was anything to go by, J.T. could smell a roast coming. He took the bag from Cobra. Crewdogs cut zero slack when razzing their own. The best way to handle it? Play along.

And plot the comeback.

Already plans formed to ink permanent marker around the earpieces on their headsets so they would walk around for hours after landing not knowing about the doughnut rings circling their ears. And the beauty of it all? Nobody ever suspected him. Usually funnyman Bronco took the fall.

J.T. fished his hand into the bag. ''Earplug holder?'' He shook the suspiciously light canister. No sound. He cocked an eyebrow at Cobra. ''Empty?''

''Bo thought you'd need earplugs to block out the baby hollering, but then Colonel Dawson reminded him that all you old guys are just about deaf anyway from so many years on the flight line. So Bronco stole the plugs out to take home for when his kid's pitching a fit.''

Chuckling, J.T. dug in the bag again, pulling out a bottle labeled…Viagra. Ah crap. ''Damn, guys, it's brutal around here today.''

Gabby leaned forward. ''Well, not totally. This bottle's empty, too, since it's mighty obvious you don't need that, either, old man.''

At least the kid had a sense of humor buried in all that chatter. J.T. jerked the two bulky remaining items, larger, soft packages.

''Huggies and Depends.'' Cobra announced the obvious with a wicked grin. ''''Cause you'll both be going into diapers at the same time.''

''Same foods, too,'' Scorch added. ''Should have thought to add some of that rice cereal and strained carrots my sister feeds my niece.''

And the roast got hotter. J.T. pivoted toward Spike. "Just decided to sit in on the class, did you?"

Spike loosened his palm-tree tie. "Wouldn't want to miss out on a good party, even brought along a subscription card for *TV Guide*," he said, patting along his jacket pockets as if searching. "For all those nights you'll be walking the floors."

More smart-ass quips rippled through the room until someone shouted over the fray, "Hey, what happened to those Viagra pills? Maybe I can find some use for them."

Cobra snagged the empty bag and dumped the "gifts" inside like a nice "hostess." "Since Tag didn't need them, we dished them out to the lieutenants for experimentation."

Rolling her eyes, 1st Lieutenant Darcy Renshaw strode across the room and plopped into the seat next to her fiancé, Spike. "Just what those dorks need, more ego inflation."

J.T. dropped the brown bag by his feet. "Well, thanks, everybody. You are all too, uh, generous."

"Ahhh—" Cobra chuckled low "—that's only the beginning."

"Seriously, man." Scorch cruised the front legs of his chair to a landing. "We'll be getting together a real celebration later. Just couldn't resist this now. Congratulations."

"Thanks." J.T. thumped his heart, plastering a sardonic smile in place. "I feel the love."

More laughter rumbled through the room as he pulled his chair up to the table beside Scorch.

"Tough crowd today." The aircraft commander smoothed two fingers along his mustache. Rumor held he'd once singed the blond stache in a bar with a flaming Dr Pepper mixed drink, thus his call sign.

"Only the strong survive around here."

Scorch's eyes flicked up to J.T.'s, held for a somber second that affirmed the truth of those words...

From inside the rusted-out jeep bouncing along the rutted

desert road in a convoy, J.T. stared back at Scorch beside him. Both of them resigned. Resolved. Scared enough to piss themselves.

Hands bound behind his back, J.T. tried to brace with a boot on the back of the seat. Shock absorbers shot, the vehicle rocked, threatened to pitch him out. The hemp cut deeper into his wrists, burning like hell, not as bad as his ribs, though. Those flamed like a son of a bitch, but the pain kept him awake.

Could be worse.

Each jolt jarred groans from Bo sitting in front, his mangled hands manacled and swelling. The young lieutenant's teeth chattered, shock setting in.

J.T. glanced back at Scorch. They would have to do something for the kid soon.

Sand caked in Scorch's mustache, the aircraft commander's Ivy League blond veneer dusty as hell. In that moment, they bridged the gap between childhoods of brownstone walk-up and mansion, between enlisted and officer. It was them against the enemy, keeping the bastards off Bo and away from Spike who carried more secrets than all of them put together.

A whistling premonition sounded.

Hell, not a premonition at all. A missile. Crap. "Incoming!"

J.T. ducked a second ahead of Scorch. The missile arced, another, both closer, taking out the lead vehicle, then the last. Explosions, one, two shook the ground.

He propped his shoulder against the back of the seat. "Bo, you okay? Damn it, kid, answer me."

A grunt sounded from the front while J.T. lay in the back seat staring over at Scorch, both of them trussed and unable to help.

Praying the rescue wouldn't end up killing them.

Only the strong survive. The words echoed from Scorch's eyes then and now.

Damn straight. J.T. nodded, shifted front for the start of class. Droning voices dwindled with the arrival of the two chemical-warfare instructors from the Civil Engineering Squadron.

At least the nighttime surveillance flights with the DEA were netting results in figuring out who sold out their flight plan. And J.T. welcomed the chance to be a part of the process to nail the traitorous bastards.

Even if the process was slow as hell.

They'd identified the two military leaks. One guy working in aerial port in Rubistan sent back vehicles to the States with the spare tire filled with drugs. The other Air Force leak—in the transportation squadron back in Charleston—took out the contraband. Their reasons were unclear, as were their off-base connections.

Neither had been picked up yet since DEA wanted to topple the whole operation. The two military links were only a small part of the larger operation.

Both men were under twenty-four-hour watch while the surveillance flights continued. Endlessly. God, the bad guys were good at this, but having closure for the shoot down would go a long way toward easing the roar in his head.

For Rena, for his kids, he would figure it all out. She wasn't the same woman he'd married, a woman who filled his life with plants and smiles and just let him be. Now she wanted things from inside him that he couldn't give. And for a man who already felt he hadn't given her near enough, damn but that blew.

Life was easier when they could use sex to work it out, reconnect while relieving stress.

By the time the training filters were being passed around, he'd decided maybe the parking idea wasn't so bad, after all, once Rena finished up with her client. Even if they didn't actually have sex. Yeah, the needy edge would still be there, but so what? Edgy was good. Didn't mean he had to act on it just yet.

He wasn't twenty anymore. He would control himself now. He would have a chance to make headway with her—without worrying about interruption. And he knew just the thing to romance her with, the last thing he would have expected to use. The toughest for him to utilize. But the only tool in his arsenal with which to breach her defenses.

Words.

Hell, talk about underarmed and untrained. He would have to bring in some emergency supplies for reinforcements to go with his pathetic stash of verbal armaments.

"Don't you want to do some word association crap or something?" Bo Rokowsky paced around Rena's sparse office space. He tapped a hanging basket in her lone little window, sent the petunias spinning into a kaleidoscope of pink and purple.

Rena tipped back in her office chair with a slow squeak and resisted the urge to tell him not to kill her favorite plant. The guy was wound tighter than the twisted macramé hanger.

For two prior sessions, her patient had tried to charm his way around answering questions. Yet if he wanted to fly again, he needed to clear the mandated evaluation. Today, she hoped for a breakthrough. She'd studied the way he operated, thought she had his number.

Scorch, Spike…J.T., they'd all been okayed after release in the psych evaluations at Ramstein AFB in Germany. But not Bo.

Every person reacted differently to stress, of course. Bo's youth, his greater injuries, his rootless past may have played a part in diminishing his coping skills. Whatever the cause, the initial debriefing called for further psychological evaluation of 1st Lieutenant Bo Rokowsky once his wounds healed before he could be returned to full flight status.

She'd been surprised when Bo requested her as his counselor since she was married to J.T. She had even gone to her boss to discuss the matter. He'd quickly pointed out that in a small base community, it was impossible to schedule around all the work and friendship connections. Doctors and counselors would forever be referring cases elsewhere. There wasn't a technical conflict of interest. The patient felt more comfortable talking to her. Budget cuts had left them short staffed. She needed to be a professional and do her job.

Bo's initial eval indicated time would likely settle his problem. Something she would have to confirm before he could return to the cockpit.

"Word association is one way to find out about you." She dropped her steno pad on the desk. "Honestly, I prefer just to talk most of the time."

"This should be pretty quick though, right? You just need to find out I'm not about to climb into a bell tower or something."

"That's one way of putting it." She flexed her foot on the chair across from her. The simple sprain, aches, immobility from her accident were making her stir-crazy. What more must Bo have gone through during the deliberate injury of both his hands? "Because of the extent of your injuries in Rubistan, the Air Force wants reassurance you're—"

"Not sporting any loose screws before they let me back in the cockpit. Yeah, yeah, I know, I'm already a wild card as far as my commander's concerned, even before this crap shook down." His dark hair gleamed in the late-afternoon sun streaming through the window as he spun the plant faster. "But you can tell the flight surgeon to tell my micromanaging commander that all the screws in my body—currently located in my arm now, by the way—do appear to be twisted nice and tight. I'm more than ready to resume flying. In fact, the only thing making me go batty these days is too much time piloting a desk.''

He abandoned the mistreated petunias for a stroll around the tiny office, combat boots giving off a muffled thud on tile. ''I'll admit, I was pretty messed up when I first got back. That was some scary crap over there. But I'm doing better now. Working. Got a new girlfriend, bounced back fast after the old one and I broke up.''

''I'll take all that into consideration when I meet with the flight surgeon for the recommendation to Colonel Quade.'' She seesawed her pen between two fingers. ''You don't care for your commander?''

Bo stopped short by her file cabinet. ''And you expect me to answer that one? Are you looking to get me booted out the front gate on my ass? Since you're married to one of us, I figured you'd know better than to ask something like that.''

So many threads to pick up on in those few words. And she'd get to them all, in time. ''Our sessions are confidential. The colonel will only see my recommendation. Not the details on how I arrived at it.''

''Since you've seen my file,'' he said, prying a magnet off the file cabinet, a clear plastic cover over a family photo taken ten years ago, ''it's probably no great leap to assume I don't have a lot of experience on how to deal with male authority figures in my life.''

''Why would I assume that?''

''How come you're getting paid for me to come up with all the answers?''

''Great job I have here, isn't it?'' She smiled.

He grinned back. ''All right. I'll play along. It's the government's nickel paying for this anyhow.'' He held up the family-portrait magnet. ''There aren't any photos like this in my past. My old man cut out on us when I was five, cracked under the pressure of paying for all those bicycles and gym shoes. My mother opened a vein rather than live without him.

Cops tracked down my old man, who still didn't want the responsibility of picking up the tab for my Nikes and Huffys."

Bo's smile, reputed to have charmed women on every continent, turned tight, hard, lending credence to his fallen angel reputation. He slapped the magnet back on the cabinet. "To give him his due, at least the bastard had enough conscience to make sure he dumped me somewhere decent rather than just cut me loose into the system."

"A Catholic orphanage."

"Ah, so you're reading my file after all. Nice work." He sprawled in one of the two government-issue chairs in front of her desk. "The sisters did good by me. I've got no complaints from then on. Guess I just relate better to women because of those hundreds of mothers in penguin clothes taking care of me."

"And that's a part of why you picked me for your sessions, because I'm a woman."

"Maybe." He grinned again, charming without stepping over the line. The guy was gifted at maneuvering.

She was better. "And since I'm married to 'one of you' then you figured I'd be more likely to cut you some slack."

His boot slid off his knee and thumped to the floor. "Hell. You're as good as Sister Nic."

Nikki? Her daughter? "Sister Nic?"

"At the orphanage, Sister Nic, short for Sister Nicotine. She said most of her prayers in the garden so she could sneak a smoke. I never could get anything past her, either. She was one tough lady, just like you."

"I'll take that as a compliment."

"It was meant as one. She's the finest person I've ever known."

"Is she still alive?"

"Oh yeah, raising hell sneaking her smokes in a nursing

home. Just hope she doesn't blow up an oxygen tank with her contraband cigarettes someday.''

''Sounds like the two of you are still very close.''

''We keep in touch.''

''How did she handle your being taken captive?'' Even J.T.'s normally stoic mama had broken down on the phone. Rena's fingers tightened around her pen.

In the most horrific call of her life, she'd finished relaying the rest of the facts to the oldest of J.T.'s eight brothers for him to pass along. The hell of it was, she hadn't realized until then that J.T. hadn't told his family about the split. Of course, she hadn't told hers, either, but they hadn't spoken to her since she married J.T.

''You're good at this talking stuff, yes, ma'am. Got me right where you wanted me in the conversation twice in less than five minutes. The government's nickel is being well spent on you.''

''Only if you answer my question.'' She set her pen aside so Bo wouldn't see her hand trembling.

''I never told Sister Nic. I didn't want to worry her. Since the crew members' names weren't on the news, it wasn't a problem keeping it under wraps.''

She recognized well that macho mind-set resistant to sharing troubles, always protecting the women without realizing the worry quadrupled without information.

And if they were so busy talking in shortened phrases punctuated with macho backslaps, where was the sounding board for what he'd been through? She would be more reassured if she knew J.T.—

Whoa. Hang on. This was about Bo. She would feel better if she knew *Bo* had vented to someone like Sister Nic, who could have perhaps drawn upon religious-counseling training.

J.T. had been cleared, right? He was fine.

Except there were levels of ''fine'' and some of them weren't so ''fine.'' Cleared to work wasn't the same as being a hundred percent when off work. Who would J.T. talk to when the time came to vent?

Jealousy pricked with thorny persistence. "When something as life altering as that happens, you should talk to someone about it."

Bo leaned back in his chair, arms on the rests, so obvious in his primal chest-puffing. "We men aren't big on the touchy-feely chitchat stuff."

Well, now didn't that sound like some other jet-jock she knew? "I've gathered that."

"Besides, while the experience sucked, and I hope like hell never to repeat it, the worst was over pretty quick."

"How so?"

"You know. Don't you?" Defensiveness faded, confusion furrowing trenches in his forehead. "Jesus, I figured J.T. would have told you all this and I wouldn't have to spill every detail."

Lightbulb moment. The real reason Bo had selected her dawned.

Too bad he guessed wrong in assuming her husband told her squat. But then if she let Bo know that, he might well reinvent the past to suit his purposes. If she played along, then at least he would be less likely to lie since he assumed she already knew.

That her husband wouldn't tell her pinched her pride and heart more than her overtight skirt constricting her breathing. "It's always helpful to hear things from another person's perspective. Adds surprising insights."

"Fine. We'll play this your way then if it'll get me out of here quicker."

Unease itched up her spine like the healing skin over her cut foot. She couldn't shake the feeling of disloyalty in hearing what J.T. had chosen not to tell her. Damn it, why couldn't this one have been shuffled to someone else? But even if her boss had relented, the move to a new counselor would mean starting all over again, perhaps delaying Bo's return to flying.

"The part where local warlords got ahold of us at first, was...tense. That's when I got these." He held up his hands. The right could have passed for normal with only one thin scar across the top. But the left shouted pain with fading incisions, the skin pale and peeling after so long in a cast. "Wondering what they would do with us was hell—fearing they might turn us over to one of their terrorist bosses. I wouldn't have made it out alive without your husband keeping them off me."

J.T.'s bruises.

The itch along her nerves turned to a vicious rash—ugly horror spreading through her as Bo confirmed all her worst fears about J.T.'s capture.

The longer her husband stayed silent, the more she'd hoped maybe the images haunting her were just the product of an overactive imagination. So much easier than admitting the worst had happened and her husband wouldn't even tell his wife.

Bo swung his boot back up on his knee, fidgeted with the long black laces. "There were already American hostages over there then, part of what we were checking up on—"

Pausing, he glanced up from his laces. "I swear I'm not being cagey. I can't say more than that for security reasons and it won't make any difference to what's going on here."

"I understand." Understood that her husband was a part of these things he couldn't talk about. Scary things that man-speak translated into the simple word *tense*.

"Anyhow, the Rubistanians intercepted the rebel caravan, and the bad guys turned us over to the good guys."

"Just turned you over?"

"Yep. They knew they were outgunned, so they gave us up rather than die."

More manspeak understatement. No doubt. "What about the days that followed?"

"Consisted of questioning while we waited for international channels to clear, and for the Rubistanians to poke around inside our plane. I don't remember a whole lot since I was drugged up for the pain most of the time."

"Does it help to downplay the events?"

He looked up, his eyes clear of the fog from reminiscing, if not the horrors of what he'd endured. "Yes."

Pain pulsed from him. She couldn't miss it even with the distance of training. The toughest part of her job. And this was a near stranger. The words would be hell coming from J.T.'s mouth.

If he ever told her.

"I don't mean to sound inane, Lieutenant, but you do realize that if you climb back into the plane, this could happen again?"

"I accept that as part of my job."

"And you're okay with it?" she asked, only noticing as the words fell out of her mouth that she'd opted for J.T.'s abbreviated manspeak.

"Only a moron is going to be totally okay with it."

The sanest response he could have given. Rena could all but see him step that much closer to his plane again.

"But I'm less okay with quitting. I owe a debt."

"The time left on your Air Force obligation can be spent in another job."

"That's not what I meant." He pushed to his feet, restless pacing resuming. "I was brought up by people who gave everything for other people, for me. I need to do something to repay that. I figured out pretty damn fast I wasn't meant for the priesthood." He tossed her a roguish wink that almost lit the dark shadows from his eyes.

Bo scooped a crystal paperweight off the corner of her desk, tossing it one-handed in the air. "And I'm too selfish in a lot of ways to go for the self-sacrificing gig. I like my toys. But I have to give *something* back. My Air Force commission allows me to settle the debt with the fringe benefits of some kick-ass toys.''

He gave the weight a final pitch, snagged it midair, then replaced it on her desk. ''I'm not as good as the people who brought me up. And I'm not some genius who can cure cancer.'' He placed his scarred hands on the edge of her desk. ''But once I left the home, I discovered that these hands that were so good at playing music also had a talent for loving a woman and flying an airplane. These hands are who I am. I won't let anyone take that away from me.''

He pinned her with his eyes, direct, no shutters or walls blocking her from seeing the man's burning drive to crawl back into that plane.

Then he spun away, hands on his hips, shoulders heaving. ''Screw this. I've had enough. Isn't the government's nickel spent out for today yet?''

She could have continued for hours exploring the Cro-Magnon implications of what he'd revealed. But that wasn't her job. Instincts told her that while this young man might well have hang-ups, they had no bearing on his fitness to fly.

And about how his hands had been broken? What had happened that day? He'd definitely closed up for the afternoon, but she'd made the break in getting through to him. They would move on to that in the next session.

Still, she couldn't help but wonder, did men really think their entire worth could be summed up with their job and sex? Did her husband think that? With J.T.'s walls so high, she didn't know how she would ever find the answer.

And at the moment, with Bo's recounting of the capture still clanging horribly in her ears, she doubted her ability to keep her own defenses in place around J.T. while finding the answer. Even a hint of encouragement from her reticent husband and she would fall into their old patterns of comforting him the only way he ever allowed.

Naked. With hot, sweaty sex.

Chapter 8

Streetlights flickering on dotted the naked horizon.

Perfect. J.T. shifted gears on the truck, whizzing past their exit. Rena frowned, but stayed silent, the low tunes of the oldies station drifting from the radio.

He'd managed to kill enough time on base to make their drive home dip closer toward sunset. Excellent for his plans. Now they cruised along over the swampy tidewaters, bridges a constant for the waterlogged region. Twenty minutes later, he pulled off onto a two-lane rural road.

"Where are we going?" she finally asked from beside him. Her window down, she tugged the two long black sticks from her bundled hair and let it ripple in the wind.

Now he really wanted that drive.

Hopefully she wouldn't nix his idea before it even took flight. "I figured you've been cooped up in the house for so long, you could probably use time outside. I thought we'd take a ride before we head back to the house."

He could talk to her at home, but not without the risk of

interruption. There were also too many doors to slam. A sunset was romantic, right? Would she agree? His period of romancing her had been so damn short, he wasn't sure what she preferred. They'd spent most of their dating days in the back of her car.

This time he would keep his hands on the wheel and his flight suit zipped.

"Take a drive?"

"Sure. Why not?" Then he would conveniently detour somewhere scenic, overlooking the water where they could talk, away from interrupting teenagers. Already moss-draped oak trees alongside the road grew thicker, more private.

He reached behind the seat and pulled out a Coke.

Rena stared at it as if he held a snake. "You brought a Coke?"

"Uh..." He dropped it between them and reached back again to select a— "Diet Coke?"

He winced. Way to go, Romeo—insinuate she needs Diet when you're already on shaky cheapskate ground romancing her with a one-dollar sixteen-ouncer.

But she would know he was up to something if he started crawling up to her window with a fistful of daisies. A drive and a Coke seemed a safer, nonobvious way to start working his way back into her good graces.

Already up to his ass in the plan, he might as well forge ahead. He arced his arm behind the seat again and pulled out a chocolate Yoohoo. "Or this can count as calcium for the baby with some chocolate for you. You'll have to key me in on what you're craving, because I'm pretty damn clueless about what you'll like."

Would she get the double meaning? Subtext wasn't his strong suit.

She stared down at the bottles resting in her lap. "Have you been keeping a junk-food stash in your car all these years?"

"I stopped by the shoppette before I picked you up." He couldn't see her face clearly enough to gauge her reaction. "That's why I was late."

"You planned this?" Still she didn't so much as glance his way, but her voice went soft.

Progress. Onward. "I wasn't sure what you would want, so I bought a little of everything." He turned off the two-lane road onto a dirt path. "When you were carrying Nikki, you couldn't get enough pizza, but then first time I brought you one when you were pregnant with Chris, you threw up all over my flight boots."

"And then we had ice cream for supper instead."

Made love. Had more ice cream. "Peach ice cream."

"You remember?" Her face went as soft as her voice.

Ooh-rah for Romeo. "I remember."

He slid the truck to a stop at one of his favorite fishing spots, total solitude with a perfect view of the inland waterway. Everything moved slow. The birds. The fish. Even the shrimp boats took their time to cast and draw back nets, cast them again or simply troll to the dock.

Why hadn't he thought to bring her here before?

Hefting the bag from behind the seat, he upended it gently into her lap, releasing a waterfall of food.

Granola bars. Pretzels. Roasted peanuts. Spanish peanuts. Chocolate-covered peanuts. Cashews. Pistachios.

"Ohmigod," she squealed, sifting snacks through her fingers. "You really did buy a little bit of everything."

"I can't take total credit. Something the guys did at the squadron gave me the idea. So do you like it?" He picked up three kinds of peanuts. "Nuts equal protein."

She scooped a bag of peanut-shaped orange candies. "Circus peanuts? And we can call this protein?"

"Hey, whatever works for you, babe."

She clasped the bag of circus peanuts to her chest. "Like

I used to tell myself the gallons of peach ice cream meant healthy milk and fruit.''

Positioning the brown sack below the edge of the seat, he raked the junk food off her lap, and hell but Rena's legs felt good even through layers of her crinkly skirt. He set the bag to the side. "What is it that you need now? Help me out here."

"So I won't hurl on your boots and mess up that nice shine?"

"I'm not talking about Coke and ice cream anymore, but I don't know how to say what you need to hear. We have to find more…neutral ground, and damn, but it was hard before and since I got back…" He shut his eyes, opened them again because the memories kept pushing through anyway. "It seems like we're more screwed up than ever."

She touched his hand. "We've never really talked about what happened to you over in Rubistan."

"There's not much to talk about." Thinking about it sucked enough. "It was scary as hell waiting for the diplomatic channels to clear, but they did. And we all came home."

She wanted more from him. Only a fool would miss that. So much for giving her words, dumb ass. But if those words would upset her? If those words scraped like a blade against his insides on the way up and out?

He would find other words for her instead. "But I made it through since I always knew I would come home again."

"How could you know that?"

"Because there wasn't a chance in hell I intended to die without making love to you at least one more time."

Her chin trembled just before she covered her mouth with a hand shaking twice as fast as that delicate pointy chin of hers. Strategy went out the open window on the marshy wind. He raised his hand, glided his knuckles along the waves of her hair.

All the want tamped down from their kiss earlier, from months, from the first time he laid eyes on her, powered to life. He held himself in check. Barely. Now his hands weren't much steadier than hers, so he let his fall to cup the sides of her neck. Her shaky fingers slid to rest on his chest.

And the next thing he knew, they were kissing again.

Not frenzied, like the out-of-control exchange in the parking lot earlier. But slow. Deliberate. No mistaking the mutual intent.

A growl rumbled low in his chest, the instinctual sound of primal possession he couldn't have stopped if he wanted to— and he didn't want to stop anything.

Apparently, neither did his wife.

She melted against him, her arms slung over his shoulders, her bracelets cool against the overheated skin along his neck. Her body flowed over his while she kissed him with all the sweet passion she'd poured over him twenty-two years ago the first time he'd persuaded her to join him in the back seat of her BMW.

Heaven help him, he would have more restraint now than he'd shown then. Even if her soft hands were crawling into the neck of his flight suit with hungry persistence.

Still in control. He could take this a little further. No problem.

Slanting his mouth over one corner of her lips, then the other, he lowered her back onto the seat, careful to keep his weight off her, for the baby, for her fragile frame. Although her hands felt anything but fragile in their strong grip on his back, his wildcat wife's fingernails digging tiny moons into his shoulders.

He deepened their kiss, explored the warm moistness of her, wanted to explore more, now, sooner, but damned if he would screw up this chance by rushing. She wriggled closer, soft body and softer breasts driving him freaking nuts. He had to touch her. More of her.

Any of her.

He stroked up her side along the loose blouse. No objections from his wife. He skimmed his hand forward and palmed her breast. A groan of contentment rolled though him in sync with the sigh escaping from her lips into him.

She arched to fill his hand, rolled her shoulders so his touch became a firmer caress. Pregnancy plumped her breasts and damned if he hadn't forgotten how it also increased her sensitivity, something they'd enjoyed to the fullest in those early days of marriage.

What a waste not to make the most of it now, and he was anything but wasteful.

He worked his thumb back and forth over the peak straining through even a bra and thin cotton, tugged it gently between two fingers. She nearly came up off the bench seat. Rena's breathy, needy whimpers encouraged him to charge ahead. Her hips rocked up and against him. She wrapped a leg around his hips.

Still in control? Barely. And fast on his way to not at all. Hell, forty-two years old and he felt as horny as at twenty. So desperate to have this woman, so tempted to let the past replay.

But even then he'd known it was wrong. He was wrong for her. Still, he'd lost his hold on reason the first time Rena—totally hot and caught up in the moment—brushed a hesitant touch over the crotch of his flight suit.

Like now. Except not in the least hesitant this time, instead confident in exactly what turned him inside out with wanting her.

Stop. He had to stop if he ever wanted a chance at more. And he definitely wanted more.

He kissed once, again, drawing away in increments, a man addicted to the taste of her and unable to make a clean break. All the more reason to pace himself.

He lifted his head and found a new resting place against

the velvet skin where her neck met her shoulder, a spot he happened to know turned *her* inside out.

Her fingers threaded through his hair, her touch anchoring him and making him fly all at once. She pressed her cheek against his head. "I'd forgotten what a great kisser you are until you reminded me this afternoon. And now."

"I'm not sure whether to be complimented or insulted, babe."

"Definitely complimented."

"If I was that great you wouldn't have forgotten."

"It's just been so long."

"Only three months." And he remembered everything about her from that time. The shape of her hip under his palm. The taste of her skin. The flowery scent of her shampoo that reminded him of all her flowers filling the dark, empty places in their lives.

"We stopped kissing a long time before that, J.T."

Hell. Turbulence ahead. And he didn't have a clue what to say next. He'd pretty much blown his wad on sensitivity with the comment just before she'd kissed him. "I kissed you, damn it."

Crap. Sergeant Sensitivity? Not.

She stiffened under him, shoved against his shoulders. "Obligatory pecks on the cheek on your way out the door don't count. And when we had sex, we pretty much went from smoldering looks to clothes off in under two seconds."

Time to shift tactics. Humor maybe. He angled up and off her. "Hey lady, are you accusing me of being a quick trigger?"

"You know better than that and don't try to change the subject." She smoothed her skirt back into place, running her thumb along the waistband. "I'm actually having a bit of an epiphany moment here and I would like to play it through if you don't mind. Besides, weren't you the one who said you wanted to talk today?"

Bitten on the ass by his own good intentions. Why the hell had he thought he wanted to talk in the first place? He should have gone straight for the one way he always managed to get through to this woman. With sex.

Except damned if she wasn't in the process of telling him how he'd screwed that up, too. "Okay, so you're saying I didn't kiss you enough. I thought I had the foreplay thing covered, but I'm sorry if I—"

"Good God, J.T., would you get your testosterone out of this conversation for a second and listen? I'm not accusing you of anything. I'm saying *we* stopped kissing a long time ago. You know full well you're an incredible lover, generous, sexy."

"Okay, Cro-Magnon level lowering, returning to the modern age." Tension waning, he winked. "And thanks."

"You're welcome." A smile quirked her kissed-poofy lips. "All I'm saying is that in some ways kissing is much more intimate than sex, and somewhere along the line we let that get away from us. It scares me to realize that because then I have to accept that we started falling apart a long time before I saw it coming, which means there's even less hope."

She was hoping?

"Rena, babe, I'm going to be straight up with you. We have our problems. I know that. But damn it, I want us to give it another try. I'm not saying we should jump right back into things. We can take it slow. Keep on like we are for a while. Cokes, circus peanuts and family dinners. More kisses."

"More kisses?"

Ah, he'd breached the defenses. He could read her so well sometimes. He leaned to kiss her again because she'd made her wishes on that clear, even for a dense male like himself. And kissing his beautiful wife was sure as hell no hardship. Her lips moved under his.

Bullet dodged. He could already envision his boots march-

ing across the hall to their rightful place beside her heels lying
lopsided, cast off beside their bed.

He skimmed a hand down her satiny arm, linked their fingers, curved them forward to rest on the slight swell of her
stomach. "It's gonna be okay, Rena. We'll work it out, make
it right, this kid's going to be a new start for us. We'll be
there for it just like we were there for Nikki and Chris."

She stiffened against him, even more rigid than before
when she'd shoved him off her. "You want to come home
for the baby."

What a damn odd question. "Of course."

Her fingers untwined from his. The fading sunset rays cast
shadows across her face while somehow showcasing the ones
in her eyes. "Did you ever really love me?"

Talk about stunned stupid.

Rena wasn't sure who was more shocked by the question,
her or her immobile husband.

He recovered faster, though. "I told you I did."

The tide shushed along the shore, reminding her she should
have kept her mouth shut.

"Forget I asked." She'd known he was coming home for
the baby, but hearing it confirmed seconds ago hurt even
more than she'd expected. "I'm being a hormonal, sentimental pregnant woman. I just want to eat my circus peanuts and
go home."

How could she trust his answer now that he knew what
she expected to hear? She'd given away her whole hand of
cards because of a few kisses. Some things never changed.

She hooked her elbow on the open window and popped a
circus peanut in her mouth just as the first stars overcame the
setting sun.

"No way, babe." He tipped her chin toward him, his touch
gentle, his gray eyes filling with storm clouds, all the more
powerful considering how rarely her controlled husband lost

his cool. "You brought this up and there's not a chance you can deny that I said the words. I know I told you. I may not have said it every time I walked in the room, but I know what came out of my mouth."

Rena swallowed down the lump of sugar too thick for her constricting throat. Did he have to sound so harsh? Pain, betrayal, frustration shifted to anger, mostly with herself for laying her emotions bare before this man. Again. "Oh, get real, J.T. 'I love you, babe, please, please let me get in your pants' doesn't carry much of a romantic punch once the horniness wears off a couple of hours later."

"But it worked," he snapped, then cursed. "I'm sorry. I shouldn't have said that."

She bit back the urge to call him a bastard, since she'd been the one to lash out first with the "getting into her pants" comment. Totally unfair since she'd been just as eager to get into his then—now, too.

His chest rose and fell with regulated frequency. Back in control. Overly so. "I'll try to translate this manspeak into something you'll understand. I gave you the best I had. I know you deserve better, but this baby limits our choices."

"This is exactly why it won't work, J.T. We haven't even been in the house together for two weeks and already we're tearing each other up again."

"And about your question…" He plowed ahead without acknowledging her point.

She didn't want to know. Either way, yes or no, truth or lie, the answer would slice through her. "I said never mind."

"But you said something else after that. Yeah, there was nothing I wanted more than to be inside you, and I intended to make damn sure once you let me get there, you wouldn't be sorry or left wanting. And then when we were together, I found all that locker-room wisdom didn't matter. I didn't need it, not when I had those breathy little sighs of yours guiding me if I just listened.'' He dipped his head to her neck. ''Do you still like it when I kiss you right here?''

The edge dulled on her anger, and God, but she resented him, herself, for the predictability of her body's betrayal.

He sketched higher to her ear. ''Or when I do this? You usually purr for me when I do that.''

J.T. nipped the lobe, continued to vulnerable patches of skin too long neglected. His hands traveled down her spine in a sensual massage that sent her bowing against him again until finally he cupped her bottom and brought her even closer. ''And what about that?''

She whimper-purred her assent and frustration.

''Yeah, babe. I heard you.'' He stared down with narrowed eyes. Pissed. Insistent, and yes, even aroused. ''And maybe I was just meeting some elemental itch you had, and I missed the big picture. But at least I was listening and trying my damnedest.''

He withdrew his hands, his body, moving away, the muggy air suddenly chilly in comparison to her overheated flesh.

Her muddled brain shouted at her to process his words while her aching heart told her to run. Her flaming body urged her to just jump him so her brain and heart would shut up because everything was crumbling around her.

''I listened to you, Rena, and maybe I'm not as good at understanding out of bed as I am in bed. But I *am* trying, damn it.''

As much as she wanted to cry or rage, at least they were talking and she wouldn't let temper or tears shut that down.

She stared into stormy gray eyes usually so steady, constant, ever honorable, and the truth deluged over her like those storm clouds opening up. In his manspeak way, J.T. had answered her question after all. J.T. didn't lie. He gave sparse accountings, but his words counted. He'd told her he loved her then. She'd just never listened.

The truth raining over her chilled to a deeper realization of icy, sheeting sleet. He'd said loved. Past tense.

Today, he hadn't said a thing about loving her still. In fact, he hadn't said those words for a long time. And she couldn't help but notice his love had stopped right about the same time as the kisses.

He'd screwed up.

J.T. lifted the crutches out of the back of the truck in their driveway, sidestepped a bush of pink flowers…azaleas maybe? Or wisteria? Hell he couldn't keep all her plants straight. Or her needs.

He passed the crutches to his silent wife, crickets sawing in the background, night traffic in the neighborhood slow and sporadic. Damn it, he shouldn't have lost his cool. He still wasn't sure exactly where he'd slid off course, but no doubt, his plan to woo Rena had been shot down.

"Thanks," she said without looking at him. She swung trim calves out of the truck, hopped on one foot taking the crutches from him.

He followed while she worked her way down the flagstone path, ready to catch her if a crutch went rogue in the soft lawn. Why did she have to make this so difficult? Everything from a simple trip inside to where he parked his boots.

Not that he intended to ask her. He kept his yap shut, because if she questioned whether he'd said he loved her all those years ago then he must have messed up worse than even he'd imagined. He'd done something seriously wrong and still he couldn't pinpoint what. He'd tried his best to keep the darker parts of his job and himself the hell out of an already strained marriage.

Opening the side door, J.T. followed her into the kitchen. "Son, we're home," he called.

Too bad he wasn't announcing the coming-home deal for real.

Stenciled ivy bordering the walls mocked him with reminders of the time he'd interrupted her painting. He could
read her lingering arousal from their kisses in the truck. They
could have been upstairs in bed now, together.

Rena rested her crutches against the counter and dragged
out a chair at the table. A sign she didn't want to go upstairs
with him? Or that she didn't want their evening to end?

She dropped into one chair, propped her foot on another.
She slipped her hand into a side pocket on her skirt and pulled
out a package...of peanuts. Honey roasted. She tore open the
corner with her teeth, poured half the minipack into her palm.

Quiet echoed through the house, dishes on the counter.
Two glasses?

One with glittery lip gloss kissing the rim. God, he couldn't
be everywhere at once checking on his family.

Chris's footsteps thudded down the second set of stairs
leading into the kitchen. "Hey, Mom. Dad. Have fun?"

"Yeah, we had a nice drive." J.T. tucked one glass into
the dishwasher, then the other. "Have someone over while
we were gone?"

Rena looked up from her snack. "Chris?"

He shrugged, shuffled across the tile floor into the pantry.
"Just a friend."

Twisting the setting knob, J.T. started the dishwasher and
flipped the magnet from "dirty dishes" to "clean." "A female friend, I'd say, based on the lip gloss on the second
glass."

"Just a friend," Chris repeated over the sound of a chip
bag tearing open.

Rena nudged peanuts around on the table. "Hon, you know
I prefer you not have girls over when no one's here."

"Sure. Sorry."

The phone rang. Lucky Chris.

J.T. yanked the receiver off the wall. "Hello?"

"Hi," a female voice crooned. "Could I speak to Chris, please? Tell him it's Miranda."

At least now he didn't have to make a room search for the girl upstairs. "Son, it's a girl for you."

Chris charged toward the phone.

"Someone named Miranda."

The boy stopped in his tracks, gym shoes shrieking on tile. He shook his head.

Cupping his palm over the mouthpiece, J.T. said, "Your mother and I will leave the room."

And go upstairs where maybe he could regain ground.

Chris stumbled back, tripping over his dragging shoelaces before righting himself.

J.T. raised the phone to his ear again. "I'm sorry, but he just stepped out. I couldn't catch him in time. Do you want to leave a message?"

"Just tell him he needs to come in to work an hour early tomorrow and run deliveries."

"Will do." He replaced the receiver. "She says you're supposed to come in an hour early to run deliveries."

Chris's face paled until acne shone double. Females could do that to a man.

"So you work with her?"

"Yeah, she's one of the hostesses." His gaze ping-ponged from one smiling parent to the other. "It's not like that."

"Okay, son. You're entitled to your privacy." J.T. hefted the transparent garbage bag out of the trash can. "But that doesn't mean I won't be curious as hell."

J.T. started for the door. Rena's gasp stopped him. "What? Is something wrong? The baby?"

"Bring the bag over here," she ordered, standing on one foot. She yanked the clear bag from his hands, tore it open.

Dumped it on the floor? She started rifling through empty cans and wadded napkins.

"What in the hell are you doing, Rena? Careful or you're
going to cut yourself."

She knocked aside his hands and pulled free from the rub-
bish...

A box for an early-pregnancy test.

Chapter 9

Hand shaking nearly as much as her insides, Rena thrust the box closer to her son.

Talk about a visit from the Ghost of Knocked-Up Teenagers Past. Nothing like having her own mistakes come back to haunt her. But she couldn't think about herself or her own fears, not with a more pressing concern on her hands.

Literally.

Chris snatched the empty box from her. "You can both quit with the freaked-out looks. It's not mine. Well, I mean, obviously the test isn't *mine*, but it has nothing to do with me. You know?"

J.T. nudged his toe along the pile of soda cans on top of an empty cereal box. "Then what is it doing in our trash?"

"It was for a good friend." Chris's words tumbled over each other. "Someone you don't know."

His squeaky gym shoes betrayed his attempt to lie, and that twisted more old fears inside her. She'd worked to teach her children the importance of honesty—a trait she so admired in their father.

Even when that honesty broke her heart.

Of course, this lie didn't rank up there with a Mob hit or money laundering or any of the other things her family had been accused of while she was a child. But she was so afraid of unwittingly passing along defective genes and shifty mind-sets to her kids.

To some degree hadn't she taught her son about shading the truth by pretending if she filled her house with plants and overbright smiles no one would notice her empty marriage?

Chris jammed his hands in his pockets. "She was worried she might be pregnant and she came over here to run the test while you were gone since there's, like, never a quiet time around her house. It's a real fishbowl over there. But she's not pregnant, so it doesn't matter, right?"

Not pregnant. Relief took the edge off her fears. If the test had been run correctly.

Rena laid a hand on her son's arm, patted until his shoulder dropped with lowering defenses. "What about false negatives on the test? She needs to be careful and take care of herself, just in case."

"A couple of hours after the test, uh, she found out for sure." Red crept up his face, tipping his ears beneath his dark curls. "She said she figured it must have been stress affecting, you know, her cycle."

J.T.'s jaw flexed. "And this makes everything okay?"

"Yeah, of course it does, Dad. She's not pregnant. Great news."

Foot throbbing as much as her head, Rena slid back into her chair, her hand tugging Chris around to face her while J.T. calmed down. "You two were lucky this time. But what happens next time? Safe sex is important for more reasons than unplanned pregnancy. There are diseases out there that can kill you."

"Like I don't know that already? They've been telling us that in school since junior high."

"All right, just doing the parent thing and checking." Rena drew in a shaky breath. "I wish you would have at least brought Miranda over to meet us."

"Miranda? I'm not seeing Miranda. She's just somebody—" Chris shuffled his feet, squeak, squeak "—from work."

J.T.'s shoulders bunched over their son's shoe squeak that chimed like a telltale lie detector. Rena rushed to add, "Okay then, whoever it is, I wish we could meet your friends."

"When?" Chris's deepening voice grew louder. "When's ever a good time around here lately? Besides, like you two have any room to preach to me about getting somebody pregnant even if I had done it."

"Enough." J.T.'s curt edict cut the air.

The air snapped between father and son. Chris's words hurt, but not as much as watching her family disintegrate under the weight of mounting tensions. "J.T., it's okay."

"Like hell it is." J.T. stepped over the pile of trash and stopped nose to nose with his son. "Don't ever talk to your mother that way again."

Chris backed until his butt bumped the counter. "Fine, okay. But I'm not dating anybody. I'm definitely not getting busy with anybody. God. Like anyone would have me. I helped a friend. That's all. You don't want me messing around in your business? Well, stay out of mine." He pivoted on his Nikes and sprinted up the stairs two at a time.

His door slam echoed.

Rena sagged back in her chair. So much for her pride in her mediation skills. Now the evening sucked on all levels. Her hands fell to her lap, peanuts and hope weighing like lumpy cookie dough in her stomach.

Kneeling, J.T. scooped up the garbage, stuffing it back into the bag until at least the floor was clear, if not their lives.

She wadded up the empty snack wrapper and extended her hand to add it to the trash. If only she could back the day up to the start of their drive, just Cokes and kisses. No stupid "Did you ever love me?" questions. "We'll talk to him again tomorrow."

J.T. gave the bag ties a vicious yank. "Damn straight I'll be talking to him. And he'll be giving you an apology shortly thereafter."

She bit back the urge to tell him to go easy on her little boy who wasn't so little anymore. More than ever she needed to let J.T. find his way as a solo parent, too, in case…

The peanuts gained fifty extra pounds of dread in her stomach.

She inched her hand up into her loose shirt and released the waist button on her skirt. She would need maternity clothes soon, new baby things. Would she and J.T. shop for a baby crib together this time? Or would they need two, one for his place and one for hers?

Reaching under the sink, he unrolled a new garbage bag and lined the trash can. He prowled the kitchen, closed an open kitchen cabinet. Smacked the lid back on the airplane cookie jar.

Finally, the kitchen immaculate, he sat, leaning down to untie one boot, then the other. "At least we have a clue now as to why he's been so preoccupied."

"Do you believe him when he says he couldn't have been the father? He's sixteen, almost seventeen. I understand teenagers have sex." She was proof of that one. "But Chris hasn't seemed to go out much in anything other than groups."

J.T. dropped the boot on the floor beside the other. "I think he's telling the truth. Except I can't help but wonder what's up with this friend Miranda or whoever she is. She's obviously sleeping with someone, and she didn't turn to the father. What the hell's wrong with the guy that she wouldn't go to him?"

The unspoken accusation of Rena keeping the pregnancy

secret flicked her conscience. "I know I should have told you about the baby sooner."

"Thank you." He nudged one boot closer to the other with his toe, lining them up before leaning back in the chair when in the past days he would have unzipped his flight suit partway, made himself at home. "There's obviously a problem there. If he's a violent type, then he's not going to like his girlfriend turning to Chris."

"You're thinking about the car accident?"

"Just running through possibilities. I can't seem to get away from the fact that you were in Chris's car, and damn it, that van swerved deliberately. Not some drunken weaving. Once the van hit you, it didn't so much as take out a trash can on its way off. The driving was deliberate and smooth."

"A disgruntled boyfriend?"

"Could be an explanation. Hormones and rage together can be a lethal combination."

"And you need an explanation."

"Don't you?"

"Accidents happen."

"And sometimes they don't." He leaned forward, elbows on his knees. "Look, I don't want to argue with you about this. Especially not now when it seemed like maybe we were making some headway earlier. We never finished our discussion in the truck—about trying to work things out."

Headway that ground to a halt when he'd made it clear he wanted to come home for the baby. She'd gone that route once and ended up with her heart shredded. "We've tried before—"

"Hold on. I'm not talking big plans. Just keep things like they are for a while longer. We still have the weekend before you can drive. There's the question of what's going on with Chris. Why shake things up?"

Because she didn't think she could survive watching J.T.'s broad shoulders walk out of her life again.

"No need to decide now. Tuesday, I have a flight I can't cancel or change. Lots of prep work, too. Why don't we regroup after that?"

Putting off answering seemed easier than discussing anything else tonight with the taste and smell of him still on her. "Tuesday, then."

"Good. This is the right thing, babe, you'll see." He scooped his boots up and stood. "'Night, Rena."

He leaned and kissed her. On the lips, lingering a full two seconds beyond a peck but not long enough for her to gather her thoughts and object.

Then he was gone, the familiar thud of his steps echoing up the stairs.

And thank God he hadn't pressed her for more, because just like twenty-two years ago in the back seat of her BMW, she was afraid she couldn't tell this man no.

"Dad, I want to quit working at the restaurant."

J.T. stared up from the weight bench at his son spotting for him in their garage workout area. "What brought that on?"

"Just don't like it there."

"You're going to have to do better than that." He extended his arms, sweating through his third set of ten reps. His job required less lifting these days as things became more mechanized, but the physical exertion still let off steam. He had steam to spare at the moment, and he needed the time to check up on his son. "A man doesn't quit on his obligations."

Accusatory brown eyes stared back down at him. "Really?"

"There's a difference between divorce and quitting." He huffed through lifts. Muggy gusts of air through the open window by the tool bench provided minimal cooling, merely moving around the scent of sweat and motor oil.

"Sure, whatever."

"Seven, eight," J.T. counted to calm his frustration as well as mark his repetitions. "Nine, ten."

He hefted the two hundred fifty pounds onto the brackets, releasing the bar with a clang. He swung his feet around to the side, snagging a towel from the floor and swiping his head. "So, son? Reason for quitting?"

Chris shrugged, baggy T-shirt rippling. "Exams are coming up. I need to study and, like, with those extra deliveries Miranda was talking about, the job's taking up lots more time. I was thinking I could, uh, quit at the restaurant for a few weeks and then find something else once summer starts."

"Why not ask for a couple of weeks off?" He grabbed the gallon milk jug filled with water and tipped it back, chugging.

Chris swiveled away to adjust the weights, decreasing to one-twenty for his go-round on the bench. "My boss, Mr. Haugen, won't go for that."

"Do you want me to talk to him about time off or cutting out the deliveries?"

He jerked around. "No!"

J.T. set down the jug on the Astroturf covering concrete. "Did he let you go and you don't want to tell me?"

"I'd just like to find something else."

The reasons made sense, but something didn't ring true in his tone. Bottom line, though, he couldn't make his son stay with the job. Chris could just screw up and get fired if he wanted out that much. "Fine. I can't argue with a kid who wants to study more. But I do expect you to find something else once school's out. You're not going to lie around here all summer while your mother and I are at work."

Chris dropped onto his back on the weight bench, feet to the side on the ground. "Is this about the stuff in the trash again?"

"Partly." J.T. stepped in place to spot for his son. "I understand you feel that you can't betray a friend's confidence.

But be careful. If this girl's boyfriend starts gunning for you—''

''He won't.''

''Are you sure, because—''

''He won't.''

O-kay. He wasn't getting any more out of Chris on that one. Although he almost hoped the angry-boyfriend scenario was true, because then there wouldn't be unanswered questions. One angry teen was a helluva lot easier to deal with than original concerns about a gang. Or that something might have leaked about his surveillance flights.

J.T. stared down at his son on the bench. ''You owe your mother an apology for what you said the other night. You hurt her.''

So did you, his son's eyes accused silently. ''I'll tell her I'm sorry.''

Chris hefted the weight bar off and closed his eyes. Concentration or avoidance? Either way, the shutout was obvious.

Two sets of ten later, Chris replaced the bar, ducked around it and sat up. ''No sweat about the summer job, Dad. I got a line on something at the squadron pool party. Spike told me he heard they were looking for lifeguards at the base pool. He said he thought I had a good shot at getting a slot.''

''Ah, now I get it.'' J.T. sat beside his son. ''Bathing suits.''

A sheepish grin twitched across Chris's face, just like the time J.T. had caught him flushing Legos down the toilet.

He hadn't thought much about Chris and swimming, or that his son might have different sport preferences than his own interest in football and wrestling. But since Spike had once been a professional diver during his stint with the CIA, if the guy thought Chris could handle lifeguarding, then it must be so. ''Not a bad way to spend the summer and earn money. Sure a helluva lot more fun than the way I spent my summers as a teenager. I'm lucky now to be doing something I enjoy.''

Chris picked up his water bottle, rolled it between his palms. ''Why did you go into the Air Force?''

''Where I grew up, it was either join the military or work in the steel mill. In my family, when we turned eighteen, we had to head out and earn a living. No hanging around to 'find yourself.' Six picked the mill. Three of us enlisted.''

''But why did you enlist instead of doing what your other brothers did?''

''You're going to college.''

''I know. But why did you decide to join up?''

''If you're thinking about the military, you need to know this isn't an easy job.'' J.T. scratched a hand up his tank top along his ribs where a phantom ache twitched. His eyes gravitated to his tome of Shakespeare's plays, currently tucked sideways between his ratchet set and buzz saw. ''Be sure you're called.''

''Were you called?''

''Not at first.''

''Huh?'' Chris's jaw slacked. ''No way. I thought you lived for this stuff.''

''I do. Now.'' Or God knows he would have never pulled his family through the moves and stress. ''Back then, I just wanted out of that town. I joined for the GI Bill, planned to get a degree, thought after that I'd work in some office. Hell, I'd run the whole damn steel mill.''

''So why aren't you?''

''Because once the airplane took off, I heard the call.'' He could still feel the rush of that first training flight, the lift, the sense of purpose, the chance to make things happen and not just have things happen to him. ''After that, I decided I didn't want to get out for the four years it would have taken me to get a degree. Why should I anyway? I was doing exactly what I wanted.''

He'd had more money, security and benefits than when growing up. He hadn't counted on meeting Rena and wanting to give her more.

"And you met Mom."

Was the kid a mind reader? "Yeah, I met your mom."

"How do you know when you meet her? The one?"

J.T. studied his son, used some of that Rena-insight stuff he'd just started to glean. And ah crap, sometimes it was better not knowing. The poor kid sure as hell wasn't the guy who almost knocked up the girl.

But he loved that girl anyway.

Clasping his hands between his knees, J.T. searched for the words to make this one better for his kid. A hopeless deal when he couldn't even make things better for himself in the woman department. "You've gotta go with your gut on that one, son. There's no clear-cut answer. You just know when you see her."

And wasn't that the truth? Rena had been so hot that day, still was. But honest to God, he'd fallen for her laugh.

"So if Mom was the one, then why did you decide to split?"

"Now, there's the million-dollar question." He tugged his weight-lifting gloves tighter on his hands. "Sometimes right for one person is wrong for another. Sometimes you meet the right person at the wrong time. Sometimes it's the right person at the right time and you do all the wrong things because you're a dumb ass. Basically, it's a real crapshoot getting all the rights lined up at the same time." He glanced sideways at his son. "Any of that make sense?"

"Yeah, it does." Chris stood, crossed to the weight rack, lifted the curl bar. "So what do I do about it...if I have that problem, right person, wrong time?"

"Hell, Chris." J.T. joined him and started alternating curls. "If I had the answer to that one, do you think I'd still be sleeping across the hall?"

''Guess not.''

Arms pumping, J.T. thought about telling Chris he didn't have to make any decisions, but hesitated. His son had asked a man's question and deserved a man's answer.

J.T. slowed the reps, replaced the weights and faced Chris eye to eye. ''The best I can offer you is the knowledge that you're in the same boat with the majority of the male population. Women are a mystery. And the guy who figures out that mystery could sell the secret for enough money to *buy* the whole damn factory.''

Something he now knew wasn't his calling, even if that factory could buy Rena everything she deserved. Damn but he'd wanted to give her more. Yet even as his gut revolted at the thought of a repeat of three months ago, a repeat of what he'd put Rena through, he knew he wouldn't walk away from the Air Force.

''My advice, son? Go ahead and quit the job at the restaurant. Study your butt off for the exams. Then enjoy the hell out of that lifeguard job. I'm betting one of those bathing suits works her way over to your tower by the end of the first week.''

He clapped his son on the back, and even though Chris only scrounged a half smile, their talk had gone well. Or at least better than any talk before.

The door into the house squeaked, opened. Rena stood silhouetted, wearing a maternity jumper.

Who the hell sucked all the air out of the garage? Because he damn well couldn't find any.

This baby was real, and getting closer to being born. A dumb-ass obvious thought, still the speed of time ticking away hadn't hit him until then.

She wasn't showing much, but nearing the fourth month, there was no question. The silky green fabric skimmed her tiny bulge. ''Supper's ready.''

Rena's eyes lingered on J.T.'s shoulders—bared by a

workout tank T-shirt. He could see her pupils dilate from clear across the garage. His heart rate revved in time with her rapidly rising and falling chest.

Chris snatched a towel off the hook. "Great. I'm starving. No surprise, huh?" their son rambled on in the thick silence. "Cool new clothes, Mom. Are you sure you're not carrying twins?"

Twins? Rena went as pale as he felt.

J.T. thumped his son on the chest. "Way to go charming your mother, bud. Are you trying to get us all killed?"

Chris winced. "Sorry. You, uh, look nice, Mom."

Rena gripped the railing and walked down the four steps into the garage with only a slight limp. Time was definitely running out before he would be asked to leave. Soon, she wouldn't need him.

Hell, she hadn't needed him at all since she graduated.

She stopped in front of her son, twisted a dainty fist in his shirt and tugged him down…to kiss him on top of his curly head. "You're forgiven for the twins comment, hon."

"And, uh," he stuttered, straightening, "I'm really sorry for what I said the other night." His thin arms wrapped around her for a rare teenager hug.

She patted his back with the same reassurance she'd given to lull him to sleep after toddler nightmares. "It's okay, hon."

"Thanks. Love ya, Mom." Toddler images aside, the pointed stare he shot his father over her head was definitely all man shouting, *Hurt my mama again and I'll take you down.* He blinked, returning to sixteen. "Catch ya' later, dudes, I'll just grab some food on my way up to my room. I gotta get some homework done. Thanks for the advice about the job stuff, Dad."

Their son's footsteps faded, but neither of them looked away from each other, her gaze still riveted on his shoulders and sweat-soaked T-shirt sticking to his chest. His eyes unable to move from the fertile curves of her body.

The primal need to protect her, have her, surged. The urge to lock that door and find new uses for the weight bench throbbed through him.

She backed, gripped the railing and found the first step. ''I'll meet you inside.''

The wind through the window molded her silky dress around killer legs and a gentle baby bulge.

''In a minute.'' Once he willed away the arousal.

Her retreat made it clear. No kiss this time.

At least he'd gotten one thing right during the talk with Chris. Chris would turn in his notice, ditch the extra delivery duties, and maybe they would use the extra time for more talks.

And since the added plans for tomorrow night's surveillance flight should net that final drug trafficking link, he would have a couple of days off to focus on his family. He could step up the pace on the romance crapshoot in hopes that someday he got it right.

Chapter 10

"No hard feelings, pal," Kurt Haugen said from behind his desk, a stuffed swordfish mounted on the wall over his head. Circling around to the front, he extended his hand for a shake. "You've always got a job here if you change your mind. I appreciate a hard worker."

Chris tried not to let his exhale of relief be too obvious. He shook hands, firm, the way his dad had taught him. "Thank you, sir."

"But I'll need you to leave now." Mr. Haugen leaned back against the big wooden desk, crossing one tasseled loafer over the other. "Once someone quits, I prefer they go right away. Not that I don't trust you. It's policy."

"Sure. No problem." Totally. He couldn't wait to get out, and this was so easy he wondered why he hadn't thought of it before. "And thanks for being cool about it. Things are really tense at home, with my mom expecting a baby and stuff."

"I hear you. I live in a house of women." He tipped a

framed family photo Chris's way, the gold rim outlining a smiling trio of Dad, Mom and little girl. "It's important to take care of them, keep them happy. You go easy on your mom, and I promise you it'll all be worth it when you see that new brother or sister."

"Yeah, uh, right." He shuffled his feet, ready to close the book on his crappy first-job experience. The lifeguard gig would have to be better.

Anything would be better.

Mr. Haugen replaced the photo and pushed away from the desk. "Well, no more of my proud-dad stuff. Take care and good luck."

Nodding, Chris backed away. He couldn't haul out fast enough. And best of all, he had some time to kill before his parents would expect him home.

He made tracks into the kitchen, the stink of fried fish sticking to him all the way through the door. Outside, he blinked against the sunlight—still bright even near sunset, inhaled a deep breath of salty air to clear his head.

Maybe he could grab a Big Mac and stop by Shelby's house, hang for a while. She was still pretty wigged out by the pregnancy scare and her upcoming move and the way Murdoch was pressuring her to change college choices this late in the game.

Chris kicked gravel. Didn't the guy realize how lucky he was to have somebody like Shelby? Pushing would just screw it all up. Which might not be so bad if it weren't for the fact Shelby would get hurt. And even if by some fluke she dumped her tall cool boyfriend for a scrawny geek, she was still moving in a few weeks.

It so sucked being a teenager stuck living with whatever the parents decided. Moving houses. Splitting marriages.

Definitely sucked.

He tucked around lines of parked cars, putting more space between himself and the restaurant. Okay, so *something* good had happened today. And the lifeguard job wouldn't be so bad.

But his dad was high if he thought the bathing suit chicks would be hanging out around Chris Price's tower. God, especially not with his bony arms and legs out there and his nose all white from zinc oxide. They'd probably think the base signed on a circus act. At least he didn't have to worry about burning since he tanned like his mom—the one good thing he'd inherited from her.

He rounded the corner to his parking spot—yeah, Dad, away from the ocean and the salt so Mom's car wouldn't rust.

Someone lounged against his back bumper. A girl someone. Shelby? Hope cleared his head faster than the beach air. He stepped up his pace to a jog and saw…

Miranda. Crap. His feet slowed.

Make it official. He now hated Lycra as much as lies.

So much for an easy home free. He'd just talk fast and leave even faster.

Chris threw back his shoulders and walked straight for the car. No hesitation. Ignoring the bodacious bitch, he thumbed the unlock button.

"Hey there, Chris." She arched away from the car and slithered into his path. "I hear you're leaving us."

"Uh-huh. Exams. New job. Less hours. That's life." He reached for the door handle.

Her hand fell on his. Held. Squeezed.

Ah crap, crap, crap. He couldn't push her away, because an honorable guy never got physical with a girl. More of his dad's teaching.

But what was he supposed to do when she got really physical with him?

Miranda slid her body between his and the door. Her cologne wrapped around him and just about strangled off air.

"You're sounding mighty cocky there, Chris. You wouldn't be getting any ideas?"

"Only about getting out of here." He pulled his hand off the door handle, which happened to be a little too close to Miranda's butt. Her gloating smile shouted that she knew it, too.

He crossed his arms over his chest.

She flicked her wavy blond hair over her shoulder. "Your quitting wouldn't have something to do with our little misunderstanding, would it?"

Do ya' think? "Nah. It's just what I said."

"About the misunderstanding part, you misunderstood that, too." She hooked a finger in the chain around her neck, sawed it back and forth, bringing the charm up from between her breasts. "So much misunderstanding going on. I'm not saying anything bad happened, but if you go around shooting your mouth off, people are going to think something *did* happen."

She kept on stroking that chain, the dangling charm swaying, the red circle with a black triangle in the middle a freaking hypnotizing eye magnet straight down to her—

He jerked his gaze away. Up to her face.

"My reputation will be a mess, Chris. Word gets around, doors will close for me. Word will get around about you, too. People will think you just got away with it, but that you're really a mule. A carrier."

He swallowed down fear and a hefty whiff of her perfume. How could he have ever thought she smelled good? "I didn't have any idea what was going on."

"If you go to the cops with what you think you saw, and say there was something bad going on, do you think they're going to believe you're innocent? They're going to think you're trying to save your skin."

She dropped the necklace back to rest against her tanned skin. "And if, just if, something big really was going on, don't you think the people you're dealing with might be smarter than you?''

Straightening from the car, she flattened a hand to his face and patted. ''But guys who play nice don't get hurt.''

Miranda stroked her fingers along his chin on her way past, leaving him standing alone by the car wondering how in the hell he ever could have thought Miranda Casale was hot. She was a freaking snake in Lyrca. His cheek itched where she'd touched him.

As his dad would say, he was in a crapload of trouble.

Chris jerked open the car door, double-checked the back seat to make sure it was empty and climbed behind the wheel.

Locked the doors really fast.

Part of him wanted to crawl away and hide. Okay, most of him wanted to do that, but he'd been hiding for a couple of weeks now. Instead of getting better, things were getting worse.

He felt like puking. But he wouldn't. He would be like his dad. This was the time to be a man.

He would have to come clean.

God, did Miranda really think he was stupid enough to believe nothing was going on? If there had been any doubts before, her little chat cinched it for him.

If he'd been a mule once—his stomach rolled—then they would use that as leverage to make him do other things. Maybe worse things.

Sweat popped on his forehead, feeding his zits. He would have to do something. He would have to talk to his dad after his flight.

Used to be he could talk to his mom easier, but his dad and even Mr. Haugen were both right about keeping women safe. A pregnant chick needed to be protected most of all. No question, his dad wouldn't want this dumped on her. His dad also wouldn't want her left at home alone with this kind of crap hanging over their heads.

The car accident.

Sweat iced. His stomach pitched. Chris scrambled for the handle, stumbling out of the car with half a second to spare before he lost his supper on the gravel.

Doubled over, gripping his knees, he gasped for clean air that didn't stink like Miranda's cologne, fried fish and a screwed-up life.

God. What a wuss. He dragged the tail of his T-shirt over his mouth and staggered back into the car.

He didn't have time to be sick. He needed to get home to his mom. And if he wanted to make it there without more pit stops to heave up his guts, he couldn't think about what might happen next.

Rena flipped pages of her gardening magazine, reclining on the sofa, her head propped by two pillows, her feet up on the armrest. Hot chamomile tea steamed on the coffee table. Cool air conditioner blew through the silence. A totally peaceful way to end the day.

If it weren't for the fact one of those pillows under her head carried J.T.'s scent.

He'd always had a distinctive air. Earthy, sexy. And, ohmigod, how pregnancy heightened her sense of smell, leaving her all the more susceptible to the woodsy soap swirl curling through her with each inhale.

She flipped pages, lingered on an herb garden layout. Odd how smells became associated with emotions. She'd been pruning her oregano plant when she'd heard about J.T. overseas. She still couldn't eat spaghetti.

But a single sniff of J.T.'s soap, and she found her eyes drifting shut so she could isolate that one intense sensation. Remember the very second she'd met the man and he'd bombarded *all* her senses. The magazine flopped onto her chest.

In those days, he'd been a C-141 loadmaster, stationed in New Jersey. She and three friends from her private girls' school had piled into her car and driven over the New York state line for a peek at those flyboys at their air show.

One look at J.T. and she was toast. She still firmly believed she would have fallen for him, no matter what her background. She hadn't felt the same tug to any of the other flyboys that day.

But her past had made her a pure sitting duck for the explosive attraction that rolled over her the first time she saw him. She didn't stand a chance thanks to the combination of her all-girl environment and lack of experience. What teenage boy would risk her father's displeasure by dating her?

J.T. had quietly dared plenty when it came to risking her family's "displeasure," and she would have loved him for that alone.

Still she could remember the feel of his hand on her elbow as he'd steadied her along the back ramp into the plane. And then he'd been waiting for her when she exited the side hatch. She never knew who he'd convinced to take over for him, but suddenly he was free to escort her around the air show.

He'd bought her a hamburger and she totally forgot what fillet mignon tasted like, just knew nothing could be as good as that charbroiled burger mixed with her first taste of love.

The telephone rang, jarring her out of her fog.

She pitched the magazine onto the coffee table, reaching for the cordless phone beside her teacup. "Hello?"

"Hey, babe, it's me." J.T.'s voice rumbled through the receiver.

Her elbow tingled with the phantom memory and damned if she didn't crave a hamburger.

Tucking the phone under her chin, she sank deeper into her pillows, releasing a fresh whiff of J.T. "Hey there to you, too. I thought you were supposed to take off an hour ago."

"Weather delay. We're leaving soon though. Thought I'd check in to see how your doctor's appointment went today."

She stifled down defensiveness. Just because he cared

about the baby didn't mean he wasn't concerned about her, too. The two weren't mutually exclusive. "Everything looks good—really looks good. They did an ultrasound."

"Ah hell, I wish I could have been there."

"I have a picture here for you. It shows so much more than we saw with Nikki and Chris. The newer technology is amazing."

"Then it's probably not a waste, after all, that we got rid of the old baby things, what with the improved stuff on the market."

"Picking out the new furnishings will be fun." Would they do it together?

"I guess it was too early to tell if it's a boy or girl."

"Yeah, in a couple more weeks, though."

"I want to go with you to your next appointment."

The quiet request shouted his resolve. He loved his kids. Her heart ached for him and what she knew he wanted. "No matter how things turn out, I understand this is your baby, too. You should be there."

He didn't answer for a second, the phone lines filled only with background voices from the squadron. Finally, his exhale echoed. "Thank you for that."

Guilt tweaked, hard, as it had done when she'd grieved over J.T. ringing the doorbell at his own house.

He was a good man. Even if he frustrated the hell out of her, she couldn't deny his honor, strength. He deserved better from life.

She could at least give him more today. "If you believe old wives' tales, then the baby's heart rate indicates this one's a boy."

"Another boy, huh? Either way's great by me. We haven't talked about names or anything yet. Do you have any ideas, family names?"

She'd named Chris and Nikki after an aunt and uncle she'd visited, respected, wanting to give her kids something positive from her side of the family. "What about your family this time? Or have you changed your mind since Chris was born about not having a James Taggart Price Jr.?"

"No junior," he answered without hesitation. "Going through school as Price Tag is a tough moniker."

One that stuck through to Air Force days with his call sign. She'd never considered the irony of it before, given his constant worries about money. "Okay, no junior. I'll pick up a couple of baby-name books and we can make lists."

A dangerous little emotion called hope started to flutter inside her. He really was trying. He'd been working hard to relate better with Chris, like during their talk in the garage.

Except she might be better off not thinking about the garage and a half-naked J.T. in workout clothes, arms and legs muscled, bared, sheened with sweat.

"Rena? Are you still there?"

"Oh, yeah, sorry. I was, uh, I don't know. I must have zoned out. No offense. You remember those near-narcoleptic moments of the first trimester."

His chuckle rumbled through the phone line and vibrated inside her. "I'll be quiet when I come in so I don't wake you."

Uh-oh. Too easily she could envision the times he *had* woken her after a flight. His eyes intense, charged, adrenaline all but dripping from him, and then he would pour all that intensity into making love to her, like in the kitchen after his return from Guam.

To this day, she couldn't look at that stenciled ivy without remembering the heat of him moving against her, in her, bringing her to a screaming release at eleven o'clock in the morning. Yeah, she even still remembered the exact time.

"Hey, Rena? I hear Scorch calling for me. Time to roll. See you when you wake up in the morning. Good night."

The line went dead.

"Good night," she whispered, keeping the phone cradled

under her chin for a silly sentimental moment before she thumbed the Off button.

Her eyes drifted closed. She inhaled his scent to mix with the sound of his voice still in her head and drifted into that twilight restlessness, neither asleep nor fully awake, when thoughts took their own direction. Remembering the summer weeks after she'd met J.T. when they'd stolen every moment possible together. Every time they'd said goodbye on her porch or hung up the phone, she'd been certain she would die if she couldn't be with him forever.

Teenage melodrama? Maybe. But also intense and wonderful.

Then one night, parked by the shore, they hadn't been able to wait any longer. Tugging the zipper down on his flight suit, her hands found their way inside.

She'd reveled in being safe and free when he held her, touched her. And yes, he'd said he loved her, those words sending showers of excitement rushing over her because if this honorable man loved her, then she wasn't tainted by her family. She'd believed the words with all her heart back then, not questioning whether or not he really meant them until many years later after too many silences between them.

How safe she'd felt in his arms, safety nearly as intoxicating as his touch, the way he seemed to know just where to stroke until her pulse pounded in her ears. Louder. Louder still until she'd thought she would shatter—

Shatter?

Rena bolted upright. Wind gusted through her front window, through the jagged hole. Glass sparkled on her floor.

Glass surrounding a brick.

Chapter 11

"Five minutes out," Scorch's voice announced through the headset.

"Roger," J.T. echoed from the metal belly of the plane. "Five minutes out."

J.T. stared at the red light posted in the cargo hold, then readied the hatch for the jump. A void of air swirled outside, soon to swallow the four jumpers waiting to hurtle out of his plane. Pitch night. Nothing but ocean below as they flew off the coast of Charleston.

Scorch flew as aircraft commander, Joker as copilot since Bo was out of commission. Their pilot's need-to-know status on these surveillance flights was low. No questions asked, they would fly the routes provided and go through the motions of a training flight as directed. His role in back handling divers and equipment called for more briefing.

Four divers stood, checking equipment, readying for their static line jump, J.T. acting as jumpmaster for the three DEA agents and Spike. The fourth DEA agent who'd been scheduled was currently curled up in the hospital, most likely in the fetal position, thanks to a bout of food poisoning.

Given the DEA's prestanding LOA—letter of agreement—with the OSI regarding this case, Max ''Spike'' Keagan had been able to step in as a last-minute replacement. Spike's diving skills and inside work on the case from the Air Force angle made him a natural choice for a quick replacement on the crucial mission.

Regular surveillance flights were still netting the same information without pinpointing that critical last link. The drugs were unloaded from the spare tires, then taken off base. The lieutenant from the transportation squadron always drove the same route to the same place at Shem Creek. Parked in the same lot out of sight and waited until a shrimp trawler pulled up.

Undoubtedly, the drugs were being loaded onto that boat. Problem was, the boat never did anything unusual afterward. No long trips. No rendezvous with another craft.

Besides, boats usually *brought* drugs to shore. Strange all the way around.

Thus the divers. The two pairs would drop into the harbor for close-up recon, and hopefully discover what the hell was going on.

''Sixty seconds,'' Scorch called.

''Roger, sixty seconds,'' J.T. repeated for the benefit of the jumpers who weren't on headset.

Geared up in a black wet suit, diving tanks, flippers, parachuting gear, Spike stared back at J.T., waiting.

Time to finish this.

J.T. nodded.

''Ten seconds,'' Scorch called.

''Ten seconds.'' J.T. listened, counted down, watched the standby light change to—

Green.

"Go! Go! Go!" He gave the first in line the traditional slap-on-the-ass signal to jump.

One, two, three, four, Spike and the other divers launched into the darkness.

J.T. struggled not to fight against the darkness. Only a slight haze permeated the hood the Rubistanians had placed over his head, but it sure as hell blocked the ability to see where they were taking him.

The very reason the Rubistanians had done it.

He kept reminding himself these soldiers couldn't know for sure who they'd captured from the warlords' caravan. Of course they would have questions and concerns about foreign military on their soil. And now that they were in official hands, chances of getting out alive were a helluva lot stronger than a couple of hours ago.

Rubistanian and American relations might be strained, but they weren't outright hostile. Rubistan didn't want to be the next Iraq.

Steady. Focus on images of Rena's face. Think about getting home. Return alive with honor.

Brusque hands guided him out of the jeep. He heard others move with him. His three crewmates?

"Stay calm," Scorch whispered. "Be low-key. Remember your training. Everybody here?"

"Roger," J.T. answered.

"Here and cool," Spike muttered low.

"Yeah," Bo grunted.

"Good, okay." Scorch's voice moved closer. "Just—"

A hand smacked J.T.'s back. "No talking!" *a heavily accented voice shouted.* "No talking!"

O-kay.

Footsteps shuffled along a dirt path. Or sand. Who knew? The guards talked back and forth, not that any of it made sense.

Hands guided them up concrete steps. Inside. The haze darkened.

The hood swept up and off. J.T. blinked against the stark lightbulb inside what appeared to be a craphole jail. Standard for this country. He hadn't expected any better from these guys than where they would keep their own prisoners.

He stared at his three crewmates, probably the last time he would see them until they were released. The interrogations would start now. Rough. But at least they were in official hands.

One of the foreign soldiers stepped forward. "We question now. You." He pointed to Spike. "We start with you."

They knew what to say, what not to say. Although Spike had the most to cover, and would benefit from more time to gather his thoughts. Hellish luck that they'd decided to begin with him.

J.T. glanced at Scorch. Their mission. Keep the enemy off Bo and protect Spike's secrets. J.T. started to speak, to divert attention and buy Spike extra minutes, but Scorch beat him to it.

"We demand our rights under the Geneva Convent—"

A rifle butt landed on Scorch's jaw.

The aircraft commander slammed against the wall. Blood spurted into his sand-caked mustache.

J.T. winced. But the foreign soldier reacted as expected. He shifted his attention from Spike to Scorch and hauled him off instead.

A minor victory, establishing some control over their situation.

The remaining soldiers led them away, separating them. J.T. watched until the last one faded…from…sight.

J.T. stared out into the dark void of the night sky. Empty. He closed up the hatch along with his memories. "All jumpers clear," he called into his headset. "Door secure."

J.T. strode back up the steel cavern to his station, the instrument panel and seat situated below the cockpit. Their part was done. He'd be home soon. Where his wife waited, something he hadn't fully appreciated until he'd screwed up his life.

He thought about fishing out his book, but found himself staring up at the tangle of cables tracking the ceiling instead. Right now, he wanted to pass out in his own bed with his own wife, against her soft body. Wake up and lose himself *in* her body.

Not gonna happen, of course.

But he would be across the hall. He was back in the house. Progress in regaining his world.

And not being stuck in a cell in some foreign freaking country.

Two hours later, he turned the corner onto his street to find police cars lining the curb. Foreboding gripped his gut in an icy, unrelenting fist. He threw open the door of his truck, boots pounding up the driveway, across the yard, just as hard and fast as when he'd run across the Rubistanian desert, raced to Rena in the wrecked car.

Control over his world shattered in more pieces than his living-room window.

Rena held on to her composure—barely—for once thankful her aching foot offered an excuse to sit in the overstuffed chair rather than stand.

She faced the two police officers in her living room, alone, except for an over-pale teenager shuffling his feet by the piano. She could do this by herself, but damn it, she didn't want to. She wanted to lean on her husband while he leaned on her.

And when this bizarre night ended, she wanted to crawl into the strength of his arms, lay her head on the breadth of his chest and listen to his steady heat thrum under her ear. She wanted him to tell her everything would be fine. It was just coincidence that Chris's car had been hit and a rock pitched through their window all in the span of two weeks.

She needed to hear that their son wasn't mixed up in something bad like her every parental instinct was screaming.

Hell, who was she kidding? She just flat out wanted J.T. with her.

And as if he'd somehow heard her, her husband plowed through the front door. Intense. Focused.

On her.

He stalked straight to her chair, ignoring everyone else in the room. Dropping to his knees in front of her, he clasped her by the shoulders, firm, solid. ''Is everyone all right? Are you all right?''

His concern pulsed into her, soothing and exciting all at once. ''I'm fine. Someone threw a brick through the window. A scary way to wake up, but nothing overly dangerous. I just thought it was important to report it to the police.''

His gaze fell to the splash of glass glinting on the floor, to the harsh gouge in the wood inches away from the couch, then up at her rumpled blanket and pillows. ''You were asleep in here when it happened?''

She nodded. Only a few hours ago she'd nestled into those pillows with plans to show J.T. the ultrasound photo.

His fingers bit into her skin. She struggled not to flinch and up his concerns.

''But I'm fine. Really. I wouldn't lie about this, not when it comes to the baby.''

Jaw still tight, J.T. stood, turning to Chris. ''Son, are you okay?''

''Yes, sir.'' Chris fidgeted from foot to foot, his baggy clothes rippling with every agitated move. ''I was on my way home from work. I would have been home sooner but there was a backup on the bridge. God, Mom, I'm so sorry I wasn't here. Maybe I could have done something.''

Horror splashed through her. ''You would have stayed

right here in this house with me while we called the police.'' She couldn't even let herself dwell on what could have happened to him out there. ''No more Price heroes for me this year, thank you very much.''

The senior cop stepped forward, hat tucked under his arm. ''Sir, we did a walk around of the yard, had a second car run a quick canvas of the area. There's nothing to report. It's probably just a teenage prank, like rolling a house with toilet paper.''

''I'm not buying that.'' J.T. shook his head. ''Didn't my wife tell you about the hit-and-run two weeks ago?''

The younger female cop thumbed through her notepad. ''We have that report, too, and will follow up. We'll schedule a car to cruise by your house. Unless you have something else to tell us, that's the best we can do for now.'' She flipped her notebook closed. ''You'll want to board up that window tonight, just to be safe.''

''No problem,'' J.T. answered, already looking in need of some physical release for the tension visibly knotting his shoulders.

The police tucked away notepads and started to pack the evidence bag with the brick inside.

''Hold on a second.'' J.T. frowned, stepping closer. He cocked his head to the side for a better look at the brick. Forehead smoothing, eyes icing, he jabbed a finger at a painted discoloration on the side. ''Damn it, that's the same symbol as on the bumper of the hit-and-run car.''

Rena leaned nearer. How had she missed the markings? The inked red circle with a black triangle inside wasn't all that large, still it niggled at her brain with familiarity. Maybe because J.T. had told her, but she'd been too foggy from the accident to process the information?

Until now. Her fears for her child grew exponentially while foreboding smothered her.

"Uh, Dad?" Chris inched forward. "Can we, uh, go in the kitchen for a minute. I really need to talk to you."

Three hours later, J.T. hammered the last nail in the plywood covering the broken window. Pounding nails didn't come close to releasing the anger boiling inside him.

Somebody had screwed with his family. Put his wife's life at risk. Dared try to suck his kid into underworld crap.

J.T. gave the nail a final whack, driving it home.

Chris had given his full statement to the police. For now, it didn't look as if they would need a lawyer, but if things shook down the way J.T. suspected, they would all be spending time testifying in courtrooms before this was over.

His son would have to testify against the people who'd threatened him. The scum-sucking bastards had come after his family, leaving him in his front yard in the middle of the night doing his damnedest to take some precautions for his family while the police looked into things.

Dangerous and scary-as-hell things.

It had taken guts for Chris to come forward, and J.T. couldn't help but be proud of his kid for making the stand. Although he wanted to shake the boy for not doing it sooner. Just thinking about what *could* have happened—

He jammed another nail home.

A cop cruiser drove past for the second time while he'd been repairing the window. Some reassurance. His military web belt now in place with his 9mm holstered provided a little more.

Except there wasn't enough reassurance to douse the fire in his gut. He'd rather be back in Rubistan sweating it out while he waited for an ass-beating thinly disguised as an interrogation than have to worry about his family. He might not have provided the most glamorous life for Rena, but damn it, she was supposed to be safe in her own house.

The hammer thunked to one side. Grazed his thumb.

Crap. He needed to get his head together before he faced Rena again. She would want to talk, and he wanted to pound more nails.

Pound some heads.

At least she was occupied now hovering over Chris. The kid was scared spitless. As well he should be. He could use some coddling from his mom and wouldn't want his dad around to witness him scared and tucked into bed.

Rena's face had been so pale when he'd walked through the door, he'd thought for certain someone had died. She didn't need this. She should be putting her feet up and banging back bowls of peach ice cream.

Instead, they were facing court cases and God only knew what from this Miranda person and her deliveries. Most likely it was a drug purchase.

How ironic. He was busting his ass trying to collar drug runners to stop that very thing from happening to other people.

He'd already left a message for Spike about setting up a meeting with the OSI to report the brick incident. Not much sleep for the OSI agent tonight after the dive, but there were too many coincidences stacking up. Even if this bore no relevance to their investigation, he was bound by his job to report any brushes with possible illegal activities. Hell, even a happenstance chat with a stranger in a bar might not be so coincidental.

Had his family somehow been targeted because of him?

Paranoid? Possibly. But he couldn't be too careful when it came to Rena and the kids.

Crouching down by his toolbox, he tossed in the hammer, nails, and wished life could be this easy to organize. He hefted the box up, nails rattling against wrenches, and strode to the garage door, punched in the code. The door rolled up and open. Inside, he closed the door and double-checked the lock. Checked the window as well, then cranked the fan in lieu of a breeze since that window would be staying shut from now on.

He ditched the toolbox on his workbench—beside his Shakespeare anthology. The book was getting dog-eared from overuse these days.

Thumbing along the edges, he slowed, flipped it open. *Two Gentlemen of Verona.* "The private wound is deepest."

Well, hell. He could use a little less insight tonight.

He smacked the book shut. He'd have to work off his tension in a more basic way. Sex would be great. But not wise. And not an option.

Exercise.

He sat on the edge of the weight bench and unlaced his boots, one, two, tucked them to the side. He unhooked his web belt, placed it within easy reach on his workbench, then peeled off his sweaty flight suit. God, how many hours ago had he put the thing on?

Wearing only his black T-shirt and boxers, he reached for a pair of workout shorts flung over a weight bar.

The door from the house opened—revealing Rena. His hands closed around the shorts. Talk about being caught with his pants down.

She startled to a stop. Tension to match his rippled off her in visible waves. Corkscrew spirals of hair all but crackled with energy.

After a quick flicker-glance down his near-naked body, her gaze met and held his. "I have something I need to say."

Uh-oh.

The determination in the tilt of her chin, he recognized well. The vulnerable glint in her eyes, however, caught him completely off guard at a time when his defenses were already somewhere in the negative numbers.

He braced his shoulders for whatever she planned to tell

him—and wished he had some pants to go along with the strengthened will.

Rena's slim fingers wrapped around the stair railing, queenlike in her garage castle. ''Temporary truce.''

Chapter 12

Rena gripped the railing until the edges cut into her palm. Swallowing her pride came hard.

Being alone right now was harder.

She moved down another stair, closer to J.T. and the weight bench. "I don't have a clue what we're going to do tomorrow. Or the day after that. I know you want to move back in for the baby, and you have to know I'm still not sure I can live with that. We haven't really resolved anything."

His face blanked, but she'd expected that once she started discussing their problems. He gave her so few glimpses into him, his feelings. She would have to go with her instincts, all of which told her to forge ahead. To take what she could right now, find something solid to hold on to.

"But I also know this is about the worst day of my life, second only to when I heard you'd been shot down."

A vein throbbed along his temple. Not as outward a sign as some of the ones Bo displayed in her office, but she read the tension in her husband well. Her arms ached to hold him as much as her body yearned to be held.

''I can make it through tonight on my own if I have to. But God, J.T., I don't want to. I want somebody to hold me for just a few minutes while that somebody tells me everything is going to be okay. I need for *you* to hold me.''

He moved toward her, slow, silent, her big stealthy husband, and yet somehow he was there in front of her before she could blink. His arms went around her, lifted her off the last two steps and clasped her to his chest, lowering her in a glide against his solid body that comforted and excited all at once. Her feet lightly touched ground, if not her senses, which were definitely still flying.

His fingers smoothed over her hair, again and again without stopping, his other hand working a firm massage against her waist that kept her anchored to him. ''I can't promise you it's going to be okay. But I can promise I'll do my damnedest to make that happen. And I can most definitely hold you for as long as you need me.''

How about forever? she wanted to ask. Except needing him meant more loss if he left again. Not that she expected him to walk out the door with the baby on the way. But she'd learned there were so many other ways to leave. He'd lived in the house with her for years while still seeming thousands of miles away.

J.T. rubbed circles on her back. ''Did everything go okay with Chris upstairs?''

She nodded. ''He actually fell asleep. I think the fear exhausted him. Is it totally ridiculous that I stood there at the door and watched him sleep as if that could somehow shift things back to when he was five and I used to do the same thing?''

''Not ridiculous at all. The five-year-old was a helluva lot easier to deal with. Bigger kids. Bigger problems.'' His arms tightened around her.

Frustration sparked inside her, the need to do something,

fix things in a way she could with a little child. "What did we do wrong that he didn't come to us right away?"

"Teenagers don't always see long-term ramifications. I'm guessing he kept slapping Band-Aids on the problem hoping it would get better on its own."

A coping method that sounded familiar. "Who are we to judge on that reasoning?"

"Guess you have a point there, babe." His chin fell to rest on the top of her head. "But bottom line, he's old enough to know better. He understands right from wrong, and whatever is going on with Miranda Casale is very likely wrong."

"He was worried about us. He was trying to protect us. That's not how it's supposed to be. We're supposed to protect him."

"And we are. He did come to us—even a little late—but he came clean on his own. He could have kept trying to bluff. I don't know about you, but I'm proud of him for standing up. He had to be scared as hell."

She turned her head to the side, resting her cheek on his chest. "God, you must think I'm a total mess. I'm okay now though. I only needed a second to find my footing again. Thank you."

He didn't let go.

And she didn't argue.

His hands kept their steady pace along her springy curls and against her back, slowing, shifting from soothing to sensual.

Still she didn't move. Couldn't speak. Couldn't do anything but stand, gripped by his arms and the fire swelling through her as surely as the proof of J.T.'s arousal. "What are we doing here?"

"Nothing yet, babe."

The promise in his deep voice strummed through her. She buried her face deeper into his chest, scent, heat. "But we're going to?"

"I sure as hell hope so." He tipped her chin until she looked up at him. "But not if it means you're going to send me packing tomorrow."

She couldn't stop herself from asking, "You would hold out to stay because of the kids?"

He cupped her face in both hands. "I would hold out so I could stay and have more time to fix this mess we've made of our lives."

Could they be "fixed," like the house or the car? She couldn't sort through it all now with her mind awash with worries for her son, her body craving the reliable comfort only J.T. could provide. And even though he'd avoided answering her question about staying for the kids, the fact that he wanted to try sent hope—and fear—lancing right through her.

Her fingers splayed across the ridged bands of muscles along his chest. "How about we cut a deal?"

"A deal?"

She smiled up at him playfully, even while the magnitude of her risk threatened to buckle her already wobbly knees. "I won't pitch your weights out on the lawn tomorrow, if you'll promise to talk to me. Really talk to me—after."

It wasn't a promise of forever. And the problems would still be there—everything from the lengthy separations brought on by his job, her temper, his hang-ups about her paycheck. But this compromise would pacify her irritatingly insistent logic enough for her to jump this man before she combusted with lust.

"If that's what you want."

She blinked, stunned by his easy acceptance. "You agree?"

His intense gaze shifted to a sensual smile to match hers. "But then I'm a guy. I'd promise to dance down the flight line in a tutu right now."

Much-needed laughter bubbled, a welcome reminder of

one of the things that drew her to this man—the surprise humor he saved for just the right moments.

Even as his blessed sense of timing had attracted her, so did his innate honor. This man would never lie to her. The promise of that talk offered her pride and common sense enough hope to let her body do exactly what she so desperately wanted.

Her forty-year-old pregnant body.

A moment of insecurity flickered. Then his eyelids went to half mast, silvery gray eyes gliding over her with an icy tickle that heated, excited. She knew. He definitely wanted her body, no matter what the age or pregnancy state.

Relief sweeping over her to bury any doubts deep, she brushed her lips across his collarbone. "Do you still like it when I do this?"

J.T. clenched his fingers in his wife's wild curls, the weight bench pressing against the back of his legs a welcome brace at the moment. A jolt of white-hot lust bolted from that patch of skin on his collarbone straight to his groin.

Hell yeah, he still liked it when she did that. His body shouted a resounding *Go for it,* while his brain insisted, *Don't forget how often sex screwed things up.*

And not the good kind of screwing.

He should take his time, do some more of that talking now to be sure she really wanted—

She licked his earlobe.

His brain fogged. The sensuous glide of her moist tongue against his skin proved too damn tempting on a night when the combination of the flight and the invasion of his home left him feeling raw. Basic. In the grips of the elemental need to stake his claim, protect what was his. "Rena, babe—"

"I still remember the first time I did that and how your eyes turned all intense and your lids went to half mast. Knowing what I was doing to you made me shiver. Which sent your eyes even grayer." She sketched his eyebrows with whisper-light fingers. "You still do that to me with just a look."

No doubts. She really wanted this, too.

He dipped his head to kiss her quiet before she could send him over the edge with only her words. The fan behind Rena blew her spiraling hair forward to tangle around his shoulders.

"Do you want to go upstairs?" Where he could give her an air-conditioned room and bed, if not roses and candles and all the things this woman deserved.

"I want here. Now. With you."

She nipped his shoulder, tunneled under his T-shirt, scored him lightly with her nails on a trek down that led her to snap the waistband of his boxers. Her hand dipped inside, found him, cool fingers wrapping around in a single stroke down. Up again.

All right then.

They'd done it in every room at some point, unable to resist an empty house when the impulse hit. But for some reason, they'd never had sex out here, in this place completely his.

Maybe there was his answer. He'd considered it too stark, messy, gritty for his wife. But with her gentle fist gliding along him as they stood right in the middle of the freaking weight room, he wondered if he'd caused them to miss out on something incredible by limiting their options.

Gripping the sweet give of her hips, he scrunched her dress up with crawling fingers, baring her legs to rub skin to skin against him. His fists full of silky dress, his legs against silkier skin, he tugged the dress up, over her head, her hair sweeping, falling free and…

Hell yeah. More creamy skin, lush woman and sensuality filled his gaze while lust filled his body. Her breasts swelled within the purple cups of her demi-bra. Generously. All those

extra pregnancy hormones worked their magic. The bikini cut
of her panties rode low, drawing a gentle line and attention
to the slight curve of her stomach.

Again that primal chord strummed inside him. She was his.
She carried his baby inside her. His heart pounded in his ears,
his hands gripping tight to the soft fabric still holding the
warmth of Rena's skin.

A final question stalled him. "Is everything okay with the
baby? You've been through a lot the past couple of weeks."

"Everything's fine." She stepped closer. "Totally fine."
Moved even closer until her breasts grazed his chest, beading
nipples peaking the lace to tease along his skin. "The doctor
said no restrictions. Although I don't think he'd be pleased
if we strung up a trapeze."

"A trapeze, huh?"

She traced the corner of his smile with the tip of her
tongue. "I'm not particularly graceful right now, anyway."

"I disagree." Something he intended to confirm. With his
mouth. Starting now.

He kissed her, deep, moist and so damn hot, hands busy
finding their way around purple lace, unhooking, skimming
down and off. Passion combusted higher than any fan could
combat.

Months of abstinence stoked the flame from red to blue.
Bluer still until nothing but white light dotted behind his eye
as he remembered how close he'd come to never being with
her again.

Rena ripped at his T-shirt, yanked it up and off while he
kicked free his boxers. Her body melded to his.

She sighed, damp breath caressing his chest, kisses and
nips following. "I've missed this so much, missed you."

They were in total agreement on that. He cupped her
breast, thumbed over the beading nipple, tugged, increasing
gentle pressure between two fingers until she arched into his
palm. "Why can't it all be this easy?"

"Shh." He soothed with his mouth and hands. "Right now it can be."

Creamy skin. All for him. No barriers. He dipped his face to her breast.

She was right. This was so easy, losing himself in the taste, scent, feel of her. No roar in his head other than the blood charging through his veins.

And even as he touched her in every place he knew she enjoyed, even as she reciprocated, somehow it all felt new. As powerful, impulsive—reckless—as their first time.

Without the fumbling.

He stroked down her side, delved past damp lace to trace along her folds, dip two fingers into even damper heat that contracted around his touch. Her nipple grew even harder in his mouth as she moaned.

Flat surface. He needed one. Now. Sooner.

His mind raced with options, the Astroturf floor too rough, the bed too far away. Time for creativity.

Turning, he backed her toward the weight bench, and thank goodness she seemed too absorbed in cupping his ass to question his intent since—oh yeah, her soft hand slipped around front—no way did he want to move his mouth from his current sweet target long enough to explain himself.

Bending forward, he eased her down along the bench, then knelt between her knees.

Her hands glided along and off his shoulders as she relaxed against the padded bench. "So much better than any trapeze."

"Hell, woman, you turn me inside out anywhere, anytime, and you know it."

Skimming her panties down slender legs and off, he flung aside the purple lace. He hooked her knees around his arms, spread her thighs slightly, her upper body totally there and on display just for him. For his hands. For his mouth.

He pressed his lips to her ankle, over to the still-pink scar from her stitches as if he could take all her pain into himself. He nuzzled the crook of her knee, worked his way up, and man, but did she ever sigh and make all those sweet sounds to guide him. Affirmations somehow became clearer, more arousing now that he realized how close he'd come to losing her.

His smile caressed her inner thigh just before he continued his path up until her scent filled his senses—roses and pure her.

''Yes,'' she sighed.

Again, he heard, agreed, settled between her legs and parted her to drink, deeper, fuller, his tongue circling the tight bundle of nerves. Her next sigh hitched on a sweet whimper-moan that encouraged. Urged. Guiding him to what she wanted, needed now, right now from his hands and mouth.

From him.

And then he heard the sweetest sound of all in her completion. But different, edgier somehow. Torn from her throat in a way he totally understood because this woman tore the breath from him sometimes.

J.T. pressed a lingering kiss that drew another tremble of aftershocks from her.

He may not be able to control forever with Rena, but he could make sure he heard that echoing completion again tonight. And again after that until she was damn near hyperventilating, if he had his way.

But first, he allowed himself a second to look at her—couldn't have looked away anyhow as more of that ''first time'' sensation rolled over him anew. Instead, he took in the image of her long dark hair spiraling to the floor. Her arms overhead, fingers still clenched tight around the steel grips, her perfect breasts rising and falling so fast, her body flushed from the release he'd brought her.

Her eyes fluttered open. A hesitant smile flickered. ''You're making me a little self-conscious here.''

He shook his head slowly, kept right on staring his fill.

"No need for that, babe. I'm just…" He paused, swallowing, words scarce for him on a normal day, and right now with so much of the past, present—damn it all—emotion clogging his throat and brain, words came tough. "There are times I can't believe I'm the lucky bastard who gets to sleep with you."

He extended a not-so-steady hand, traced the fragile line of her hipbone up, along the curve of her breast. She gazed back at him, her eyes unwavering, unblinking, glistening with tears when he'd vowed never to make this woman cry again.

She arched up and he forgot how the hell to think. One of the things he appreciated most about losing himself in Rena. She scooched toward him, wrapped her legs around his waist and guided him home. Oh yeah.

Gripping her hips, he steadied her, nudged into the tight fist of moist heat. Waited for her to accommodate, waited for her sigh. Then moved. Again, in time with her, their bodies in sync if not always their minds.

He kept his pace slow, controlled, careful. Her heels dug into the small of his back, urging him deeper, and he let her take the lead, let her body dictate, easy enough since they wanted the same thing.

Eventually, as always, he couldn't tell who controlled anymore. Neither probably, because the driving need had hold of both of them. Something that had controlled them for years.

Eyes closed, his face settled against the damp curve of her neck, his skin equally as slick, growing wetter as she rocked against him. More of that frantic edge slugged through him, the sense that he had to hold on to this moment because he might never have another chance with this woman.

An unacceptable thought.

"Don't stop." Her nails jabbed into his back with urgency. "Not yet."

"Don't worry, babe," he growled into rose-scented hair. "I have no intention of stopping or going anywhere."

Damn straight on that.

She pulsed around him, harder, massaging him in her release that threatened to send him over with her. Still, he held back, took her cries into his mouth, absorbed her trembling, drew out her fulfillment until his body roared for relief. Her cries building, fading, she sagged against him.

Only then did he allow himself the final thrust that would send him flying into the mist. Rena's husky voice and sighs, right there with him, steered him through the haze. Damn, but he loved listening to her.

Shuddering, he gathered her close, his face still in her hair. How long? Who the hell knew? Finally the world, concerns, their son, his work—the promise of Rena's talk—all started echoing through the fog to drag him back. And he would deal with all of it.

He knew his duty, never cut out on responsibilities, always kept his word. But for right now, the world could just shut the hell up, and Rena's talk would have to wait.

He reached for more of the total escape he could only find in his wife's body.

Sprawled on top of her husband on the floor, Rena tried to ignore the dark cloud edging into her brain. It had to be because of Chris's mess. Not because of anything to do with J.T. They'd made progress. They were both on the same page now about talking, working to improve things.

Then why was she afraid of tomorrow?

Their legs tangled, she listened to the percussion of his heartbeat in her ear. "The Astroturf must be giving you a serious case of carpet burns."

"Worth it."

"We could go upstairs," she felt obligated to offer even as she yearned to stay here, in the moment.

"In a minute," he growled, his eyes still closed, hands warm on the small of her back. "Don't want to think enough to walk yet. Not sure I could put my shorts on to head that way anyhow."

She swirled a finger through the hair sprinkling his chest, his skin slick with sweat. "It's cooler upstairs."

His eyelids snapped open. "Ah hell, I'm sorry." Bracing her waist, he sat up. "I didn't even think about how uncomfortable this must be for you. Let's go."

He stared back at her in his lap, his gray eyes intense, resigned and fortified for what would come next.

Déjà vu left her swaying, transporting her to nearly four months ago when he'd worn that exact same heartbreakingly intense expression. Just before their final argument that had sent him walking.

Her throat closed as if to hold back words and the possibility—probability—of a repeat showdown. Something she couldn't face yet with her emotions so bare. Vulnerable.

To hell with getting cerebral right now. Surely she could enjoy the physical nirvana of just lying with J.T. after how many hours she'd dreamed about touching him, tasting him. "No, really. I'm okay. I wanted to make sure you're all right." She tickled his chin with a lock of her hair. "Let's stay here a while longer."

"How much longer?" He nipped the tip of her finger.

She wriggled until her knees landed on either side of his hips. "As long as you can last, flyboy."

"Now, what man could resist that challenge?" He cupped her breasts while she rolled her hips until he throbbed hotter, harder against her. He lifted, shifted, guided her down.

So what if this was a reliable delay to their talk? It was an incredible way. And she would get around to doing the right thing soon enough.

Damn. She hadn't changed one bit in twenty-two years.

She was still totally at the mercy of her body's craving for this man.

Right now she wanted to enjoy the shimmering sensations and connection and a blissful moment when she was absolutely certain they could work things out because they couldn't have something this perfect that wasn't meant to be. They couldn't deny this connection for the rest of their lonely lives.

Yes, she understood it was carnal and elemental, but this wasn't just sex. It was almost as if when reason, defenses, human foibles and stupid, stupid pride fell away, their souls recognized each other at the most simple level, so right. Mates. For life.

She wanted to believe they would make changes this time, but her wary heart couldn't escape a fearful sense brought on by years of experience with this man. That as soon as the sweat chilled on their sated bodies, they would hurt each other again.

Chapter 13

Morning sunlight streaked through the bedroom curtains, throwing lacy patterns on the walls. A familiar enough image for J.T., but one he hadn't experienced in nearly four months. Not in this room, with his wife curled against his side. Naked. Something he intended to enjoy for a few more minutes before life intruded.

J.T. stroked her arm, watching the digital clock blink away minutes. They'd never gotten around to a conversation the night before, and he couldn't say he regretted the delay.

He'd braced himself for the discussion, even to the point of planning where it should take place. At the kitchen table with a bowl of peach ice cream. He hoped the ice cream would remind her of happier times and soften her up before the tough talk.

Only, she'd faded into one of her pregnancy narcoleptic naps. He'd wrapped her in a quilt, scooped her up and carried her to bed. If he'd even considered sleeping elsewhere, she'd put an end to that with a groggy arm around his neck pulling him down to join her.

Fair enough. No need to ask him twice.

His gaze skated from her feet peeking out of the covers, along her curves draped in a sheet patterned with a thousand little flowers, up to the creamy skin of her shoulders and neck.

Damn, but her hair looked good on his pillow.

His hand explored her arm, along her hip. Sighing, she flipped onto her back, landing his hand square onto the tight curve of her belly. Shock stilled him. Longing held him there.

He'd been careful the night before not to touch her stomach. Only a bonehead wouldn't realize she had hang-ups about reconciling because of the baby after their shotgun wedding. Hell, maybe he had a few of those hang-ups himself—wondering if this was the only way to work himself into Rena's life.

But for now, while she slept, he allowed himself a moment to meet his new kid. He palmed the slight swell, turned onto his side until his face rested against the top of his wife's head while he rubbed a slow circle greeting.

Rena snuggled closer, still asleep and warm, mumbling stuff he couldn't make out.

He smiled into her hair. "It's okay, you have a while longer before you need to get up."

"Hmm. Good. So sleepy. Love you."

Sucker punched, J.T. couldn't move. She rolled to her other side, away, and clutched her pillow while her breathing resumed a steady snoozing rhythm.

She was probably stuck in some time-warp dream state from twenty years ago when she'd said those words all the time and he hadn't appreciated how much they meant. But did she mean them now and if so, how would he keep from hurting her this time, too?

Swinging his feet to the floor, he sat on the edge of the mattress, scrubbing his fingers through his hair. Minutes ago he didn't want to leave the bed and now he couldn't haul ass out fast enough. What the hell was wrong with him? The truth blindsided him like a bogey sneaking in from his six o'clock.

He'd fallen in love with his wife all over again.

His head fell into his hands. Hadn't he always loved her? He'd told her so. Sure as hell thought so. But somehow those feelings paled in comparison to the gut-gripping emotion twisting through him.

And that scared the crap out of him.

Now he had to accept the fact that she had been right about demanding more over the years—and about the ways he'd hurt her through a distance he hadn't even known he'd put between them. He had a helluva lot more backpedaling to accomplish than he'd thought.

Okay, so the stakes were higher. At least he had his feelings lined up. He would just tell her when they talked and make damn sure she listened.

Except he couldn't help but wish he had more to carry into this confrontation than three little words he'd used before without realizing their full importance.

Shoving to his feet and away from the temptation to wake his wife up with sex, a reliable connection, he headed for the bathroom and a lonely shower. Maybe the showerhead would beat some inspiration into his brain.

Dressed in a fresh flight suit, he loped down the stairs, his socks making no sound on hardwood. He wasn't sure he wanted to face the garage and all the hot memories there. One look at the weight bench and he would be right back in a world of hurt. But he needed to snag his boots and swap out the Velcro patches off his dirty flight suit onto his clean one.

J.T. paused at the base of the stairs. Maybe he could bring Rena breakfast in bed first. That would start the day on a nicer note.

As long as he didn't pick something that would make her hurl on his socks.

Around the corner, into the kitchen, he stopped short at the sight of his son. "Good morning."

Chris slouched against the counter, spooning a bowl of Frosted Flakes into his mouth, eyeing his dad with confusion. "'Morning."

"You sleep all right?"

"Yeah, how about you, uh, I mean—" Red-faced, he looked down and stuffed his mouth full of another bite.

The bed shuffle hadn't gone unnoticed. Hell, the door to Nikki's old room had probably been standing open. Keeping things low-key for his son had been the last thing on his mind when J.T. carried Rena up to bed the night before.

Still, Chris kept quiet. Shoveled cereal. Didn't ask if his parents were back together, which stung worse than facing the question, because silence meant the kid had stopped hoping.

Breakfast in bed with Rena would have to go on hold for a few minutes. J.T. poured a bowl of cereal and a glass of milk for himself and leaned back against the counter beside Chris, crossing his feet at the ankles. "You okay?"

He stirred soggy flakes. "I'm sorry for screwing up with the stuff at the restaurant."

Not the subject J.T. had been thinking of, but then Chris obviously wanted to ignore the other topic. "I'm not going to lie to you, son. It would have been better if you'd come to us right away."

"Because of Mom's accident?"

No soft-soaping that. His gut burned. J.T. tipped back half a glass of milk, without relief. Hopefully Spike would have some good news for him when they met in a few hours. "Yes, and also as far as having the authorities believe your side of the story."

Nodding, Chris shoveled another spoonful of soupy cereal

into his mouth. J.T. waited, ate, the clock ticking by seconds over the door.

Pivoting on the heels of his athletic socks, Chris dumped the rest of his cereal down the disposal and made an overlong production out of washing the bowl. "When you were over there, in Rubistan, I mean—" he paused, washing the spoon—twice "—did you, uh, get scared?"

Water running, he eyed his dad sideways.

"Yeah." J.T. nodded, the understatement of the century. A dry smile tugged one corner of his mouth. "Sometimes so much I thought I'd piss in my pants."

Chris stared back. Shock sent his jaw slack. He dropped the spoon and shifted to face his dad full on. "Really?"

"Really." He'd always thought children needed to feel parents were invincible. Maybe finding out parents were human might not be so bad, after all. Sure would have helped prepare the kid for the breakup. "Only a fool wouldn't have been scared. Anyone can be brave when the odds are in your favor. It's what you do when you're scared that's the true measure of courage."

"Is that from Shakespeare?"

He hadn't even realized Chris knew he read the Bard's works. "Nope. Actually, it's from my old man."

One of the few conversations they'd had. Right after he'd found out Rena was pregnant. Strange how he'd forgotten about going to his father at that time until just now.

Other talks with his dad shifted around in J.T.'s head. Short exchanges, sure. His parents were just as closemouthed as he was, but they made their words count.

Had he done the same? "You don't have to go to school today."

"Yeah, I think I do have to go."

His son was becoming a man. "Okay, then." The kid was probably safer there than at home, anyway. "But remember, you can call me if you have any problems. I'll be there in minutes.''

''Thanks, but I'm okay.'' He pushed away from the counter and started toward the door.

Make the words count. ''Son?''

Chris turned. ''Yeah?''

''Love ya.' J.T. hooked his arm around Chris's neck and pulled him in for a hug.

His son hugged back. Thumping. Rena would have laughed over the fact that men had to hit while they were hugging, but hey, guys understood the lingo.

Thunking his son once more on the back, J.T. pulled away. ''And you're still grounded 'til the end of time.''

Grinning, Chris shrugged, baggy clothes rippling. ''I figured as much.''

''Go grab your backpack and I'll see what's keeping your mother.''

Scooping a muffin off the counter for his wife, J.T. hoped the upcoming talk with Rena could go even half as well as the one with his son, simple, low-key. Otherwise, they were all screwed.

She was so screwed.

Inching back from the kitchen door, Rena steadied her steps if not her pulse. The image of father and son, standing together, white athletic socks on crossed feet side by side, squeezed all those pregnancy emotions until she could barely breathe. Watching J.T. and Chris in sync like that was… perfect, the family she'd always wanted.

Well, without bricks flying through her window.

The fear from the night before quivered through her again. Followed by the oh so vividly red memories of how she'd escaped that fear.

Slumping against the wall by a wrought-iron plant stand, she let herself enjoy looking at J.T. Waking up alone had been disappointing. But then she'd realized J.T. probably couldn't have woken her anyway, as deeply as she slept. She'd squelched down hurt, forced herself to think clearly. He was being considerate by letting her sleep.

Quit thinking with her hormones and start using her brain or she'd never get through this with her heart intact. But oh, as she stared at J.T., freshly showered and shaved in his flight suit, strong jaw and handsome face that only grew more appealing with age, her emotions did so want control over her.

She'd always enjoyed J.T.'s body; however that body became all the more tempting when the man inside was being so incredible. Of course, he'd always loved his children, been active in their care, took his turn walking the floor. But the talking? He'd left that up to her.

Until now.

Seeing him become the father she'd always known he could be made her wonder what their lives would have been like had he shared some of that openness with her over the years. She'd lost count of all the arguments and reconciliation talks—actually mostly *her* talking. And even if he was talking now, too, was it realistic to expect they could patch this up themselves?

This possibility of reconciliation screamed, "last chance." Which meant going for broke on the fix with the one thing they'd never tried.

Marital counseling.

How strange that she of all people should be scared of the prospect. Scared of what she would hear. Could that be why she'd avoided it?

God knows, J.T. wouldn't want to go. Even laid-back Bo dragged his boots at the prospect of spilling his guts and having his brain picked. Hell, she was frightened to her roots just thinking about it, too. But the more she considered the idea, the more certain she became that this offered their only hope.

Of course, that meant delaying any talk for a while longer, waiting for the perfect time rather than some car discussion to and from work. Logical, right?

Not a scared-as-hell stall tactic.

She entered the kitchen before they could come out into the hall and realize she'd been watching them. "Hey, guys. I'm ready anytime."

Chris's gaze ping-ponged from one parent to the other. "Uh, I gotta get something from upstairs."

He angled past and out before she could even hug him.

Rena stopped by the table, couldn't move anyhow. Facing J.T. after making love shouldn't be this…tummy flipping. Exciting. Scary. Much like after their true first time when she realized what they'd done changed everything.

Except after the real first time, he'd held her, kissed her. Damn it, if she couldn't have the holding, she at least wanted her morning-after kiss.

"Hi," she said softly, words suddenly drying up.

"Hi back." J.T. smiled, extending one hand with a muffin, the other with a glass of milk. "Breakfast? I was going to bring it up to you."

Emotions squeezed tighter.

He leaned down over the chair between them while she moved closer and, yes, she had her good-morning kiss even if he couldn't touch her, the chair between them and his hands full of her breakfast. And how sweet was that?

His lips moved over her with a firm, deep, slow kiss as if they had nowhere to go, no real world concerns. A kiss, right in the room where they'd enjoyed a hot encounter after his return from Guam when there had been plenty of sex but, heartbreakingly, no kissing.

His tongue coaxed her lips open, swept inside, connected, explored, sending her tummy into a flat spin. Then he kept right on kissing her so she couldn't say something that would mess this up, and God, but she was relieved.

With a final skim of his lips over hers, he stepped back. "I need to grab my boots and change patches." He placed her muffin and milk on the table. "Be back in a few and then we can leave once you're dressed."

Watching him stride into the garage where they'd made such passionate love the night before, she reminded herself that she had kisses back. That was a positive step. And now she knew what to do to keep them once they both finished their half day at work.

She also knew how hard her reticent husband would resist her solution. Which scared her all the more because this was it. Their last chance.

J.T.'s words echoed through her mind. *Anyone can be brave when the odds are in your favor. It's what you do when you're scared that's the true measure of courage.*

She sunk into the chair. Great.

With the way odds were stacked against her, her bravery points must be off the charts.

J.T. stood to the side while Spike clicked through the cipher lock at the OSI building. The opening door—thick metal like a safe—hissed with the release of air from the area sealed tight for soundproofing.

He followed Spike through security, down halls and past a mix of workers in uniforms and civilian clothes—the heart of military counterintelligence keeping base personnel clean. He hated like hell that anyone around him might have a part in drug trafficking.

At least he had the connections here to learn the worst his son could face.

Spike swung a door open to a small interrogation room, sparse, stark and a helluva lot less dirty and dark than its counterpart in Rubistan. They'd already exchanged the basic info on Chris's situation out in Spike's office before the OSI agent had gone silent, then suggested they take the rest of the conversation to a more secure part of the building.

J.T. dropped into one of the unrelenting chairs in the windowless room in a completely windowless building. "Thanks again for coming in early after pulling an all-nighter."

"No problem." Spike sat across from him, coffee cup in hand, dark circles of sleeplessness lining sharp, clear eyes. "Had to come in anyway after how things shook down last night."

"I'll take that as a good sign." J.T. downed the dregs of his java, his fourth cup of the day.

"You'd be right." Spike tipped back his coffee. "DEA cameras confirmed the boats were picking up the drugs and coming back clean. Until last night, we couldn't figure out how they were offloading the drugs. Turns out, they were packaging up the stuff and placing it in the shrimper nets. They cast the net out, but with the webbing loose on one side so the drugs drop into the harbor. Net comes back empty. Looks like a bad throw to the casual observer. They repair the net and keep right on trawling for the rest of the day— or in this case, evening."

"And how's the exchange made?"

"We're still tracking that, but we're pretty certain a small underwater craft, minisub, retrieves it and runs it up the coast. It's freaking genius when you think about it. Without this tip-off, who the hell knows how long it would have taken us to figure it out? Now we just need to pinpoint who's receiving on the other end. We've already connected two independent shrimpers and a market here. We expect more to fall."

"And do you think this ties in to what Chris saw?"

"Could be. Based on your message, I made a few calls before you got here. The young woman, Miranda Casale, has already been picked up for questioning. Everyone at the restaurant will be questioned sometime today. A lot of base kids work at that place. Could be coincidental. Could be someone looking for a new contact. With any luck, that common symbol on the bumper sticker, the brick and the girl's necklace will lock in the final connection.''

J.T. nodded, crumpling the disposable cup in his fist. These bastards had come after his wife and kid. He hoped they fried. His job might have brought stress to his home life, but at the moment he couldn't help being damn glad he'd played a part in bringing down scum like these.

Spike placed his cup on the table. "Hey, dude, no matter how this shakes down, you're going to be okay and your son's going to be okay. Chris stepped up in time. Plenty of military kids get in trouble—just like anybody else's kids. He gave us a heads up on another lead. He's a good kid who got stuck in a bad situation.''

"Thanks for looking out for him.''

Memories of those days in a Rubistanian cell hummed in the air, whispers of the minor victory they'd all silently celebrated by diverting their captors enough to buy Spike an extra couple of hours before his round of questioning.

Now the time had come for J.T. to buy some of that time for his family. To keep the heat off them until the threat passed.

Spike smiled. "Hey, dude, it's what we do for each other.'' He drained his coffee and stood. "Your part's finished here. Go home and hang with your family.''

Chapter 14

Exchanging her work clothes for stretch pants and an overlong T-shirt, Rena turned her back on her reflection in the bathroom mirror. Facing herself and her mistakes wasn't easily done, and she would have plenty of that soon enough.

Time and excuses had run out. She and J.T. would have to come to a firm decision on their future. It wasn't fair to Chris to string things out.

The trip to and from the base had been quiet, as if J.T. understood any talk would require full attention—and likely be too long to accomplish during the short ride.

She tugged her hair free from inside the overlong T-shirt and searched through a basket by the sink for a matching hair scrunchie. Purple? Black? No. Gray, like her mood. Maybe she could just entice J.T. into having a quickie before they opened Pandora's box. Rena gathered up her hair and—

Huh? She focused all her attention inward—

There it was again. The tickle inside her. Gasping, she dropped the hair scrunchie and savored those butterfly whispers of life within her she'd never expected to feel again.

She pressed a hand to her stomach and didn't even breathe for fear of missing repeats. Her baby became all the more real—hers and J.T.'s—this new person who deserved so much more than a couple of parents who pitched plates and stormed out of rooms.

"Are you all right?" J.T. asked from the open door connecting the bathroom to their bedroom.

She hadn't even heard him walk up.

Rena nodded, her hand still cradling the sensation inside her. Her lip trembled. "The baby moved. I'd forgotten what it felt… How incredible… I just…" Her chin trembling, she shrugged. "Our baby moved."

His throat convulsed on a long swallow. His hands clenched and she knew he wanted to touch her, even if he wouldn't be able to feel the flutters yet.

She hated that he had to be hesitant, but if he touched her right now, she would weaken. She would forget all about her resolve and give in when she needed to make a stand more than ever for the baby. For them.

Still, this was his child, too.

She angled past into their bedroom and slid the ultrasound photo from her dressing table. "I never got the chance to show you this last night."

He took the slick black-and-white image and stared at it for so long she grew dizzy holding her breath.

A smile dug dimple brackets around his mouth. "You're right. This is incredible. Even more than I remembered. Thank you."

"There's nothing to thank me for."

Slowly, he set down the photo, his gray eyes somber. "There are many things to thank you for."

Oh God, he could be so sweet sometimes. She walked into his arms, where she'd wanted to be all day anyway. Tension left his bunched muscles, his eyes softening but losing none of their impact.

She guided his hand to her stomach, placed and held it against their child. Cars drove past outside. Trees rustled in the breeze. But they both stood still and quiet for—she had no idea how long.

His hand slid away and up to sketch knuckles along her cheekbone. "I've loved you since the first time I saw you. No matter what happens, no matter what else we might say to each other, I want to make sure you know that."

She melted. Like a bowl of peach ice cream abandoned on the table, she melted into a puddle of emotions. Arching up, she met him as he angled down to kiss her.

With her defensiveness washing away, the hope shone clearer. Tempting her. Maybe things really would be okay this time without pushing him.

But then she remembered his words to Chris in the kitchen about fear and bravery. In the face of J.T.'s strength and courage, how could she be anything less? This was her defining moment. If she wanted to be a woman worthy of this so very special man, she needed to be brave enough to make the tougher choices.

Resolve stronger than her shaky knees and quivering belly, she eased down from her toes, broke the kiss. She caressed J.T.'s bristly jaw up into the silver flecking his temples. "I'd like us to attend marital counseling."

Predictably, he turned stone still in her arms. "Why? Things are back on track now. Didn't you hear what I just said?"

Hear? Of course she'd heard. And it scared the spit out of her because she wanted to chicken out and just take what she could. But she knew now that would only delay the inevitable. "On track? J.T., we had great sex."

He quirked an eyebrow, not smiling. Already she could feel the restrained irritation resurrecting within him.

"Fine. Incredible sex." Better than anything she could remember, sex that touched places of her soul she didn't know existed. "That hasn't helped us before."

Still, he kept his temper reined, cupped her shoulders, his hands on her always a distraction. He almost certainly knew that and was using it, damn him.

"I get your point, babe, but we're talking like you always wanted. Hell, I've talked more in the past two weeks than I did the whole time I was growing up."

He had a point, and she wanted to be swayed as much as she wanted to dig in her bare feet and stand her ground. Problem was, when this man finally decided to speak, he could talk her out of her good sense as fast as he could her clothes and heart. "We need an impartial third party to help us sort through some tough issues."

"I figure we've passed a few landmarks," he continued as if she hadn't even spoken. "Sure we've had arguments, but I haven't walked out of the room and you haven't thrown a dish. That's progress."

"Not funny."

"Yes, it is."

Her lips twitched. "Maybe a little."

"So what's the problem? We've got a good thing going. Let's roll with it."

"Yes, things are improving. We both still have feelings for each other." She kept her eyes on the neck of his flight suit rather than risk falling into his smoky eyes. "But we're deluding ourselves if we think everything's magically going to get better. This—" she waved her hand in the general direction of their bed—a bed that was waiting too conveniently close for her peace of mind "—is wonderful, but it's a Band-Aid fix. What's changed to keep us from landing back in the same hurtful place?"

"We're older. Smarter."

She snorted. "We're older, anyway." Grabbing hold of her resolve while sticking strong to her decision not to grab hold of him, she stared straight into his eyes. "Jesus, J.T., can't you see that even with progress, we're also still making some of the same mistakes?"

He exhaled long, slow, pissed. "So use the counselor degree and tell me what I should do."

She forced her own arms to stay at her sides as much as she wanted to cross them, close herself off. "It's not you. It's us. And you know I can't do that, anyway. It's like telling a doctor to diagnose and treat herself. There's no way to obtain impartial distance."

"You're great just the way you are."

"Quit BSing me, J.T." She resisted the urge to stomp her foot, which would only hurt and not accomplish squat except to give away her frustration level when it came to this infuriating, sexy, heartbreakingly wonderful man. "I may not be able to heal my own family, but I know enough to realize it takes two to make or break a marriage."

"We can't afford it," he said, thumbing the ultrasound photo off the dresser, "especially not with a new kid on the way."

"We can't afford not to, especially with a new baby on the way."

He replaced the photo, sliding a crystal ring dish to the side and out of her tossing reach, a smile playing with his dimples.

Damn it, she would not be charmed by his quiet humor. Not now. His dimple deepened.

Maybe she was a little charmed.

She closed the distance between them and flattened a hand to his chest. "It's free at the base clinic, covered as part of your benefits. Family Advocacy is there for a reason."

How could dimples turn to a scowl so quickly? "I'm not putting my problems on record there."

"Confidentiality applies."

"Yeah, right. Until someone sees me walking out of there. Fliers can't afford a hint of personal problems."

"And a broken marriage isn't a hint?"

"No."

Deep breaths. She toyed with straightening his collar while she regulated her breathing and organized her thoughts. "All right, you have a real problem with counseling. I'm trying not to be insulted that you think so little of my career field."

"Don't look for a fight." He lifted her hand from his chest and pressed a kiss against her wrist, playing havoc with her heartbeat. "Let's both take time off from work, spend it with the kids and each other like you wanted before. I'd already decided during my flight tonight to take leave."

His concession surprised her, big-time, since it would involve dipping into her paycheck to finance the trip, a definite step forward for them. Enough to relent? Hoping that she could soften him up later on the counseling issue?

If only he weren't nipping at the sensitive inside of her wrist in an obvious, calculated effort to distract her. "And we would go somewhere. We would use *our* money to pay for it."

"Yeah, sure." He dropped her hand and made a big freaking production out of brushing away a few dead leaves from around the base of a begonia plant in the window. "Let's rent that cabin like you wanted to for Christmas. We can have that family time together once Nikki and Chris finish up exams."

He'd agreed, even if the prospect left him looking itchier than one of her kids after a roll in poison ivy. Why couldn't she stop reading something into the fact that his restless movements straightening things in the room took him closer and closer to the hall?

The vent by the door captured his attention and he stretched up to adjust the open/shut lever. "Or if the cabin thing doesn't appeal for summer, make whatever arrangements you want. Anything's fine by me.''

His left foot landed in the hall.

''Since you're walking out the door, does that mean I get to throw something?''

That stopped him. He looked back over his shoulder. Turned. ''Real funny, Rena. I'm trying to be accommodating.''

''Accommodating? Sounds to me like you're trying to placate me so you can get the hell out of the room.'' Deeper breaths. ''This is exactly what I'm talking about when I mention marriage counseling. We could probably use some family counseling, too, with Chris's situation.''

''Well, hell,'' he snapped. ''Didn't we get anything right?''

Old habits slid into place too easily and she refused to let them take over. ''I'll ignore that comment since I'm trying here. But it's obvious you're only agreeing to the vacation to placate me.''

''You won.'' He crossed his arms over his chest. ''Be happy.''

Bad-body-language alert. And her temper was sparking, ripe and ready for anything to fuel it to life. Two weeks of holding her tongue, walking on eggshells, terrified to hope and terrified not to, all sliced at her paper-thin control. ''I *won?* Good God, do you hear yourself? It's not about winning. It's about both of us being happy.''

''I'm happy if you're not pitching plates.''

''You deserve more than that and so do I. I want us to go to marriage counseling.''

His arms unfolded and he gripped the top of the door frame, the hall sealed from sight. ''Oh, I see how it is. I agree to what you ask by talking—like how I'm finally agreeing to the vacation you wanted so damn bad last year. So you up the request until I say no. Then it's my fault things fell apart.''

Was there truth in that? Maybe. But if so, then it only solidified her surety that they needed help. "How could you think I would wish for this hell? Don't you realize how much our split hurt me? More so the second time, even, coming so close on the heels of what happened overseas. Do you have any clue what it was like thinking you'd died? Imagining what was happening to you if you hadn't?"

His hands fisted against the frame.

"We were both a mess when you came home. And as much as I want to hope nothing bad ever happens to us again, that's unrealistic." The fear of a repeat swamped her until she used the excuse of her sore ankle to sit on the edge of their bed. "We need to be rock solid to face the future. We need to be open with each other, not just winning and losing. Do you realize you still haven't even told me what happened over there yet?"

"We already covered that in the truck."

"Do you actually believe that constitutes a real conversation on the subject?"

"You already said imagining it hurt you. Why would I want to make that worse?"

She flattened her hands to the giving softness of the quilt as if pressing the wedding ring patch pattern could somehow imprint the premise and promise into her. Talk about a Freudian slip in buying the thing in the first place. "Because being married means sharing burdens. And if you won't share yours with me, then I can't share mine with you. I need someone to lean on, too."

"More upping the ante to make me walk?" Hands falling from the door frame, he reentered their room, one step, two. "You want to hear all about it? Fine. We were in Rubistan on a mission that looks like one thing but really is about something else. We were stressed. Ready to get the hell out and back to our families."

He paced the room, back to the ultrasound photo. "We

figured we were almost home free once we crossed out over the water. Instead, we took a missile hit that would have sent us into the gulf if anyone other than Scorch had been flying the plane.''

The reality slammed into her as if she'd been hit, too, but she forced herself not to sway, an outward sign that would make him stop.

God, she still couldn't quite believe he was actually talking after all this time. She wasn't sure whether to be relieved or more scared than ever.

''But we made it, landed. Got picked up by some tribal warlords who beat the crap out of us, broke Bo's hands.'' He glanced sideways at her. ''Bo's great act of resistance? Looking up.''

She blinked down the tears clogging her eyes and throat, air heavy. Heart heavier for the young pilot not much older than her own children. For her husband.

''Lucky for us, the Rubistanians arrived within a couple of hours and shot the hell out of our caravan so we could have the marginally better option of being interrogated by them instead.''

She flinched, couldn't hold it in anymore, but stayed silent, her hands digging deeper into the quilt.

''You want more from me?'' He stalked toward her, toe to toe. ''A pound of flesh like in that Shakespearean play? Well, I'll just cut myself wide open for you, babe.''

Scrubbing a hand over his face, he spun away on his boot heel, stalked, glanced back over his shoulder. ''Scared? Hell yeah, we were scared. Scared of dying.'' His feet took him clear across the room to the window shrouded with lace curtains. ''But most of all, I was scared of what you and the kids would go through when you got that front-door visit.''

His fist met the wall.

Tears burned acid paths from her eyes and down her face. As a counselor, she knew this outpouring was the right thing

for him, pain concealed being far more lethal than pain released. But as a wife, God, she hurt for him.

Familiar features assumed a stranger's cast with harsh an-
gles. ''Is this sharing deal working for you? Are we closer
now? Do you feel better about us? I hope someone's happier,
because I sure as hell am not feeling at all better.''

A thousand words jumbled through her head, a thousand
different ways to try and make this better for him, except
what if she chose wrong and hurt him worse? Objectivity
wasn't even an option at the moment, but the pain in his eyes
was killing her. She had to do something.

Rising, she reached to hold him.

His hands shot up. Backing, he shook his head. ''You want
me to make this easy for you? No problem. I can do that just
like I did a few months ago.''

Pivoting away, he walked out the door.

Her eyes flooded, and she wanted to run after him and hold
him. Not that he would let her.

Which frustrated her all the more and left her itching to
throw something. No dishes though. She'd grown beyond
that. Her hand settled on the pillow sham made to match her
spread and she allowed herself the outlet of a hefty pitch.

Whoomp.

The pillow thudded against the door frame, slid, plopped,
quilted linking rings mocking her from the floor.

Damn it.

J.T. descended the steps two at a time, boots pounding
hardwood and releasing none of the roaring tension kinking
every muscle in his body. He shouldn't have lost it.

Duh.

But somehow that woman always knew how to crawl under his skin and peel everything away until his emotions lay
out all raw and exposed for the sunlight to burn. He should

have just agreed to her counseling suggestion and made nice with the shrink of her choice.

So why hadn't he?

Hand on the end of the banister, he stopped, truth delivering a helluva gut punch. He'd shut her down because he was half-certain a shrink would tell them they didn't have a chance. At least this way, he kept control over the situation.

Control?

Then how had he ended up out in the cold again like after his return from Rubistan? His fingers closed around the wooden knob at the end of the banister, light slanting through the hall window like the open load ramp of his plane.

J.T. clanked down the belly of the C-17, the Charleston sunlight blinding through the open hatch. Almost bright enough to wipe away the darkness of days spent in a hellhole cell before diplomatic channels cleared for him to come home.

Home.

An efficiency apartment not much bigger than his cell, except he had no one to blame but himself for landing there. He'd let his stupid-ass pride propel him when Rena tossed his crap on the lawn. How could he be so proud of her and so freaking pissed at the same time over the fact that she didn't need him?

J.T. slowed his steps, not in much of a rush to get out of the plane now, after all. He paused alongside Bo's litter. The flight surgeon, nurse and techs worked the transfer while the kid groused about not being allowed to walk out under his own steam—as if he could anyhow, all drugged up and casted during their layover and assessment in Germany.

As J.T. waited and watched through the open load ramp, Scorch cleared the load ramp first. Steps steady, the five stitches along his jaw the only visible sign of their ordeal. His sister, brother-in-law and baby niece met him with hugs and crying and a quick hustle off to leave all this behind for a family reunion.

Spike, in civilian clothes now that he was back on base and not in his overseas undercover role anymore, strutted straight into his waiting fiancée's arms. 1st Lieutenant Darcy Renshaw kissed him hard, unmoving and eyes shut tight while tears streaked free and fast down her face.

Happily ever after around this place still came with heartaches along the way. Only the strongest relationships survived.

Damn, but he'd hoped his and Rena's could be one.

He looked down at Bo, the lieutenant pale but outwardly cocky on the stretcher. "Do you need somebody to hang with you until you're settled at the hospital?"

"Are you kidding? Have you seen the hot new flight nurse over there? I'm figuring I'll need a bed bath before supper." He winked up at the flight surgeon keeping pace alongside. "Right, Doc?"

Bo laughed, a hoarse croak but damn clear about the need to keep things light, superficial, something J.T. totally understood. Too much emotion, adrenaline, anger rumbled around to be processed yet.

Spike and his fiancée broke apart. Arms around each other's waists, they strode away. Clearing sight lines to reveal something J.T. hadn't even dared let himself hope to see.

His family.

He'd been fairly certain Rena's big heart would bring her here, as well. But on the off chance it wouldn't happen, he hadn't let himself think about it. He didn't have room in his head to process even one more emotion—especially not disappointment.

He left Bo to the tender ministrations of the flight nurse and walked forward, his boots landing on the tarmac. American concrete. Relief tingled over him like the start of a sun-

burn. He was pretty sure his feet kept moving, because his family drew closer.

Then they were all in a group huddle of hugs and words he couldn't hear because the buzzing in his head was so damn loud.

One thing about that afternoon stayed clear. How Rena trembled, those emotions churning through them all, multiplying until it even rattled his teeth. If he hadn't been holding on, Rena probably would have fallen off her high heels.

Right then, he knew. He couldn't put her through this anymore. She'd wanted him gone and maybe that was the best thing after all.

But not just yet. He hated himself for being a selfish bastard, but he couldn't walk today. The kids deserved this homecoming, Rena, too. And, damn it all, he couldn't make himself walk away from the chance to lose himself in her body one more time.

They would have their homecoming, before he left for good.

And what a homecoming it had been, so perfect, and somehow he'd felt like a freaking black cloud walking through the clean light of his house. Like now, standing in the hall, wanting to go back up those stairs and wondering if staying away was better for her in the long run.

He glanced upstairs, frowning. Had he started to understand, then, this deeper love he felt? God knows it confused the hell out of him now, and he'd been too much of a mess then to process much of anything.

Holy crap. He slumped against the wall, bracing his foot on the banister across from him for support. He hadn't walked away to protect her. He'd left because the dawning realization of how much he loved her scared the hell out of him.

He couldn't reconcile it all then. Still wasn't sure he could.

Except now, he wanted to.

At least he was home. Alive. He could—and damn well

would—deal with the rest. Once he got his head on straight. He needed five minutes to pull it together again and then he'd go back upstairs for damage control.

He opened his office door.

To find a man dressed in black and a ski mask sitting at his desk, rifling through drawers. What the hell?

The man looked up, eyes narrowed in the ski-mask slits.

Anger, rage, raw emotions still stark and ugly on the surface roared to life. J.T. launched forward.

The man's hand slid into sight—holding a Glock, the big nasty-looking 9mm stalling J.T. quicker than a brick wall in the face.

The dark eyes blinked from inside the mask. "Well, hello, Sergeant. I was hoping to finish up here before you came in, but now we're out of luck."

Options raced through his head. If he called a warning, Rena would come downstairs. As much as he hated having made her cry, at least it might keep her safely upstairs.

One-on-one odds he could handle. Hell, right now he welcomed the chance to fight back, better than being stuck in a cell with his hands tied behind his back.

The man's attention shifted. J.T.'s muscles bunched for action.

The gun twitched. "Well, hello there, ma'am."

Ma'am? Rena? Adrenaline turned to icy heat. A trick? Maybe, but with that gun possibly pointed at Rena, J.T. couldn't afford to act until…he…looked…

At his wife standing red-eyed and horrified in the doorway. *Oh God, babe, I'm sorry.*

Pain exploded in his head. J.T. managed a half turn toward his attacker before…

Everything went dark.

Chapter 15

Rena screamed. Ran forward. Tried to catch J.T. as he fell toward the ground. God, he was heavy. She crumpled to the floor with him, hard, but at least she'd kept him from cracking his head on the desk on the way down.

As if he hadn't already taken a hard enough hit to the skull when the guy looming in dark clothes and a ski mask had knocked J.T. out with the butt of his gun. Bile bubbled up, scalding her throat.

She cradled her husband's head in her lap, fear snaking through her, gripping, like poison ivy to fertile ground. "Take whatever you want. I'll tell you where everything is in the house, the keys to the car. Just take it all and go, but please don't hurt us."

Don't hurt J.T. again.

Gun level, the lean man skirted around the corner of the desk. "I need your husband's flight schedule, ma'am, for tonight and tomorrow, and then I'm out of here. Out of your hair. It's really simple, actually. I have everything under control."

What the hell did this guy want with a flight schedule? His flat accent gave her no hints of his background other than that he sounded educated, not some street thug in search of a quick pawn. Something niggled at her about his voice, but she couldn't place him as anyone she knew well.

Rena studied his clothes for clues, black pleated pants and T-shirt, nice cut and make on a tall, fit frame. Not someone she had any real hope of taking out.

Her world had gone crazy in a couple of weeks.

She didn't know why this man had a gun pointed at her, but she knew enough to realize this was bad. Really bad. "And if I find whatever schedule it is you're looking for, you'll let us live?"

"You don't have a choice but to believe me. Of course, I could start by killing your husband, and then wait for your son to come home. What do you think?"

She thought all the options sucked. Him knowing she had a son scared her even more. Was he someone they knew? Maybe his voice sounded familiar, after all, or maybe her frightened-as-hell mind was playing tricks on her.

That she didn't have any idea where J.T. might have a flight schedule made things worse. She feared he didn't have one at all, because hadn't he talked about taking leave? That his schedule was clear now?

What did this guy need a flight schedule for, anyway? If she was sure she would live, she could give it to him and then let the base know it was gone.

But if she gave it to him and then he killed them... She would have put crew members' lives at risk. Furthermore, giving it to him would constitute treason. A line neither she nor her husband could cross.

Think time. Start with the truth, about her only option since what more could she do? Bash him over the head with her begonias? "We don't have it. J.T. is starting leave now. There's nothing in this house for you."

"Like I believe that. Try again, ma'am."

Apparently this overpolite scum didn't recognize truth. She burned to take this guy on with a lamp or ashtray upside the head for a chance to protect J.T. and Chris. Too bad she hadn't pocketed the crystal dish she'd longed to lob at J.T.

Except she also had to protect the baby she was carrying. She needed to buy time for J.T. to regain consciousness.

If he regained consciousness.

Oh God, she couldn't even think about that.

Time to pile on the lies. Because no way would she let J.T. die before they'd worked things out between them and until he'd apologized for walking away from her again, bless his stubborn soul. They deserved forever.

"Okay, fine. What I said was true, but there's more. The schedule isn't here—yet. J.T. had to leave work early to bring me home. I'm on half days because of a car accident—and I'm pregnant," she rushed to add in hopes that even if this slime didn't respect her condition, he might fear the harsher legal ramifications if he killed a pregnant woman.

She watched her assailant for hints of his personality, weaknesses, anything to provide an edge. If only she could see his facial expressions. Instead, she had only body language and flickers of emotion in those narrow eyes peering back at her through the slits in the knit mask. Gun steady, he smoothed his other hand along the wrinkles in his black T-shirt.

Fastidious? Obsessive-compulsive? Or just plain freaking amoral that he would think he could break into her home, hurt her husband.

She frowned, watched. "J.T. left early, and someone from work is supposed to bring his schedule by later."

Geez, that was lame and so not how things worked, but hopefully this person would buy it anyway, the best she could come up with while under so much crushing pressure.

"Why don't they e-mail the schedule to him?"

Why hadn't she thought of that? "Because the computers were down today. One of those out-of-control virus things. You'll probably hear about it on the news in the morning."

She'd never tested her aptitude for her family's shady penchant for lying, but obviously she'd picked up some of the skill by osmosis from years of exposure while growing up. One thing to be grateful for from her childhood.

His eyes squinted in the mask. "Okay, I'm not saying I trust you, but what you say sounds possible. You're going to help me tie up the big guy here and then you're both going to hang out secured in a closet while I look. If you're actually telling the truth, I'll let one of you get the schedule at the door. But I'll be holding a gun to the other one's head. Understand?"

Rena nodded. God, had he actually stolen a glance of himself in the windowpane as he walked? She was worried about dying here and he was checking himself out?

Rage threatened to blind her. Come hell or high water, she was taking down Mr. Narcissist.

He looked around the room, knelt, unplugged a short extension cord. "Now tie his hands behind his back with this. And do it tight, because I'll be watching."

Rena hefted her husband's limp body to his stomach, stalling as best she could, an easy enough prospect since he was heavy. Gently, she pulled his limp arms behind his back. How long had he been out? Was he awake now, faking to listen, plan, establish an edge?

If so, he was doing a helluva good job with the act.

Once she finished, she glanced up, exhausted, scared. And determined not to fail.

Mr. Narcissist waggled the gun toward the hall. "Drag him into the closet."

"You have got to be kidding. There's no way I can manage that. No way." If she could get him to put down his gun...

"I see your point. But I want you to sit there."

He pointed to J.T.'s recliner in the office, a butt-ugly green chair she'd made fun of just before she'd jumped her husband's bones on the eyesore.

"And don't move, ma'am," Mr. Stuck-on-Himself added. "I'll be able to see you. One twitch from you and I'll crack your husband's head open this time."

She shivered. Nodded. Started to move for the chair, but suddenly found herself reluctant to leave J.T. She pressed a kiss to his head and whispered, "I love you."

"Touching," Mr. Narcissist mocked. "Now get in the chair while I lock this guy up. Then you're next."

She inched away, careful to keep her moves smooth, predictable. Her captor tucked the gun in the small of his back, in his belt, his gold buckle and design catching the light...

A red circle with a black triangle inside.

What did Chris's mess have to do with someone wanting J.T.'s flight schedule? And damn, damn, damn, why couldn't she figure out why that symbol looked so familiar?

The man rolled J.T. onto his back again. He gripped under J.T.'s shoulders, dragging him into the hall, straining and scooching backward.

What a dumb ass. He should have put her in a closet first so she wouldn't be free while he maneuvered J.T. Not that she intended to mention the oversight. Instead, she processed the new insight. The man wasn't as smart as he thought.

Rena studied him closer, saw sweat seeping through his mask. Stress or heat? His hand fidgeted with his belt—again. Stress. Definitely.

While that edginess could be dangerous, it could also be her weapon since it impaired his logic. Playing him, outsmarting him would be a tightrope walk, but he had her on size and firepower.

When he turned his back to open the door, she snatched a paperweight off the edge of J.T.'s desk and tucked it in her pocket.

Mr. Narcissist shifted back, huffing. He tugged his gun out again. "Okay. You next. Closet."

At least she would be with J.T. again. She crossed into the hall.

"Are you nuts, lady? You get your own closet."

No damn way could she let that happen. She needed to talk to J.T. when he woke, update him, reassure him. She extended her wrists. "Tie me up before you put me in there, but I'm not leaving him. You're the one with the gun, all the power."

"You're damn right." He pressed the gun to her temple, a cold, lethal kiss. "And you'll do whatever the hell I say."

Childhood memories shivered over her, visions of the soulless eyes of her father's friends who carried weapons like these. Panic thrashed against reason, threatening any hope of calm. She had maybe three seconds to figure something out. Her gut churned. The baby somersaulted.

The baby. The man had seemed to shift his focus when she'd mentioned being pregnant.

"I have to go to the bathroom," she blurted.

"You're joking, right?"

"I'm pregnant." And damn, but this might work. "I swear there's no way I can hold it a minute longer. If my husband doesn't come to in time for delivery of the schedule, don't you think it'll raise a few questions if I answer the door with wet clothes, not to mention the smell, and it's not like I'll have time to change my clothes once the doorbell rings—"

"Okay! Okay, lady, I get the point." Gun waving, he grimaced. "You can go to the bathroom, for God's sake."

A small victory, but she'd take it. Plus, every time she pushed and won, she discovered more about her enemy.

"But I'm going to search you when you come out."

She pulled a weak smile. So much for the paperweight she would have to ditch now.

He kicked the door shut on J.T.'s prison and followed her to the half bath around the corner.

Rena stepped into the bathroom and closed the door. Exhaling, she sagged against the door, searching for ideas. But there weren't any convenient guns in the toilet tank.

She considered writing Help on the window in lipstick, but he might check the bathroom and she couldn't risk triggering his anger.

Yanking open the medicine cabinet, she scanned the metal shelves. No nifty drugs to drop in his drinks. Nothing but a soap refill and the nail-care products from Julia Dawson's gift at the hospital a couple of weeks ago.

Rena snatched up the metal nail file, bent it into a curve and slipped it into her bra down near the underwire. Uncomfortable as hell, but not visible in the mirror. At least her swollen, tender pregnancy breasts offered better hiding.

Wouldn't that make an interesting headline for tomorrow's television news flash? Pregnant housewife takes down abductor with her killer bra...more details to follow at eleven. Stifling a hysterical laugh, Rena ditched the paperweight in the trash.

Rena flushed the toilet and turned on the faucet. She needed to get a grip.

She twisted off the water, gripped the doorknob. Fear sliced through her with every tight breath. What hell J.T. must have gone through overseas. She'd known, of course, but hadn't really *known* until this moment.

Guilt crawled over her. She hadn't been there for J.T. when he needed her. Sure, she'd gone through the motions when he'd lumbered off that plane. But when he'd walked out of the house a couple of days later, she should have chased his ass down. Dogged him until he came home where he belonged, until he had time to come to grips with his hellish experience.

He'd braved her family, offered her safety, a haven. Love. He deserved the same from her.

She'd fought for her marriage. She'd fought for herself.

Now it was time she fought for J.T.

J.T. fought the fog.

God, his head hurt. Groaning, he rolled to his side, off his numb hands. Still they wouldn't move.

He was tied. Ah hell.

He blinked against the dark, his eyes slowly adjusting with the help of a thin bar of light slanting under the door. Small space. Hands tied. Rubistan? His brain logy, he battled with now and then. Wrestled down dread. Forced even breaths in and out to stuff down the swell of nausea. From a concussion?

He filled himself with air. Smells, too. Smells of home. Rena's cologne. He struggled to sit, canting up closer to the scent wafting off…wool dangling overhead.

A coat. Hers.

He was in a closet, not a cell. Relief washed away nausea. Memories blasted through of the man at his desk. Rena walking in. And then… What?

J.T. jerked against his constraints. He had to get out. To his wife. He couldn't allow thoughts of what might be happening to her.

And then he heard her. Her voice pierced the door, growing louder.

He slumped back against the wall. She was alive. For now.

With slow, controlled moves, he worked to free his hands as he grounded himself in the husky, vibrant—alive—sounds of Rena's voice.

"I'm telling you, if you put me in another closet and my husband wakes up without me there, he's going to flip out. He gives new meaning to the word *overprotective*. You won't have the chance to convince him I'm all right or bring him to me, or me to him. He'll cause a ruckus that will alert anyone who's anywhere near the house. Then there's no way you'll get that flight schedule you want.''

Flight schedule?

Realization dawned through his clearing brain. She was feeding him information in case he was awake. Warning him. Damn, he loved this smart, spunky woman.

''Your best bet is to put me in that closet with him. You can tie me up. But you need to keep things level until the guy from the base comes with the finished schedule.''

What the hell? She had to know that wasn't true.

Of course she did. She must be stalling. She had to be scared to death and still she stayed calm. Pride for her clenched inside him, a welcome break from the other emotions pummeling the hell out of him.

''We really shouldn't wait much longer to open the door,'' she continued. ''Do you think he's hurt badly? I should check him. Since you're wearing that mask, I'm hoping that means you genuinely want us to live. So why not—''

''For God's sake, lady.'' A male voice cut through. Familiar? Tough to tell with the pain and door muffling. ''Will you please just shut the hell up for a minute so I can think?''

A smile so damn incongruous with the nightmare situation tugged at him. God love his wife's ability for gab.

''Okay,'' their captor conceded. ''You can go in the same closet. But you will be tied.''

''Fine. We all want to get out of this alive. You're making—''

''Tied *and* gagged.''

The bastard was dead.

For now, he needed to make the most of the window of opportunity Rena had bought them. J.T. slumped back onto the floor and waited.

The doorknob snicked. He closed his eyes, forced his muscles to relax.

Light flooded through his eyelids. Rustling sounded. No more talking from Rena. The son of a bitch had truly gagged her. A tic tugged at J.T.'s eye.

More rustling. The heat of another body drawing closer. Settling against him. Rena.

Tension seeped from him.

More heat, another person. "So, Sergeant," said their captor, hot breath blocking out the scents of home. "You wouldn't be faking, would you? I should probably check."

Ah crap. J.T. had one second to prep himself before—

A fist slammed into his ribs.

Pain rocketed through him. A moan slipped free, from him, from Rena, too. He forced himself to relax again in spite of the pain howling inside him.

"Guess he's still out, after all." The sounds of popping knees creaked as the man stood. "I'll be close by and checking. Often. So no tricks or stupid heroics."

The door slammed shut.

J.T. listened for the sound of retreating footsteps, his head and ribs throbbing. He blinked to adjust again, swallowing back the reflexive need to vomit. He didn't dare risk more than a whisper, and damn it all, she wouldn't be able to answer. But at least they were both alive. In the same place.

He wasn't alone in the cell this time.

"Rena? Rena, babe, I'm okay." He angled up to sit, the pain nothing in comparison to the need to comfort her. "We're okay. We're going to get out of this."

She wilted against him with a whimper.

Glancing down, he could almost make out her face in the murky closet. Best he could tell, she wasn't hurt, other than a bandanna tied tight around her mouth.

He wanted to put his arms around her so damn bad. "You did good. Real good, getting him to do what you wanted and feeding me information. I'm proud of you, babe." Understatement. "Now, here's what we're going to do. Are you listening?"

She nodded against his chest, nuzzling deeper as if she wanted to burrow inside him.

"We're going to shuffle back-to-back and untie each other. Can you do that?"

She nodded again.

Shifting, scooting, trying like hell not to make noise, he moved. His feet bumped old gym shoes, rain boots. An umbrella toppled.

Crap.

He froze. Stopped breathing, waited. The umbrella rolled down his arm to a whisper rest against the floor.

J.T. inched again until his fingers touched Rena's. She linked hers with his for three precious seconds before she picked at the binding.

He searched by touch along her wrists…hell. She was secured tight with some kind of rope. How she made her fingers bend and maneuver along his binds he couldn't even imagine. Her hands must be numb. And then there was the baby, too.

Damn it, he needed to do something, but all he could do was talk. A wry smile kicked in. That's what she'd always wanted from him, after all, and he could come through now, reassure her if nothing else. Say all the things she needed to hear.

Say all the things *he* needed to say to her in case he never had the chance again. "I still remember the first time I saw you. It was like somebody colorized a black-and-white movie. A hokey thought, huh?"

She melted against him a little and he thought maybe it wasn't so hokey, after all. Too bad he'd never thought to say it before.

"I'm committed to my job, don't get me wrong, and I love the hell out of it. But there are parts that are…tough. Dark. The things that we do and places we go, it's so—" he struggled for the word "—opposite of home. I don't know how else to describe it. Even when I'm enjoying the job, the whole time that I'm away I still look forward to coming home, flipping the switch that shifts from there to here, dark to bright colors."

Her breathing grew quieter, her fingers slower for a second before she picked at the cord around his wrists again. Her smaller hands pried at the knots better than his fumbling ones, much the way she'd always been able to work free those strings of knots that seemed to build into a chain on the kids' gym shoes.

He leaned forward to give her better access to his bound wrists. "Problem was, sometimes the switch got stuck, my head was there even though my body's here. And I don't know how to be in both places at the same time." A low laugh climbed free. "I can already hear you asking me why the two have to be separate. But there are things I don't want in my house. Things I don't want touching my family. Or touching you."

The cord fell free from him. His fingers burned with the rush of returning circulation. He tried to flex, but couldn't order his hands to move yet. Kinda like how he'd known he should act and say certain things when he'd returned but his body just stayed…stuck.

He couldn't afford the luxury of time now.

J.T. shook his arms and gritted through the fiery pain. "It's not because I didn't think you were strong enough. God, babe, what you do holding this family together year after year while I'm gone… How you held it together today…"

His fingers twitched, clenched, slowly listened to his brain. He reached behind Rena to untie the bandanna gag. "You're the strongest person I've ever met, but you shouldn't have to be." He fumbled, yanked, untwisted the knot. "You didn't sign on for this. I did."

The bandanna slipped free and landed around her neck.

Rena leaned forward, forehead to forehead, tears glinting even through the dark. "J.T.? I didn't sign on for a job. I signed on for you, wherever you are, good or bad places, I want to be there, too."

Her hands still bound, she toppled forward to kiss him and he thanked God for the chance to hold her. A privilege he wouldn't throw away again.

Rena skimmed her lips over his once more, then rocked back on her heels. "Now, what are we going to do to take out that bastard before our son comes home from school?"

Chris flung his backpack onto the ground by the park bench outside school.

Okay, he was trying not to be an ungrateful brat. Geez, he was already lucky his parents hadn't killed him for holding out about what happened at the restaurant. But like, couldn't they at least pick him up on time? As if it wasn't bad enough everyone would see his "mommy and daddy" drive up to get him.

At least no one had tried to pound him today while John Murdoch was absent and couldn't stick up for him.

Chris slouched lower on the bench. He was really, really trying not to screw up and piss off his folks. He'd actually turned down four different rides because, if his dad didn't think it was safe for him to drive himself, then he shouldn't take rides with others his age—even if one of those "others" was this really cute babe from his Spanish II class.

Nope, he'd called Bo. A mature choice. Right? Since that's who Dad picked to stay over when Mom was in the hospital.

And at least Bo drove a cool Jeep with the top down most of the time rather than a dorky parentmobile.

"Hey, Chris?" Shelby leaned over the back of the bench into his sight line. "What's going on? I thought you were using your mom's car 'til everything works out with buying you another one."

Geez, her dark hair smelled good swinging right there beside his face. He could even remember how soft it felt when he'd hugged her while she cried.

He looked away, down, scuffed his gym shoe over gum stuck to the concrete. "Dad drove me in today. He's late picking me up."

She slung her backpack over. "Do you want a ride home?"

Make that *five* ride offers and one of them from Shelby. And he couldn't accept even one. The day just got suckier by the second. "Nah, thanks. I already called Bo to come get me."

"Bo? He's cool. Great Jeep."

"Yeah. He got a Jet Ski to celebrate his cast coming off."

"Really cool." She circled around to the front and plopped down beside him. "How about I wait around with you?"

There wasn't any reason he couldn't talk to her. School was safe or his dad wouldn't have let him come. "Sure. Thanks."

A bus chugged by. Arms hung out the windows. The shouts and laughs and we're-free noises carried on the wind.

He lifted his shoe off the gum, a long stream of hot sticky pink stretching. "Everything going okay?"

"Great. Really great." Turning, she hitched a knee up onto the bench, a megahot knee pressing against his thigh. "Listen, Chris, I just want to say thank-you for being there when I needed a friend. I mean, I don't know who else would have been so cool about everything and not judged me and just helped me—"

He kissed her.

Oh God, he was really kissing Shelby Dawson. He didn't remember leaning or even deciding to do it. But her face was right there and Murdoch—the lucky bastard who got to do it with her and probably didn't appreciate her—wasn't around.

And her lip gloss was all shiny and he had to know what it tasted like before she moved or he would die.

Strawberry.

Her breath hitched. He heard it. A tiny gasp thing that said maybe this was okay and she wasn't saying no or pulling back. Her mouth softened a little and he leaned forward, angled his mouth over hers more fully.

She jerked away. "Ohmigod."

Crap.

Her eyes widened. She touched her lips with a hand that shook.

Double crap. He was so screwed. "I'm sorry. I'm not sure what I was thinking by—"

"I had no idea."

No idea he liked her or no idea she would like him? His heart shifted from double time to triple, pounding like the bass drum rallying the football crowd.

"Chris, you are absolutely one of my best friends in the world."

Thud. Stop. The friend word.

His heartbeat started again, slow, pushing against the ache in his chest. "Your friend, huh. Gee, thanks."

"I'm so sorry if I did anything to lead you on."

Get it together, Price. Salvage some pride. "Hey, chill. It's no big thing. I totally understand. Just thought I would see, if, well, before you move—"

"Stop, please." She clamped her hand over his mouth and blinked back tears. "God, Chris, I'm really sorry."

That she felt this bad over trampling his heart to bits notched his pride up a little. He clasped her wrist to pull it away from his face and tried not to get too hyped by the way her pulse throbbed so fast against his fingers.

He placed her hand on her knee and gave it one more hinting try. "Since you and Murdoch are hardly together anymore, I wondered—"

"Uh, Chris?" Her gaze shot down to the sticky gum before coming back up to him. She winced apologetically. "John's not here today because his dad took him for a late registration at the college I'm attending. He changed schools for me."

That was it then. Shelby was moving and John Murdoch was going with her and the guy deserved her because he'd made the tough choice to be with her. "I'm glad for you two that everything worked out."

"Are you okay?"

"Of course I'm okay. It's not as if I was in love with you or anything. I like you, all right? And I thought if Murdoch was out of the picture I'd better make my move fast before some guy moved in ahead of me. I mean, Geez, Shelby, you're hot."

She gave him a watery smile. "Okay. Enough. Stop it. And thanks."

"Sure." He tracked his eyes back to the Bazooka bubble-gum blob, not a big fan of seeing her pity-stare right this minute.

Yeah, the tree, bus stop, road hurt less to look at, especially now that he saw a Jeep rounding the corner, a guy in a flight suit driving who—the black vehicle revved closer, clearer—was Bo Rokowsky. "Hey, there's my ride. I gotta go."

Chris hooked his arm through his backpack on the ground by the bench and stood.

Rising, Shelby stopped him with a soft hand on his arm. Her eyes went from sad to kinda confused. "And Chris? About what happened just now, you know, with the kiss." Confused changed to—surprised? "For what it's worth, you're really good at it. I mean *really* good."

Pink popped along her cheeks before she started looking over at the tree, bus stop and road before her gaze fell somewhere short of his face, more like his shoulder. "Well, uh, I need to go, okay?"

"Sure, catch up with you later." Chris shuffled backward

toward the Jeep, watching until she got in her car and drove away. His dad's words niggled to the surface, bringing understanding, if not peace.

Right person. Wrong time.

He pivoted toward his ride. "Thanks for coming over, man," Chris called out. "My folks aren't answering at home or on their cell phones."

Bo downshifted to a stop. "No problem. I'm still flying the desk. Just tapped someone to cover me for a few." Snagging the green flight bag from the front seat, he pitched it into the back. "Hop on in and let's get you home."

Chapter 16

"Ready whenever you are." Rena clenched her fingers in J.T.'s flight suit.

His heart pulsed steadily against her fist as she sat with winter coats and sweaters tickling her head. At least they weren't helpless anymore. They had a plan, a chance, hope. The nail file had even helped saw and pry at the persistent knots binding her wrists. They'd kept the ropes loosely in place, would soon slip her gag back up too so their captor wouldn't be alerted.

Part of her wanted to stay inside the closet until the very last second possible to stretch her time with J.T. But they couldn't afford to wait much longer and risk Chris coming home. Already, he must be questioning why his father hadn't arrived. Please, please, please, Lord, let Chris be irresponsible and just go hang out at a friend's house.

Not something they could count on.

J.T. tunneled his fingers into her hair, locating the knot in her gag. His hands hesitated, stroked along the sensitive nape of her neck. "I'm proud of you, babe, and how you handled that bastard out there. We have this chance because of your quick thinking."

"I hope it's enough." She allowed herself one precious last minute to look at J.T.'s face in the dim light, checked that he wasn't hiding some injury from her. His pupils appeared evenly dilated...but his eyes seemed different somehow, distant. Not cold, but focused, steely.

Ready for battle.

And finally she understood about that mental switch of his. How could she have lived with this man, slept with him for twenty-two years, carried his children, and never have seen such an integral part of him?

How utterly ridiculous to think that even though her mind had always understood he served in the military, until now she'd never known the warrior. She'd prided herself on her love for this man, only to find she'd missed out on half of *who* he was.

Footsteps sounded.

Rena startled.

J.T. lifted the bandanna. "Time's up, babe."

Panic, adrenaline, resolve washed through her like sheeting rain. She wanted to shout for fate to wait. She needed another moment to process these new emotions, just one minute.

Thudding steps grew closer, louder.

Eyes closing, J.T. slumped back against the wall, but with adjustments, angled to spring faster.

The door jerked open. Their captor's body blocked the bulk of the light, only a few beams streaking around him. Even so, spots danced in front of her eyes, finally clearing.

"You." He pointed the gun dead center toward her chest. "Get up."

Why was he coming for them? Although this certainly worked better than concocting some reason to kick the door and draw him over.

Rena shifted awkwardly, as if straining for balance but in reality shielding her body from the gun's line of fire, shielding her baby. Giving J.T. a clear path to launch.

She could see J.T.'s muscles bunch. Anticipation pulsed from him.

"Damn it, come on," Mr. Narcissist barked, all mannerly pretenses gone. "Apparently you weren't lying, after all, about the schedule. Some guy from base just pulled up in your driveway."

What?

He waggled the gun, gesturing for her to rise. "The doorbell will be ringing any—"

The back door opened. "Mom? Dad? Everything okay? I tried to call."

Dread pierced her more effectively than any bullet. In seeking to protect one child, now she had another just as precious in danger.

Mr. Narcissist jerked to look—the perfect chance to jump him. Except now he had his gun pointed at Chris, her son standing pale-eyed and swaying in the archway from the kitchen to the hall, with Bo stunned to a stop a few steps behind him.

Damn. Damn. Damn.

"Chris, get back," she shouted.

"Don't move, pal." Gun level, the man reached down and jerked Rena to her feet. Her hands still tied slackly, she stumbled up, her knees protesting after so long folded. "I'll put a bullet right through your mother."

"Mr. Haugen?" Chris gasped.

Chris's boss? Hadn't that guy already been questioned in regards to the Miranda Casale issue?

And likely released. Hell *and* damn. Their hope of getting out alive evaporated now that they had a name for their attacker. He couldn't let them live. And obviously everyone would know that.

An exasperated sigh slid through the mask right before he peeled it off, sandy-colored hair standing on end. ''You never could learn when to keep your mouth shut, could you, pal?''

Kurt Haugen pitched aside the mask, grabbing her arm again before she could inch more than a whisper away. The barrel of the gun cut into her side. She didn't dare risk more movement even with his attention focused on Chris and Bo.

She stole a quick check on J.T. in the closet. His eyes opened, not much but enough for her to know he was awake and plotting. He stared straight at her, two fingers flicking. She frowned. He repeated the flicking gesture until she understood.

He wanted her to lead the man away, keep him occupied. Give J.T. a chance to slip out and catch him unaware.

At least that's what she hoped he meant.

They had a single edge. Haugen didn't know J.T. was awake and untied—an edge that wouldn't last long once Haugen regrouped.

She prayed Chris wouldn't ask about his father and remind the man. ''Hon, I'm okay. Everything will be fine as long as we stay calm. And now that Bo's here, maybe he can help Mr. Haugen with the information he needs. Is your flight bag in the kitchen or the Jeep?''

''Whoa. Hold on a minute,'' Haugen interrupted with an easygoing smile, as if doing nothing more than asking friends to wait up for him on the golf course. ''Nobody goes anywhere unless I say so. And I say we go to the kitchen and figure out what the hell's going on.''

He jerked her forward—without sparing so much as a backward glance at J.T.—and ushered them all into the kitchen.

''I had a good thing going, pal,'' Haugen tsked at Chris, ''until you opened your mouth.'' Frowning, he glanced back over his shoulder.

J.T.

She had to keep this guy talking. Narcissists loved to talk about themselves, right? "What do you mean, a good thing?"

"The drug running, of course. Well, until your kid got weirded out by moving a little money for us. Geez, we would have paid him well. The two military dudes were more than happy to figure out a way to pay their maxed credit cards."

"Why not leave the country? Why take a chance breaking into our house, holding us this way? It sounds like you're smarter than that." Keep talking. Cover noises.

"Because I can't just run off, even if there was somewhere to hide from my boss. I'm accountable to people, people who expect something from me on this end—which I will have once I have the flight schedule. The feds are getting a little too snoopy after those surveillance flights. Once I have the schedule in hand, we can reroute our guys' paths and times accordingly for a final big payoff. Then the family will relocate me."

Like a kaleidoscope, his words and images jumped in her mind—drugs, family, threats, emblems…

Her gaze dropped back to his belt buckle. Finally she remembered why it had seemed so familiar painted on the brick. "Ohmigod."

The red circle, black triangle inside.

Revulsion shuddered through her. She knew exactly where she'd spotted those markings before, symbols that were well-kept secrets known only to those on the inside. This insignia represented one of the most powerful Mob families.

A perverted coat of arms she'd seen as a child while peeking through the banister rails at her father's "business" guests.

Voices fading with footsteps, J.T. shook his hands free of the loosely wrapped cord. He crouched low, peering through the thin gap between the hinges of the open door.

Haugen stood in the kitchen archway with Rena at his side. He jammed his gun deeper in her side.

J.T.'s hands fisted. He channeled the rage, training never more important than now.

Instincts. Breathe. Assess.

Rena asked Haugen some question that left the man furrowing his forehead in concentration. Good job, babe.

Sliding into the hall, J.T. kept his observation peripheral now. No looking at the bastard and setting off the internal radar that might cause him to check his six o'clock.

Haugen chuckled. "So you recognize my belt buckle, Mrs. Price. Not many would. Maybe it was a little egotistical of me to place it on my calling card through your window, but I figured your son would make the connection with Miranda's necklace."

J.T. processed the periphery view. Rena and Haugen in the doorway. Chris by the table. Bo, to Rena's right, by the refrigerator. Moving infinitesimally. Trying to work a rescue solo? Or had he seen J.T.? And what about Chris?

Come on, somebody. Get back to distracting Haugen. J.T. wound his way through the hall, grateful for the clutter and oversize plants that provided a helluva lot more cover than desert. This was his turf, damn it.

Chris backed until his butt bumped the counter. "You've been running drugs? And now you're going off with Miranda Casale?"

"Miranda?" Haugen's face whipped up, his body moving forward, deeper into the kitchen—way to go, Chris. "God, no. Aside from the fact that she's the don's niece, I love my wife. Why would I screw around with Miranda Casale? Besides, she's too young and too obvious. She was sent down to keep an eye on her uncle's interests."

Rena leaned on her right foot, the gun barrel inching out of her side. "If you love your wife, how could you leave her like this?"

Damn straight, Rena. Good men don't leave their women behind. He heard the message loud and clear, and wouldn't be repeating his mistake.

"I'm taking my wife and daughter with me."

Bo stepped closer. "Your wife's a part of this, too?"

J.T. flattened his back to the wall. Angled around a picture frame. Only five more steps and he would be hidden on the side of the archway. Out of Haugen's sight line.

"Of course not." Haugen looked past Rena to Bo, the man's gestures growing more erratic as Rena, Chris and Bo had him ping-ponging responses around the room. "They think it's a family vacation. No need to worry them. I'll explain things when we get…where we're going. They'll realize I did this for them, to give them the things they deserve. I'd do anything for them."

Two more steps. Past a plant stand.

Bo inched closer. "Even sell drugs and pump money into terrorist accounts?"

"If I don't do it—" Haugen shrugged, his gun pulling out of Rena's side, but his grip on her arm still tight enough to dig into her flesh "—they'll only find someone else."

Bo's chest expanded with outrage, bravado, as he strutted closer, an arm's reach from Rena. "That's a bullshit excuse to justify your own greed and you know it."

In place, J.T. nodded to Bo. Knew the young officer caught the movement even though he was smart enough not to alert Haugen by looking away.

"Are you an idiot or what to tick me off this way?" Haugen advanced around Rena.

No, Bo wasn't an idiot. But Haugen was. This time, the enemy was going down.

Bo sprung toward Rena. Body blocked her out of the line of fire. J.T. launched through the cleared archway, tackled Haugen. They hit the tile. Hard. Teeth jarring as they skidded across the kitchen, bashing into chairs, the table. He pinned Haugen's gun hand to the floor.

Rena? He wanted to check. Didn't dare lose focus.

Haugen arched, swung his other fist. J.T. blocked. Slammed Haugen's hand against the saltillo tile floor, once, again and again until the gun clanked free.

J.T. channeled the roar, instincts honed and focused. This was home turf and damn anyone who threatened what was his.

Haugen panicked, bucked, tried to twist.

J.T. coldcocked the son of a bitch with an uppercut to the jaw. Haugen's head smacked tile, lolled to the side. Chris scooped up the gun, his too-long legs and awkward teen body never exhibiting more speed and grace.

That fast, it was over. Battles often were, and thank God this one ended with no shots fired. Rena? He searched, saw her shielded by Bo's body behind the pantry door.

Rocking back on his haunches, J.T. shook out his aching fist and extended his other arm. Rena untangled herself from Bo, shook loose her ties and flew forward. She landed against J.T.'s chest. Into his embrace. Covering his face with kisses.

"Ohmigod, J.T., you did it, holy crap, you really did it." She reached for Chris. "Come here, kiddo."

J.T. glanced over her shoulder to their son. "You okay?"

"Yeah, Dad, I'm cool." The teen passed the pistol to his father. "I'm okay, Mom. Geez, no need to pump out the tears."

"Shush up." Her arms closed around both of them. No arguing with a determined Rena. "I'll cry over both of you as much as I damn well please. And Bo, too, oh God, thank you."

Bo's face creased into his best bad-boy grin. "No problem. And as much as I'd enjoy a hot lady like you crying all over me, I'm not overeager to meet up with Tag's right hook."

Winking, Bo yanked up the phone, dialed, relaying clipped details for 911.

J.T. trained the gun on Haugen's prone body while keeping Rena tucked close.

Adrenaline still surged through him, but aftermath stripped away the numbness of battle focus. Emotions blazed through him—good, bad, some raw primal, some even downright Shakespearean poetic. And yeah, the force and collective roar still scared the crap out of him.

But not enough to make him run for the quiet of cover anymore. Not now that he understood exactly what he'd been missing by closing himself off from the full power of his love for his wife. Her love for him.

With the joint forces of Rena's indomitable will and his determination, they could accomplish anything—even rebuild a marriage made to last a lifetime.

Lounging against the porch post, J.T. sucked in a drag of pure night air as the last cop cruiser pulled away from the curb. Adrenaline still singed his insides, but tonight he would find peace with his wife rather than through the Bard.

Once he thanked Bo for a debt he could never repay.

The young officer leaned against the opposite post, flexing his fingers. Yeah, crap like this brought back some bad memories.

Crickets and june bugs hummed above the minimal traffic. Street lamps glowed into empty yards, lights flickering off in the windows of a neighborhood going to sleep. Chris, upstairs being fussed over by Rena, would likely be asleep soon, as well, the teenager exhausted, relieved. There would still be trial testimonies, but the badasses had been nailed.

Rena's surprise ID of the circle/triangle symbol even offered Spike the final link he'd been seeking. Now authorities knew where to look in tracking the drop-off point for the drugs once they'd been run up the coast.

And all without a bullet fired.

J.T. rubbed his hand along the tender knot on the back of his head. A small price for putting this all to rest. One of the flight surgeons had even made a house call for him, checked him over, deemed him perfectly well thanks to his thick head.

And hadn't Rena laughed at that pronouncement?

Damn, but her laughter sounded good. God willing, he was through making her cry. "Thanks, Bo, for everything today. You really put your butt on the line for my family."

"I owed you."

"Well, we're definitely even."

"Nobody's keeping score. It's what we do for each other," Bo said in an echo of Spike's same words, not surprising since the credo ingrained itself in all of them.

Bo studied his bootlaces. "Besides, it felt damn good to strike back at the bad guys on this one. Makes everything that happened to us over there mean something."

"Yeah, I hear you." Understatement. It had taken them nearly four months, but finally, they'd completed their mission.

J.T. drew in a little more of that magnolia-scented air to ground himself in home.

Home.

It was time to return.

Bo pushed away from the post. "Well, man, I should hit the road. I'm betting I can milk this for a little TLC from someone of the female persuasion. What do you think?"

J.T. thumped the young officer on the back on their way down the flagstone path. "I'm thinking that you better stay the hell away from my daughter, *sir,* or I'll tell people your real name."

"Yeah, yeah, I know." Bo swung up into the front seat. "No crewdogs for your little girl."

"No players."

"A player? Who me?" Winking, he cranked the Jeep. "Catch ya' later, dude. I'm off to romance my lady friend."

Bo revved the engine, shifting into reverse and roaring out of the driveway into the night.

Romance. Chuckling, J.T. shook his head. He and Rena had pretty much skimmed over that part, jumping from shared hamburgers to a shared kid, family, apartment, day-to-day get moving with life.

More lights along the rows of houses switched off, reminding him of his explanation to Rena about his work/life switch, his inability to blend the two worlds.

Had he somehow segmented his relationship with Rena, as well? Dating, one switch. Flick the switch to husband, another mind-set, being a provider like his father.

Recreation had never played a big role in his life. He'd found a job he enjoyed, productive hobbies like rebuilding his house or his car. And for smiles? Light? He had Rena.

But what had he given her for light in return?

Well, hell. He stared down the empty road. A few weeks ago he'd been beating his head against the wall at the prospect of entering the "dating" world again. But now, the idea sent one helluva thrill through him—when the right woman was involved.

The romance gig wasn't a crapshoot, after all. As much as he wanted to present Rena with diamonds and fancy vacations, the incredible woman he loved enjoyed circus peanuts, too.

He wasn't giving up on draping her in a diamond or two someday. But he'd finally learned he could also drape her in plenty of romance now.

J.T. fished into his back pocket for his cell phone. After twenty-two years, it was about time he asked his wife for a date.

* * *

Rena rapped two knuckles against her son's open bedroom door.

"Yeah?" Chris called from his bed, pitching a magazine to a floor already covered in clothes, a towel and schoolbooks.

Her heart rate still thumped an extra couple of beats every time she remembered how close she'd come to losing J.T. and Chris today.

Rena tiptoed over a discarded backpack on her way to her son's bedside. "Are you okay, hon?"

"Still a little wigged out, but it'll be better in the morning. Just need to sleep. Maybe swim some laps tomorrow. Get my head together."

She perched on the edge of his bedside table. "Swimming laps is a good way to relax."

"Yeah. Gotta work out the stress somehow." He crooked both arms behind his head. "Dad's probably down in his office veging with the Bard."

"Excuse me?"

"You know. How he always reads Shakespeare and junk like that to chill."

But she didn't know.

How could she have missed that about her husband? A sad commentary on how little she and J.T. had communicated over the years. She would have cried her eyes out over the discovery a couple of days ago. Now it only fueled her resolve to learn more about this fascinating man she'd married. And along the way let him learn some more about her, as well.

"'Night, hon." Rena leaned to skim a good-night kiss on her son's forehead. "I love you."

He hooked an arm up and around for a hug. "Love you, too, Mom." He pulled back, mock surprise on his face. "Gee, when did you get so little?"

"When did you get so big?" She grinned.

Laughing, a deeper sound these days, he flopped back. "G'night."

"Good night, hon."

Clicking off the overhead light, she left, closing his door on her way out. Finally, she and J.T. could be alone. Would they talk? Or just cut straight to mind-blowing sex? Or pass out from exhaustion?

Her tummy tumbled in nervous flips.

Rena padded down the stairs, toward the computer room, refusing to let the ghosts of their afternoon horror haunt her home. She peeked into the office. No J.T., but sure enough, right beside the butt-ugly green chair rested a thick tome.

She stepped closer, her hand falling to rest on the volume of Shakespearean plays. She thumbed through, some pages highlighted, her husband's spiky scrawl beside passages. She let the book fall open as if it might give her a glimpse into J.T., a hint for what she should do next.

"Our doubts are traitors, and make us lose the good we oft might win, by fearing to attempt." *Measure for Measure*. Rena traced a finger along the words. No more waiting. She knew exactly what she needed to do and finally had the confidence in herself to go for broke.

Rena snapped closed the book. She had a husband to welcome home.

Making tracks back up the stairs, she headed straight for the bedroom closet. First on her welcome-home agenda, clear room for his flight suits and Hawaiian shirts.

A swoop of her arm smooshed her work dresses to the side. She didn't intend to give up pushing for marital counseling. But in the meantime, she could still go on her own, work through some of her issues from her childhood. Straighten out her insecurities and need for control.

A starting place.

Kneeling, she lined her heels up in double rows to empty space for his boots and gym shoes.

The phone jangled from beside the bed.

A call? This late?

She eased to her feet and rushed to scoop the cordless phone from beside a pot of mini-mums. "Hello?"

"Hi, is Rena there?" her husband's deep voice rumbled through the line.

Huh? Had he hit his head harder than she'd thought? Maybe she should have insisted the flight surgeon take another look at him. "J.T.? Are you all right?"

"I'm totally all right. In fact, I've been more than all right since I saw you at that air show."

Okay, now she was really getting worried. "J.T., where are you?"

"Turn around."

She spun—to find him lounging against the hall door, cell phone at his ear. One black leather boot pressed to the wall, his knee bent. His flight suit stretched across mile-wide shoulders. "I was hoping you'd remember me, because since the second I saw you, I've been hoping like hell you'd go out with me. So, I decided to give you a call, see if you're free this Friday for a date with a local flyboy."

God, as much as she drooled over those shoulders of his, he really took her breath away when he smiled. Damned if she didn't feel eighteen again.

Phone pressed to her ear, she smiled back at him, flicked her hair over her shoulder, played along. "I might be free, if the right flyboy asked."

"Well, babe, I'm asking." He angled away from the door frame, ambled closer, his big, muscled body drawing nearer, filling her eyes and her heart. "And I intend to keep right on asking until I can convince you to go out with me."

He stopped inches away.

She clicked off her phone but kept it cradled against her neck, soaking up the silly romantic gesture a little while longer. "You are so crazy sometimes."

"Not often." He set his phone on the end table. "And only for you, babe. Only for you."

He reached for her phone, as well, and placed it beside his before lifting her hand, kissing her palm.

Definitely eighteen again, but with a forty-year-old's wisdom on how to do things better this go-round. "I want you to come home. For good."

"That's where I want to be." He folded her hand against his chest, against his heart thumping along at a pace as fast as hers. "Not just because you're pregnant, but because I can't stand the thought of living the rest of my life without you beside me."

She gathered the beautiful words up into her heart with surety and happiness, because, by God, J.T. never lied.

He stared down at their linked fingers and rather than pushing him to talk, she knew now to wait. He would come around to filling the silence if she simply gave him the chance.

"I spoke with the flight surgeon when she checked out the lump on my head."

Her racing heart stopped. "You're okay?"

"Totally fine." The twinkle in his eyes jump-started her heart again. "Although you'll have to keep me awake all night."

She sagged closer, her hips rocking against his. "I think that can be arranged."

"Thank God." His forehead fell to rest against hers. His chest expanded with two hefty sighs before he continued, "About my discussion with the flight surgeon. I asked her to recommend a marriage counselor."

Rena's throat went as tight as her chest. She'd been prepared to wait, work, hope, pray that things would work the way that she wanted. But to have him make the huge step on his own... Oh God, she loved this man.

Steady gray eyes stared down at her with no doubts to

cloud their beautiful-sky appeal. "Up the stakes as high as you want. I'm not walking again."

Sometimes hormones were a wonderful thing. Letting all those happy tears well up and flow free, Rena flung her arms around his neck. "Oh God, J.T., I love you."

J.T. felt her words rocket right into him, straight for his heart—where she belonged. He wrapped his arms around her and pulled her against his chest—also where she belonged. "I know, babe. And I don't ever intend to take that for granted again."

He dropped a kiss on her head while her sighs caressed through his flight suit, still so damn stunned and glad to see over her shoulder where she'd made room for his clothes in their closet again.

"Hell, I can't believe I'm the lucky bastard who stole your heart when you could have had anybody." His fingers tangled in her hair. "There are so many things I wanted to give you over the years. Still things I wish I could give you. But you can be certain I love you. Always have, and it only gets stronger with time."

"Things?" Her stunned response drifted up.

"Yeah, a bigger house, trips, a grocery budget that didn't include coupon clipping."

"I never asked for any of that."

"But you deserve it all."

She angled back, hints of her fiery temper sparking in her chocolate eyes. "Do you really think that little of me?"

"What?"

She thunked his chest. "Do you believe I'm so shallow that I would only be happy if we had more money? I think I'm insulted here, J.T."

Rena clasped his flight-suit collar in two determined hands, strong hands that nurtured, loved and, yes, even demanded. "Do you have any idea how proud I am of you, hell, of myself, too, for that matter, and everything we've built over the years?''

The words rolled out of her, ringing with a conviction he couldn't fight even if he tried. And he definitely didn't want to fight with her anymore.

Her soft hands caressed up to his face. ''We started with nothing, and in twenty-two years you've risen to a rank most in your profession never see. You've given me three precious babies, and we've brought up two of those children. They may not be perfect, but then neither are their parents and I'm still proud of who Nikki and Chris are becoming. Even our house, we did this from the front porch you replaced to that ivy I stenciled.''

Those words rolling from her settled into him with a rightness that brought peace. Yeah, he still wanted to give her more, but now knew he could keep her happy while they waited.

He turned his face to kiss her hand again. ''I'm partial to that ivy.''

''Me, too.'' Her arms looped around his neck. ''You've given me something I never had as a child. The chance to hold up my head. To be proud of who I am.''

Studying her dark eyes, he found flecks and sparks of pain he'd seen reflected in the mirror and in the eyes of his crewmates. He'd understood about Rena's upbringing and had been determined to take her away from the ugliness of that world. But he'd never realized until now that his wife had also spent time in a war zone. With guns. Deceit. Danger. What a scarring way for a child to grow up, now that he actually thought about it.

In flipping his switch, maybe he'd closed off the chance for his wife to share some burdens with him, too. Something he now knew to fix.

Rena's arms slipped forward and she lifted his hands, kissed each palm as he'd done to hers. ''I love your hands and what they do for me, but I need you for so many reasons that have nothing to do with what your body can provide." She tapped his forehead. "What are you thinking?"

A thousand things, about their past, her past, all things they could share later in bed. And with the counselor. And on moonlit nights by the shore.

For right now, he'd settled for the obvious, most important answer and a piece of himself to share with her. "You reminded me of a quote from a Shakespearean play, *A Midsummer Night's Dream,* I think. It goes something like, 'Thou art as wise as thou art beautiful.'"

"Wow. Am I ever one lucky lady or what?" She arched up against him, whispering against his mouth. "I get love, a hunky flyboy and sensitive poetry all in one fella."

His mouth found hers, settled, held while relief over their new start swept through both of them.

And then the chemistry soared. Ooh-rah.

Her lips parted or his mouth opened. Who could tell what happened first? And what the hell did it matter? Because he was too busy exploring the warm, moist heat of Rena.

She tipped back, tugging him down onto the bed with her. Definitely ooh-rah.

He caught himself with his elbows against the bounce of the mattress, careful of the baby, of her. "You still haven't answered my question."

"What question was that?" She tickled her fingers along the nape of his neck.

"Will you go out with me this Friday?" Gathering a fistful of her hair, he kissed along her jaw, her ear, not at all averse to using a little persuasion. "We could catch a movie, go park by the shore afterward."

"Yes, I would love to go out with you, anywhere, anytime. Surprise me." She stroked her delicate foot up the length of his leg, slow, deliberate, until her leg hooked around his hip. "And it's a sure bet you'll get lucky on the first date."

Epilogue

How could a guy get so lucky in one lifetime?

Smiling, J.T. followed his wife up the stairs to their bedroom, the gentle sway of her hips, the swing of her spiral curls along her back drawing his eyes as always. Framed pictures of kids marked the years. And soon, another photo would be added to the collection once the hospital's newborn picture taken just last night was developed.

He cupped his hands around his son's tiny back, securing the baby to his shoulder with a seasoned grip. Like riding a bicycle. J.T. remembered the parent-hold well. One hand cradled under his son's bottom, the other hand cupping Jamie's dark, curly head.

Jamie. James Renard Price. Not a junior, but rather James for J.T. and Renard as a masculine form of Rena. Their two names blended for this baby who had brought them together.

He and Rena had come a long way in the past few months with the help of their marriage counselor. Not always easy, spilling their thoughts, but well worth the effort in the payback of a solid relationship. He'd learned to open up more. She'd learned that his quiet moods didn't mean distant. Rena had even told him she'd gained all the more faith in her abilities now that she'd seen how effective counseling could be from the *other* side of the desk.

So much love flowed freely these days, for his wife, for his new son, his other children, too. Life was good.

And about to get even better once Rena saw the surprise waiting to welcome her home.

Like a teenager ready to impress his first girlfriend, he followed her up the last stair, down the hall, to their bedroom. He stopped his wife before she could open the closed door. "Wait right here."

"How come?"

He sealed a quick kiss on her lips. "Trust me."

Her smile caressed his mouth. "All right then, flyboy. I'm waiting."

Tucking inside their room, he placed their sleeper-clad son in the middle of their bed, on Rena's favorite quilt with rings. He tugged Jamie's tiny foot. "Hold on for just a second, little man, while I go back for your mama."

J.T. made a quick sweep of the room to ensure everything was in place before sprinting to the hall where his wife waited with suspicious, but twinkling eyes.

"Okay, babe. Ready now." Gently, he swept her up into his arms.

Her hair trailing over his wrist, she laced her fingers behind his neck with a squeak and laugh. "I really can walk."

"I know you can." He settled her closer, enjoyed the scent and softness of her. And yeah, he wanted to pamper her a little. He'd forgotten how tough childbirth was on a woman, even with a quick four-hour labor like Rena's. He needed to hold her close. "But can't a guy be romantic?"

Ah, he loved how she melted against him. Hell, he just loved *her*.

Sighing, she relaxed in his arms. "By all means, then, carry away."

He stared down into the dark eyes of this woman who'd stolen his heart at an air show nearly twenty-three years ago. "I love you."

She stroked his face. "I love you, too." She nestled her head under his chin. "Now let's enjoy the peace and quiet while we can."

Amen to that. Nikki would be home soon to meet her new brother, and Chris would be bringing his girlfriend over to see Jamie as well.

Since his older friends had graduated and left for college, Chris seemed to have come out more, found his footing, especially once the police had fully cleared him. The lifeguard job had brought a girlfriend to his tower and into his life. He was calmer, more settled.

Knowing the possibility of a swim-team scholarship loomed in Chris's future calmed a part of J.T. that would never totally stop worrying about money. Of course, he worried a little less now that he'd made Chief Master Sergeant.

J.T. shuffled aside other thoughts, focused on his wife instead. He didn't want to think of anything except the homecoming surprise he had planned for Rena. Romancing his wife was turning out to be fun as hell.

Since folks from the squadron would be showing up to drop off dinner soon, he needed to get moving with his plan. He toed the bedroom door open wide and waited for his wife's reaction.

Flowers bloomed on every surface along with her potted plants—all mixed among candles. By the bed, bottled water perched in an ice bucket beside a plate of strawberries and grapes.

Rena's gasp of surprise, of happiness, told him all he needed to know. Romance rocked.

"So, Jamie," he called to his son, the little guy pumping

his tiny feet in response to his father's voice. "Do you think your mama likes the flowers?"

"She most definitely does." Rena snagged a pink rose from a vase as J.T. carried her toward the bed and inhaled the flowery scent. "Who says you can't have kids *and* romance? Thank you."

"My pleasure." And he wasn't done yet.

Carefully, he placed her onto the mattress against the piles of pillows, pulled her shoes off. J.T. stretched on the other side of the bed, while they watched their baby as they'd done in years past with Nikki and Chris.

His wife cooed and conversed with their newborn son, adjusting his lightweight blanket, tickling his toes and glowing even more than she had while pregnant. She would enjoy these next couple of months off before going back to work part-time.

Rena tugged the loose tail on J.T.'s Hawaiian shirt. "I think Jamie likes the crazy colors."

"Seems so." J.T. reached into his back pocket for the small box tucked away and hidden beneath the loose overshirt. "Remember how Nikki and Chris used to track things with their eyes early on?"

"I sure do."

Behind his back, he flicked open the box and pulled free the gift. He brought his hand forward and let the chain slowly slide loose, pendant swaying. "What do you think of this, little man? Will your mom like it, too?"

Her eyes glinted with tears. "Just when I think my heart can't get any fuller, it stretches even more."

J.T. winked at his son. "I think that's a yes." The jeweled charm continued its pendulum swing above the entranced baby. "I saw this while I was TDY to Spain a couple of months ago. The stones aren't as big as I would have wanted to get to celebrate something so damn awesome. But I actually put some sensitive-guy thought into it. Thank goodness the kid was born on time so I didn't have to change the birthstone.''

He looped the chain up to show her the circular mother charm crafted to look like a woman holding her children, each child a jewel stone. Their three children-gems winked back—a diamond, sapphire and topaz.

She touched each of the jewels with a trembling finger. ''It's perfect. You're perfect.''

Leaning over Jamie, Rena kissed J.T., a warm kiss, nothing passionate given her recovering state, but warm was good, too. Especially when there was the promise of so much more in a few weeks.

And judging from the glint in his wife's eyes, she was already anticipating six weeks into the future as well.

Ooh-rah.

She sagged back onto her pillows, the necklace clutched in her hand to her heart, the rose resting in her lap. ''God, it's good to be home.''

Home. Rena. Two words with the same meaning for him now.

He'd found that just as it was okay to bring darker parts of his military career into his relationship with Rena, into his house, he now always carried a part of her with him wherever he went. It had been a long journey across the years, across an ocean, but finally he was where he belonged.

''Yeah, babe, it sure is good to be home.''

*   *   *   *   *

OUT OF UNIFORM

BY
AMY J FETZER

Amy J Fetzer was born in New England and raised all over the world. She uses her own experiences in creating the characters and settings for her novels. Married more than twenty years to a United States Marine and the mother of two sons, Amy covets the moments when she can curl up with a cup of cappuccino and a good book.

For my mother-in-law

Leah Catherine Fetzer

For easily dispelling the stigma
that goes with the words "mother-in-law"

For teaching me the art of canning without explosions,
making "sliders" during a winter storm and for
raising terrific sons and daughters…
One in particular

And mostly, Leah, for welcoming me into your family
and teasing me just like I was your own.

I love you

Amy

One

Marines didn't like sitting still. Give them an objective and they'd take it on, grab it by both hands and improvise, adapt and overcome.

Rick's objective was simple. Open a pickle jar. However, his thickly bandaged shoulder and the cast from elbow to knuckles with a half-dozen pins with rubber-stopper tops in his wrist were the obstacles.

A one-armed Marine wasn't overcoming a damn thing. And the possibility that he wouldn't be for a long time left him in a perpetual bad mood. It hadn't let up since he'd been wounded and taken off Force Recon's active list. He wanted back in, wanted his wounds to hurry up and heal so he could get back to his company. Back into action.

But that wasn't getting him pickles.

The simple task had suddenly become like reaching for the Holy Grail. He knew his wounded hand wasn't strong enough to grip the jar. Besides, it hurt like hell the pins just made it worse. His shoulder was already throbbing, the pain working its way up to his head. He loosened the sling that secured his arm to his side like a straight jacket, and the weight of the cast pulled on his shoulder enough to make him suck in his breath. Determined to get the damn pickles, he tucked the jar under his arm, wedging it against his body, and with his good hand, twisted the cap. The lid popped and liquid spilled down his side and onto the floor.

With a patience he didn't normally have, he removed the sticky jar and set it on the counter, staring at the puddle. He smelled like the mess hall. It was going to take him half an hour just to clean it up. He hated being like this. He'd never been helpless in his life.

He was supposed to be the first man into war, leading his company and taking out a few enemy targets before the battalions landed. Reconnaissance. Not be the invalid. He was glad no one was around to see this.

The doorbell rang.

Great.

Witnesses.

He debated answering it, then after the third chime, tightened the sling and headed to the door. He hoped whoever was on his doorstep would just go the hell away. Since his right arm was locked over his stomach, he had to shift, use his good hand, and the awkwardness reminded him that he couldn't manage the simplest thing without rethinking the process.

He opened the door, already scowling. The last person he expected to see was his estranged wife standing on his porch.

"Hey, handsome."

Kate.

Like the pelting of shrapnel, everything he'd ignored for the last year pinged back into his mind. Attacking him from all sides. His body went into a hard lock-and-load drill, reliving every time he'd touched her, the things they'd done together between the sheets—and everywhere else in this house. Biting waves of longing crashed over him and made him realize how much he'd missed her. That she was still the most beautiful woman he'd ever laid eyes on. Still sexy, vibrant.

And *not* his.

"What the hell are you doing here?"

His gaze raked over her body, and he tried not to

notice how great she looked. But it was useless. He had
radar where she was concerned. He took her in like
breathing, the way her red hair framed her face and
curled like liquid fire over her shoulders to lay over the
lush swells of her breasts as if tease him; the way the
green shirt set off her eyes and cupped her torso like
nobody's business. Did she wear those low-riding
cropped pants, and expose her tanned tummy, along
with that delectable navel, just to taunt him with what
he couldn't have? The discomfort in his jeans went instantly from a twinge to downright painful.

Which just pissed him off. Since he couldn't do
anything about it with her anymore.

Kate cocked her head and smiled. "You know, Rick,
that's what I always loved about you—your warm
friendly greetings."

Smart mouth. "Very funny. Now just take those
suitcases—" he gestured to the two at her feet "—and
pack your little Irish behind back in your car and go
home."

"This is still my home, too."

He stiffened, his eyes narrowing. "No, it's not. Not
anymore." Because she'd left him. A year ago she'd told
him their marriage was beyond repair and she was tired
of being the only one fighting to make it work. The
woman didn't know what real fighting was, he thought.
And he hadn't seen a damn thing wrong with their marriage.

"Yes, well, I'm not here to rehash our marriage. I'm here to take care of you."

"I don't need it."

"Really?" she said, and he recognized that smug tone. "Is that pickles I smell?" Her gaze lingered for a second on the splatters on his pant leg.

Rick's eyes thinned to slits. "Yes, it is. Now if you'll excuse me…" He started to close the door.

She slapped a hand on the panel and stepped closer. "Not so fast, Marine. I have direct orders."

"Yeah, right."

"If you don't let me take care of you, Rick, then you have to go back to the Navy hospital. Today."

He yanked the door back open, wincing as needles of pain shot up his shoulder to his neck. He wanted to rub it, but the plaster-covered bandages prevented even that simple relief. "Says who? I'm fine alone."

"Your commander and your doctors say so. And oh, here's a stretch—both of them outrank you." She produced a letter and he snatched it, reading it quickly.

"Damn."

"Yes, I knew you'd be just delirious with excitement." She shivered dramatically, then delivered a devious grin that almost made him smile. Almost.

But all he saw was the prospect of having her here, twenty-four–seven. They'd kill each other before the week was out. "Why?"

"Because they both know you as well as I do. You'd

be up, walking around, not taking your medication and trying to tough it out like a hard corps Marine."

"That's my job."

"Not this week, or for the next couple months, at least. And that's *if* you play your cards right and behave."

His gaze thinned. Kate Wyatt knew her husband would rather chew glass than admit he needed anyone. Especially her. "You need help, Rick. I'm a nurse. Since you refused to remain in the hospital, your commander has ordered it." Her gaze moved past him. "And from the looks of the house, well, let's just say that for a man who prides himself on spit and polish—"

"So it's a little messy." Man, that sounded too defensive even to his own ears.

Kate lifted the suitcases. "Back up and let me in. Face it. I'm here for the duration."

He didn't move, debating how to get out of this. The last thing he wanted was having the only woman who could make his blood roar within shouting distance. Hell, his heart was already thumping just looking at her.

"Would you like to read the orders again, *Captain?*" she needled.

Caught between a rock and a command order, Rick knew when to retreat, if only temporarily. Besides, he didn't want the neighborhood getting a load of this. He moved out of the way, sweeping his good arm to welcome her inside. Into a house she'd helped decorate and take care of, then had left.

She passed close in front of him and he caught a whiff of her perfume, felt the heat of her body like a sting. He ground his teeth, resisting the urge to lean closer and inhale the scent that was all Kate. All woman.

All hot, ripe body and great smiles.

Man, seeing her shouldn't be this hard.

When he went to take her bags, she backed up and snapped, "No, you're not to use that arm at all if you want to be fit for Force Recon again. And that includes both arms."

"I can use this arm fine." He wiggled his fingers, then flapped his left elbow.

"The muscles are connected, Rick, and straining your good side in deference to your wound will mean you just take longer to recover. And look a little lopsided, too," she teased, swinging her arm like a monkey. He wasn't amused. "Is that what you want?" He let his hand fall away. She dragged the heavy suitcases farther inside, then, leaving one, took the other to the guest room.

Rick didn't move while she carted off the second, and he felt very unchivalrous just standing there.

Hell, he felt like a five-year-old—and lucky he was dressed.

When Kate came back, she stopped in front of him. "You look tired." He wore a T-shirt with one sleeve cut out so he could get it around the cast and thick bandages. All it did was stretch the fabric tight across his bulging chest muscles. The couple days' growth of beard only added to his rugged do-or-die appearance, which she'd fallen madly in love with four years ago.

"I'm annoyed," he said pointedly. "And I feel fine." But he wasn't. He rubbed his jaw, ignoring the pain throbbing steadily in his shoulder. The cast felt tighter, but he'd be damned if he'd let her see he wanted to curl up in a ball and whimper like a swabbie.

"When did you last take your medication?"

He didn't respond, and Kate had her answer.

"Rick," she groaned. "It's to fight infection from the surgery, jarhead." She went to the kitchen, slipping on the pickle juice and grabbing the counter.

She met his gaze. "I see we've had an accident."

"I swear if you talk to me like you do your patients—" he pointed at her, the twinkle in her eyes irritating him even more "—I'll throw you in a closet and never let you out."

She hid a smile and muttered, "Sorry."

She took inventory of the bottles of pills on the counter, read the labels and then dispensed them onto the counter with such efficiency Rick *felt* like one of the faceless people in the hospital. Which was why he'd chosen to return home and sleep in his own bed.

And now had his very own soon-to-be-ex wife stand-ing in the sticky kitchen, looking like she had in his dreams.

Hell, she was always in his dreams, but dreams didn't account for much in his book. They were fan-tasy. She needed to look more like a nurse, he groused silently. Because with every ripe, well-defined inch of her packed into that cute outfit, she was sending his imagination down the road to ruin. And she'd been here, what—two minutes?

She handed him his antibiotic pill, then a glass of water, standing guard as he took it. Satisfied, she went to a drawer, pulled out a notepad and pen and jotted down the time, date and dosage. That she remembered where the pad was and that he hadn't changed the location of anything in the house said something to him—he was clinging to something he didn't have anymore. A wife. Someone who loved him.

But she'd left him, and the old resentment rose in him.

She dispensed a painkiller next, holding it out to him. He didn't take it.

"You're in pain."

"I'm fine." Great. Was that all he could say in his own defense?

Her voice went liquid soft. "Rick, you had major surgery less than a week ago, and already this morn-ing you're perspiring." She touched his cheek. Her hand was so cool on his face, he nearly moaned. "Take this and go to bed."

If you come with me, an inner voice shouted. He grabbed the pill and, like a child, jammed it in his mouth. "I'm going to watch the game."

"That's fine, as long as you get off your feet and rest." Kate went for the mop and bucket as he walked out of the kitchen. When he was out of sight, she sagged against the counter, fighting tears.

Oh, it was so hard seeing him like this. He was barely standing on his feet. Dark circles made his blue eyes look hollow, and his skin had lost some of its usual tan. Other than that, he looked pretty good for a man who'd been wounded enough to need a couple of blood transfusions.

He had no idea how difficult it had been for her to stay away this long. Or that she hadn't.

She'd been working for her civilian doctor when Rick's commanding officer had called her. Hearing the words *he's been shot* had shattered everything inside her. They'd stabilized him in a field hospital and then airlifted him from somewhere in the Middle East to an Air Force base in Germany for surgery.

Kate had been on a flight within an hour. She'd sat outside the OR during the surgery and was by his bedside for two days until he was off the critical list. He'd been too deep under with morphine to know she was even there, and she'd made the staff swear not to tell him. He wouldn't want her to see him like that. But watching him lie in the hospital bed hooked up to IVs, a monitor beeping out his heartbeat, and bandaged from throat to fingertips…all she could do was thank God he was alive. And realize that she'd never stopped loving him.

Not living with him anymore hadn't lessened the worry. Because she still *felt* married, felt connected to him, she thought, pushing away from the counter and grabbing the mop.

She'd handled having him walk out their door and into danger for years during their marriage. She even understood that he could never talk about the missions; there were some things wives and the American public didn't need to know. So she'd kept her worry capped, not wanting to be a distraction for him while he was on the battlefield, but it wore on them because Rick would never open up to her. About anything. Not even his feelings for her.

That was the reason she'd left. She'd been doing all the work, all the talking. And that shield of his made her doubt his love for her. Or if he even needed her in his life.

She rubbed her face. Why was she analyzing this again?

If he'd wanted her to stay, he would have fought harder for her. He'd have picked up the phone at least once and asked her to come back, to try to work it out.

But his pride was too big and his heart too tightly sealed.

That hurt the most.

He'd fight for his country, die for it. But when it came to her and their marriage, he just let her walk out the door without a word.

That was the last time she'd seen him until he was on a gurney being wheeled into the O.R. by two Corpsmen.

Still exhausted from the long flights and jet lag, Kate battled with the memory as she finished cleaning the floor, then went to the guest room to unpack her things. It felt strange to be back in this house. She struggled for focus, reminding herself this was a job. In-home care. The navy was paying her. She had to get Rick back in fighting form so he could return to what he really loved.

She wandered through the house, straightening up and gathering laundry he'd left in some of the strangest places. Then she made the mistake of walking into their bedroom.

His bedroom, she reminded herself. A wave of longing hit her, making her grip the door jamb. They'd expressed so much love in this room. She looked around at the rich eggplant-and-taupe decor of the room, at the grand four-poster Rice bed they'd picked out a week before the wedding. As he'd paid for it, Rick had whispered that he was going to make love to her every way imaginable in it. Her heart clenched with something close to pain as her body remembered he'd made good on that promise. She touched the tall mahogany post, leaning into it.

The bed was haphazardly made, but it was the matching dresser she noticed instantly. There was nothing on it—none of his things—and after investigating, she learned the drawers were empty. Why didn't he use it? She went to the closet. One half was filled with pressed uniforms, from his evening mess dress to his "jungles," the camouflage utilities he wore in the field. His combat boots were in perfect alignment, varying colors from his black jump boots to buff desert suede. His covers were aligned on the top shelf. His "civvies" filled the rest of the closet, equally as neat as a wall locker in a barracks.

While they were married he'd stored his many uniforms in the guest room closet so she had some space. Except for moving them in here, he'd changed nothing. It was as if he didn't want to acknowledge that she was gone.

Well, she *was* gone. She had a new life, an apartment, she thought, almost angrily stripping the bed, replacing the sheets with fresh. She dusted the room before heading to the garage to start a load of laundry, frowning at the new woodworking tools and chunks of wood on the workbench. Must be house repair stuff.

Satisfied she had a jump on the disorder, she fixed

Rick a sandwich and brought it to him. He was
slumped on the sofa, asleep, the remote control in his
hand, the TV stuck on a news channel. She set the
sandwich down on the side table and drew a blanket
over him, then checked his pulse. On a whim she sat
on the edge of the sofa by his hip. Reaching out, she
grazed his face with her fingers, pushing his short,
dark hair off his brow and noticing the cut near his
hairline before sweeping her palm over his whiskered
jaw. Unconsciously, he turned his face into her hand.

Her heart skipped a couple of beats. He didn't have
to say a thing and she was already coming apart inside,
as if she were falling under his spell all over again. His
quiet strength had first attracted her, then his smile. It
changed his whole appearance and always made her
stomach do a little flip. He'd done everything right—
nothing mushy, just straightforward love that showed
in the way he looked at her, the way he touched her
body and reached into her soul.

She missed that. The little sparkle, the devilish teasing that overflowed with raw sexuality. Unwisely, she
let her gaze run over his body; so sculpted and hard,
the thin T-shirt ridged over his six-pack abs. She didn't
have to see more—every solid muscled inch of him
was imprinted in her mind and invaded her dreams.

Her gaze moved to the pins in his wrist, and for his
sake, she hoped his shattered bones healed. If he
couldn't function with a weapon, he'd be medically

discharged. It would destroy him. The Marine Corps was his life. His entire life.

If the Corps wanted Marines to have a wife, they'd have issued them one. She'd heard that a thousand times from male Marines—most of them married. It was their way of not letting the fact that they had someone at home waiting and worrying get to them when they were in the field. It ticked her off sometimes, too. She'd been as much a part of the Marine Corps family as any Marine. Honestly, the toughest job in the Corps was being a Marine's wife and watching him walk so willingly into danger.

She studied Rick now, her throat closing over a hard lump that hadn't left since she'd learned he'd been wounded. She didn't want him to see her crying over this. He'd shrug it off, tell her he was fine, no big deal. But just the same, she wondered what it was like to take a bullet. To know that you might not make it home. *And that home was empty,* a voice in her head screamed.

I know, I know. But I tried.

When she'd married him she'd known he wasn't the kind of man who talked a lot about himself, or his feelings, and she didn't set out to change him. She'd hoped that he'd feel secure enough that he would at least not shut her out, and would perhaps turn to her when he was hurting. But not Rick. Even when he'd lost one of his men in combat, he still hadn't confided in her.

He'd barely spoken at all. Instead, he had gone out in the backyard and chopped wood for two days, gotten drunk with his buddies. Afterward, he was back to the same man she'd always loved.

She swore sometimes that when he was hurting, he moved on autopilot.

Heck, he never even told her when he wanted her. He'd just pull her into his arms, kiss her, and that was it.

Well, she thought, smiling, that hadn't been *it*—sex had always been so exciting between them. She missed it. But she needed words. It was so female, she admitted. So girlie to need it, but she couldn't get around the fact that the last time she'd heard him say he loved her was when he said his wedding vows. She needed to feel as if she meant as much to him as his military career.

Duty is to God, country and Corps. Everything else is just gravy, Marines said.

Kate didn't want to be gravy—she needed to know she was equally important to him. But when he didn't fight for her, she understood she wasn't.

Damn him.

Just be his nurse, she told herself resolutely, laying her hand on his chest and feeling him breathe, absently counting off the times while she looked at her watch. When she looked up, his eyes were open.

His lips curved in a sleepy smile that was too sexy

AMY J. FETZER   23

for his own good. Her heart tripped all over itself to catch up with the lost beats.

"Hi, baby," he murmured groggily.

Her heart clenched hard. "Hey yourself, handsome."

A year fell away, a year of being alone without him in her life, in her bed. Kate's eyes burned. And when his good hand moved up her back, a familiar heat slid over her skin, awakening her.

"So, is this what it takes to get you back here?"

It would have taken so little, she mused. One phone call. "You're telling me you got wounded just so I'd come be your nurse?"

His lips quirked. "I've done dumber things for you."

"Yeah, sure. When?"

"How 'bout the time I wore that stupid underwear for you?"

"But you looked *so* sexy in it." Just the memory made her heart pound.

"Glad you were the only one who saw it. Imagine the ribbing I'd have suffered if my teams knew I wore a gold thong for you."

"It's called a slingshot, and you don't wear any underwear except when you're in uniform, anyway." That had always turned her on.

He gave her a devilish look. "I'm not wearing any now." He applied pressure to her back, drawing her near.

She didn't know what made her say it. "Funny, neither am I."

Rick groaned and pulled her closer, laying his mouth over hers. Their first contact in a year was electric, the rawness of desire spiraling out of control. In seconds, he was devouring her.

"Oh, man," he murmured, and kissed her hungrily.

Kate sank into it, her body screaming recognition as his mouth made a slow, luxurious slide over hers. His tongue, dipping and sweeping made her spine tingle with a pulse of need that wrapped around her and settled between her thighs. His free hand swept her spine to her breast, cupping it, his fingertips making slow erotic circles over her nipple. Fire radiated, her response consuming her and pouring into him. His kiss grew stronger, raw and devouring, then he tried to draw his bound arm around her, and flinched, growling in pain.

She lurched back as he grabbed his shoulder.

"Dammit," he muttered.

Kate shot to her feet, guilt pinging through her. "It's just as well. We shouldn't have done that, and I didn't come here to pick up anything, Rick. I came here to help you recuperate."

"Well then, be a damn nurse and stay away from me!" he snapped angrily. "You might have called it quits on us, but that doesn't mean I *ever* stopped wanting you!"

Wanting her? Not needing, loving? She couldn't allow herself more than nursing him back to health. He wouldn't change, and he'd break her heart once more. She couldn't live through that. Not again. She'd never survive. She'd already lost something more precious than her marriage, and she was barely surviving now.

"You're just horny," she said tightly. "Don't confuse lust with anything remotely resembling actually *needing* me, Rick." She spun around and headed for the kitchen, her body still stinging with desire and her hurt burning her throat.

Two

Rick felt like a prisoner in an enemy camp.

The only problem was he knew he couldn't make an escape. And the camp commander was like a demon on wheels.

From his "cell" on the sofa, Rick watched Kate move around the house with military efficiency, cleaning, rearranging things back to some semblance of order. His uniforms and gear might be able to pass inspection at any given moment, but when it came to dust bunnies, Rick had his priorities.

Since her last remark, she'd moved around him as if he wasn't there, and Rick savored the small pleasure of simply watching her. She was graceful, so feminine and curvy in all the right places. She had a gorgeous hourglass figure like a movie star, and he knew when he held her he held a woman—round, soft, sweet smelling. His body sat up and took notice, which wasn't surprising. He'd always had a perpetual hard-on around his wife.

But she wasn't his wife now.

Somewhere in the legal system there were separation papers saying just that. His brow knit as he remembered her call, telling him it was best if they ended it. He hadn't pleaded with her to come back, though he'd wanted to beg. He'd figured if she'd talked to a lawyer, her mind was made up and there was no changing it.

That said a lot to a guy.

Old anger festered, resentment stewing in him, and though he itched to pull her into his lap as she passed close, he distracted himself with flipping through channels for something more interesting.

It wasn't happening.

"Rick, that's annoying. Pick something," she said as she passed. Watching her go just reminded him of all the good times they'd had, how much he'd loved her and how easily she'd left. There wasn't anything wrong with their marriage that he could point a finger at—except that she always wanted him to tell her what he was *feeling*.

Rick wasn't a sharing kind of guy, unless he was furious with someone. He'd been raised by people who didn't give a damn if he was hurting, having been passed from foster home to foster home, then to an unfeeling uncle who'd told him to deal with it. So he did. Alone. He'd let his guard down once, and the lousy reception he got was enough to make certain he didn't do it again. He considered feelings a weakness, and he didn't need to get "in touch" with any part of himself. He knew what kind of man he was, and was content with working things out on his own. Why couldn't Kate understand that?

Why couldn't she see that he didn't want her to experience the burdens and, sometimes, the ugliness he had?

Her last comment played through his mind again, and frowning, Rick left the sofa and headed into the kitchen. She was filling the dishwasher with the sinkful of dishes he'd left behind. He didn't want her cleaning up after him, taking care of him. He wanted her sweet little ass out of this house, so he'd be left alone.

"What was that last crack about?" he demanded.

Kate glanced over her shoulder, confused for a second. "It wasn't a crack. It was…insight. Don't confuse wanting sex with actually needing me."

"I've always needed you."

Her heart clenched a little. "You've wanted me. In your bed, in this house. But you don't really need me."

"I say again, woman, what does that mean?"

Woman? She knew he was mad when he said that.

She threw the dishrag in the sink and walked up to him. "It means you survived quite well without me for nearly a year, and now that you're injured, you need help. I'm here to give it. But that's where it has to stay. Nurse to patient. Because it's obvious you still aren't willing to open up to me." *And let me into your heart. Deep in.*

"Kate, baby, I loved you."

She arched a brow. "Past tense?" The sting of that nearly made her legs crumble.

"What the hell do you expect? You left *me*." The humiliation of that failure was enough to make him grind his teeth.

"Because you wouldn't talk to me, Rick. You keep everything locked up so tight I don't think *you* even know what you feel."

"Dammit, what do you want from me? To tell you I miss you? I do. That I want you? Like crazy. But don't tell me you're here for any reason other than you feel sorry for me."

She blinked and reared back. "Pity? For you? A man who can hold his breath underwater for two minutes? Who jumps out of airplanes into heavy combat because it's the quickest way into the front lines of battle? A man who survived a week in the Iraqi desert, alone, with a K-bar knife and a canteen? No, I don't feel sorry for you in the least."

"Then why are you really here?"

She hated that his voice went soft and tender; she wanted to stay mad. "You love the Marines, and I'm here to see that you get back to what you love most, as soon as you can and in the best shape possible. Because that will make you happy." *Even if it's without me.*

"Okay, I can buy that," he said after a moment.

Were all men that clueless? "Good. Are we done jabbing?"

"I doubt it."

She made a frustrated sound as she turned away and left the kitchen. He followed her to the bathroom and watched her gather his shaving supplies.

"You need a shave," she said, noticing his frown.

"I shave when I shower, you know that. Or have you forgotten everything?"

An image pierced her anger, of her shaving him in the shower before they'd made love against the wall like wild, hungry teenagers. She closed her eyes for a second, the frantic pulse of the memory shooting through her body like a rocket.

"No, I haven't." *Not a single moment.*

He moved closer, hemming her in, his towering strength nearly smothering her. "Me, either," he said, his voice a husky growl that make her skin tingle.

Unable to help it, she reached out and touched his jaw. "So do you want to bathe and shave? Or is that cowboy stubble a new look for you?"

"Hell no, makes my face itch. But I have to do it

left-handed because of this." He knocked on the cast. "I'll turn my face into hamburger."

"Lucky for you I'm here, then. I have something that will help."

She brushed past him out the door, and a couple seconds later was back with a cellophane wrapped hospital pack. Breaking it open, she flipped out a plastic sleeve.

"This goes over your hand and shoulder and will create suction on your skin, so water won't get in."

He was relieved. "Outstanding. I didn't think a plastic bag was going to keep this thing very dry for long."

"If you were in the hospital, they'd have helped you shower with this."

"I don't need help to take a damn bath."

Her expression told him he was pushing his luck. "Stop fighting me, Rick." Then she looked him in dead in the eye and ordered, "Strip."

Rick stared at her for a second, thinking she was trying hard to be impersonal now. *We'll see.* Not bothering to struggle with the T-shirt, he grabbed a handful of the front and yanked. The garment tore from his body with one pull. He dropped it to the floor.

Rick, taut and tight with pounds of rippling muscle, was about as good as it got, Kate thought, wanting to be wearing nothing but her skin, and pressing it against him.

"It will make a good rag," she said blandly, and

knelt, untying his sneakers and removing them. When she glanced up, she found him staring down at her with a hooded look. Then he pulled at his belt buckle, jerked it open and unzipped his pants. Kate stood abruptly, and the hint of a dark, sexy smile curved his lips. Her toes practically curled. He was teasing her, knowing she was a sucker for his body.

Not one to pass up an opportunity, Rick gripped her hip, pulling her closer, and when her hands splayed over his chest, he felt seared all the way to his spine.

"Didn't we just discuss this?" Kate said, feeling the length of his arousal between them. "Or are you still that hardheaded?"

Scowling, he let her go. "Apparently."

She moved around him and turned on the bathwater.

"No, a shower."

"No," she said patiently. "You won't have the balance on a wet floor. This has a rail on the wall at least. And it will do your muscles good to have some heat on them. I'm betting your shoulder and arm isn't all that hurts." The bruises on his spine were still discolored and ugly. She sat on the edge of the tub, testing the water, adding a packet of something from the hospital stuff she'd brought.

"Epsom salts," she said, swishing it around. "If you have any cuts it might sting a little, but it will feel great."

You in that tub with me would take the sting away,

he thought, then cursed when his groin thickened. He was going to be a blathering idiot by the end of the day.

"Leave me alone, Kate. I can manage."

"Really? Try." She handed him the protective sleeve and watched him struggle to get it over the pins. When he sucked in his breath, she took it and gently worked the plastic sleeve over his hand and up his shoulder. She pressed on it tightly and it adhered to his skin.

"Okay now, git." He wasn't about to let this humiliation go on with her watching.

She ignored him, taping the open edge for extra protection. "You could slip."

"Then I fall."

"And it will set you back a month. Is that what you want?" She pressed the last piece of tape in place.

That was the second time she'd asked that, Rick realized, frowning. She looked up at him, hands on her trim hips. Hell, if she was going to be a pest... He tugged his trousers farther open and let them drop to the floor. His eyes almost dared her to inspect him as he stepped out of them.

Instead, Kate swallowed, avoiding a glance at everything he owned. But standing in the bathroom with her handsome, naked, soon-to-be-ex husband was something she hadn't really considered when she'd agreed to this. Oh, he could really do some damage to her protective armor if he kept this up.

When he climbed into the tub, the intense urge to

pat his tight behind nearly overpowered her. He groaned as he sank into the hot water. The tub was custom made because he was so tall and he'd wanted it to accommodate both of them. It reminded her that their marriage had included a lot of sex and very little deep verbal communication.

He braced his injured arm on the edge and let the other sink under the cloudy water. Kate pulled a stool close, laying out bath items, then leaned over to gently lift his head and cushion his neck with a rolled towel.

Rick closed his eyes, tempted to nip at her skin, since she was pushing her breasts in his face, but instead sank deeper into the water. "Thanks. Man, this feels great."

"Soak for a bit. I'll be back in a few minutes."

"Running off so soon?" he challenged.

Already at the door, she turned back to look at him. The water was above his waist and cloudy white, but did nothing to hide what lay beneath. "I'm not running anywhere. I thought you'd like privacy." She sure as heck needed it.

"You could wash my back?" He grinned.

Her heart did a quick tumble in her chest to see him smile. "There is a back brush beside you."

Rick snatched up the soap. She was acting damn impersonal for a woman who'd made incredibly erotic love to her patient for years. Left alone, he tried lathering up the washcloth with soap but couldn't manage the simple task. The harder he struggled, the more he ended up chasing the bar around the tub. It reminded him that he was a nonfunctioning Marine.

Useless.

Hell, he'd like nothing more than to pull Kate onto his lap, but couldn't do anything about it once he got her there. He stared at the soap and washcloth, then clamped the cloth between his knees and rubbed it with the bar. Eventually, he managed to scrub himself, and satisfied he was decently clean, he reached for the shampoo.

Kate stood outside the bathroom, hearing him curse, ready to pop in and help whether he wanted it or not. He could tease her all he wanted, but it just made her heart feel bruised. Giving in to him would accomplish nothing except a little temporary satisfaction. Good satisfaction, but still temporary. Like picking up the best parts of their life and not dealing with the bad.

Well, it wasn't *so* bad, she thought. Much of it had been great. Until she'd started feeling as if she were an appendage to his life, and not really in it. She didn't have any foolish dreams of getting him to share himself with her this time.

She heard a thump and looked in. Seeing him struggle to reach the shampoo bottle, she stepped inside.

When he looked up, it was to glare at her as if his inability was her fault. She ignored it, used to that kind of frustration from patients, and sat on the stool.

Taking the shampoo, she lathered his hair and rubbed his scalp, avoiding the cut on his hairline. He moaned like a tired bear. She smiled, remembering when they'd shared this tub, how he liked conditioning her hair because it made his hands so slick they skated over her body. He had great hands, knew all the right places to stroke and tease until she was quivering and begging him to push inside her—

Abruptly, she picked up the hand-held sprayer and rinsed his hair, wanting to douse herself. He tipped his head back, letting the water cascade over his face.

Then those deep blue eyes zeroed in on her, making her insides spring apart for the hundredth time that day.

It felt like Chinese water torture to Rick. A beautiful woman—one he'd explored thoroughly for years—was treating him like a patient, and he was so hard for her right now, he could crack walnuts. He tossed down the washcloth strategically so she wouldn't notice.

Fat chance.

His gaze lowered. "You're wet."

She looked down. Her shirt was soaked, her nipples straining against the wet cloth. When he started to reach for her, she slapped the razor into his open hand. He clutched it, and she filled her palm with shaving cream. She knew him; he'd have to try shaving himself before asking for help.

"Kate," he warned.

"Oh, for pity's sake, this is getting old. I swear, I've never heard you gripe as much as you have in the last couple hours. Why struggle when you don't have to?" She lathered his face.

"It makes me feel like a child."

She let her gaze slide up and down all the man and muscle exposed, then simply arched a brow. "You mean there's a sweet infantile innocence in there somewhere?"

He snarled something under his breath and she held up a mirror for him, watching him scrape away a couple days' worth of beard. His gaze flicked up, catching hers. She was inches from him.

All Rick had to do was lean in a bit to kiss her. Yet he kept shaving, and when he couldn't adequately reach one side with his left hand, she took the razor.

She shaved him carefully, smoothing her fingers over his skin to be certain she got all the bristles. She cupped water, rinsing, sliding her thumb over his chin, around his lips. He nipped her fingertip, his flashing eyes meeting hers, and Kate experienced the power this man had over her. He sucked the tip for a second, and she hesitated, wanting his mouth on hers, wanting every part of him connecting to her. Right now. When the back of his knuckles grazed her breast, a bolt of hot need slammed through her. She jerked back, blinking.

Oh, for pity's sake. If he kept this up she'd be on the floor spread-eagle, begging him to take her.

"We're done. You need to stand," she said coolly, grabbing the hand sprayer.

Angered at her indifference, he snarled, "Dammit, Kate, get the hell out of here! I'm not completely helpless."

She tossed down the sprayer and stood. "Call me when you want the sleeve off."

"I can do that."

"No, you can't. I taped it on, *Captain.*" She stormed out.

Using the rail for balance, Rick stood slowly, rinsed himself, then stepped out and reached for a towel. He dried off and was struggling to wrap the towel around his waist when she walked back in. He glared at her as, with a flat expression, she strode up to him and adjusted the terry cloth. Her fingers grazed his groin and it jumped to life again as she tucked the towel tight.

Damn thing had a mind of its own, he thought a second before she yanked off the tape in one shot.

He winced. "You liked that too much."

"Yes, of course. I so enjoy seeing you torn, bleeding and in pain."

Her voice fractured a tiny bit, and Rick wanted to kick himself. Kate was not a vindictive person. There wasn't a mean bone in her beautiful body. It was the reason he'd never confided in her about some of the things he'd done. She wasn't strong enough to hear it. She would turn away. *And what did* not *telling her leave you?* a voice asked. *Except alone?*

She removed the sleeve and draped it over the shower stall, then gathered up the debris. "There are fresh clothes on your bed in your room."

Your bed, *your* room, he thought, remembering when it was "ours."

She left him alone, and Rick decided this had to end. He couldn't take her being here without touching her, without wanting to be inside her and feel her grip him, hear the delicious little sounds she made just before she climaxed in his arms.

God, he wanted his wife. Bad.

And all he got was Florence Nightingale in tight pants.

Dressed in sweatpants and a T-shirt Kate had cut the arm out of, Rick sat on the edge of the bed. She was out there somewhere fussing over something, thinking she was helping when she was just driving him closer to insanity.

Checking his watch, he grabbed the phone and dialed, asking for his battalion executive officer. His C.O. was still with the battalion overseas, but the X.O. had come back with the advanced party to set up the battalion again.

"Sir. I have to inquire, is this nurse necessary?"

"Yes. I've spoken to your surgeon. He let you go home with the express condition that you return to the hospital every two days for a checkup. You missed it, which was a direct order, Marine." Rick winced. Though he'd called, the fact that he'd fallen asleep facedown in his bed for an entire day wasn't excuse enough. "So Dr. Fisher contacted me."

"I don't need a nurse, sir."

"I would think, son, that a pretty woman caring for you would be better than a corpsman in combat boots."

Kate's image burst in his mind, and Rick glanced toward the door. Somewhere in the kitchen, she was clanging pots. Frustrated and annoyed. "Yes, sir. Roger that, sir."

"The fact that it's your wife—"

"Begging the Major's pardon, sir, but she's my ex-wife."

"Not according to the Marine Corps and this state. Not yet. Is that something you can't handle, Captain? She took leave from her job to fill in, at Dr. Fisher's request. The Navy didn't have any nurses to spare."

Rick didn't want any of the troops or their families neglected because hospital personnel were leaving their positions to come check on his sorry butt.

"Recuperate, Captain. We need you back in fighting form."

"Yes, sir."

"And Captain?"

"Sir?"

"Maybe you should take advantage of this opportunity?"

Rick couldn't stop his smile. "You don't know my wife, sir."

"Apparently, Marine, neither do you."

With that, the Major hung up. Rick stared at the receiver, then put the phone back in the cradle.

A pot clanged, dishes chimed.

Yup, he thought, *I'm in the enemy camp with no reinforcements in sight.*

Three

When Rick entered the kitchen, she was prowling through the cabinets, the freezer and fridge, the air punctuated with the snap of cupboard doors and a whole lot of muttering.

"What *are* you doing?"

"Looking for something to cook! Do you know you have only a six-pack of beer, one egg and a jar of pickles in there?" She pointed to the fridge.

His brows shot up. "There's beer?" He crossed the kitchen.

She barricaded the refrigerator door. "Not with painkillers, you don't."

"Kate…" he warned, reaching around her.

She shifted her hip, cutting off his approach. "It'll raise your blood pressure."

She was raising his blood pressure, he thought, and had images of backing her up against the nearest counter and kissing her till she melted.

"When you no longer take them, you can have a beer."

Rick pushed his fingers through his hair. "Jeez, you're a tyrant." Her chin tipped up and he wanted to nibble on it, and keep going—all the way down to the curve in her hip where she was ticklish.

"There isn't any chow," he said patiently, "because I've been deployed for over five months."

"Oh." She knew that, Kate told herself. She'd known exactly where he was, even if she wasn't here. "Well, then it's take-out, I guess."

"I have some MREs in my gear locker."

She made a face. Field rations? "Meals Ready to Eat? Yuck."

He pointed to the bottom drawer near the stove. "Take-out menus are in there."

She opened the drawer and grabbed a handful, sifting. "Pizza, Chinese, Thai, Mexican, sea food?"

"T & W has the best fried oysters in the state."

She glanced at him, arching a brow. "Oh, really?"

"Yeah, I have a standing order." He said it just because he knew it would tick her off. She was too practical to have take-out unless it was a special occasion.

He'd been eating it since she'd left. He could have gone to the mess hall, but he didn't want anyone knowing about his private life. A company commander eating alone in the mess hall would open up too many doors to gossip.

She ordered Chinese, and by the time it was delivered, she had the table set. He was used to eating it right out of the carton, but then, he'd bet she knew that already.

"I'll grocery shop in the morning."

"There's cash over there." He nodded toward the ceramic jar on the counter.

She didn't look, knowing the pretty little tulip-shaped jar was where she'd kept her "house cash."

"Want anything special?" she asked.

"Anything would be great, Kate. But I wonder…is cooking in your job description?"

She made a face at him, spearing her chicken and cashew nuts. "If MREs are the option, it is."

"They taste like heaven in the field. If anything, just to wash away the taste of dust."

"Where were you on deployment?"

He hesitated, then jabbed a piece of food with his fork. "Afghanistan."

Her breath rushed in.

He didn't look up. "I can't tell you any more, Kate, you know that."

"Well, now I know why all the plants are dead."

He glanced at a fern that was so brittle a slight wind would make it disintegrate.

"Why didn't you ask Candice next door to water them for you? I'm sure she would have."

He simply shrugged and Kate studied him.

"You didn't tell anyone I wasn't here, did you?"

"Not anyone's business."

"Not even Jace?" Jace was a lieutenant, Rick's company executive officer. And his friend.

Carefully, he set his fork down, wiped his mouth with a napkin and looked up. "No. Not even him. But they aren't stupid. When you weren't there when I left on the plane, I think they figured something was up."

Kate's face reddened. He'd left for war, and she hadn't been there to see him off.

Rick sensed her pity, and hated it. "They asked. As far as I was concerned the subject was off-limits."

Well, that didn't surprise her. "I see," she muttered, and if she could feel worse, she did. She'd thought about the position she'd put him in many times over the last few months. The Marine Corps was a tightly knit group. They took care of their own. And when it came to gossip, discretion was not the better part of valor.

"It wouldn't have mattered," he said.

"How so?"

"Because *I* still don't get why you left."

Her head jerked up. "Then we really haven't progressed, have we?"

"How about you tell me why you felt the need to walk out on our marriage?"

Why didn't you come after me? she wanted to snap, but said, "I did, Rick, a thousand times. You won't share anything with me."

He made a snide sound. "We talked all the time."

"Sure, we did. About average stuff, what to do on the weekend, what flowers to plant, but I never heard what was in your heart. I don't even know that much about your past."

His features tightened. "It's not as nice as yours. Let's leave it at that."

"Oh, for the love of Mike, this is what I mean. You know, I can even count how many times I've heard you say you loved me!"

I do, she wanted to hear. *I do love you.* But he said nothing, staring. Fuming. He hadn't said how he felt when she'd left, any more than he'd missed her.

"Every time I thought we were finally communicating, that you'd open up and be comfortable enough to share more than the mundane, you'd be off on a deployment and we'd be right back where we were."

"Which was?"

"Not being close enough for two people who planned on spending the rest of their lives together."

"Well, that's not the case now, is it?" He stood, shoving in the chair and picking up his plate. "We aren't sharing our lives anymore, Kate, because *you* split."

He didn't love her enough to stop her. He hadn't even tried, dammit. It would have taken so little, she thought, her eyes tearing up. One call. *Anything.*

"I may have left, Rick Wyatt, but you know what?"

"I'm sure you'll tell me," he snapped, then noticed the tears in her eyes.

"You didn't do a damn thing to stop me." She rushed from the room.

Rick dropped his head forward, exhaling a long, tired breath. He hated himself for making her cry, and she was right, dammit.

He rubbed his face, then drove his fingers through his short hair. If this kept up, it was going to be a long and difficult recovery. And by the end, they'd be shredded.

At three in the morning, Rick stood outside the guest room, watching Kate sleep. If his shoulder wasn't throbbing he'd still be asleep right now.

It felt natural to go find her. How could he resist when she was this close again? She looked like a wood sprite curled on her side, her red hair spread over the pillow. The room was filled with her fragrance, and he stepped inside, lowering himself into the padded chair near the foot of the bed.

It felt familiar, watching her sleep. When they'd first married, he'd lain awake sometimes for hours just staring at her, thinking he was the luckiest man on the planet that she'd fallen in love with him. The day he'd married her he'd thought he'd finally have what he'd dreamed about as a kid.

Someone to love him. Someone who needed him.

He'd grown up without love, and for a while, he'd given up looking for it. Sure, foster parents liked him well enough, but that wasn't the same as when Kate stared into his eyes and he knew she loved only him.

Rick rubbed his face, wondering how everything had gone so wrong, and what he'd done to cause it. It had to be him, he thought. Kate was a man's dream in a wife. A great wife for a Marine, too. She knew damn near every individual in his company by name, plus their families. She'd had the wives over for coffee, checked on the young troops' families when they were deployed.

She'd made Rick look good.

The best thing to happen to him in his life was right now lying in a bed ten feet away, and somehow, he'd let her slip through his fingers. He wanted to grab her back, keep her.

She stirred, shifting from her side to her back. Her thin nightgown strap slid off her shoulder, exposing the lush round curves of her breasts. Like a moth to a flame, he was drawn, moving to her bedside and staring down at her. Moonlight from the window streamed across her body, and his heart ached for her.

Just plain *ached*.

He wanted to crawl in there with her, feel her against him, feel whole again. He'd tried to tell himself he didn't need anyone, but he needed Kate. She'd been the only anchor in a very lonely life. The last year was proof enough. He'd felt lost until he opened the door this morning.

As he stared down at her, a hundred thoughts marched through his brain, torturing him. Good grief, he didn't even know where she lived! Had she dated anyone in the last year? Was she in love with another man? Did whoever it was touch her? The thought of another man putting his hands on her made Rick's stomach tighten, his heart constrict. She was his!

Face it, Marine. You lost her. You screwed up and lost her.

Yet here she was. When he needed her, she'd come running, wanting to take care of him, but not wanting to love him again.

It killed him to know that.

And he was tired of dying a little each day.

He turned away, stopping long enough to grab a painkiller, then headed back to their bed. Alone.

Showered and dressed before dawn, Kate grabbed the copy of Rick's chart and headed for the master bedroom to check in on him. Her brows shot up when she found his bed empty, and she hurried through the house, searching for him.

A little needle of panic shot through her when she couldn't find him.

She stood in the kitchen and shouted, "Rick! Where are you?"

She heard a tap on glass and her gaze shot to the multi-paned window that looked out onto the porch and backyard. He was on the screened porch. She let out a breath, then, grabbing a cup of coffee and tucking the chart under her arm, she stepped out onto the porch. He was on the wicker sofa, his bare feet propped on the matching coffee table, a mug in his fist.

He looked up and she noticed the dark circles under his eyes.

"How long have you been out here?"

"A couple hours."

"You couldn't sleep? Are you in pain?" She touched his forehead, then set the cup down to take his pulse.

He pulled away. "I'm fine. Stop hovering and sit."

Her brows rose. *Unusually grouchy this morning,* she thought, and stepped over his legs to sit.

The sun was just rising, the land coated in a purple-orange haze. It felt familiar, the silence, the glowing sky—Rick beside her on the wicker sofa. If he didn't have to leave at the crack of dawn for some training operation, they'd shared that first cup of coffee right here. Although his time at home was rare, they'd made it a ritual.

She put her feet up, wiggling into the cushions.

"It's been awhile since I had a relaxing morning like this."

Rick glanced to the side. She had her head tipped back, her eyes closed. He wanted to kiss her senseless. "How so?"

"I'm working for two doctors. One's a surgeon. I'm constantly running between the offices and hospital to check on patients, and most times end up with the night shift."

That didn't sound fair to Rick, but then maybe she didn't have anyone to go home to, either. *Don't open that can of worms,* he warned himself, and kept his mouth shut.

"Civilians?"

"Yeah, and they like giving orders just as much as the military. But they're great people." A smile curved her lips and he wondered if she was thinking about some man. One he'd like to pound into the dirt right now.

A fresh headache brewing, he went to rub his forehead before he remembered he was laced into the sling like it was a straight jacket.

"I need to look at the stitches today and change the dressing."

"Later."

She lifted her head to look at him, rebellion in her green eyes. "I have a job to do, Rick." She reached for his coffee cup, eyeing him when he held on to it.

His eyes went dark and dangerous. "You're coming between a Marine and his cup of joe."

"Better call in reinforcements, then." She wrestled the nearly empty cup from him, set it aside, then reached across him and grasped his wrist. She took his pulse.

"God, what a nag," he teased.

She flashed him a smile, her hair falling over her shoulder. "I'm Irish. It's an art form." She let him go, gave him back his coffee, then opened a folder and jotted some notes.

Rick tipped his head to read. His name, rank and serial number were on the edge. "What are you doing with my records?"

"It's just a copy of your surgery report and instructions from Dr. Fisher."

Rick gave her a sidelong glance. "Studying up?"

"It helps to know exactly what they did." She closed the file, clipping the pen to the top. "And Dr. Fisher will want a report." Fisher was a Navy Captain, the equivalent to a Marine Colonel. "Full bird," as they called them.

"Heck, I don't even know what they did. It was a haze."

"Do you want to know?" She offered him the chart.

"Nah, as long as it'll heal, I don't care if they used staples and glue."

"Not quite, but close." Three different teams of doctors had kept him alive, but Dr. Fisher had taken over once Rick was stateside. He'd been sent back to the U.S. for the simple reason that there were so many wounded, they needed the space in Germany. Kate still didn't know the details of how he'd been wounded, and she told herself she probably didn't need to know.

Tossing the folder on the table, she stared at her cup, toying with the handle. "If you want to talk about it, I—"

"No," he interrupted. He wasn't about to tell her that one hellacious Technicolor nightmare had shown him every second of the attack last night. She'd want details. It was too ugly to share.

"I didn't think so."

He opened his mouth to say something, though he didn't know what, but she cut him off. "How about a fresh cup of coffee?"

Rick drained the dregs of his coffee as she stood and tried to maneuver around the table, then decided to step over his legs instead, just as he slid his feet off the table. She lost her balance, and with his good arm, he caught her around the waist and pulled. She landed on his lap.

"Whoa. You almost kissed the concrete."

"Yeah, thanks. Keep those gunboat feet out of the way, huh?" She wanted off, now. A second more and she'd be all over him.

She shifted to push off, and Rick groaned a curse.

She looked at him. "Did I hit your shoulder? Your hand?" A muscle in his jaw worked and Kate frowned, touching his face. "My stars, Rick, you're hot."

"You got that right."

His hand splayed over her hip, the warmth spiraling through her with the feel of his arousal against her hip. The fact that he was hard for her, right now, made her body hum.

"Rick. Let me up, you're going to hurt yourself."

His eyes darkened and he bent his legs, toppling her against him. "Not any more than I already am." His hand moved up her bare thigh.

Desire tumbled through her and she wanted his kiss, his touch. Right now, all over her. Yet she covered his hand, a warning in her eyes. "This won't solve anything, you know."

"It'll help a couple things." His fingers slid under the edge of her shorts, against naked skin. Kate was frozen, hunger battling with common sense. Then his hand moved, his fingertips sliding over her center, pressing, sending hot liquid shots of desire through her body. *More,* her mind begged. *More.* Then her brain kicked in.

"A temporary fix," she managed. With Herculean will, she gripped the arm of the sofa and pulled herself up, then looked back at him, noticing the bulge in his sweatpants and the look in his eye.

Hard and intense. She wondered if he was angry with her or himself. "Try to think of me as a…corpsman."

His gaze roamed her body in its shorts and T-shirt, her nipples outlined through the fabric. Knowing she was aroused made his own body flex with need. "That'd be easier if I didn't know what you look like naked."

His fierce gaze slid over her like warm wine, intoxicating her. Before this got dangerous, she picked up his cup and headed into the kitchen.

Rick stayed where he was, needing time to get a handle on his hunger, deciding he was behaving like a hormone challenged teenager around her. When he could stand, he went into the house, hunting in the cabinets for a toaster pastry. It tasted like ten-year-old MREs, and he reached for his coffee to wash it down.

Kate was rooting in the fridge, her behind displayed for him.

"Trust me, Kate, the grocery fairy didn't show up during the night."

Suddenly she popped up, as if she'd suddenly thought of something. "How about pancakes?" She stepped to the cabinet and pulled out an unopened box of pancake mix. "I forgot I saw this in here yesterday. No doubt it's been here awhile, but it's unopened so it should be okay."

He nodded, watching as she moved around the kitchen, dragging out bowls, a skillet and syrup.

He missed seeing her in here, moving like a professional—efficient, quick. Sexy as hell. She'd fallen in love with the wide-open kitchen with the view to the backyard the instant the Realtor had shown it to them. Rick glanced around. Everything was exactly as she'd left it, minus a couple of burned potholders.

"Sit down, Rick. Before you pass out."

He gave her a sour look, but sat on a stool at the end of the island. He simply watched her, remembering her cooking Thanksgiving dinner for her family the first time. She'd been a nervous wreck, making way too much food. But it had been picture perfect. He'd been so proud of her.

He missed her family, too, he thought. Loud, Irish and happy to argue good-naturedly at the drop of a hat, they'd welcomed him into their fold so easily it had shocked him. Before Kate, he'd been on the outside, and now he was there again.

"How're your brothers?"

Finished preparing the batter, she ladled spoonfuls on the hot griddle. "They're fine. Mom and Dad are on a cruise. Their third." She shrugged. "The Yucatan this time, I think. Connor's working on the West Coast, enjoying being single. We've resigned ourselves that he will never marry." She flipped the pancakes.

It was on the tip of Rick's tongue to say her brother hadn't found the right woman, but he kept his mouth shut. Rick had found the right one and look where they were.

"Sean and Laura are in Texas. His construction company's doing well enough. And Michael…"

She stopped, staring down at the pancakes, then quickly put them on a plate before him.

"Kate? What's wrong? What's up with Mike?"

She lifted his gaze to Rick's as she handed him silverware and syrup. "Nothing. He and Carol are fine."

Rick frowned, cutting into the pancakes. "That's not all, is it?"

"No." She took a deep breath and ladled more batter onto the griddle. "It's good news, actually." Her voice had gone unusually bright. "Michael's going to be a father for the first time."

Rick's features tightened, the words hitting him like a frontal assault. Kate had wanted children. Rick hadn't. He'd felt that the two of them were enough, and admitted that he didn't think he was father material. He hadn't had a role model to know what being a parent was, not to mention a good one, but that wasn't the main problem.

Little kids scared the hell out of him. Give him a hundred raw fresh-out-of-boot-camp Marines and he was fine. But turn a baby loose anywhere near him and he was useless. He couldn't keep his wife; what made him think he could ever be a dad?

His career was too risky for kids, he reasoned, just

as another voice screamed that most Marines had families and did just fine. He jabbed at the pancakes, eating without tasting. But Kate had accepted his feelings on the subject before, and if she didn't understand them, the fact that she wasn't living here and his recent, almost deadly injuries were speaking loud enough now.

Kids would have been a huge mistake. Especially caught in this mess. "That's great for them," he said, focusing on his meal.

"Carol will deliver around April."

Rick looked up, noticing a strange look in Kate's eyes. Slowly, he set the fork down. "They'll make great parents."

"Yes, they will. Michael said he was scared and excited. He's never even held a baby before."

Neither had Rick. "Tell them congratulations for me, will you?"

She nodded, her gaze on the pancakes sizzling on the griddle. He stood, brought his plate to the sink and thanked her for the meal. She murmured something unintelligible, her back to him as she scooped up the remaining pancakes. She slid the pan off the burner and faced him.

When Rick expected a confrontation, he got cool and dictatorial.

"You need to take your medication." She stepped around him, doling it out.

Rick took the painkiller, wanting the foggy oblivion right now. Anything was better than seeing the heartache in her eyes. He headed out of the kitchen.

He was heading for cover, Kate thought, watching him go. Whether Rick admitted it or not, she knew the real reason he didn't want to discuss kids. He didn't want a permanent tie to anyone. Because to have a baby with her would be creating a solid, unbreakable bond even he couldn't ignore.

For a man who'd grown up alone all his life, she'd have thought he would jump at the chance of being a father, making a family, putting down roots. But not Rick. She'd come from a large family and wanted one of her own, but his attitude sent that dream up in smoke.

It was probably good he didn't know that a couple weeks after leaving him, she'd learned she was pregnant. She'd tried to reach him, but he'd been on a mission, out of contact. Telling him now would be pointless. And painful. He didn't want her enough to come after her, but a baby would have made him feel obligated. She didn't want him that way, as if it was a duty.

But then, she didn't have their baby anymore, did she?

And she didn't have him, either.

Four

Rick knew when it was wise to retreat and duck for cover. So when she started barking orders like a drill instructor, he complied, lying on his bed so she could change the dressings. She'd been quiet for the last hour and it made him wary. A quiet Kate O'Malley Wyatt was not a good thing.

It meant that an explosion was coming. Which usually involved a short quick argument ending with some wild sex. It's what he loved about her. When she wanted to kiss and make up, she left nothing to chance. But now she wore that determined look of a trained nurse ready to do battle.

With a stack of sterile supply trays wrapped in plastic, she sat beside him, removed the sling, his shirt, then peeled back the bandages above the cast. Her touch was delicate and careful, but he couldn't look at her.

"How many have you got of those?" He nodded to the sterile packs.

"The Navy hospital gave me several. They were generous. But then, you hold a special place in Lieutenant Roker's heart."

Rick made a face. "She's a warhorse who doesn't know the words *let me sleep*. That woman poked and prodded at the strangest hours." It was the reason he'd asked to leave the hospital. That and sheer boredom.

"You loved it. She was quite taken, mentioned something about a sponge bath."

His gaze zeroed in on Kate like a heat-seeking missile. "I like the one I had with you more."

Something momentarily softened in her eyes, dived right into his heart and stirred him up. Then she was all-business.

"Be still. When you get the stationary pins out it will be easier to move around without them bumping into things."

As she spoke, she opened the pack, arranging mountains of gauze, then unrolled what looked like surgical instruments. "You know how to use all that?" he asked.

"Of course. We use them in E.R., most times we have to do triage surgery. But I've trained as a surgical nurse for the past year." She'd had to do something to use up the time alone or she'd have gone crazy. Watching the door, listening for the phone that never rang.

She placed his cast on a pillow. "You have to keep the shoulder immobile so the internal stitches can heal. Moving it around will tear them, and you could end up back in surgery. So promise me you won't try to use this arm."

When he didn't say anything, she looked at him.

His brows shot up. "You want actual words?"

"Yes."

"Don't trust me?"

"When it comes to you not pushing yourself to heal faster than you can? Nope, not a lick."

"I promise."

She made a comical noise like a crowd cheering. "Victory! Ohh-rah." She grinned, then said, "Now just relax and this will go a lot easier."

"They always say that when it's going to hurt."

"Is that fear I hear?"

"Do your worst, Miss Nightingale."

Carefully, she peeled back the layers of padding, and when she saw his wound, she swallowed and forced her features to remain still. "Looks like someone already did." He'd been shot in the back, and while there was a clean hole there, the exit wound was tattered.

Rick watched her, and while he admired her

methodically efficient nursing skills, it felt cold to him. As if his Kate had stepped out and someone else was within his grasp as she leaned over him, cleaning the wound, inspecting the stitches.

"It's looking good. Can you lift your arm a little?" He did, but when it started to tremble violently, she laid it back down on the pillow.

He cursed.

"It will get better, Rick," she told him. "The wound nicked an artery. You're lucky you didn't bleed to death."

He knew that, and thanked God for the Navy corpsman attached to his unit who'd rushed through gunfire to help him.

Kate sterilized the area, not at all shocked when he didn't flinch, didn't move. After redressing the wound, she helped him back into the sling. She knew he was in pain, his breathing hard, yet his expression didn't change. She collected her instruments and left to put them in a basin, and when she returned, he was out cold. She checked his pulse, satisfied the painkillers had kicked in.

She left him to sleep, but stopped in the hall, grabbing the wall and covering her mouth, muffling the sobs trying to escape. Her heart broke for him. Rick was a Marine down to his bones, in his soul, and from the looks of that wound, he might never be one again.

It would destroy him.

* * *

Rick woke to the sound of voices. Women's voices.
Lots of them. He managed to dress in jeans and a
T-shirt, but skipped the shoes and socks. He moved
down the hall cautiously, waiting for the attack of females he could hear laughing and chatting away in the
kitchen. Some voices sounded familiar, and when he
stepped inside, he wasn't as stunned as he might be.

Marine wives had infiltrated his kitchen. They'd regrouped and brought supplies. The island counter was
laden with covered dishes and cakes, plastic containers of food. There was even a couple bottles of wine
and a stack of books. Kate stood near the end of the
counter, smiling, pouring coffee, slicing a breakfast
cake someone had obviously brought. She looked so
happy right now the sight struck him in the chest.

His gaze moved over the group of about a dozen
women, recognizing his commanding officer's wife,
and the Sergeant Major's wife, right beside her as always. The room quieted as one by one they noticed
him. They all stared, and he felt suddenly self-conscious of his bare feet.

"Good morning, ladies."

They murmured a greeting, looking back and forth
from him to Kate. He felt as if he were standing inspection, they were staring so hard.

Kate heard a couple envious sighs from the women.
Rick's snug black T-shirt and worn jeans were enough

to give her palpitations. Add to that the sexy, sleepy-eyed look and he made her want to drag him into the bedroom and have her way with him. Rick caught her gaze and, as if he recognized the look, he winked.

The Colonel's wife, Janet, stood, coming around the table edge. "How are you feeling, Captain?" She moved toward him, deep concern in her eyes.

"Better than I was a few days ago, ma'am."

"Alan called me just afterward." Her gaze flicked to the cast and bandages. "You look better than I expected."

"Thank you, ma'am."

"Look, Rick. Food." Kate glanced at her friends. "Apparently they're aware of your culinary skills and sent in rations."

"Honey, we did it for you," Kelly, the Sergeant Major's wife, said. "We're all so glad you survived, Captain."

There was a collective nodding of agreement.

"It could have easily been one of our husbands."

"I appreciate this, ma'am, ladies." He nodded to the others, still feeling on display. It was tough being the only one of the battalion back home, even if he was wounded.

"Well, you have the best of care with Kate. In that we won't worry."

"When we didn't see Kate at the predeployment formation, we wondered why," a young wife said. A couple other women nudged her.

Kate blushed and started to speak, not knowing what she'd say that wouldn't embarrass them both, but Rick spoke up.

"We said our goodbyes in private the night before." With a devilish grin, he slipped up beside her and put his arm around her shoulder. "And Kate had an emergency at the hospital that morning. I figured saving a life was more important than seeing me off with a thousand smelly grunts."

They laughed, but Kate stared up at him, realizing he'd saved her many uncomfortable questions about their relationship—maybe even her reputation—with that bald-faced lie. He kissed the top of her head, and when she looked up at him, she wondered just how much of Rick she wasn't seeing because she wanted to *hear* him express his feelings.

What if she was the one who'd failed them? She'd hoped that by her leaving and spending some time apart, he would have been moved to action. But what if he was just as scared as she was? She felt suddenly ashamed of herself. As if sensing it, Rick stayed beside her, leaning on her, touching her and joining in the conversation. When the Colonel's wife stood to say goodbye, like a well-trained squad, the women all headed for the door. Kate saw them out, hugging each one.

After they'd left she closed the door and looked at him, grinning. "Want to pig out? Janet, Kelly and Christine are the best cooks in the battalion."

Like kids cut loose from the shadow of a parent, they went into the kitchen, investigating the dishes and sampling everything.

"You're a better cook."

"I won't tell the Colonel's wife you said that." Kate glanced up, her smile mischievous. "But thanks, I haven't cooked in a while."

"No fun doing it for one, huh?"

She went still for a second. "No, Rick, it's not."

He heard the bite in her tone, and sighed. "Kate, how about we call a truce?"

"I wasn't aware we were at war."

"If we keep butting heads we will be, and I don't want that."

"Yes, you need to rest."

"It's not that," he snapped, then took a breath. More softly he said, "I just don't want to walk around on eggshells—and you shouldn't have to, not when you're helping me."

She met his gaze over a pot roast that was still steaming. "Agreeing to disagree?"

"Yeah."

"Deal."

He dug a fork into the center of a cherry pie, and she shrieked. "Rick, stop that!" She cut a generous slice and served it on a plate. "Your manners have gone to the dogs. Next you'll be drinking right out of the milk carton."

"Possible. No one around to keep me in line." He winked again and her heart dipped.

"Go to the couch." She pointed the way.

"Ma'am, yes ma'am."

Rick smiled on his way back into the living room, thinking it had taken so little to get a rise out of her again. His mind latched on to the other ways he could do that, and he sat, groaning, and eating cherry pie without really tasting it.

This is your mess, he thought, and not for the first time. *How are you going to fix it?*

It was after midnight when Kate heard a strange noise—a deep groan laced with agony. She left her bed and hurried into the master bedroom. In the dark, Rick twisted and writhed, a nightmare locking him in its grip. She came to the bedside, calling his name, afraid that his thrashing would break the stitches or bump a pin. She leaned closer.

"Rick, honey, it's over. You're here with me."

Yet the dream raged on. He twisted on the sheets, muttering something that sounded like commands. *He's reliving the battle in his dreams.* He was breathing hard, his face contorted, his fist clenched. She pressed a knee to the mattress and started to wake him, then remembered that when she'd startled him awake in the past, he would come up swinging, fist primed. He could injure himself further, she thought, and bent low, whispering his name.

It hurt to see him so tortured, straining against invisible bonds, damning the gunfire going on around him in his dreams. She leaned close to his ear.

"Rick, it's a dream. Wake up."

"My men," he muttered.

"They're out of danger. Reinforcements are here," she said, hoping he'd calm down. He was going to rip the stitches open. He arched sharply, flailing, and Kate shifted closer, laying her hand on his brow. He was sweating, but clammy and cold, and her eyes teared up. What had he suffered?

"It's over," she said softly.

"Kate," he moaned, his eyes still closed.

"I'm here, darling. I'm here." She curled in beside him, reassuring him. He calmed, his breathing softening, and she kissed his cheek, pressing a hand over his wildly beating heart. "I'm here, Rick."

"Don't leave me." His voice broke.

And her heart shattered, her eyes burning. Suddenly, she needed to hold him, and settled closer. She laid her head on his uninjured shoulder, stroking his face, his arm, waiting until he drifted into a peaceful sleep.

A serene contentment enveloped her, warm and safe and needed. It was deceiving, and she fought the urge to stay right there and sink into her own dreams. Certain he was sleeping peacefully, she slipped off the bed and padded back to the guest room.

She wanted to stay, but Rick wouldn't want her to know she'd seen him like that. It brought new questions. Was she hoping for a change in him that wasn't going to happen? He was a private person, but she felt it was from years of being so alone and isolated, tossed through the foster care system, then dumped on an uncle who couldn't have cared less about him.

Maybe Rick had expected her to leave, too, and had kept himself back in case she did?

And then, damn her heart, she'd gone and done so, confirming his worst fears by walking out.

Rick was groggy when he woke the next morning. That was the reason he hated talking pills. It felt like a cloud fuzzed his brain, making his reactions slow, his thoughts jumbled. Nightmares did that worse than the drugs, yet last night's dream hadn't been as bad as the others. Vaguely, he remembered dreaming of Kate's touch, hearing her voice drift through his mind. He could almost feel her body pressed to his side. He shook his head, deciding that he was fabricating it all because she was here, so close and so untouchable.

He walked into the kitchen and poured a cup of coffee. When he heard music, he followed the sound to the back porch. He stopped in the doorway, smiling.

Now that was a pleasant sight—Kate bent over the lawnmower, adding gas. But his attention zipped right to her shorts, frayed cutoffs hinting at the curves of her behind. The skin-tight pink tank top hugged her breasts, proving she wasn't wearing anything under it.

Going to be a helluva morning, he thought, already feeling the strain to his body.

Not making himself known, he sat on the wicker sofa and propped his feet on the table, his arm on a pillow. No reason to piss her off when she was giving him such a nice view. He wanted to help, but knew she'd force him into submission.

As she had last night. They'd sat around like pals, watching movies, not getting too near, not touching the topic of their impending divorce. It made Rick sick to think about it, but he was treading carefully, and wisely, kept his mouth shut and just enjoyed being with her again. He'd missed her so damn much, and for a while there it felt like it used to be—a little exciting to be near her, and comfortable knowing she was around.

He nursed his coffee, watching as she pulled the rip cord and started the engine. She wore a pair of women's combat boots he'd bought for her, and a red USMC baseball cap. She mowed the back lawn around the small swimming pool while Rick admired the muscles in her thighs and her tight behind in the sexy shorts. He'd been so proud to have her as his wife— not because she was drop-dead gorgeous as much as the fact that she had a heart as big as the country. Being here, despite their troubles, proved it again.

The engine stopped and she moved the mower to one side. When she saw him, she stopped in her tracks.

"How long have you been up?"

He told her. "You've been at it early." He gestured to the couple dozen nursery pots of flowers ready to be planted.

She shielded her eyes as she walked closer. "Already out to the grocery store and back. I thought these would look nice. You don't mind, do you?"

"Of course not, and stop asking me about stuff like it's not your home, too." She opened her mouth, and he shot to his feet. "I know what I said, but it is."

"Does that mean I get to take over the bathroom?"

He groaned. "God, no."

Smiling, she dusted off her hands as she entered the screened porch. "How are you feeling?"

"Outstanding."

She eyed him, then frowned. "Sit down."

"I'm tired of sitting. I'm tired of doing nothing."

"Too bad. Play a video game."

"With one hand?"

"Duck hunt?"

He smirked. "Not a challenge."

"Janet left books. Read one."

"Maybe later."

"What can I help you with?" she asked.

"Nothing," he fairly snarled.

Kate let that glide off her, knowing he'd had a nightmare last night. "Then come out and sit while I plant."

She grabbed a lawn chair and a pillow and he followed her out into the sun. Rick took the pillow, his gaze warning her away, and she knelt and started digging.

"Seeing anyone?" he asked.

She jerked around to stare at him. How could he ask that? she thought in annoyance then she took a breath. "No, you?"

"Obviously not, if you're here and she's not."

"You're a lousy patient. I'm not surprised."

"There isn't anyone else, Kate. There never will be."

She froze and met his gaze. He hadn't said anything like that to her in a long long time. What was she supposed to say? Thanks? Good to know? *If there won't be anyone else, then why can't you confide in me?* He was her husband. In some ways they'd shared as much as two people could, and knew each other intimately. Rick's "keep it all in" was what had ruined the core of their marriage.

She didn't say anything, but stood, leaning down to kiss him tenderly. She couldn't form words, couldn't express what that meant to her in any other way.

Then she went back to planting.

But Kate was having more than second thoughts. Heck, they'd plagued her for days after she'd left, when she'd learned she was pregnant with a child he'd never wanted. She'd lain in a hospital knowing she was losing the only connection to him, and that he hadn't wanted any bonds that tight.

And if the last few days were any indication, those bonds were still unwanted.

Five

Rick didn't know what was ticking him off—her re-action to what he'd told her, or his inability to understand his own wife after all this time. He'd expected more from her, and for a woman who wanted him to express himself, she wasn't upping the ante any. He'd spent far too much time dissecting that kiss, and by dinner, he was sawing one handed into his sirloin steak as if he was cutting barbed wire.

He was being stubborn by refusing her help—that much he recognized—but as if fate interfered, his weak grip slipped.

The knife clattered to the floor just as his fork went airborne like a grenade, arching high.

"Incoming," Kate said, and they both watched it land on the kitchen floor. She looked at him, her lips twitching.

"Go on," he groused sourly. "Let it out. You look like you're going to bust a gut."

She lost it, her laughter filling the house like music. He'd missed that sound.

"I'd say my point was made rather well," she teased.

He pushed the plate toward her. "Fine, go ahead."

She retrieved the flying fork, set it in the sink and then pulled her chair close to cut his steak for him.

"Want a bib, too?"

"Want me to stuff a rag in your mouth?"

"Like that would do any good." She grinned, speared a piece of meat and held it poised at his mouth.

"I can manage from here." He snapped up the bite anyway, then took the fresh fork from her.

"I saw new woodworking stuff in the garage."

"It's just some basic tools, and a project I'd started."

"I didn't know you liked building things."

"I didn't, either. It was sheer boredom and watching way too many home and garden shows that did it."

"Garden?"

"I was making a window box." He thought for a second. "I think that's what it was. I didn't get very far before the last deployment. The Sergeant Major was teaching me. He's a real whiz at it."

"I've seen some of his recent work."

"Yeah? When?"

"When I was at Kelly's for a coffee with the wives."

"You haven't been for a year."

She arched a brow. "Says who?"

He frowned.

"I still keep in touch. I didn't want them to know, either. It's not like they wouldn't speculate when we weren't seen together."

"At least my men keep a lid on talk."

She laughed shortly. "Ha, who are you fooling? They're the worst. Oh, they'll never reveal classified stuff, but if you think men don't gossip, you're wrong. Everyone has an opinion, and everyone is looking for something to pick at to avoid looking at their own lives."

Rick winced, thinking how he'd immersed himself in work rather than come home to an empty house. Avoiding the issues, he thought sourly. "Well then, my men are still over there, *gossiping* and not cleaning their weapons."

She liked his teasing smile. That was the Rick she remembered. "They've only got a couple weeks till they return. And I'm betting they're anxious to know how you are, though I'm sure Janet reported to her husband, and Kelly to the Sergeant Major. You'll be the talk of the camp."

"What a thrill."

There was a stretch of silence before she said, "Were you afraid?"

He looked up. "No."

She made a face, clearly not buying that.

"I wasn't." He shrugged. "Not till I got hit. I was afraid I'd lose consciousness and someone else would die because I wasn't watching their six." *And that I'd never see you again,* he added silently. She'd been his only thought the instant he'd realized he was shot. He'd had to force her out of his mind, tend to his wound until the corpsman reached him. But she'd never left his thoughts, and he'd prayed he'd live long enough to have another chance to hold her.

Hadn't he sworn to himself that he'd take that chance when he was well enough to get to her? That he wouldn't let her slip away again? As if he'd *let* her slip away. She'd been right before. He hadn't stopped her; he had just accepted. Why, when he wouldn't accept defeat on the battlefield, did he give up so easily with the only person he loved more than living?

War and love were not fair.

"You're such a hero," she teased, batting her lashes and fanning herself.

"Yeah, but I can't cut my own steak."

"That's why you have me," she said primly.

"I can think of other reasons to have you."

She looked up, and his gaze locked on her like a target. Kate could almost feel it touch her skin, and every inch of her body sprang to life with a desire so strong it demanded satisfaction. *Right now.* Her skin tingled; the area between her thighs flushed. Before their separation, Rick and she would have been tearing at each other on the floor by now. But that was then.

"Or rather, *ways* to have you."

"Rick…"

"I won't hide the fact that you light me up like a nuclear warhead, Kate."

"So you like walking around all…" She gestured to his jeans.

"Hard for you?" He grinned at her sweet blush. "Better than being dead."

Her teasing smile melted instantly. "Don't say that!" She stared at him, her lower lip trembling, memories of seeing him torn and bleeding ripping through her mind. "Don't ever say that!"

She started to leave the table, but he covered her hand with his and kept her there. "I'm okay, baby."

"But you could have *died*."

"We both knew that could happen."

"Yes, I knew that! But I don't want a folded flag, Rick. I don't want the regrets of a grateful nation. Don't do this again."

"I can't promise that and you know it."

She let out a breath. She should be used to this, and wondered if the Sergeant Major's wife ever was. Or Janet. Their husbands had been in the Marines for over twenty-five years. Kate didn't bother to remind herself that she and Rick were legally separated. Her feelings were strong and wounded, and still focused on him.

She didn't want to be free of him, and as she lifted her gaze, she knew she *had* to use this chance for something more than helping him get back to the career he loved enough to take a bullet.

"I know," she muttered as she stood to gather plates.

He caught her around the waist, pulling her close.

"I'll watch my six, I swear. If for no other reason than not to see that look in your eyes."

Her throat tightened and she leaned down and whispered, "Right now, *I'm* watching that six. And it's such a nice backside to see." Then she kissed him.

Rick didn't let it stay chaste; pulling her down on his lap and devouring her mouth. He was starved for her, his hand sliding up her bare thigh to her breast. He cupped her, massaged her and her soft moan was a gift. His hand roamed, his tongue dipped and teased. He could feel the heat building in her.

"God, I've missed you."

"Sex or me?"

"I'm a guy. I can't separate the two."

She smiled against his mouth, still balancing the plates and kissed him some more. Then she stood, and as if nothing had happened, she went to the sink.

"Forget those, I'll help with them later."

"They're my grandmother's dishes, Rick. Did I ever let you handle them?"

"There is a first time for everything."

"Yeah, sure. When you have two working hands, maybe."

That hit him hard, again. "God, I hate being helpless."

She sighed, dropping her head forward. "You know what?" She faced him. "I'm sick of this bitching."

"Excuse me?"

"So you can't do for yourself and you don't like it. Big deal. Get over it, Marine. In the grand scheme of things that *could have* happened to you, not being able to cut meat or shower without falling is pretty minor."

He blinked up at her. It was the explosion he'd been waiting for.

"Is that who you are, Rick? Two hands? I sure as heck don't see you that way. You're a Marine. Improvise, adapt, overcome."

"With you jumping down my throat when I try to do anything?"

"Because you're fighting your own recovery!"

She moved in like a wild tigress—in his face—and he fought his smile. She looked magnificent, her eyes flashing brightly, her cheeks flushed.

"You were shot, for pity's sake. You can't expect to magically be in peak Marine condition because it annoys you. Part of improvising is asking for help. Part of overcoming pain is doing the things you need to so you're *not* hurting. You have three more days of complete rest, and when the stitches come out—if you be-have—I'll ask the doctors to cut down the pins so they won't be in the way so much. Once they're removed, it's smooth sailing till you start with therapy. So—" she cocked her hip, folded her arms "—how about you make this a little easier on both of us and stop re-fusing my orders, and just do them!"

"Anything else, ma'am?" he said, his lips stretch-ing in a wide grin.

It startled her. "Yeah. Behave. Don't try to lift any-thing, do anything, with that arm, so I can take a bath without worrying."

"I will park my six on the sofa." He crossed his heart.

She eyed him doubtfully.

"Unless you're going to let me watch."

Her cheeks reddened.

He leaned down in her face, his husky voice driv-ing through her like a blade. "It's not like I haven't seen and kissed *and* tasted every inch of you."

Kate sputtered, then simply pointed to the living room, but her hand trembled. Heck, her whole body trembled.

Rick arched a brow with a sexy look, giving her an-other chance to reconsider.

Kate knew she was about to give in so she straight-ened her shoulders and pointed harder. "Go, now. Sofa. On the double. Or *I'll* take those stitches out with a butter knife!"

He spun around and marched out, smiling to himself over that little outburst. Even if she tried to smother her feelings now and then, he'd seen them in her eyes, and it gave Rick a sense of purpose he'd lost when she'd walked away.

Kate came out of the bathroom feeling relaxed and ready for a glass of wine. She poured one, taking it with her to the living room. Rick was sifting through movie DVDs when she sat on the sofa.

He glanced up, his gaze traveling swiftly over her Doris Day pajamas, the satin thin and clinging to her curves.

"Is that chick camouflage?" he said.

She glanced down. "Comfort."

"I remember a little red number you had." He wiggled his brows.

"Little is right."

"It looked good tossed on the bedroom floor."

Inside she went absolutely giddy with desire, then smothered it, leaning over to look at the movies. She plucked one out, waiting for some grief from him. But he took it and loaded it in the player.

"You'll like it."

"I doubt it. Nothing explodes in this movie."

She nudged him. "Give it a chance." Kate busied herself with propping pillows for him and fussing during the credits.

He caught her hand. "Are you going to hover all the time?"

"I'm a nurse. It's what I do best."

"No more nurse tonight, okay?"

She sat down on the sofa, then propped her feet on the coffee table.

A half hour later, Rick was still watching. Kate was sound asleep beside him. Smiling to himself when she wiggled into the cushions, he scooted closer and she snuggled to his side, her hand on his stomach. He wouldn't wake her. She'd been doing so much since she showed up, besides driving him nuts.

After the movie, which was good even if nothing blew up, he turned off the set and shifted so she was more comfortable. His uninjured arm around her, Rick closed his eyes, thankful that she was in his arms, even if she didn't know it or want it.

Early in the morning, Rick was dangling his feet in the pool, reading the latest thriller and trying not to drop the book in the water, when a sudden blast of noise from the house made him glance up.

What the hell?

He was up and moving fast, the book discarded. He burst in the back of the house and winced at the music combined with the vacuum. He didn't know which was worse or louder, but when he walked into the living room, Kate was dancing to some old Temptations music as if the vacuum were her partner. She looked like she was having a blast.

She'd always cleaned or cooked to music, just not quite this loud.

He leaned against the nearest wall, watching her hips gyrate, her breasts bounce quite nicely. And when she did that hip curling motion that was too much like she did when they were making love and she was on top, Rick decided he was just asking for punishment.

He called to her.

She paused and looked around, smiling when she found him. She shut off the vac.

"Is that necessary?" He gesture to the stereo.

"Just putting a little do in my honey-do list. Breakfast is on the table for you."

He smiled as she turned back to the world's most boring chore, then went into the kitchen. He sat down to the enormous meal she'd prepared, catching a glimpse of her through the doorway as she bebopped down the hall. Amused, he shook his head.

He felt better this morning, less groggy. No nightmares. Kate had slept beside him on the couch until three in the morning, and when he woke, he was covered with a blanket, his legs on the sofa, and she was gone. Dammit. How was he supposed to win her back if she kept her distance?

A few minutes later all was quiet and she started to join him, then noticed a lightbulb was out in the kitchen.

"I can do that," he offered.

"Orders…" she reminded him, and grabbed the step stool and bulb, climbing up. She wasn't tall and had to stretch. Rick rose out of his chair just as she lost her balance. She shrieked and he caught her with his good arm. Her feet dangled off the floor.

"Rick! Put me down. You'll hurt yourself."

He met her gaze head-on. "I'll never let you fall," he said, setting her down.

Her breath caught at the strength of his tone. She stared at him for a long moment, then said, "Let me check your stitches."

He snatched her wrists. "I'm fine, no pain. I swear."

"Okay, okay." She climbed onto the step stool again, and this time Rick held her steady. The bare skin of her thighs was cool beneath his hands and he wanted to stroke her a little higher, under those shorts, but she'd probably fall again.

"How about a swim after breakfast?"

She eyed him and stepped down.

"Okay, I'll sit, you swim."

Good grief, he was really bored, Kate thought. While the house had come with a pool, Rick rarely used it because it wasn't long enough for laps. Floating around lazily wasn't his idea of fun.

"Sure. I'll get the sleeve." She smirked up at him. "Think you could manage getting those jeans off, or do you need he—"

He eyed her.

"I'll let you slide this time."

He went to change and when he returned, she was already out by the pool, a couple of lounge chairs set up, with towels. Rick stopped short when he saw her in her bathing suit—if that's what you'd call it. She couldn't put on a one-piece? Did she have to wear that skimpy thing? Then he remembered she'd bought it for him, swearing she wouldn't be seen in public in something so sparse.

It barely covered her.

And she must have seen something in his expression because she adjusted it and said, "I found it in an old beach bag. I didn't bring a suit."

Like that mattered?

The bright pink flowered bikini was nothing more than a couple of triangles. Rick groaned as he sat in a lounge chair, wondering how long it would take for him to go clinically insane with hunger for his own wife. He lay back, closed his eyes and absorbed the sun. When he heard the splash of water, he cracked open one eye. Okay—wet, she was worse. Well…better, actually.

Diving off the board wasn't much help, either. Everything bounced. If he wasn't half covered in plaster and stitched up, he'd try his damndest to get her into bed.

She swam to him, leaning on the edge of the pool.

"You can get in with the sleeve, you know. I can blow up an inner tube or the float."

"Maybe later. The flowers look nice." He nodded to the flower beds she had planted the day before.

She glanced around, admiring them. "Till I kill them."

"Your green thumb is a little tainted."

She made a sour face, but didn't deny the truth.

"You have other talents. Want to test them out?"

Her attention snapped back to him. "Are you trying to provoke me?"

"I guess that depends to what end."

"I'm not sleeping with you. That won't help things between us."

"You're avoiding the question."

"I refuse to answer on the grounds that it might ruin this lovely day."

He shook his head. "Not good enough, babe. Truth."

"Oh, we're doing truth or dare?"

Oops, he thought. "One truth."

"Yes, I still want you." Like mad, like crazy. It was taking everything she had to keep from provoking *him*.

Explosions went off inside him. "Now?"

"Don't go there. My turn. A truth."

He braced himself.

"What was the first thought that went through your mind when you realized you'd been hit?"

He leaned forward in the lounge chair, his gaze locked with hers. His voice was smooth and buttery soft when he said, "You, Kate."

She blinked.

"I wanted to stay alive to see you again."

Her eyes burned, and she saw the honesty in his expression. Kate felt as if she'd just been given a gift.

His gaze raked her as if he was *seeing* her for the first time. "God, I've missed you. *You*," he stressed. "Not sex. Well, there is that." He flashed a devilish smile. "But I've felt…"

She waited, breathless.

"…empty."

Kate glanced away, her throat tightening. It was a step, she thought, looking back at him when he spoke again.

"It was like being thrown back into the orphanage or foster homes. I didn't have a place anymore."

Her heart aching, she left the water, grabbing a towel and wrapping it around herself as she sat beside him. He lay back in the lounge chair, holding her hand. "When I was on that plane from Kandahar, I was so doped up, but I kept thinking, I'll never recover enough for Recon again. And I didn't have you, so then what?"

"You will be fit. I'm here to make sure of it."

"Why are you doing this, Kate? I know it's not easy for you. It sure isn't for me."

"Because no matter what's happened between us,

I know being a Marine is what you love. You won't stop being a perpetual grouch till you're back to full speed."

His thumb made a slow circle over the back of her hand. He leaned forward, bringing it to his lips for a kiss. "Thank you."

Kate's heart tore a little. She wanted to beg him to tell her more of his feelings, but she suspected they were locked up in some private spot that he didn't even share with himself. Part of her said, *Leave him be, it's just the way he is.* But pure Irish stubbornness told her that this was where they went wrong. She'd never felt totally his, never felt completely intimate with him because he wouldn't share his past. His pain. She suspected there was more to his reasons for not confiding in her, a little insecurity he'd never admit to having, maybe. Yet she savored this moment more than anything. It gave her something she hadn't thought she'd find again: hope.

A dark cloud moved into her thoughts, and she wondered what would happen when he learned she'd been pregnant with his child.

A day later Rick was wondering if she was deliberately torturing him. A week later he was an idiot.

She pranced around in the sexiest clothes, showing off more skin, and he was almost willing to give up national secrets if she'd stay closer, kiss him like she had before.

He stood in the shower, knowing she was outside the door. He could hear her humming. He was managing fine. She'd installed one of those soap dispensers for him, but insisted on being nearby in case he needed anything. He didn't mind, except his thoughts were locked on dragging her into the shower with him. Of course, he couldn't actually *do* anything worthwhile, and that put a damper on his desire. A little. Very little. But things would change. He was getting the stitches taken out this morning.

He felt like a kid going to see Santa.

Not that he'd ever done that when he was a child. Although Kate could take the stitches out herself, the surgeon had to give the okay. Kate had gone beyond the call and had given him a decent military haircut, but she'd convinced him that as much as he wanted to be back in uniform, it just wouldn't work around the cast, pins and bandages.

He shut off the water and stepped out. She was there with towels, and he let her be Nurse Nelly. He'd been doing anything to keep her by him, to provoke her care. And the way she was drying him off said he was getting to her.

As she was to him.

All day, every second. Man. He wanted her. So much that all he had to do was think about it and he was ready.

She wrapped the towel around his waist and then worked the plastic sleeve off.

"I've got to change. You going to be okay?"

"Sure, fine. But you look nice now," he said, taking in the miniskirt and sleeveless top she was wearing.

"Oh, I don't think so."

"Why?"

"This is not the attire of a Company Commander's wife."

"But we're separated. Legally."

She looked so hurt just then, he could have kicked himself.

"Not to anyone in the battalion. And it doesn't matter." She turned sharply and left.

She was dressing up for him, he thought, giving the public the best impression. It made him smile, even as he decided their relationship was like one of those spinning plates balancing on a stick. Keep the stick wiggling or they'd crash.

A half hour later, he was pacing by the front door when she came out, looking too damn sexy in a red blouse and skirt. His gaze lowered to her stocking-covered legs and the high-heeled pumps. He whistled softly and she blushed, smoothing the line of her skirt.

"You know…I don't have a weapon to fend off the troops. I'd hate to have to clean someone's clock today."

She rolled her eyes, smiling and nudging him out the door. "Me too, since that would be disobeying *my* orders—*command* orders—and you'd end up in the brig, ruin your reputation and wouldn't get that cherry lollipop after you get your stitches out."

He chuckled. "I think I'd risk it. Even for a cherry sucker."

Kate smiled and climbed behind the wheel. Yet Rick's mind locked on one fact.

With the stitches out and all the heavy bandages gone, he could do more. Not much, but whatever it was, he planned on doing it with her.

Six

In the kitchen, Kate had the radio going as Rick moved in behind her, swift and silent.

"What's up?"

She hopped out of the chair so fast it fell back. "For heaven's sake, Rick. Don't creep up on me like that!" she said, covering her heart.

"Sorry." The apology lost something when he gave her that sexy lopsided smirk that sent her pulse into overdrive. Then he examined the fabrics and machine on the kitchen table. He'd forgotten that she'd left it here. "Sewing? I haven't seen you sew in years."

"I know. If it's straight lines, I can manage."

"What's it going to be? Because I can't tell." He lifted the corner of some fabric and foam.

"It's a pad for your shoulder and neck," she explained, as if he should know. When his brows shot up, she added, "The sling strap is chafing." She reached out and touched his throat where it was already red this morning. "Since you have to wear it for a long time, I thought…" She shrugged, suddenly feeling silly.

"It's better than the towel I was going to stuff there. I didn't think it was the manly thing to do."

"Unless it was camouflaged?"

He grinned at her.

"The hospital has pads for things like that. Lieutenant Roker should have seen to it."

"I guess that sponge bath wasn't as exciting as she thought." He winked and Kate's insides clenched.

"I don't see how." Good grief, she thought. She was breathless just thinking about him wet and soapy and naked.

As if he could read her mind, his expression grew somber and heated.

Immediately, Kate sat down at the machine again, trying to catch her breath. He was her husband, for heaven's sake. It wasn't as if they hadn't had some exciting sex in the last few years, and right now she was feeling as if she'd just met him. She glanced at him as he sat in a nearby chair, then she continued sewing.

He was behaving a little differently. Ever since he'd had the stitches removed, his mood had changed, almost overnight. Kate couldn't be more pleased, because a grouchy Rick was no fun at all. But this man was just, well, more at ease. It made her wary. She was already weak for wanting him, and inside she was terrified that everything would go wrong and she'd get her heart broken once more. She didn't want the fantasy of being with him again to cloud her thoughts. But it was.

She sewed faster, the machine vibrating the table. Then, when she was satisfied with her work, she went to him, unlacing the sling and sliding into place the small pad that would protect the side of his throat and the back of his neck.

He stretched his head like an ostrich, testing it. "That's great, babe. I didn't realize how much it irritated till now."

"With the grump level at an all-time high, how could anyone tell?"

He gave her a sly look. "I'm not a grump."

"Of course not." She patted his head, then cleaned up her mess.

Rick moved as if to help with the machine, but when she eyed him pointedly, he sank back into the chair, enjoying watching her move around.

"Hungry?"

"God, no, after that breakfast? I bet I've gained a

couple pounds already." He patted his stomach. Her gaze stopped there, and he felt heat charge through him when it traveled lower. Then, suddenly, she was looking around as if searching for something to do or, God help him, clean.

"You want to help me finish the window box?" he said abruptly.

She looked at him. "Using a saw? I don't know—"

"The wood is already cut. It just has to be assembled and sanded. I think with vise grips we can manage."

We. Kate was too pleased about this to balk at being around power tools.

"Sure." She grabbed a soda for each of them and they went into the garage. While he pulled out some planks of wood, Kate started some laundry and puttered.

"Come on, don't be afraid."

She thrust her chin up. "I'm not."

"Hell you aren't. Remember when you tried to hang a picture in the back hall?"

"Don't remind me, please." She'd swung the hammer so hard she'd missed the nail, smashed her finger and worse, put the hammer right through the wall. He'd teased her mercilessly for the two days it took him to repair her mistake. Kate acknowledged her limits after that.

Rick instructed her on how to clamp the planks in the vise to sand the edges, then together they worked to nail together and clean up the window box. It seemed like such a simple thing, her nailing as he held the wood, Rick teasing her not to nail his only working fingers to the board. Yet it gave her so much pleasure just to be near him without thinking about their problems.

It also made her aware of his scent, of the pure masculinity of him she'd fallen in love with. She glanced to the side, catching his eye, and suddenly remembered the moment she'd first seen him on a beach in California, near Camp Pendleton. It was such a lark, because she'd been living in Northern California at the time and was in the area attending a nursing conference in San Diego for a few days. Rick had been surfing, or as he later claimed, *learning* to surf, and her first glimpse of him was as he peeled off his neoprene wet suit and she got a load of that body. He'd looked at her, a stare so dark and powerful she'd stopped breathing.

Then he gave her that half-smile that still made her heart tumble in her chest, and although the Marines with him had started up a volleyball game, he'd ignored them and walked right up to her.

He'd introduced himself and asked if she wanted to take a walk. She wasn't about to go off with a stranger, and told him so. He'd promised to keep her in sight of her friends, but said that if they hung near his fellow Marines, she'd get a lesson in teasing and catcalls. By the time they'd walked a half mile down the beach she was sinking fast for him. He'd been so intense. In the way he looked at her, as if delving into her soul. He hung on her every word, his strength of character defined in so few of his own.

She was pretty much a goner even before he'd driven hours up the coast to surprise her. She'd been shocked to see him, and all he did was walk right up to her, take her in his arms and kiss her like no one had before.

Rick had always been a man of few words.

Was she trying to find what wasn't there? Did she want something from him he didn't know how to give?

"Earth to Kate."

"Hmm?" She dragged her gaze to his, smiling.

"You tired?"

"No, why?"

"You seem, I don't know, a little dazed."

"Just thinking."

"About what?"

"A beach in California."

His smile widened as he understood. "I still say it wasn't the bikini that got my attention."

"So it was the boobs falling out of my top?"

He gazed down at her, stroking her red hair off her face. "It was this." He rubbed a strand between his fingers. "Every man there wanted to get his hands in your hair. And on other parts, too."

She blushed. "And you're the exception?"

"No, I'm the only one who had the guts to go talk to you."

"Guts? Why?"

"Come on, babe, you're not that innocent, now. Men are intimidated by beautiful women. It's the rejection factor," he said.

"Ah, yes. Sort of like death before dishonor?"

"I wouldn't go that far." He handed her a piece of wood. "We can put this on the front in the center."

It was the Irish Claddagh symbol—of two hands, holding a heart. "It looks hand carved?" She turned it over in her hands.

"It is. Like I said, too many home and garden shows and too much time on my hands."

"*You* did it?"

His face reddened a bit as he nodded.

During their marriage, Rick had done lots of household stuff—the usual things, minor repairs and maintenance. But he'd spent his free time playing sports or working out. Or with her. He'd never been the hobby type.

But creating something new, out of raw materials, was more than just boredom, she thought, staring at the carving.

"It's beautiful, Rick! I'm amazed and, well, impressed. I knew you were handy with a knife, but you've never done anything like this before." The Irish emblem was perfectly carved on wood so thin she thought it would break. She carefully set it down. "Why the Claddagh?"

When he shrugged, she stepped near and met his gaze.

"You did it for me, didn't you?"

"Yeah."

Kate's heart tripped all over itself. "Why?"

"I was thinking about you at the time, I guess. You have that symbol everywhere." He tapped a finger on her silver Claddagh necklace.

She cupped the side of his jaw. "Thank you."

Rick swallowed, wondering what to do, what to say. She looked as if she was about to cry, and all he wanted to do was hold her. It wasn't right that he couldn't just do it, but he was afraid she'd pull back, and he didn't know if he could handle a cut like that.

Then he knew if he wanted her back he had to do what she needed: talk. He took a leap of faith and jumped. "I started carving that piece to get you out of my mind. I needed a distraction. All this was a distraction." He gestured to the wood and tools. "The harder I tried to ignore that you were gone, the more you haunted me," he said almost like a curse. "And just…"

He hesitated.

"And just what?"

"Just picturing you in this house, in our bed, made me feel as if I'd lost my entire world because I wouldn't talk."

Soft green eyes stared up at him. "You're talking now, Rick."

His gaze scored her upturned face and he stumbled over his thoughts and said, "I've really missed you, baby."

A tear spilled and rolled slowly down her cheek. The sight of it caught him in the chest like a well-placed hammer.

"Aw, Kate, honey." He slipped his good arm around her and she laid her head on his shoulder.

"I'll cherish this Claddagh, Rick," she muttered into his chest.

"It's just a silly window box."

"I know that. Oh, men are so stupid sometimes," she muttered tearily, and Rick thought, *We'll never get it.* How could something so trivial move her like this? Was it really that easy? Women. He'd never figure them out, least of all his own wife.

He pressed his lips to the top of her head for a moment, inhaling her perfume, then tipped her chin up.

She wet her lips, and it was all he needed. He captured her mouth and hunger exploded. Floodgates opened, pouring a torrential flood of desire and passion over him. Like a serpent it snaked through his blood, and she held on as his tongue plunged between her lips. He took control, devouring her, taking what he'd missed so much he'd thought he'd die. He needed her to breathe, to survive, and wanted her closer, cupping her round behind and pushing her into his erection, letting her know she had control.

But he wanted to be inside her, he pressed deeply, stroking her into the sweet madness and watching her pleasure erupt.

Then something hit the floor, and they parted, breathing heavily. He glanced at the screwdriver rolling across the concrete.

"Think that's a message to get busy?" he managed, smoothing one hand over her hair.

"I thought we were busy." Her teasing smile lit up the darkness inside him, pushing it aside.

He kissed her softly, delicately, this time, then said, "It won't look so good if we don't paint it."

She nodded, sniffling as she stepped back and focused.

"The Claddagh goes on last. Pick a color for the box." He showed her a number of unopened paint cans.

"Good Lord. Rick!"

He shrugged. "I couldn't decide."

She picked out a soft gold color for the box and a cream for the Claddagh, to blend with the house exterior, and he stirred while she wiped off the sawdust from their sanding.

"Where should we hang it?"

"I made it for the front, under the bay window in the living room." She agreed, and he watched her paint with small precise strokes.

"No one's going to look that close, Kate."

"I'll know."

"You are so ana—"

Her look stopped him from finishing the unattractive description. "Don't say it! I know. Drove my mother nuts."

"Everything is by the rules with you."

"Oh, look who's talking, Captain Spit and Polish, with his boots lined up in precise even rows."

"That's training."

"And who's going to inspect your gear in this house? At least my focused ways," she said before he could supply another word, "are a Zodiac thing. I'm a Scorpio. Nothing is ever as good as we think we can make it."

"Don't I know it."

She glanced up. "You're talking about us?"

"You want perfect."

"Nothing is ever perfect, least of all a marriage. I just want you to trust me enough to confide in me."

A little wall shot up in Rick's mind, blocking the pitiful past he'd tried hard to ignore. "You wouldn't want to hear it."

Her gaze narrowed. "Don't assume. Or would you like to test that theory right now?"

"I'm having fun, and since I've been bored silly for weeks now, let's not spoil it."

"Avoidance never solves a problem."

"Let's give it a try for today, huh?"

She eyed him for a couple of seconds, then conceded and went back to painting.

It was just plain interesting to watch her do even that.

Rick smiled to himself, loving the way her tongue rode her upper teeth in sync with the brushstrokes. His gaze swept her. Her ripe little body was wrapped in shorts and a tank top that fit snugly and outlined every delicious curve he wanted to possess. He swore she was wearing stuff like that just to raise his blood pressure. God knows it was reaching its limits this close to her. He wanted his hands on her, wanted to feel her grow wet and hot with the desire she kept locked up just for him.

He took a deep breath, shifting on the stool. This dangerous mind binge was not helping, he decided, and looked for something to do.

"Put your finger on this, will you?"

Kate snapped around to look as he started painting the Claddagh. "I can do that."

"I know, but I want to. Sort of like finishing my masterpiece." And not think about making love to her, he thought.

"Feels good to create something, huh?"

"Yeah. I never got to make anything when I was a kid unless it was in art class in school or shop class. When I was little I never had a backyard. Most of my foster homes were in apartments."

"You missed out on a lot. Brothers and sisters especially."

"I told you it wasn't heartwarming. And you fought with your siblings."

"What kids don't? Mom and Dad were referees most of the time."

"That's because guys don't want girl cooties."

She laughed shortly. "Yeah, my brothers would barricade themselves in a tree house and hoist the rope ladder so my sisters and I couldn't come up."

When Rick was done, she took the brushes to the utility sink to rinse them. "They always seemed to be having more fun than us."

"They were talking about bringing girls up there, and what they would do with them once they got them, trust me."

"They did. I caught Sean once."

Rick smiled, curious. "Doing what?"

"Making out."

"Learn anything?"

"Not anything you didn't show me," she blurted.

"I wasn't done."

She went still. Then her gaze jerked to his, his eyes gone smoky and piercing.

Kate felt riveted to the floor as he rose from the stool and moved toward her. Her heart did that double thump when he looked at her like that—as if he wanted to eat her alive. She'd enjoy every second of being devoured.

She licked her lips and he made a sound, of frustration and want. She recognized it. The same feelings were working their way through her right now.

"Dammit, Kate." He swept his arm around her, sandwiching her between the worktable and his long, lean body.

The brushes tumbled to the floor seconds before she put her hands on his chest. "This won't solve—"

"You're so sure?" He cut her off.

"No," she confessed.

"Neither am I."

His head dipped, his mouth swooping over hers. The crush of heat and hunger that had been building all day rippled through him and into her. She felt it, the tight muscles of his body, the long length of his thighs against hers. The need to wrap her legs around his hips made her arch into him, his kiss going wild and almost fanatical.

Her lips burned and his tongue slipped between, stroking her into madness.

"I want both hands on you."

Her own slid up and curved around his neck, and Rick moaned, feeling truly alive for the first time since she'd left. Heat pulsed through him in heavy waves, churning his blood and thickening his groin. He cupped her behind, pressing her to his hardness, letting her know just how she controlled this.

"I want to touch you again," he said against her lips. "There."

Kate moaned, her body on fire, her hand moving to his chest, nails circling his nipple. Rick felt longing rush through him, and opened her shorts, wanting to remind her how it was between them.

Then his hand dived inside, his finger sliding smoothly into her.

"Rick!" she cried, startled.

But then she relaxed as he moved in and out, circling the tender bead. He tortured her, loving the way her hips flexed and retreated, the way she gripped his shoulder. He kissed and kissed, sliding wetly, wishing he could open his jeans and bury himself inside her.

"Let it go, honey. Come on, I can tell you're so near. You can't hide it from me."

She was holding back, afraid to step into this part of their relationship again. Rick tried to understand it, knowing he'd have to win her back. Differently this time.

He introduced another finger, watched her eyes flare, felt her quicken with the coming explosion.

"Rick. Oh, it feels so good."

He smiled. She was leaning against the table, practically on it, one leg hooked around him.

It would be so easy to slide inside her, yet he dipped to her nipple, which was peaking against her tank top, and closed his mouth over it, wetting the fabric and sucking deeply.

She came unglued, and he experienced her pleasure—the shuddering gasps, the tiny moan of triumph as her body tightened down to her toes. The rush of heat and liquid warmth. It had always fascinated him, seeing her climax. It was never the same, never precise. She flowed with it, thrashing, leaning up to cup his face and devour his mouth.

Let him feel it, fusing and hot and passionate.

He held her tightly, kissing her until the fire simmered and faded.

"Oh. Rick."

"I love seeing you like that."

She blushed and pressed her head to his chest. "That was unfair, you know."

"I know. But I've missed you too much to apologize. And I won't."

Kate's throat burned with tears as she held on to him. She'd missed him, too—like breathing. Even while she slept she was reaching for him, and in the morning she was always wrapped around a body pillow. That emptiness was another reminder that her isolation was her own fault, and she squeezed him closer.

Rick tightened his own embrace, wishing for two good arms to hold the woman he loved.

So she'd never leave him again.

Seven

Rick winced as the glass slipped from his hand and hit the floor. He glanced over his shoulder, knowing Kate was out in the front yard planting flowers in the window box they'd made.

Hurriedly, he grabbed the broom and started sweeping up the mess. If she caught him without his sling, she'd read him the riot act in four languages.

The air was still crackling from their lovemaking in the garage, and though he wanted to take her to bed, he was literally an arm short. He didn't want to spoil it by screwing up.

He put his foot on the dustpan, sweeping the glass

up and hiding it in the bottom of the trash can. She'd been taking him to therapy and working with him to get his strength back, but she wanted him to go slow. Rick knew he was an impatient man and wanted it all done now.

When he heard the front door open, he quickly stashed the dustpan and grabbed a soda, trying to look nonchalant.

Then Kate came walking in, barefoot.

Oh hell. "Don't! Stop!"

She halted instantly, muddy hands in the air. "What?"

"I broke a glass," he confessed.

Her eyes narrowed and Rick knew that look. "And you don't have on the sling."

Oops. Immediately he put it back on.

She backtracked and slipped on sandals, then went for the broom and swept again. Then she mopped. Rick just watched her, shaking his head and accepting her uncompromising nature. Like she accepted his impatience.

"Don't push it with that arm, Rick, or you'll be sorry." She washed her hands and was about to give him another earful of her patience-is-a-virtue speech when the doorbell rang.

"Saved by the bell."

"Not hardly. I'll be watching you," she warned, then went to answer it. He followed.

Rick stood back. When she flung open the door, she shrieked and launched herself into a man's arms.

"Jace! Oh, I didn't know the advance party was back."

"What a shock, since you know everything."

The Marine Lieutenant set her back down, kissing her cheek, then lifting his gaze to Rick.

Rick smiled. "Get your hands off my wife, Marine."

Jace threw them up in the air. "Yes sir, Captain sir." Then he crossed to Rick, accepting his awkward handshake. "Man, you look great. I thought you'd be in the hospital still."

Kate moved between them, explaining that the only reason he wasn't was because she was a nurse.

"Lucky dog," Jace said with a glance at Rick. "I think I need to go out and get shot." Jace gave Kate a long, admiring look that set Rick's teeth on edge. He should be used to Jace's flirting with every woman he saw. The man had it down to an art form.

"Don't say that!" Kate gave him a playful shove.

"I wouldn't recommend it." Rick slung his good arm over Kate's shoulder. "She's a dictator."

Jace grinned at them.

"Hungry?" Kate asked.

"For your cooking? Yes, ma'am."

Kate smiled, glancing at Rick.

"What?" he said. "I can see something hatching in your mind."

"I was thinking that if the advance party is back that

means more men are hanging around on a Saturday, alone."

Rick doubted they were hanging anywhere, but said, "I'll make some calls."

"Nah, I will," Jace exclaimed, whipping out his cellphone. "It will cost you a beer, though."

Kate shook her head, heading for the kitchen and pulling out some steaks.

Jace was still on the phone when Rick handed him a beer. The last time he'd seen him, Jace had been beside the gurney, lifting him onto the evac chopper.

Jace tipped the phone away from his mouth for a second. "The place looks great, Rick."

Rick inclined his head toward Kate as she put potatoes and eggs on to boil.

Jace looked at her. "Figures."

"Do I have to beat you, Lieutenant?"

Jace grinned. "Like you could with that arm?"

"Stop looking at her like that."

"Then you shouldn't have married someone so pretty." Ending the call, Jace went to Kate, leaning against the counter. "Count four more, that okay?"

"Oh, sure."

"They're bringing beer and dessert."

"Good, because I wasn't planning on baking today."

"Santiago's fiancée is in town, too."

Kate glanced at Rick, smiling. "And here I thought

it was going to be me with six Marines. The testosterone level would have surely killed me."

Laughing, Rick came to her, standing behind her and sliding one arm around her as if staking his claim. It was the first time he'd been this close to her since the fun in the garage. He wanted more, wanted Kate naked and panting beneath him.

She glanced over her shoulder, touching his face, then said, "Why don't you two go outside? I have lots to do and you'll just be in the way."

"Sorry, we didn't mean for you to do all the work. We can call out for something, you know," Jace said.

"Take-out food after a six-month deployment? I *so* don't think so."

Rick knew she'd say that, and inclined his head to Jace. They went out to the back porch, and Kate got busy preparing potato salad and dragging out the partyware she'd bought just for get-togethers like this.

A half hour later the porch and yard were filled with single Marines relaxing and enjoying the day off before getting back to organizing the battalion. The advance party, a small group that always left a few weeks before the bulk of the troops to set up a mission command post, also came back to do the same before the rest returned. With her in the kitchen was Rachel, Gunnery Sergeant Mitch Santiago's fiancée. "You don't have to stay in here, Rachel. Go out there with Mac."

"And listen to all that Marine speak?" The pretty

blonde jutted her chin toward the backyard as she chopped vegetables. "They're talking shop and I still don't understand half of the abbreviations. PMO, TMO, BX, APC."

"Provost Marshal Office, Transportation Management Office, Base Exchange and Armored Personnel carrier," Kate said without thinking.

Rachel laughed. "How did you learn it all?"

She looked up, realizing how it rolled off so easily. "I had to learn it when Rick and I married." She shrugged. "Then more along the way. If you need to know anything, ask the Sergeant Major's wife." Kate told her the Marine Corps had actually developed a course, LINKS, to teach the lingo to Marine wives now. "We take care of our own."

"Well, I know *you* do."

Flattered, Kate put together some chips and dips and looked at Rachel. "We need to bust up that group and get them to talk about something else. Like your wedding?"

Rachel smiled. "I wish. I've been trying to get Mitch to decide on things for months."

"Well then, I'd say that's our mission?"

Rachel rushed to get her wedding planner and grabbed the dips, following Kate to the backyard.

The men stopped talking instantly and Kate knew they'd been discussing a mission that was classified. She whispered the same to Rachel as she set out the food, then looked at Mitch.

"Come on, Gunny, sit. You need to make some choices or you'll never walk down the aisle with Rachel."

Mitch smiled at his bride-to-be and came to her, kissing her softly. They were deep in a discussion when Jace said to Rick, "Your wedding was videotaped, right? She could watch it and see what a military wedding is like."

Rick looked at Kate, noting her startled expression. "I don't even know where it is," she murmured.

"I do," he said. She blinked up at him.

They moved into the house, and Rick went right to the tape and popped it into the player. Jace had been his best man, and as the couple sat on the sofa, the other Marines scattered around as Jace gave blow-by-blow comments. Rick and Kate stood back, watching the scenes unfold.

Her throat tightened as she saw herself meet Rick at the altar, how he took her hands in his and kissed the backs before the priest started speaking. She glanced at him. He was leaning against the wall, watching, then his gaze flicked to hers. Her eyes watered and Rick held out his arm to her. She came to him, sighing against his chest.

He dipped his head. "I watched this a lot after you left," he whispered.

She'd thought as much, since he knew where the tape was. "Why?"

"I was wondering how it started so great and ended so badly."

She held his gaze, stupid, silly tears blurring her vision. "Maybe because that was the last time I heard you say you loved me."

He groaned, squeezing her, and kissed her deeply, oblivious to Jace's comments, or the applause when, in the video, she and Rick ducked under the arch of swords and Jace whacked her on the behind, welcoming her into the Corps.

Sounds faded and Kate's fingers were in his hair, his mouth rolling over hers. Rick pulled her between his thighs, focused solely on her. "It's not over, Kate, you know that, don't you?" he said against her mouth, for her ears only.

"I don't want it to be."

He kissed her again with more power, as if doing so would brand her as he had on their wedding day.

Till someone said, "Jeez. Get a room, you two."

Rick pulled back, smiling over her head at the group. "I would if you guys weren't here."

Kate gathered herself together, feeling out of control with the kiss. Yet her mind snagged on his words. *It's not over.* But when he didn't need her help anymore, what then? When he recovered completely and was back in action, would that change? Revert to the way it had been?

And when she told him of the child she'd lost? She

looked up at him for a long moment, scared inside, then turned her attention to their guests. "Who's ready for chow?"

"Oh no, you don't, Marine," Kate said, coming into the garage like an F-18 jet at Mach 1.

Rick was on the exercise machine that was as big as a car, which was why it was in the garage. The instant the stitches were out, his mood had changed. He envisioned his recovery coming a little closer. That was great, but it meant she had to watch him. He'd overdo it because he was impatient. Being up at the crack of dawn and sneaking a workout proved it.

"You heard the doctor. It's too soon for that much weight. Get off that machine and put this on."

She shoved the sling at him, trying not to notice how sexy he looked bare chested, wearing nothing but black shorts. The muscles of his thighs flexed with power as he pushed on the pedestal, bringing an unbelievable amount of weights up the pulley system behind him.

He shook his head. "It'll get dirty."

"I'll wash it. Stop. Now, Rick."

He let the weight down and took the sling. "I'm done, anyway."

She smothered a shriek and whirled back into the house.

Rick smiled to himself and grabbed a towel, wip-

ing down. He'd left the sling in the bathroom on purpose, knowing she'd come charging after him. She
was spending way too much time cleaning stuff that
didn't need to be cleaned, to avoid him. For a woman
who'd been in his face twenty-four–seven for three
weeks, she had made herself scarce in the last couple
of days.

He knew exactly why.

They'd gotten past the uncomfortable newness of
being together again. Her barking orders, him obeying
them because, well, she wouldn't give him a choice. All
she had to do was brush past him, touch him, even in
a medical manner, and he was lit up like a firecracker.
And so was she. Even looking at her across the dinner
table was tough because he could remember how many
times dinner went cold while they'd made love—all
over the house.

He scented her like a stag, his body so aware of her
that his heartbeat thumped like a hammer. Yet now that
he wasn't covered in bandages, the tension between
them grew to abominable heights. He could move
more, and he was making good use of the mobility.

When he entered the kitchen, she was slamming
cabinet doors and moving around without accomplishing anything.

"It's way too early for this, Kate. Calm down."

"I knew you would do this."

"It was just some leg presses."

"Without a spotter. You weren't supposed to—" She clamped her lips shut and closed the cabinet so carefully Rick could feel her fighting her temper.

He tried to adjust the sling straps and she moved closer, helping him. It was exactly what he wanted. Her, closer.

"I'm going to glue that sling on you. You can take it off when you sleep if you prop up the cast." She shook her head, adjusting the straps for him. Her face was inches from his as she reached around. "I swear, Rick, you're so stubborn."

"Look who's talking, Irish."

Her gaze flashed up, and in her eyes Rick saw that she remembered. Remembered how it was between them, the heat and passion, the ravenous need for each other. And that that was when he called her Irish.

A nervous little smile curved her lips. "Work out only the legs, okay? No sit-ups."

Rick couldn't if he tried. It put too much strain on his shoulders. He wanted his energy for other things. "If I don't do something, I'm going to get fat and sloppy."

Kate's gaze moved over him. "Not a chance." He was used to running every day. A body like Rick's didn't happen overnight.

When she started to move away, he snapped his arm around her waist and pulled her close.

"Ew, Rick, you're sweaty." Her hand splayed over

his chest and all she wanted to do was burrow into his arms.

Rick felt gut punched from the need pouring through him. "Get sweaty with me."

"I don't even know how to use that machine."

His voice was whiskey rough as he said, "I didn't mean with the equipment."

She stared owlishly, and before she could think, he'd backed her up against the island counter.

"Rick."

"I've missed touching you," he said softly. He cupped her jaw. "Every time I look at you I remember what you taste like, what it feels like to be inside you. You're driving me crazy." His gaze slipped over the short satiny nightgown and robe, her hair tossed from sleep. There was a lushness about her that humbled him.

"I don't mean to." Giddy pleasure swept through her as she stared up at him.

"Honey, you don't even have to try."

His free hand roamed her shoulder, dribbling down her breasts, pausing to tease and stroke, and her breath came faster. But Kate didn't stop him. She wanted his touch. Months without him had been like losing a limb, had robbed her of feeling anything except the loss of him in her life.

He took her mouth like he owned it, like he was dying for her, his hand slipping under her nightgown to her naked behind. Warm and seeking.

And she devoured him back, a wet slide of lips and tongue that pulsed with hunger.

Rick thought he would disintegrate right then, a year's worth of need crashing through him in hot liquid waves. She moaned deeply, and he cupped her center, rubbing.

"Rick," she said against his mouth. A meager protest, she knew. Being near him was turning into torture, till she welcomed sleep only to have him appear in her dreams, reminding her of the passion they'd shared. Yet dreams never satisfied, leaving her wanting him so badly hunger struck like a slap, and nursing him was the last thing on her mind.

"I want to touch you again, baby. I need to." Under her nightgown, he palmed her bare skin still warm from sleep, and her kiss grew hungrier, a message Rick wouldn't ignore. Her heat pressed to his erection sheathed in dark cloth, searing him.

He throbbed for her.

She'd have to be numb not to know it. Kate did.

It fueled what was already there, bringing awareness to an overpowering level. And her will, her misgivings, slipped from her grasp, her desire filling the space and reminding her that he was still *hers*. She knew this wouldn't fix anything, but he'd been the last man to touch her body and the only one to touch her soul. Rick made it so enjoyable to be female, she thought as his hand slid to her shoulders, pushing the robe off. The satiny fabric whispered to the floor as he hooked her straps and pulled them down.

Kate couldn't move, couldn't speak, the heat in his eyes imprisoning her where she stood. He dragged the fabric low, letting it tease her breasts as he leaned in. He met her gaze for a second, then wrapped his lips around her nipple.

A bolt of heat spiraled through her like a pulse sonar, her head dropped back and she arched, offering herself. And he took, devouring her with a desperation that drove all thought from her brain.

Throbbing pleasure pricked her skin.

His nearness was like a drug, teasing her with the addiction.

His teeth nipped at her rib cage, her waist as he pushed the nightgown to the floor. It pooled silently as his mouth moved lower, boiling the blood racing beneath her skin. Then his fingers teased her center, making her flex.

"Rick," she gasped.

"Want me to stop?" His finger dipped and her breath shuddered.

"No."

He kissed her deeply, then slipped his arm under her rear and lifted her onto the counter.

"Rick!" He would hurt himself.

He didn't seem to care, stripping off the sling, then immediately wedging himself between her thighs. He drew her against him, letting her feel his arousal.

"I've been this way since you walked through the door." He kissed her thickly, his hand mapping her body, spreading her thighs wider. "I've been just *existing* without you, Kate."

"Oh, Rick."

She shouldn't. She really shouldn't. This wasn't going to help anything except the desire flooding through her. But being with Rick like this again made her lose all reason. She moaned and her insides clenched, warming with wet heat, her hips pushing on the demanding hardness between them.

"You taste so good, better than before."

She laughed softly.

And Rick feasted, ravenous for the taste of her. He nibbled and kissed, sucked until a luxurious moan spilled from her lips. He caressed her contours, loving her curves, his fingers brushing over her center, teasing her.

"Touch me, Rick," she whispered in his ear, and he felt unhinged. "I want to feel you inside me."

His fingers stroked over her hot center, a rush of honeyed heat answering him. Her scent drove him mad with want, and he slid one finger inside her— slowly, watching her shudder and arch.

"That feels so good." Her hips rocked and he introduced another finger, pushing deeply, then withdrawing, hearing her breath catch with the motion.

"I want to taste you, all of you. Show it to me,

honey. I know you're close." Just to taunt her, he pushed inside slowly and withdrew with equal patience. Her entire body quivered under his touch.

He pushed her back, bending. "Do you remember when we did this the first time in here?"

"Yeah."

"And the second?"

"Why are you talking *now?*"

He chuckled and leaned forward, tasting the joint of her thigh. She was breathing hard, her body tense. Rick knew this woman, what she liked, and he tempered his need for her. "Outside at midnight under the stars?"

The memory flashed through her brain. "Oh, yeah." It had been so erotic, so decadent, the threat of being caught heightening their senses.

"I want that heat." He dipped his head and covered her softness.

She shrieked and laughed, throwing her head back. He cupped her buttocks, holding her for his assault, and brought her closer to rapture, her hips rolling in a sensuous wave with each stroke of his tongue. Kate was always vocal and this time was no exception. She whispered that her toes curled when he did that, that her heart was in her throat. That her body was his.

Then she didn't have to tell him anything more.

He knew.

Her spine curved, her sculptured body flexed. Then

she found it, and stiffened, shivered delicately, calling his name and begging for him to push inside her. He didn't, and an incredible feeling washed over him as he watched her pleasure erupt, felt it, tasted it. She was a wild creature trapped in the throes of her own passion. He didn't want it to fade, wanted to experience it with her again and again, smiling at her mewling cries of pleasure even when she was spent and panting.

She collapsed, melting. Rick swept his hand over her body, laid bare for him.

"Oh, Rick." She rose up and reached for him.

He went still, his eyes intense as he suddenly experienced the enormity of the moment. She was in his arms, wanting him as badly as he did her, but he realized he'd let their marriage take second place, like a misplaced toy, and it wasn't going to come back with simply being found again. He hadn't a clue how to give her what she needed. Except this way.

Her fingers on his jaw brought him back, and he kissed her softly, then pulled her off the counter, letting her fall against him.

Kate stepped away, taking his hand, tugging him with her toward their bedroom.

He stopped and she looked back. "Don't ask me if I'm sure, Rick."

"I won't," he said, drawing her into his arms, his hands everywhere. He could barely breathe with wanting her so much, and backed her toward the doorway.

Kate plunged her hand inside his shorts, sweeping around to cup his tight behind. He ground himself against her, then staggered to the bedroom. Falling back on the bed, he smiled up at her, and was surprised he felt a little nervous.

She was like a gift he'd seen, unopened, knowing it was for him, but denied the thrill of discovering what was inside. And now he could.

Eight

Kate hovered over him, naked and beautiful, and his throat tightened. His fingers sank into her hair and he cupped her face, trapped in her liquid green eyes.

"Don't talk. Don't question. Please, baby. We should, right now."

She smiled. "I was just wondering if you have any protection?" As she spoke she pushed the dark shorts down, inching back enough to flick them off. Her gaze slid over his body like honey.

Leaning forward, she opened the nightstand drawer and found the condoms right where they'd left them, untouched. Grabbing one, she met his gaze, climbing to straddle his thighs.

"I'm not gonna last," he groaned.

His back against a mound of pillows, Rick watched her slither sexily on top of him, peeling open the little packet. He flinched wildly when she enfolded him, obviously taking pleasure in sheathing him.

"You're killing me!"

She just grinned, sliding warmly on him, teasing him. Rick squeezed his eyes shut at the sensations burning through him like fire.

"Kate, honey. I want to see you remember." He thrust upward, cupping her face, his gaze locked with hers as he filled her.

His throat burned. She'd kept such a distance between them lately, and he wanted her to remember it all, miss nothing. He gripped her hips, giving her motion, and absorbed her like fresh rain, feeling the broken bond reforge.

Her body sang, calling to him, and he thrust again, entranced by her expression.

She chanted his name, her hips pumping wildly. Rick clutched her and watched her explode, her hips shoving, then her mouth ravenous on his. She was vocal and animated.

He loved that about her. It excited him, how sexy and untamed she was. For him. Only him.

His shoulder throbbed from the effort it took to keep from gripping her with his wounded hand as she pushed against him.

"Rick. Rick."

"Look at me. Now." She obeyed, cupping his face in her palms, her eyes hazy, her body pulsing as he pushed deeper, harder. Her panting undid him; the pawing of her feminine muscles around him drove him wild.

Rapture hovered, then fractured. She cried out, clinging, kissing him. Pain and passion blended as he stared into her eyes, felt his climax claw up his body and demanding his attention. He thrust, then withdrew slowly, then plunged again into her hot tight haven.

The summit beckoned.

Fiery ecstasy climbing.

She buried her face in his chest and held on tight. "Rick."

"I know, baby. I know."

The ride continued with his heavy length pulsing inside her, touching her womb. Then Kate came apart and he bucked, his hand stroking her tender nub.

"I want you to remember this, baby. Never forget this."

Tears seared her eyes. "I never did, Rick. Never."

She loved him: she'd never stopped. As the crest of desire peaked and shattered over them, Rick felt the depth of his loss, the love he'd hadn't cherished enough, hadn't held on to. Ecstasy filled him, along with despair.

* * *

Kate woke before Rick. The last hours had been a physical strain for him, she knew. He hadn't done so much as move from bed to chair since the surgery.

She sat back on her calves, watching him sleep, thinking he was the best-looking thing on the planet—and that she'd probably made a big mistake by forgetting their problems and making love to him.

Yet she felt complete, the missing part of herself back where it belonged.

Nothing was resolved, except they were physically close once more. Not that she was complaining. Just looking at him made her want him again. But she knew she had to dump some of her perfectionist attitude, and not push him so hard to talk. Perhaps she'd have to face the fact that Rick would never share parts of himself, while she shared everything.

Well, not everything, she thought, her heart clenching as she remembered their baby, of being so alone when she'd lost it, and wanting to tell him. To be held and comforted by him. He'd been out of the country on some mission, she knew; they wouldn't contact him or tell her where he was.

Telling him about their child was still a block between them. She couldn't bring herself to do it yet. Everything was so fragile....

"Hi," he said.

She met his gaze, and he smiled sleepily, reaching

to run his hand over her bare hip. "Every man's fantasy is to wake up with a beautiful naked woman beside him."

"Good afternoon." She glanced at the clock. "Or should I say evening."

"Time flies." He wiggled his brows.

"Hungry?"

"Yes. Starved. But I have a better plan."

He pulled her down on him, his hands mapping her naked spine. He kissed her slowly, then met her gaze.

"I know, baby, you don't have to say it. Here, we're great. It's out there we have trouble."

"You didn't think we did."

"I'm seeing it a little differently now."

She smiled, being content with that for the moment. She kissed him, working her way down his throat, his chest, then tenderly she kissed his wound.

"I'll heal by tomorrow for sure."

She laughed lightly, snaking her tongue over his nipple. His breath sucked in hard. She was sliding down his body, laying wet sultry kisses across his flat stomach, when the doorbell rang.

She looked up.

"Great," he said. "Someone has lousy timing."

Kate rose up, searching the covers. "Where's my robe?"

"In a puddle on the kitchen floor," he said, rolling off the bed, grabbing a pair of jeans and pulling them on. "Sit tight, I'll get it. You're not answering the door looking like that."

His gaze melted over her and Kate smiled. "Naked?"

"Freshly loved." Rick winked. He walked out, already too damn hard to appear before visitors.

Kate searched for something to put on and slipped into one of his worn Recon T-shirts. She was still sitting on the bed when he came back, holding an envelope and a stack of papers. It was his expression that caught her in the chest.

He lifted his gaze. He looked so wounded. Hurt.

"Rick, what's the matter?"

He didn't say anything as he dropped the papers on the bed between them.

Kate frowned, snatching them up. She didn't have to read past the heading. It was the divorce papers.

"I didn't know you'd filed."

"I didn't. The attorney must have done it after a year of no contest."

Rick's features pulled taut. It was as much his fault. He'd never contested, just agreed and went along. He had no one to blame but himself.

His gaze stayed locked on the tattered manila envelope. "Papers, hell." He sat on the bed and rubbed his face. "I suddenly feel like a kid."

"A kid? Why?"

He was quiet, not saying anything, and Kate slipped

from the bed, convinced that he wouldn't. Little pricks of pain tortured her with his silence. It was so like before, where he'd just shut her out.

Then he spoke, and she looked at him sharply.

"When I was a kid, everywhere I went in the foster system I came with papers." He gestured to them. "One beat-up bag, and papers telling them who I was and some report from a social worker. People didn't even talk to me, they just read the papers and shuffled me in or out. I think it's why I hate writing fitness reports on my men. How can you tell who a person is from a two-paragraph summary?"

"You can't."

"Well, they did. I didn't have such great reports, either. I read one when I was about fifteen. Antisocial, unruly, refuses to talk."

It was the first time he'd revealed anything like this, anything deeper than just the vague summaries he disliked. Kate took each word as a little treasure.

"It didn't matter."

"Yes, it does. Don't tell me it's not important, because you haven't gotten past it." She moved beside him, making him look at her, and she was struck with the haunted expression in his eyes just then. "I'm not afraid to hear it."

"I am."

"Why? It's part of who you are."

"No it's not!" He stood abruptly. "I worked hard to

get out of that hellhole and I've come too far to look back." She couldn't handle it, he thought. He had to be the strong one. He had to carry the ugliness of his past and his career. She was so loving and gentle-hearted that he knew hearing the details would destroy that innocence he loved about her. She'd come from a big loving family and had no idea what it had been like. Besides, he was over it, had dealt with it in his own way.

Rick sighed, rubbing his face and thinking this was exactly why there were divorce papers sitting on the bed between them.

"Looking back is not the same as *going* back. I have things in my life I don't want to examine, either. But they've made me who I am right now," she argued.

"Oh, yeah? What things? Being cut from the cheer-leading team? Beaned your brother with a rock when you were in the third grade? How about not knowing your real name till you were six?"

Her eyes flew wide and she stepped back in shock.

Rick saw it, felt it cut into him, and if he needed proof that she'd react like the last woman he'd confessed to, he had it.

He left her without a word, and Kate sank slowly to the bed, the tangle of sheets still warm from their bodies. There was more to his experience than he'd ever let on, and she hopped off the bed and chased after him. She found him on the back porch, staring out at the pool.

"You can't leave it at that, Rick."

"Wasn't that enough?"

She grabbed his good arm, forcing him around only because he let her. Then she moved in closer, touching the side of his face. "I don't know what holds you back every time, but you have to trust me."

"What holds me back is that the last woman I told about how I was raised disappeared real quick."

Kate stepped back. "Don't insult me by comparing me to some woman you never mentioned before."

He looked above her, staring at nothing for a long moment. "I've made a lot of mistakes, Kate. I know that."

"Yes, you have. So have I. How about you stop trying to hide everything from me? I'm stronger than I look."

His eyes were hooded, so solitary her heart ached.

She'd left him, so what made her think he'd believe her? Regret swept her and she tried another tack.

"You know, Rick, I knew who you were when I married you. I knew what being married to a Marine entailed. I didn't walk in blindly. Have I ever been a bad Marine wife?"

"No, of course not." She was the best, he thought, keeping their life in line and marching on while he vanished for months at a time.

"Then why do you expect me to react like that witch?"

He let out a long, tired breath and stared at the rippling water of the pool. "I didn't want to risk losing you by telling you all of it. Can't you see that?"

"I do now. But you *didn't* tell me."

"And you left, anyway."

Her face flamed. "I said I made mistakes. But you didn't come after me, Rick. That spoke really loud."

"I did."

Her features went taut. "What?"

"I did go after you. A day later. I went to the hospital. I was outside the E.R. You were working, and smiling at everyone, and I thought, I'm dying inside and she's fine without me."

"Damn it, Rick, you should have come talk to me. Those smiles were for show, for the patients. I wasn't fine." She'd kept it all in, hoping he'd come for her.

He turned his head, met her gaze. "You're right, I just accepted it."

Because everyone had left him in the past, she thought. Why would he expect otherwise?

"I figured you just couldn't handle military life, being alone all the time, doing everything." And didn't love me enough to hang around and try, he added silently.

"I did and you know it, dammit. You didn't trust me or *us*."

"No, I didn't," he admitted. "I knew I'd sent you away, Kate."

"You *pushed* me away. Don't you think we have a chance now?"

He looked at her with such hope in his eyes her stomach clenched. But he only nodded.

She swallowed hard, then ventured to say, "How is it that you didn't know your name?"

Rick was quiet for a moment, his brow knitting. "I was three or four when I was abandoned into the system. I didn't have any records, but the cops tried to find my mother. It took awhile, but they did. She was dead." His shoulders moved as if shrugging off the pain of a child. "Drugs, I think. I don't know. Nor do I care. But before they found her, I was entered into a computer, with reports. Some clerk simply typed in something and I suddenly had a new name. It wasn't until they located my birth certificate that I learned my name was Richard Wyatt. Before that I was Johnny, John Smith, John no one, whatever."

She pulled him down to the wicker porch sofa, sitting beside him, her heart breaking for the little boy no one wanted. He kept staring out at the yard.

"Thanks for telling me that much, but how rough you had it isn't the point, Rick. It's part of who you are, but not the man you are now. What matters is that you think you have to keep everything inside and not talk about it that hurts you. You lost men and didn't talk to me, or anyone. I hurt when you hurt, Rick. But

I know now that you don't want to tell me everything, and I won't push anymore."

It was the resolute tone that made him look at her. "Yeah, right, you're the pushiest woman I know."

She sighed, laying her head on his shoulder. "It's the Irish in me."

"It's what I loved about you."

Loved. Past tense again. Kate's heart tore in half and she wondered if her pestering had ruined everything between them.

"You see everyone as good, Kate, before you see the bad. Even then you won't face it."

"You make me sound like a first-class sap."

Smiling, he threw his arm around her and pressed his lips to her temple. "No, it's innocence, a trusting nature." He looked down, tipping her chin up. "I adore that in you. Your energy. The room is a little brighter when you walk in."

A lump swelled in her throat and her eyes teared up. He leaned forward and kissed her softly.

"I need that," he whispered against her lips. "I need that so badly."

She was a bright star, and Rick felt as if he cut her off at the knees every time he didn't talk things out with her. He admitted it was harder to *not* talk than talk. "I didn't want to spoil it, Kate. And I did, didn't I?" He thought of the divorce papers in the bedroom, like a snake about to strike.

"No." She leaned to kiss him. "No."

She'd been shocked by his statement, the pain in his tone slicing through her soul. This little bit of his past told her there was more. Oh, she knew about his uncle, that when they'd found he had a living relative, the welfare system had brought him to his mother's brother. Rick rarely said more, dropping only vague pieces of information over the years. His past wasn't what had made her fall in love with him four years ago.

It wasn't a weakness.

It was his strength.

This ability to grow beyond his troubled past. He'd gone to college on scholarships, been selected for Officer Candidate School, graduated number one and was instantly selected for Force Recon. That said a lot about a boy who'd been abandoned with nothing but the clothes on his back and no one to love him.

Everyone had abandoned Rick at some point. Foster parents, his unfeeling uncle. And now her.

Shame and regret welled through her, because when she'd left he'd probably expected it, so he didn't fight. It hurt that he hadn't bothered to chase after her, but in the past days, she'd come to understand that Rick might be an iron man on the outside, the tough, strong man he showed the world, but inside he felt like the kid who'd been shuffled around with a stack of papers.

When it came to fighting for love, he didn't know how. Because no one ever fought for *his* love.

She was trying. "I had a hand in it, too. And I'm sorry."

Rick stared down at her, his broad hand enfolding her delicate jaw. Just looking at her made his hope flare and he decided that if they were on their way back, it was going to be different this time. It had to be—he wasn't going to lose her again. He'd die before he let that happen.

Then he kissed her softly and whispered, "Me, too, baby. Me, too."

A few days later, the stationary pins were removed. Rick swore the process was worse than being shot, and while there would always be a couple of pins in his wrist, the doctor declared that his bones were knitting well. He felt almost bionic, but before he could get excited about being out of the cast, they put another one on. This one didn't restrict his fingers so much and was lighter, the weight no longer pulling on his tender shoulder.

While Kate was off running some errand, Rick worked to regain his strength. She'd go bezerk if she knew he was doing exercises. But impatience was his worst enemy. He had a few days before the battalion returned and he wanted to be in uniform for the occasion.

He set the fist grip down, looking around the kitchen. Then he started to drag out pots and pans, practically clueless as to what he was doing. But he wanted to give Kate a break. She'd been working like a madwoman, feeding him so much he'd gained weight. If he hadn't appreciated his wife before, he did now. She'd worked a full-time job, and could manage more in a day than his whole company. Being around her, he saw what she did to make their house a home—noticed she'd brought in flowers and put up pictures. She was moving in with him again, he thought. Rick opened the fridge, wondering what he could manage to cook without blowing up the house.

An hour later, Kate returned home and rushed into the kitchen, waving her hand in front of her face and wincing at the shriek of the fire alarm. She grabbed a cookie pan and waved the smoke from the fire sensor.

When they went off she heard him say "thank God," and she laughed. He spun around, looking guilty. And ridiculous in the cobbler's apron.

"What are you doing?"

"Making a mess, can't you tell?"

She walked closer, noticing the very nice salad in the bowl, then the broiler with something shriveled and burned in the center of it.

"I know it doesn't look like it, but I started off with good intentions." He shook his head sadly.

She peered, trying not to laugh. "Chicken?"

"It was. I think an arson squad will determine how it ended up like this."

She laughed softly and looked up at him. "Why are you doing this?"

"You've been working so hard, and well," he shrugged, almost bashful, "I wanted to give you a break."

She glanced at the mess. "Take-out would have been a break." She met his gaze again.

"What's the matter? It's not that bad, is it?" She looked as if she was about to cry.

"This is so sweet, Rick." Kate was touched beyond measure. "I can see the cast wasn't what was really stopping you from cooking."

"Obviously I'm the one who lacks this talent in the family."

Family. Kate felt suddenly stung again with the fact that she hadn't told him about the baby she'd lost.

"MREs are so much easier." He tossed the burned food in the trash and set the broiler pan in the sink. "Kelly dropped by to get the other containers, by the way. The guys come back in a few days."

"You're excited."

"Yeah, just need some news." He went to the stove, stirring something.

"Been pretty boring here, huh?"

He glanced at her, his velvety gaze sweeping lazily

over her from head to toe, making her remember the last time they'd made love, wild and outrageous in the tub. "I wouldn't say that."

She stepped close, peering in the pot. "And this is?"

"Fettuccini Alfredo."

"Really?"

"That's what the Sergeant Major's wife said."

"Bet that's not all," Kate muttered, heading to the phone and dialing, holding a finger up when he started to ask. Then she ordered an entrée from a local restaurant.

"I'd rather take you out."

"Not with your fingers swelling like that."

He looked at his hand, then frowned. They were a little puffy.

Rick expected her to rant at him, but instead she went to the freezer, pulled out an ice pack and ordered him to sit. He obeyed, and she packed his arm in ice.

"No tirade?"

"Would it do any good? You're paying for your crime right now, Marine."

"Where did you go?" he asked when she started cleaning up the mess.

"To get some more clothes."

He frowned, adjusting the pack. God, his hand was throbbing. "Where do you live?"

She looked up. "I was wondering when you'd ask that."

Rick felt a stab of shame. Another fact he hadn't bothered to learn. "Well?"

"I have a one bedroom apartment about a mile from here."

A mile? She'd been that close and he didn't know it? Rick rubbed his forehead, thinking what an ass he'd been. "I'm sorry. I don't know why I never asked."

"You just didn't want to acknowledge I was still near, Rick," she said, her voice fracturing a little.

"I didn't. I kept thinking you'd come back."

She stared at him over the counter. "We're a team. Your missions are classified, not your feelings. When you hurt, I feel it. Don't you understand that? You're not alone."

"I was never sure about telling you any of it, Kate. I guess I felt that if you saw the worry, then you'd be afraid, and I didn't want to leave you like that every time I deployed."

"Oh, give me a break. It's not like I don't have tons of people to talk to—the other wives, my family. My friends to turn to. I'm a damn good Marine wife and I'm perfectly capable of handling anything, and you know it."

"I've seen a lot of ugly things, and I didn't want to lose that way you looked at me."

"What way?"

"I don't know, it's sorta…" He stopped, and Kate walked over to him.

"Hero worship?"

He made a face. "Nah. Like I was special."

She had a feeling he didn't mean in a loving way, but something else. "Special how?"

He slipped his arm around her, pulling her between his thighs. "Like I was good enough for you."

"Oh, Rick." She sat on his knee, gazing into his eyes. "I wouldn't have fallen in love with you if you weren't. And you don't have to be so inflexible, either. I never expected that of you. You did that to yourself."

"And I lost you, anyway."

She blinked. "After the past few weeks, you really think that?"

"You were divorcing me." His tone was bitter with hurt.

She stood and Rick frowned, following right on her heels. The papers were in the bedroom, like a sore that wouldn't close. Kate marched in there and picked them up.

Then she went to the fireplace and set a match to them, tossing them in. She watched them flame, while he moved up behind her.

Rick was still as glass, so silent he could hear his own pulse. "Kate…"

She looked up. "We aren't there yet, Rick."

"Thank God." He gathered her in his arms and kissed her deeply, with a gentle tenderness that melted her bones.

Nine

Rick woke abruptly, sweating. He sat up, bracing his back against the headboard, and stared into the dark.

His gaze shifted to where Kate lay beside him. Even after they'd started making love again, she'd slept in the other room, yet tonight she'd ended up here. He cherished the fact, watching her sleep. When he swiped at the dampness on his forehead, she stirred, rolling over and blinking sleepily.

"Nightmare?"

"Not really, just a rehash of it all." His bad dreams had eased over the past weeks, giving him an analytical perspective instead of having him in the midst of turmoil.

She shifted, gathering the sheet to her breast, and he leaned over, kissing her, smoothing her hair back. She looked so much like a little elf sitting there that he smiled.

"I know it's pointless to ask, but—"

He eased back, holding her gaze for a long moment, then sighed and said, "We were in the hills outside Kandahar."

Kate held her breath, as if she were about to leap into the unknown.

"It's cold there now. Wind howls like crazy through the mountains. We were to dispatch a group of rebels in the hills. We had them surrounded and they panicked, firing blindly. I had two teams forward. They were supposed to get inside the caves and draw them out. I was covering them with my team."

Kate listened to him, not so much his account of the ambush, which had come from behind, but how he told it. In between details he related what he'd felt, heard, not just the mission report he'd give his commander. She listened about how he'd been hit by a sniper and crawled out into the open to eliminate the threat to his men.

"Never thought I'd seen anything so wonderful as that corpsman hovering over me."

He stared at his fists the whole time he talked, and then he lifted his gaze to meet hers. His voice was solemn as he said, "I thought of you, Kate, only you. I knew that even if you weren't in this house, you were somewhere safe, and that was good enough for me."

Kate felt the ache in his words.

"I kept telling myself I'd find you as soon as I could. That I wouldn't waste time, and I'd make you come back." He grasped her hand, holding it to his chest. "Then here you were, never too far away."

Kate's lips trembled and she inched closer, kissing him and whispering a teary, "Thank you."

She knew she should tell him about their baby right now. But she felt as if they were still walking on eggshells that were about to crack. Just because they'd crossed a bridge didn't mean everything was fine.

She wanted a big family and he didn't. How they'd managed to avoid bringing up the subject in the past weeks was a work of art in evasion. Rick had grown up without anyone around and didn't know how much fun it was having brothers and sisters. He didn't even want one child. And he hadn't wanted that close tie to anyone, she knew. Yet when he scooped her onto his lap, smiling at her, all thoughts of anything but him vanished.

She shifted, straddling his thighs.

Instantly his hand went under her nightgown. "You're so warm and soft." He stroked the curves of her behind, then palmed her breasts. She tipped her head back, covering his hands with hers.

"I love when you touch me."

"I want you again."

"Really? I wouldn't know." She ground against his hardness under the sheets, then reached between them, grasping him.

"Kate." He said it with a groan.

"Now, Rick. I want you, now."

He stripped the nightgown off over her head, the idea of having her pulsing through him like a thunderbolt. He pulled her closer, his tongue laving her nipple, feeling it peak beneath his touch.

He slipped his hand between her thighs, spreading her, positioning, and Kate thrust against him. He filled her hotly, eliciting a long moan from her, and she was on him like a wild creature, kissing him, retreating, then thrusting her hips and taking him away from their problems.

She was untamed, in control, and he let her have it.

"Rick."

"Come on, honey. Don't stop. Whatever you want, I'm game for it." He wanted her energy, wanted to give her everything she needed because she gave every part of herself to him.

He regretted not cherishing it, thinking he didn't deserve her, but Rick understood, finally, that Kate was meant to be his. She'd been trying to tell him that, in her own way. He just hadn't listened very well. She needed him to need her. He did, like breathing, but he'd never told her, never spoke the simple words that would have kept her with him and given her what she wanted. It was so little to ask.

She cupped his face, her gaze locked with his as she rode him passionately. She begged for more, shivering in his arms, going tense and tight, rocking wildly.

He'd never seen anything so beautiful as her climax, the expression on her face, the glazed look in her eyes. He watched her release shatter through her and it sent him over the edge. The coarse hardness of his passion erupted, a storm pulsing with their tempo, and he thrust upward, his arms clamped tightly around her, their bodies fused with energy and pleasure.

He choked on the emotions bombarding him and ran his hand up her spine, feeling her shimmer in his arms.

Then softly, like a flower spent for the season, she collapsed.

Rick didn't let her go, the silence of the night coating them.

He loved her. More than anything in his life.

Now he had to find a way to prove it.

Visitors were starting to stop by.

It was something Rick hadn't really thought about until it began. Whether he or Kate wanted to think that no one knew they'd been apart, this told him the truth. They all knew.

They hadn't come to seek her out before, either

knowing she wasn't here, or not wanting to intrude. But the trickle of visitors had become a constant influx in the last couple of days, because the battalion was returning. Families were gearing up for the landing.

Rick was eating a quick sandwich when Kate went to answer the door. The sound of excited voices drew him out of the kitchen, and he found her with a blond woman who looked familiar. Kate was holding a small bundle.

"Rick, you remember Tina? Staff Sergeant Ridge's wife?"

He nodded, greeting her.

"And this—" Kate pulled back a blanket to reveal a tiny baby "—is Emma."

Rick moved close, staring down at the beautiful infant. "She's so small."

"Makes it better for giving birth," Tina said. "Want to hold her?"

"Oh, hell, no." He backed away, but something in Kate's expression tightened his gut. "I don't know the first thing about babies."

"Hold her like a football," Tina said.

Rick flapped his arms. "My football arm is broken." He was saved when another child inched around his mother, peering up at him.

"This is Thomas. Say hi to Captain Wyatt."

"Hullo."

"Hey, sport."

Tina patted his head. "He misses his dad."

"I bet."

Kate looked at Rick for a long moment, and he felt she wanted to say something, her eyes were so sad just then. Instead she invited Tina into the living room.

Kate sat, nuzzling the infant, and Rick was riveted by the sight of her cuddling the tiny newborn.

"I'll leave you two ladies," he said, and went to the kitchen.

When Tina frowned, Kate said, "Kids scare him."

Then Thomas wiggled off the sofa and headed toward the kitchen. His mom started to call him back, but Kate stopped her. "If he can face armed rebels, he can face a four-year-old."

She wanted to go in there and watch him with the child, but she turned her attention back to her friend. Rick didn't want children. She did. With him. And even as they were patching up the holes in their marriage, she wondered if she'd ever be truly happy if being married to him kept her from her dream of having children of her own.

In the kitchen Rick sat in his chair, toying with the salt shaker. Seeing Kate with the baby made him want to see her hold his child. Which was stupid, since he'd never had a role model to help him be a father. He wouldn't make a good dad. He didn't even know how parents were supposed to behave.

Suddenly there was a little face beside him.

"Hi," a small voice said.

"Hello, Thomas."

"What are you doing?

"Eating lunch. Want some?"

"I had hamburgers. I get to have a lot of them when Dad's not here."

"How about dessert?"

"Whatcha got?"

What did they have? "Cookies?"

The boy shrugged and Rick stood. The boy barely came to his knees, for crying out loud. Rick bent, meeting his gaze at eye level. "Want to sit on the counter?"

"Really?"

Rick deposited the boy on the counter near the fridge. Then he poured a small glass of milk and brought over the cookie jar. The child seemed to inspect the contents for a lot longer than Rick thought was necessary before he selected one.

"Take two, they're free."

He giggled.

"My mom said you got hurt, huh?"

"Yes. I did."

"Shot with a bullet."

With a rifle, he thought, but didn't correct him. "Yes."

"Did it hurt?"

"Sure it did."

"Did it bleed?"

"Yes," Rick said, and wasn't sure how much a kid his age should know.

"Did you cry?"

"No."

"How come? I cry."

"Didn't matter. I was alone."

"Mom says just 'cuz you're a boy doesn't mean you can't cry."

"Your mom's right."

"So did you cry?"

Clearly he wasn't giving up on the subject. "No, I bit my tongue."

"Lemme see."

Rick showed him.

"I don't see nuthin'."

"See anything," Rick corrected, "and it's all better."

"Can I see the scar?"

"Why?"

The boy shrugged. Rick slipped his arm free of its sleeve and showed him.

"Is my dad gonna get one of those?"

Oh hell. "No, Thomas." He righted his shirt quickly. "I don't think so. Your father is smarter."

Thomas smiled. "Yeah, he is."

"Are you excited about seeing him?"

"He comes home in three days and a wake up."

Rick grinned. The military countdown. Kate once had a chart on the wall that had the Marine emblem divided like a puzzle. Each day she'd color in a numbered block. The "wake up" was when the day finally arrived.

"We're going to play games and eat pizza and all sorts of stuff."

The boy chatted fast and furiously, telling Rick everything he wanted to do with his dad. Rick leaned against the counter, watching the kid drink his milk and jam in the rest of the cookie. He took one for himself, asking Thomas a couple of questions. The kid was sharp, and talking with him was surprisingly easy.

When he looked up, Kate and Tina were standing in the doorway. Tina held the baby. Rick nudged the boy and he looked up.

"Uh-oh. I'm not supposed to be sitting on the counter."

"Yeah, me neither." Rick took the empty glass, then lifted the child down. "I think we're safe, pal," he said in a conspirital voice, glancing toward the boy. "They don't look mad."

Kate stared at Rick, unable to take her eyes off him and his ease with Thomas.

"We're leaving, Thomas," Tina said.

"Aw, man," the boy groused.

They saw Tina and her children to their car, Rick helping strap the boy in. Kate and Tina hugged, made vague plans to have lunch sometime after her husband came home.

"See you later, Capt'n," the boy said.

"Bye, Thomas. Watch your six."

The boy saluted him and Rick's smile widened. As the family drove off, Rick looked at Kate. "Sweet kid. Did you know he can read already?"

"Bet his father is proud of that."

"Yeah. Thomas talks a mile a minute. It's hard to keep track."

"Yes, they're like that. Everything is new and exciting to them."

Kate bit her lip to keep from blurting out her secret. Seeing Rick with the boy gave her a little twinge of hope, but then Thomas was another man's child, not theirs. Big difference.

"Kate? Something wrong?"

She glanced at Rick as they went back inside. "Why would you ask?"

"You look, I don't know...funny."

"I'm fine. How about a workout with weights?" she said, changing the subject.

Rick nodded, trying not to frown. He was more in tune with her emotions now and he knew there was something she wasn't saying. He almost dreaded hearing it, and decided to count his blessings and go with it till she was ready.

But suddenly it felt like a timed charge was about to go off between them.

On the flight line on the base, the crowd of people and the noise were almost smothering, an excited happiness permeating the air making everyone smile.

Kate glanced at her husband, standing proudly and looking sexy in his jungle uniform as he saluted Marines that passed him. Kate wondered for a second if he'd knock himself out with the cast. The airplane opened and Marines rushed across the deck to their families. She and Rick waited patiently amid the throngs of children running toward their fathers.

He smiled down at the kids. "You know, I used to look at your parents and think what a great childhood you must have had. I was almost jealous." Rick looked at Kate. "But I knew you loved me, and when you said you'd marry me I was glad I'd get to know your family."

"So you married me for my dad, huh?"

He chuckled. "My uncle didn't want a kid around. He was young, and being a surrogate father to a boy with a bad attitude wasn't easy for him. He didn't hit me or anything—I was bigger than him, in any case. But he just didn't care. Plus I don't think he liked his sister very much."

"So you were more or less on your own?"

"Yeah."

"You changed everything yourself."

Rick frowned at Kate, pouring himself a cup of coffee from the service set up for the troops and families.

"Look where you are now. A college graduate, a highly trained and decorated Marine commander. That was inside that boy all the time. So what pushed the unruly kid to make a change?"

"I guess it was Alice."

Kate arched a brow, looking a little jealous.

"My girl in high school. Her family didn't want us seeing each other, and looking back, if I were a dad, I wouldn't want her seeing me, either." He frowned. "I was hotheaded and reckless. So they forbade her to see me. We toughed it out for a bit, then she went with some ball player."

Kate nudged him to go on as they strolled the circumference of the flight deck, away from the troops still unloading from the plane.

"I hated it, that my looks and attitude marked me as trouble in sneakers. So I studied. I didn't do much else except work a weekend job."

He'd earned scholarships with his grades and had been selected for a free ride to the Naval Academy. He'd told her about his life in college, but not much before that.

"You said once that you fit in right away at the academy. That it was like a family."

"I knew someone there actually gave a damn."

"Someone here does, too."

"Ah, baby, I know." He slung his arm about her. He looked around and, surrounded by these families, soaked up the scene.

"So what about this woman you told about your childhood? Why did she turn and run?"

"Hell if I know. I didn't expect it, that's for sure. She wanted someone with a…" He stopped, thinking.

"A pleasant uneventful childhood," Kate suggested, and he nodded. "Oh, for the love of Mike, like that makes a difference? Who's childhood is pure? What a horrible, self-centered—"

Rick could tell she was getting mad on his behalf, and he smiled widely. She clamped her lips shut, laughing at herself.

"Her loss," she said with feeling. "I don't see how she could have resisted you. You were too intense to ignore, so passionate about your devotion, your duty, your men. I admired that. Even the way you went after me."

"I thought I'd scare you off."

"You said as much. You used to hold my hand as if you wanted to. Not to make a pass."

He took her hand now. "I was trying *to* make a pass."

She nudged him and walked back toward the crowd. "When my dad first met you he said, 'Grass doesn't grow under that man's feet, lass. Marry him fast.'"

Rick felt the warmth of pride. Her dad was a fine man. "We used to have some great talks."

"Lectures."

"To *you,* maybe. Not me."

"My Da has a glib Irish tongue. He was lecturing you, you just didn't know it." A silence stretched, and Kate said, "Why couldn't you tell me this before?"

"I thought…well no, I didn't think. Strong and silent seemed better than unloading because of the last time I told—" He stopped abruptly and looked at Kate. "I didn't want to see pity in your eyes."

"So what do you see now?"

"That you're…" he searched her face, searched for the words "…in my soul."

Kate felt something move through her, straight into her heart like an arrow. She loved this new man who was emerging. She touched his jaw and curled her fingers around the back of his neck. "No public displays of affection?" she said, a breath away from his mouth.

"Risk it, please."

She laughed against his lips, then kissed him, and he drew her to his length. He wanted more, wanted her alone again. Then he heard his name being called.

Rick looked up, easing back. Jace was gesturing to them and together they met with his troops. Kate listened as Rick spoke frankly with his men, then thanked the corpsman who'd saved his life. The shock on their faces when Rick spoke so openly about his feelings was enough to boost Kate's spirits. She didn't mind being pushed aside. There was a bond between these men a wife would never understand.

Kelly stepped up beside her, offering her coffee from a thick paper cup. The sounds of laughter and babies crying, some being held by their fathers for the first time, filled the air around them.

"He seems different, Kate."

"Really? You think?" She didn't know anyone else had noticed.

"Oh, honey, give yourself a break, will you? You can't change this part of them, but the time at home—that's your business."

She glanced at the Sergeant Major's wife. "You knew."

"What battalion doesn't know everything?"

Kate groaned. "Yeah, I guess. He had the nerve to say the men don't talk."

They laughed over that bit of garbage.

"I'm glad to see you helping him with this."

"He needed a watchdog."

"I'd say he's the watchdog right now."

Kate's gaze was on Rick as he glanced over the crowd. She was almost breathless as she waited until he found her. Then his gaze locked on her like radar, and her heart gave a little skip. She hoped that sudden feeling of excitement never went away. Then he simply held his hand out to her. She excused herself and went to him. That gesture, him wanting her near, told her that Rick *was* different now. Whether it was his wound, the threat to his life or her, she didn't know, nor did she care.

After an hour and some motivating speeches from the battalion commanding officer, the crowd thinned, the families eager to bring their Marines home. Rick was in the passenger seat as Kate drove off the base.

"They did well, really well."

"You trained them."

"Ha, the Gunnery Sergeants did."

He stared out the window at the passing scenery, noticing the banners on the fences declaring love and welcoming the troops home.

"I've got the best troops," he said. "God knows I'm tested just as much as they are."

"What do you mean?"

"My judgment is," he explained. "I have to stay so focused, so objective, and give orders without emotion, but knowing them and their families as I do, it's tough. I could be ordering them to die."

"I know what you mean."

He looked at her, a little skeptical, and she shrugged. "Well, it's sorta like in the O.R. or the emergency room. One mistake and, well, same thing. I have to trust my training, though it's not the same as battle, of course. I do get a little too involved with my patients. But that lack of emotion is what makes you a good leader."

Rick flushed, then reached for her hand. "I'd rather be a good husband."

She sent him a sexy smile full of promise. "Are we home yet?"

"Drive faster."

Rick slid his hand over her thigh, under her skirt. She wriggled in the car seat, speeding, then slowing down. "Stop! This is dangerous."

"I want you."

Her entire body clenched like an unsprung coil. Rick kept talking, telling her what he would do to her once they were in their bedroom. Kate's breath came in tight gasps, and when his hand moved higher, a fingertip stroking her, she thought she'd spin the car out of control.

"Rick. Please."

"Oh, yeah, I plan to."

"I mean—"

"I know exactly what you mean."

She turned down their street, careful of the kids playing, and pulled into the drive. Rick was out of the car and beside her door before she could collect herself. He grabbed her hand, unlocking the house and pulling her inside.

She dropped her purse, then was in his arms, kissing him. "We've made a spectacle for the neighbors. I heard Candice next door laughing."

"Ask me if I care," he said, walking her backward,

unbuttoning her blouse as he did. He worked it off, flinging it aside.

Kate felt giddy, so like a teenager, as if they were getting away with something they shouldn't. When they reached the bedroom, her skirt was somewhere in the hall with her shoes. He backed up against the bed, falling on the mattress and taking her with him. His hand cupped her behind and she started on the thick buttons of his heavy camouflage shirt. He rose up just enough for her to peel it off him.

Then he smiled, sliding his fingers inside her panties. "I love these little lacy things."

"I know." She yanked the green T-shirt over his head, then kissed him.

Rick felt torn apart, her kiss was so eager, so strong, so devouring and erotic.

"Hurry, Rick, please." She was suddenly wild, desperate, and he responded, loving that she was showering this on him.

"Rip them," she said into his ear, sending chills down his body.

He yanked and the thin material shredded in his fist. Then his trousers were open, her hand stroking him. "In a hurry?" he murmured.

"Oh, yes, I don't know why, but yes!"

He rolled her to her back, spreading her thighs, then pushed inside her in one hard stroke.

"Oh, Kate," he groaned.

She whimpered beneath him, thrusting her hips forward, and he understood what she wanted, needed.

Fast, hot and right now. Rick obeyed, making love to her, experiencing the tidal wave of passion as it roared to life and raced toward the explosions.

Then it happened, taking them by surprise, and Rick realized they weren't using protection. And in his heart, he didn't care.

Ten

Rick watched the corpsman cut off the cast. "God, I've been looking forward to this for so damn long."

The doctor stood by, making notes in the chart as the corpsman worked. "You'll be ready to return to duty in a couple weeks but you're not to use the arm to lift anything more than a coffee cup till I give the go-ahead, Captain. It stays in the sling."

"I can live with that." He'd been doing weeks of physical therapy since the first bandages had come off, and he was ready to dump the cast and get back in uniform. Back to work.

"Do I need to give the orders to your wife?" The doctor flashed a cheeky grin.

"She'll demand them, anyway."

"I'm not surprised." The doctor set aside the chart and manipulated Rick's wrist and shoulder. "A woman who flies to Germany to meet the medical plane is not a woman I'd want to argue with."

Rick's head jerked up, his features taut. "I beg your pardon?"

The doctor looked uncomfortable for a moment, then sighed. "She met the plane from Kandahar, Captain. She was outside the O.R. during surgery and by your side till you woke from recovery."

Rick scowled, glancing at the door and knowing Kate was on the other side.

"She never mentioned it to you?"

"No, sir."

"I'm not surprised. She asked us not to tell you. I didn't question it. I figured she had her reasons, but I thought you should know what kind of woman you have for a wife."

For a brief moment, Rick wondered why she hadn't told him. Then he realized that when he hadn't gone after her when she'd left, she'd thought he didn't want her in his life.

"Thanks for telling me, sir. Don't let on that I know, okay?"

The doctor nodded and the corpsman helped Rick into the sling.

He'd keep this secret to himself for now.

It proved a couple things: that she hadn't come to help him out of pity or obligation, and that all he'd really had to do to bring her back was reach out.

When he flung open the door, she smiled and rose from her chair. And he and the doctor exchanged an amused glance when she asked for his prognosis and instructions. For once, Rick was damn glad she was a pill about it, and just accepted that his wife was a perfectionist.

Yeah, he thought. He could live with that.

It was an impromptu surprise for Rick. He didn't know the wives of his staff NCOs had called ahead. Let him think the parade of friends and food was spontaneous, Kate thought. The house and yard she still thought of as hers was filled with people again. There had been lots of welcome-home parties. Some private, some not, but seeing her loved ones again was like renewing a part of herself she'd lost when she left.

Kate ignored the regret that buffeted her, and brought a tray out to the porch, then went into the yard, where Rick was grilling burgers on the barbecue. A couple of wives were in the pool with the kids, and Kate was refreshing drinks and beers when she heard Jace.

"I'll take that bet."

She glanced at the lieutenant. "What bet is that?" She handed him a fresh beer.

"The baby pool. You know, how many deployment babies we get by next rotation. Can't collect for at least five months, though, when the girls start to show, but I have odds on at least ten babies."

"And you think it's not *planned?*" Kate said. But it happened so much that when the troops returned, there were a lot of surprise deployment pregnancies. Kate kept her features impassive as she thought that she'd been one of them. She'd gotten pregnant just before Rick left for six months.

"I lost last time," Staff Sergeant Ridge said. "And I'm glad." He glanced over at Tina, who was holding Emma's feet in the water, and winked at her. Thomas, not to be left out, rushed to his dad, and his father scooped him up, wet bathing suit and all.

"You going to be part of the pool odds, ma'am?" Ridge asked.

"No, not this time around," Kate replied, trying to keep the pain out of her voice.

Over the grill top, Rick met Kate's gaze. She could tell by his expression he was thinking of the line he'd drawn between them because he didn't want kids.

"I don't know about that," he said, and her brows shot up. The shock on her face was readable to anyone, even Thomas. Rick put out his hand, keeping the boy back from the grill. "What would you like, Thomas?" he asked quickly, wondering why he'd opened that door. "Hot dogs, hamburgers?"

Kate turned away, feeling the euphoria of the past few days slipping away as she brought drinks to her girlfriends, then eagerly took baby Emma from Tina so she could have a break. Dan came to his wife, sliding into the water with his son to play while Kate nestled under the umbrellas with the infant. She chatted with the baby, who didn't know her voice from Adam's, and her throat tightened as the child latched on to her little finger.

How could Rick not want this? she thought, and kissed Emma's downy hair. She lifted her gaze.

He was watching her, the grill smoking, and he didn't take his eyes off her until Jace nudged him to pay attention.

Rick flipped the burgers, laying some on a platter, but seeing Kate again with the baby struck him like a slap. He felt as if he were cheating her out of something wonderful. All he had to do was look at her face and see how much she wanted a baby.

His baby.

His. The words kept repeating in his mind and a strange feeling made his skin chill. "Jace, you ever wonder if you'd make a good father?"

"No, not really. I haven't found Miss Right yet. And I'd like to have her alone for a while first."

"But if you did."

Jace frowned and Rick wasn't sure he should get into this conversation right now.

"I think I'd be a good dad, yeah. My dad was great. But I don't think that has anything to do with it. You have to want to be a father, and want to be able to change your life for them." Jace glanced at the kids whooping it up in the pool. "They're pretty easy to please. I'd just want to be sure, though. It's not like you can give them back, you know."

Rick dragged his gaze from Kate and smiled. "I can't picture you a father."

"I can picture you, though."

Rick's head snapped up. "Why?"

"You're fair with the men, you give them all equal respect. You know their families, you consider their lives and troubles."

"That's my job."

"Hey, the younger men idolize you, Rick. And I've had other commanders, believe me. They weren't as attentive or considerate."

Rick shut off the grill and called out that chow was hot and ready. Kate rose and moved close, handing out towels, and Rick swept his arm around her, his gaze on the little girl all in pink. Emma fussed, and Kate lifted her to her shoulder. The little girl looked up at Rick with that wide-eyed innocence he found so rare, and he felt as if he were drowning.

To be responsible for someone so small, he thought. Kids depended on you for everything. Did Kate want a baby for them or because she wanted to feel needed?

"Why do you want one, Kate?"

She turned, her eyes locked with his. "Because our baby will be a part of us both. Our future. And don't tease me like that again."

He heard the bite in her tone. "Who said I was teasing?"

Kate moved away, angered that he'd dangle the promise of a child in front of her like that.

The doctors Kate worked for called her to assist in surgery, and she went, needing to be out of the house. Being around Rick twenty-four hours a day was great, but she'd been away for two months now and needed to return to her job, needed to reestablish the connections. Or lose her seniority. Aside from that there was only so much house cleaning and errands she could do without going crazy and feeling a little useless.

Rick didn't mind, promising to not do any handsprings in the backyard. He was healing faster, his strength returning with therapy and weight training. He'd even gone into work for a couple of hours.

They'd talked more in the last weeks than they ever had, and Kate felt the solidity of their marriage had grown. It was she who was keeping them apart.

She knew she should tell him, and as she passed the nursery on the maternity ward, she felt the pangs she'd pushed aside for years now.

For Rick.

How was she supposed to convince her own husband that she wanted to have his baby, without sending him off in the other direction? How was she going to tell him she'd been pregnant once before? She'd tried twice since the party and couldn't muster the nerve, not when he looked so happy and contented. It wouldn't be long before he sensed something was up and turned the tables on her.

Kate dreaded it. It didn't take long for a powder keg to go up in smoke.

Rick tossed the rubber ball, catching it, then flung it up behind his back and caught it again. Kate was at work for a few hours, which was good. Aside from the fact that she was getting cabin fever, she'd yell at him for this. He worked with a hand vise and could crush a tomato with two fingers, but that wasn't how you handled explosives.

He didn't hear Kate come in the house.

She stepped into the kitchen, watching Rick juggle fruit in the air like a circus performer. "Well, I see you've been up to no good."

He spun around, looking so guilty she almost smiled. Fruit hit the floor and rolled under the table.

"Why didn't you tell me?"

"I was hoping it would be a surprise."

"It is. You don't need my help if you're that strong again."

Panic shot through him. Did she really think he

wanted her here just for physical therapy and sex? "I'm not one hundred percent. This is just dexterity."

"Fine."

Rick scowled, scooping up the fruit as he came to her. "Something's been bothering you lately. What is it?"

Kate let out a long-suffering breath. "We might be talking more, and God knows making love is incredible, but today I realized again that we still don't want the same things."

A chill wrenched though him. "Whoa. What brought that on?"

"I was in the maternity ward."

"Oh."

"It wasn't just that. Do you know how hurt I was when Ridge asked if we were going to have a child and you said, 'I don't know about that'?"

"Yes, I think I do."

"No, you don't. It hurt, Rick. Because I know you don't want kids. It hurts even more because—" she met his gaze and sucked in a breath "—I was pregnant with your baby."

He went pale. "Oh, God." Rick did the math, and since she wasn't presenting him with a child, he understood. "You miscarried."

"Yes."

"You didn't bother to tell me? Talk about me shutting *you* out, Kate."

"Don't even start, Rick. I tried to tell you. You were

on some mission and couldn't be reached. Ask your Major. I tried. But it was classified."

He thought back and knew she was right. "Why didn't you tell me when I came back?"

"Why? I'd already lost the baby, and telling you would have just made things worse. What was the point?"

"I had a right to know."

"Really? You didn't want babies with me. You didn't even come after me. What was I supposed to think? A baby would have made you feel obligated."

The last word came out like a curse, and Rick winced.

"I didn't want you that way and I still don't."

"And if you're pregnant now?"

Kate inhaled, her look so frantic and lost that Rick stepped toward her. She backed away. "I'm not. I'd know, so don't dangle a 'maybe baby' in front of me, Rick. It hurts."

"Who said I was? I've been thinking about it a lot."

"Why?"

"You want a child."

She shook her head. "It has to be mutual. I want to have *your* baby." She said the words around the knot in her throat. "Not any child."

"What do you want from me?"

She lifted her gaze, tears spilling. "I want my husband to love me enough to want roots with me. To make the family you never had." She took a breath. "You would want that, too, if you'd just let yourself believe you're capable. I think you'd make the best father in the world because you wouldn't neglect your child. You would never do what happened to you."

"Kate, honey, I don't have any experience—"

"Neither do I! Who really does? I was willing to take a chance on us. Wanting a family is saying what I've been trying to tell you for years—that I'll never stop loving you. I'm not going anywhere."

"But you did."

"Yes, so you'd come after me, show me you loved me."

Rick scraped a hand over his short hair and cursed. "I didn't think you loved me enough to stick around."

"Oh, Rick."

He gathered her close, holding her. "If I don't agree to babies, you'll be gone?" He held his breath.

"No, of course not." *He's still afraid,* she thought.

"But you won't be happy."

"Yes, we will," she said bravely, "and that means more to me than children." Kate choked on her tears, pushing out of his arms and rushing from the room.

Rick dropped into a chair, his head in his hands, wondering how he could screw up a good thing so fast.

They walked on pins and needles.

Rick could kick himself for not being careful when he spoke. Kate wasn't mad, she wasn't sullen, she was her same old self. But he knew what was beneath, and it wasn't the woman he'd been falling in love with again for the past two months.

"Kate," he said, walking into the living room.

She was curled on the sofa, reading a novel.

"We need to talk."

She set the book down, inviting him to join her. Her smile was forced, but so pretty his heart ached. "I'm sorry you had to suffer alone. Losing a baby couldn't have been easy."

Kate looked away, remembering. "I felt so alone and scared. Then when it was over, I felt just…empty."

Rick grasped her hand. "That's how I felt when you were gone. Hell, every time we're apart." He struggled for a second, then blurted, "I'm scared."

"Of kids? I know."

He shook his head. "No, not because of the responsibility, or whether I'd make a good father or not. I think I would, actually, but I'm terrified of leaving you alone with a child."

"Because you were shot?"

He nodded.

"If it happened, I could handle it."

"I know you could, but I wouldn't want our child to have to grow up without a father."

She blinked. *Our child?* Was he really coming around? She wouldn't get her hopes up. "But they'd have a mother. I understand your feelings, Rick. It will take me a little bit to accept it in here." She touched her heart. "I already knew it in here when I married you." She tapped her temple.

"No, baby, you're stronger than I thought, and what I mean is I—" The phone rang, cutting him off, and Rick cursed under his breath, then grabbed it up. "Yes, sir." He frowned at Kate. "With my wife, sir? Yes, sir." Rick hung up. "The C.O. wants me at the base with you. In twenty minutes."

Kate hopped off the sofa and dashed into the guest room. Rick had a quick shower and shave, and found his uniform laid out. He could still smell her perfume in the air. It made his arms ache for her.

Kate waited by the door, checking her appearance in the hall mirror when Rick's image appeared behind her. She turned, her heartbeat tripping a little. "Feel good to be without the cast?"

She tried to smile. It didn't quite reach her eyes and it hurt Rick to see it. "Yes, it does."

She handed him the car keys. "I think you're well enough to drive." She turned away and he felt the chill in her tone. As if she were leaving him, though she was still here.

At the car Rick grasped her arm gently and she lifted her gaze. Her eyes were glossy and Rick groaned. "Honey, talk to me. We can't go on like this."

"I know, we'll talk. But duty is calling."

They got into the car and Rick started the engine. They made idle talk till they reached battalion headquarters.

"Rick? Look." She pointed to the men in formation. Rick parked and got out, but a Marine rushed to open Kate's door before he could, then escorted her to a small covered area filled with chairs. She frowned at her friends there, at the C.O.s and Sergeant Major's wives, then looked out on the parade. The battalion was stretched out over the length of a football field.

Rick was ordered to report to his C.O. When he stopped in front of the Colonel and saluted, the Colonel returned the salute. Then a voice over a loud-speaker called attention to orders. The entire battalion snapped from parade rest to attention.

As Rick stared straight ahead, he could see Kate in his line of vision. He listened to the citation for bravery, then the awarding of a Purple Heart—to him.

All Rick thought of was Kate.

As the account of the attack was recited, his commander pinned the medal—a purple heart with George Washington's silhouette in gold in the center—to his uniform. Then the band struck up the "Marine's Hymn," and the men were dismissed. Troops converged on Rick.

Kate stood with her friends, tears in her eyes. She was so proud of him, of his survival, of how much they'd grown in the past months. She could live with the love of her life. She could accept that kids weren't in the cards for them, perhaps until much later. And she wanted to tell him that.

Rick instantly missed her presence and after shaking hands with several comrades and well-wishers, he excused himself from the conversation that normally got his blood pumping. He found her surrounded by other wives.

Rick murmured, "Excuse me, ladies," as he made his way among them. "I need to speak to my wife."

"Rick, what is it?"

He gripped her arms, planting a strong quick kiss on her lips. "Don't give up on me."

"What?" She glanced around at the others, her face flushing.

"In the past couple of months I've learned a lot about myself, and you, but I'm still learning." To her astonishment he removed his Purple Heart, slipping his fingers inside her blouse to pin it on her.

Kate looked from the pin to him and back. "What are you doing? It's yours!"

"No honey, it's yours."

"I didn't earn it."

"Yes, you did. I might have been shot, but there are all kinds of wounds." She softened, staring up at him. "You're the one who braved mine. You're the one who faced an opponent." He gazed tenderly at her. "You healed more than my shoulder."

Kate swallowed. A small crowd listened to his words, but she hung on each one, the onlookers fading away.

"I've been alone all my life and when I found you I stopped looking."

"Oh, Rick." She couldn't get past the knot in her throat, resting her hands on his arms as he pulled her close.

"When you walked through our front door, I was

angry and yet so happy that I could breathe again. You're my air, my life. You're the reason I fought death in the field. The reason I wanted to *live*." He cleared his throat, his every emotion sharp and bright in his eyes. "You rescued me from a place I didn't know I was hiding in, and now that I'm out of there, I want to make roots with you." He leaned closer, his eyes dark with promise as he whispered, "And babies with you."

Kate choked on her breath. She didn't expect him to change overnight, but that he'd opened the door made her deliriously happy. "I love you so much, you know that?"

"Yes, I do. You flew all the way to Germany for me, didn't you?"

She blinked, then her smile widened. "Doctors can't be trusted with secrets."

"No more secrets. We say what we mean." Rick fished in his pocket, then took her hand. "I love you, Kate. I love you more now than the first time I put these on you."

He slid her wedding rings back on her finger. The clear white stones sparkled in the morning light as the crowd around them roared with Oh-rah and applause.

"Me, too, Rick. Always, always."

He grinned, the dazzling smile surprising some people, but not Kate. She knew him better than he did himself. In or out of uniform, Rick was still intense and powerful.

And the love of her life.

* * * * *

DOWN TO THE WIRE

BY
LYN STONE

Lyn Stone is a former artist who developed an avid interest in criminology while helping her husband study for his degree. His subsequent career in counterintelligence and contacts in the field provide a built-in source for research when writing suspense. Their long and happy marriage provides firsthand knowledge of happily-ever-afters.

This book is dedicated to the retired
Special Agent Ray Mixon and his family,
Molly, Joyce, Donna, Debbie, Eddie and Billy.
Thanks for being such good friends all these years.

Prologue

"Corda never should have gone to Colombia in the first place, considering his past three assignments. He hasn't had more than five consecutive days off in the last three years. DEA's using him up." Holly Amberson tossed the classified folder she was holding onto the table, shook her head and clicked her tongue. "You'll have a dead body or a burned-out shell if you don't extract him now."

"Thank you, Holly," Jack Mercier said, appreciating her concern for a fellow agent she had yet to meet. If she had a fault, it was the fact that she wanted to mother them all, even though at twenty-eight Holly was the second youngest person in the room. But profiling was her main trick, so her take was very credible.

He looked around the circular conference table at the new team he was forging, a conglomeration of exceptional talent gleaned from major government agencies in an attempt to pool those contacts and resources for Homeland Security, its Terrorist Threat Integration Center in particular.

The concept was not unique, but the personnel present were. The team, named Sextant, Latin for the six segments of a circle, would have carte blanche to combat terrorist threats any way they saw fit, hopefully before any acts were implemented. Almost six months old, Sextant was a civilian special ops prototype meant to erode the rivalry that currently existed among the agencies of the government. Its success was essential.

He had given them Corda's file and they'd had overnight to consider what they thought should be done. Now he was addressing them in order of hire. Though Jack was the leader by virtue of appointment from his position at the National Security Agency, and had the final say, their ranks were equal and their opinions crucial in forming this and any other decision affecting the team. "Will, your input?"

"I say let Corda finish up or all he's done so far down there will be for nothing and he'll be mad as hell. Probably with *you* for pulling him out."

Jack gave only cursory notice to the playful, nearly concealed kick under the table Holly issued Will for disagreeing with her.

Camaraderie had formed already, amazing Jack with how well they all got along considering their diversity. And how accustomed they were to calling the shots in their former jobs.

Holly, his first recruit, had been Special Agent in Charge of an FBI counter-terrorism team based right here in McLean, VA. Will Griffin had distinguished himself with the ATF in Houston, rising to a supervisory position very quickly.

But there were the others to hear from on the issue of Joseph Corda and his final mission for the Drug Enforcement Agency. Clay Senate was formerly with the CIA in covert ops and would know more about Corda's actual situation than any of them. "Your assessment, Clay?"

"Make contact. Give him the choice. I agree with Will. Corda will turn his resentment this way if we yank him now."

"Clay's right," Eric Vinland said before being asked. "Besides, if Corda's to be a member of this outfit, he's supposed to get a vote, too. Right?"

Eric's boyish smile flashed. Clay couldn't get over how young Vinland looked compared to the others, even Holly. And how deceptively naive he could seem. Yet he was a master player when it came to infiltration, blending with the enemy, as he had done for the Defense Intelligence Agency during the past six years.

"I'll go," Eric said, as if it were a done deal, the decision already made. He was good at reading faces and Jack suspected his own had just been read.

"No, not you. We'll contract this one out," Jack told him, watching for any sign of resentment or surprise. He purposely didn't give Vinland his reasons. Maybe it was unnecessary to keep testing them the way he did, but the overall mission of the team was vital. He needed to examine every nuance.

Instead of arguing, Eric shrugged, as if he had fully expected that answer. "Then I've got just the person."

Eric casually slid a file past the one empty chair at the table, the vacant place waiting for Joseph Corda to complete the circle and make Sextant complete.

Chapter 1

By all rights, he should be dead as a doornail.

Joe Corda lay where he had fallen during the attack, his 9mm as empty as his soul, the last round spent. He surveyed the clearing full of bodies. Five, by his count, maybe another one over in the bushes.

They were new recruits, all of them, little or no training, couldn't shoot worth spit. Half of them probably shot one another. Some death squad. He had heard them coming for a quarter of a mile.

Joe felt the sting then. A ricochet must have caught him, or maybe a graze. The nick on his forehead oozed blood, already drawing flies. The whole blamed country was filled with flies. And damned mosquitoes the size of bats. He slapped at his neck, swatted the insects away and wiped the blood off on his sleeve.

Close call, he thought. Close, but certainly acceptable when this was practically a suicide mission to begin with. The chief hadn't called it that, but Joe had known going in that it would be worse than dicey. This was the fourth such assignment he had survived within the last couple of years. The third one to end on a similar note. This script was definitely getting old.

"Just ain't my time right now," he muttered. His own words, even spoken that quietly, rang clear in the silence around him. God, he had sounded almost disappointed.

Hearing what he'd said and how he said it suddenly tripped some trigger within him, alerting him to the fact that death no longer bothered him all that much. Even the flashes of precognition he'd had the night before hadn't upped his pulse rate. They came as he had hovered on the edge of sleep, two brief still shots. One, of the business end of an automatic staring at him like a big round eye about to wink out his life. The other, a quick glimpse of Humberto's woman looking scared to death.

He usually didn't waste time dwelling on death, especially his own, but for some reason, now it was hard not to. He had been teasing it, maybe even courting it this time. Probably on the other missions, too, now that he thought about it.

"The big sin," he grunted.

He was no stranger to sin, of course, even big ones. In his thirty-two years, he had broken just about every commandment sent down from the mountain and a few he was sure God forgot to tell Moses to write down. Not that Joe claimed to be all that religious. Not even close to a good Catholic anymore. But early lessons stuck and he did recall that suicide was the one biggie that kept you out of the churchyard.

Joe shook his head, realizing he was a little out of it right now. The adrenaline still pumped through him like a shot of pure horse.

"Good thing I'm quitting," he muttered aloud. He'd gotten reckless. Cocky. It was time to get out of the business. And he was going to. This was his last gig with DEA. His papers had gone in. It would be official now that this mission was over. He would go home, do his report and be done with it all. He wondered if the new job would be something where he wasn't so tempted to dare the devil the way he'd been doing. If not, he'd decline it.

The shine had rubbed off his enthusiasm pretty early in the game, but he liked to think the core of it was still in there somewhere. He just couldn't find it anymore.

Dad sure would want it to be there. Giving up on anything was not an option for him. His native Cuba had at least one refugee who'd become American all the way to the bone before he reached puberty. José Corda was a Yank for sure, and he had bred his son to value freedom, to fight for right and be a stand-up guy. Two voluntary stints in 'Nam and a chest full of medals said a lot about what the old man believed. Joe had spent most of his life just trying to measure up.

The mission here was straightforward enough: get inside the cartel, pinpoint the fields for destruction, wreak all the havoc he could at the compound and destroy Carlos Humberto.

Drugs were now the main export here. A damned shame as Colombia was a beautiful country rich with emeralds, gold and even platinum. Paramilitary groups were everywhere, all financed by the drug trade, all unstable as a crate of Mason jars filled with nitro.

Three months were enough. Joe was off the clock as of today. He'd cut it very close, satisfied everything would hit the fan in less than a half hour after he left. He glanced at his watch. Yeah, the truck would have blown by now. The sheds had gone up. He'd heard the explosions not long before these shooters showed up. The crop dust would happen tomorrow or the next day.

Joe had effectively cut off the head of one snake, for all the good it would do in a country writhing with them. Humberto's current shipment of heroin had blown sky-high before it reached the plane. He'd take the heat from higher up when his coca and opium poppy crops fell to the aerial eradication.

Joe only wished he had been able to make the payroll in Humberto's fireproof safe disappear, too. But what he had accomplished should do the trick.

He wiped his face again and reached in his pocket to find his extra clip.

"Ah, amigo, do not trouble yourself to reload," came the silky dark voice of Humberto.

The rascal spoke English, which he had never done before within Joe's hearing. Joe was supposed to be Cuban, highly recommended to Humberto by one of his main contacts in the States who had turned helpful after he had been apprehended with a suitcase full of uncut heroin.

Joe's vision from last night had just become reality. He had known it would.

Humberto held the automatic loosely, but his finger was twitching on the trigger. The deadly eye of the barrel stared at Joe.

He looked away, nodding in the direction of the bodies of Humberto's men. "You got here a little late for the fireworks, Slick."

Humberto's black eyes were menacing, his teeth gritted. "You have destroyed my life, Corda. I shall enjoy killing you. It is the one pleasure left to me now."

"Found out my name, huh? Somebody been telling tales out of school?"

Humberto nodded slowly. "Oh yes. Someone you trust."

"Well, that really narrows it down. Humor me. Curiosity might kill me before you get the chance. Who was it?"

"Very well, why not? The final word you hear, Corda, will be the name of your Judas." Humberto stepped closer, firmed the grip on his weapon, pointed it directly at Joe's chest and opened his mouth to speak.

Joe instinctively ducked to one side just as a single round barked. Strange, he should have felt the impact before he heard the sound. And there should have been more than one.

"God, don't tell me you missed at that range," he said, laughing, waiting for the burst of fire that would finish him off. This was it. He braced.

"I never miss," came the soft, calm, unaccented voice of a woman.

Joe jerked upright again. Humberto was gone. Instead, cool as the proverbial cucumber, there stood the goddess. She kicked at Humberto's dropped automatic with the toe of her boot and strode over to peer down into the ravine where Humberto lay. "Chest shot. Dead center."

That's what they all called her at the compound, *The Goddess.* She was a knockout. Long wheat-colored hair, sea-blue eyes, perfect build—not skinny, certainly not fat. Perfection. Humberto's houseguest or hostage or mistress. No one was quite sure. Maybe even Humberto hadn't quite made up his mind about that yet.

Joe blew out the breath he'd been holding, then laughed again, more rationally this time. "You be sure to tell me what old Hummy did or didn't do that pissed you off that much. I'll make a note."

She almost smiled, but seemed to think better of it. Considering what she'd just done and since her Beretta now rested beside one well-shaped thigh, Joe didn't believe she intended to carry out Humberto's plan for him.

Instead, she gave him her free hand. "Get up. It would be a good idea to leave now. Morales will send someone else out if the men do not return soon. He will probably do that anyway. For Humberto. The place was an inferno when I left. No one even noticed me leaving."

Joe struggled to his feet, weaving a little once he was standing.

The hand she had offered him felt cold to the touch, even in this heat. And it had trembled just a little. Ms. Sure-shot obviously wasn't quite as unaffected by all this as she would like him to think she was.

"You coming with me?" he asked as politely as he knew how. She was holding a pistol, after all.

"I can hardly go back," she retorted, but her voice remained pleasant. Almost too deliberately calm. She looked over at the ravine again. "I got rid of the money. He'll be blamed since only he and Morales had access to it. Supposedly."

"My my. I wonder how you managed that." He smiled for real. "And why you did it."

She gave a half shrug. "I figured it was time someone made a move. It seemed you were planning to retire there."

"Not hardly." There was no sound in the ravine, but it wouldn't hurt to make sure Humberto was dead. He started to go check.

She grasped his elbow, halting him. "Forget it. We don't have the time. Grab another weapon and let's move out."

"You're not Spanish," he observed as he scooped one of the automatics off the ground and checked the magazine. In the week since she had arrived at Humberto's stronghold, he had never heard her use anything other than Spanish, pure and accent free. Now she spoke English like a Vassar graduate.

"Brilliant deduction," she replied, plowing through the undergrowth ahead of him.

"Are you somebody's little agent, by any chance?" he asked.

She scoffed. "I am no one's *little* anything, Mr. Corda."

He brushed aside a prickly frond and turned sideways to slip between two trees. She *was* little and cut a narrow path. "A freelance…what, then? Mercenary?"

She stopped for a second to adjust her boot. The woman had a wicked, dimpled smile that turned a man inside out and left his guts exposed. Anyway, that's just what it felt like when she turned it on him now, and she wasn't even applying it full force. However, her eyes weren't playing the same game as those lips of hers.

"Think of me as a student of human nature." She had pocketed her pistol after shooting Humberto, and picked up one of the AK-47s. It now rested in the crook of one arm, the barrel pointed too close to his foot.

Joe backed up a step, pursed his lips and fitted the automatic he had chosen into a more comfortable position to carry. "You picked some strange specimens to study," he observed with a heavy sigh.

She brushed aside the bushes with her forearm. "I'm not quite finished yet," she informed him. "I have one left to dissect."

"You talking about me?" he asked. She was having to work at being clever. Working damned hard and pretty much succeeding, he had to give her that. But he sensed something in her that she wasn't about to reveal to him. Her movements were a little too studied. But there was no point in provoking her right now by calling her on it. "You can't be talking about me."

Her low, sultry laugh sent chills down his spine despite the intense heat of the jungle at midday. He got the feeling she was already taking him apart, piece by piece. Trouble was, he didn't mind it. Not at all.

She pushed past him to take point. He didn't mind that either since it sure improved the scenery up ahead. She looked pretty damned good in those jungle fatigues Humberto had provided for her. *Hot* was the word and it had nothing to do with the weather.

"Would hanging out with you count as a death wish?" he asked just to make conversation.

She stopped and turned all the way around to face him again, her eyes narrowed as if she really were studying him. "What makes you ask such a thing?"

"I'm drawing the line at suicide," he told her. "I just decided that a few minutes before you showed up."

He watched her prop a hand on her hip and incline her head as she shook it. "One of a kind, aren't you?"

Joe grinned at her assessment. "I devoutly hope you believe that. You have a real name, or should I just keep calling you Goddess like all the other *bastardos* around here?"

"Martine," she admitted after a few seconds of dead silence.

"Great, can I call you Marty?" he asked as she turned to take the lead again.

"Not while I'm holding a weapon," she replied wryly. "Last warning."

"Martine it is." He could be agreeable when necessary. "Do you have a last name, or are you so well known you only need one, like Cher or Sting?"

"Just Martine for now. We'd better go find Vargas."

She said nothing else until they reached the outskirts of Paloma Blanca. Neither did he. Joe knew she was psyching herself up to deal with what might happen next, just as he was.

Things were about to get even more interesting.

Miguel Vargas, whom the natives knew as Father Miguel, was Joe's only contact in the area, though he hadn't had the chance—or even a good reason—to meet with him yet. He had received a spiel about Vargas's background and mission before coming down here since they were supposed to be coordinating their efforts. It had been as brief as the one Vargas probably received on him, Joe was sure. There was that old thing with the agencies divulging as little info as humanly possible to each other, even when lives were at stake.

Martine obviously knew that was where Joe was headed and why and who Vargas really was. It was time she explained a little more fully how she had found that out.

"Hold up a minute," he demanded before they left the shelter of the forest and entered the village.

She stopped until he reached her side. She was no longer smiling, which didn't surprise him much. There wasn't a helluva lot to be tickled about in their situation. "Let me see Vargas alone first," she said.

"Why? Confession?"

"Trust me."

Joe snorted. "Yeah, right."

She said nothing.

Vargas was no more a priest than Joe was. He was with the Company, the CIA. Joe figured he probably did some good for the natives just to kill time. You had to walk the walk in a situation like this.

"Why don't you tell me exactly what you *are* doing here, Martine. If it's classified, just say so and I'll shut up."

She blew out a sigh, then tightened her lips.

"C'mon," he urged. "What's the deal?"

With a quick glance toward the village, she then looked back at him. "I need to ask Vargas something." She moved on as she spoke, walking a few steps ahead of him. There was this little hitch in her voice. Just a quiver like women sometimes got just before they let loose with the tears.

Joe didn't believe she was going to cry, not for a hot second. A woman who could shoot a man and not blink would hardly be the weepy kind. He'd give Martine the benefit of the doubt. After all, she could have blown him away just as easily as she had Humberto.

The trail widened, so Joe moved up to walk beside her.

"So, how'd you hook up with Humberto?" he asked, trying his level best not to sound judgmental, even though he was.

"He found *me*," she told him as she looked him straight in the eye. "I was on my way to find Vargas. The jeep I hired in Bogotá hadn't quite made it to Paloma Blanco when Humberto intercepted us. He obviously knew the driver who must have alerted him I was coming. I had no choice about going with him to the compound." She hesitated, just a beat. "So I complied."

"Played along, huh? You must have had a good reason to leave Bogotá when you know it's so dangerous outside the cities."

"Yes."

"Want to tell me what it was?" he asked.

"Not yet."

Joe clicked his tongue and pursed his lips. "O-kay. You haven't seen Vargas at all, then?"

"No," she said. "That squad you took care of back there—" she said, nodding the way they had come "—they knew this is where you were headed."

"So you followed...and armed. How resourceful of you," Joe said without sarcasm.

"I listen a lot," she admitted. "And I'm very good with locks."

"That how you got to the money?"

"Precisely," she confessed. "I figured Humberto would have a hard time explaining what happened to it. That the rebels were likely to take him out of commission permanently. It was slated for the purchase of weapons. But you knew that."

"Yeah. What did you do with it?"

"I hid it under the seat in the truck that was leaving."

The truck he had set to blow sky high. Joe laughed out loud. She had a mind on her, this girl.

"You don't believe me?"

He just smiled. Hell, he wanted to kiss her senseless. She was his new best friend. She had wrapped up his assignment as if they'd planned it out together in detail.

"All right," she said with an air of nonchalance that made him see red. "Believe what you will. I only have to see Vargas and then get us out of here."

"Then let's do it," he suggested, stepping into the clearing ahead of her. Maybe he was taking a chance, having her at his back with a loaded weapon, but her leaving the country within the next twenty-four hours probably depended on his staying alive to help make it happen. *Probably* being the key word, of course. She could have other plans.

"I called for a pickup. In code, of course," she said in a low voice as they wound around through the ramshackle huts to Vargas's temporary home.

"You simply phoned home, I suppose?"

"Exactly. I called my contact in Bogotá from the compound and gave a prearranged signal."

"So where's the rendezvous?" he demanded.

"We'll discuss it later." Her tone did not invite a debate, so Joe let it be. Anyway, Vargas would have something arranged in the way of transportation.

The villagers they encountered seemed very careful not to notice them. Joe could hardly blame them when both he and Martine were wearing the green camouflage uniforms worn by the paramilitary ELN faction. *National Liberation movement, indeed.*

Though she'd been nervous before, Joe noticed she had suddenly stopped trying to hide it from him. "Does it seem unnaturally quiet here to you?" she whispered.

"Wouldn't *you* cut the conversation if two armed strangers were prowling your streets? There was a massacre in La Gaberra not long ago. A few of General Silva's guys strolled in and wiped out every living soul, right down to the old folks and the kids. I'm just surprised these people aren't already running for the hills.''

Joe saw no reaction of horror from her. Either she didn't believe him, she'd already known about the event or atrocities didn't bother her. She was hard to figure.

''Where are you from?'' she asked, forgetting her suggestion that they not exchange biographies at the moment. She didn't sound all that interested anyway. She was too busy checking doorways and rooftops for threats. It didn't look like she was a novice at that, either.

''California,'' he lied. Turnabout was fair play. She'd know he was lying, of course. He was about as south-in-the-mouth as Andy of Mayberry when he wasn't speaking Dad's Espanole.

She halted, her gaze fastened on the largest of the shacks, and threw out an arm to stop him before they left the alley. ''That must be it.''

He smiled down at her. ''Yeah, well, there's a cross on top so it's safe to say it's not the grocery store.''

She looked up, biting her lip for a minute as if she had something she wanted to say. Then she sighed and tucked the Beretta in the back of her belt. ''Wait here for me.''

He figured the worst that could happen was that she would turn over her information to Vargas and Joe wouldn't get to hear what it was. That was okay by him. She had her own agenda, he had his.

Joe just couldn't imagine any agency he knew sending a woman like her down here to take care of business. *Any* business at all, but especially this kind of thing. Her beauty would make her too vulnerable, no matter how well trained she was.

''Sure, go ahead.'' He looked at his watch. ''Five minutes?''

''Five's good,'' she said, sounding distracted. ''Thank you.''

He nodded and watched her cross the road and disappear into the open doorway of the ramshackle church.

Had someone sent her here to check his progress? Or maybe Vargas's? Was she with the Company? She had obviously known what Joe's job was all along.

Five minutes, hell. He wanted to know what was going on here. Cursing under his breath, he readied his weapon and headed for the chapel.

When he ducked to enter, a bullet thunked into the door frame just beside his ear. Two more rounds echoed the instant he dropped and rolled. Damn, it was so dark in here after the bright outdoors, he couldn't see.

"Hold your fire," she shouted. "He's dead."

Joe's eyes adjusted rapidly. The agent cum priest lay sprawled across the floor in front of his rough-hewn pulpit, pistol still gripped in his hand. Another man lay across the room, also dead.

Question was, who had fired first? And why?

Chapter 2

Joe lowered his own weapon. Maybe not a smart move. She could do him next, but he figured if that was her intention, she would have done it before now. "What the hell happened?"

She shrugged and pursed those tempting lips. Like that was supposed to shift his attention? He had to admit, it did just a little and that made him mad.

"The other man shot Vargas when he leaped to protect me. And I just…reacted."

"Oh, what a relief it wasn't planned," Joe said sarcastically. "Never mind that Vargas was the one who was supposed to get us a ride out of this drug den."

"I told you we have a way out." There was the slightest hitch in her voice again. "You still believe Vargas was one of the good guys?" she asked. "I think he might have turned."

"Might have?" Joe looked at the dead man again.

That sort of brought up the question of whose guys *she* might be one of, Joe thought with a grimace. He'd hate to kill her. Never had killed a woman. But then again, he'd never had real reason to. He sure hoped he didn't have one now.

It was then Joe recalled again the vision he'd had of her face. Probably only a dream. He'd been half asleep at the time, had even had a drink with Humberto before he went to bed. It was impossible to know if it had been an actual flash, one of his blinks of the future like the one of Humberto's gun staring him in the face. But he could see the one of her even now in all its detail. The face of the goddess, frozen with terror.

He almost laughed. What a crock. This woman would never wear an expression like that even if he held the gun to her head and meant business. He shook off the memory.

"You want to tell me what's going on or are you waiting for me to guess?" he asked.

She ignored his question as she removed the weapons from Vargas and the unknown corpse. When she gave them to Joe, he noticed her hands. The long fingers were graceful, yet not delicate. Her nails were beautifully shaped, yet not overly long, the smooth ovals devoid of anything, even a coat of clear polish. The outer edges of her palms, like his, were ridged, a result of intensive, long-term martial arts training. Trouble was, hers were shaking. Just a little bit, but the tremor was there.

He thought about turning one palm side up and checking her life line, then decided he didn't want to know if the crease had a sudden break in it. His own fate seemed directly related to hers at the moment. Living was looking better and better.

"Vargas could be the one who gave you up. I was present when Humberto received a message from someone here today that gave him a heads-up on what you were doing. But whoever sent it didn't know your face, couldn't describe you. When you left the compound and headed for Paloma Blanco, Humberto figured it must be you. He decided to terminate you in private, just in case there was another operative within the compound he didn't know about.'' She shrugged. ''Then after you left, all hell broke loose, and Humberto knew for certain you were the one.''

''If that's true and you already have a chopper coming for us, why did we come here? To get rid of Vargas?''

''No. I needed to talk to him. Ask him some questions. Too late for that now.'' She shook her head.

''Well, one of them would have killed me if you had let me walk in here with you. So you saved me again,'' Joe said. ''Jim Dandy to the rescue.''

''What?''

''Old song. I'm into golden oldies. What do you like? Classics? Salsa, maybe?''

She frowned. ''Jazz. What does that have to do with anything?''

Joe sighed and stood up. ''Nothing, I guess. Just seems a shame to be dodging bullets in the company of a total stranger. They'll be coming after us, Martine. Now would be a good time for us to get acquainted. Who are you with?''

''I'm with an independent contractor. Your boss hired us to see that you made it home.''

''Which boss?''

She shrugged. ''Mercier.'' When Joe didn't reply, she added, ''With Sextant.''

''Wrong answer. Mercier already sent someone to give me a hand and extract me early. I declined.'' Too much info to part with, maybe, but Joe wanted some answers.

''He actually made it here? Contacted you?'' Her blue eyes flew wide with what looked like hope. ''When?''

''Two nights before you showed up, I think. It was dark as pitch. I never saw him. No one did. In and out like a shadow.''

''Thank God,'' she murmured, crossing herself. ''That

was Matt Duquesne. My brother.'' She shrugged. ''We were to meet back in Bogotá but he was gone too long. I figured he must have run into trouble. He must have opted for a route out without involving Vargas. He might have sent a message I didn't receive. Or sent it after I left the hotel.''

''That's what you were going to ask Vargas? About Duquesne?''

She sighed. ''Yes. Unfortunately. When Humberto brought me to the compound, there was no indication Matt had ever been there. And of course, you still were. So I thought Matt might have been…'' She let her voice trail off as if he should be able to fill in the blanks. Then she abandoned her search and looked directly at him. ''You're sure he got out without being caught or followed?''

Joe shrugged. ''He was invisible and split right after we spoke. No shots, no ruckus. Yeah, I'd say he made it without a hitch.''

She cleared her throat and continued searching the place. ''Humberto found out pretty quickly who I am. My prints are on file and the man had connections in the States you would not believe. He emailed my employer and demanded a ransom for me, meanwhile knocking himself out trying to convince me to stay voluntarily.'' She scoffed. ''Such a charmer, wasn't he?''

Joe didn't want to talk about Humberto charming her. Humberto had been pretty close-mouthed about it himself. Joe had just assumed the Goddess was simply Humberto's new mistress. He didn't want to think about that at all. Or the things she must have had to do to get virtual freedom within the compound. Damn, she'd even read the man's email?

She rose and dusted her hands against the legs of her pants. ''All right, we can go now. Time is short. I'll need to call as soon as we get safely away and see if Matt made it.''

"No one but me ever realized your brother was there. He must be damn good at what he does. He might have run into a little trouble on the way back, but I expect he could handle that, don't you?"

"I hope so," she said. "He's all I have."

It all sounded plausible the way she told it. Whatever the truth, the man who was supposed to be Joe's only means out of Colombia was dead. Vargas was an agent with a proven track record. But he could have turned.

Joe had come to neutralize Humberto and disrupt operations. The CIA—namely Vargas in this particular area—was more concerned with the state of the government, which faction would prevail and figuring out how to control that faction if possible. Maybe Vargas resented Joe's intrusion or simply gave him up to cement relations with Humberto. Stranger things had happened.

At any rate, the mission was over and it was time to go home.

The DEA had a presence in Bogotá, a carefully controlled presence maintaining strict cooperation with the government forces. Joe was unsanctioned as far as they were concerned. On his own. He couldn't go to them for help. If caught, he would be labeled CIA, even though he wasn't. The interference of a CIA operative would generate some truly bad press, both here and at home. The CIA *was* here, after all. Dead on the floor.

A mere DEA agent was expendable in the grand scheme of things. There was no love lost between the two agencies. That was one reason for organizing the new Sextant team, promoting cooperation. It seemed unlikely to Joe that it would work after so many years of rivalry and jockeying for jurisdiction, but ever since he'd been approached about joining he'd been fascinated by the concept.

"Ready?" Martine asked, interrupting his thoughts.

"The chopper is meeting us in half an hour and we've got about a mile and a half to run."

Decision time. Humberto's drug operation helped finance a rebel faction while he still held rank in the regular army. He had played both sides of the fence. Martine could be with either side, sent to eliminate him. She'd done that. She had probably killed Vargas, too, and had definitely shot the unidentified man who lay in the corner.

She knew about Mercier and the job and what Duquesne had been doing here, but if Duquesne had been captured, getting that information out of him would have been simple enough. Anyone under enough pressure or the influence of certain drugs would spill his guts all over the place.

That left two options to consider. She was leading him into a trap, to take him alive for purposes of embarrassing the American government, or she was exactly who she said she was and was getting him out of Colombia.

Could he afford to trust her? He closed his eyes, hoping for another quick flash of precognition, but nothing came. So much for the infamous Corda *gift*.

That aside, his ordinary instincts were usually pretty good.

Martine practiced patience while Corda made up his mind. She understood his dilemma and admitted to herself that he would be a fool to take her at her word. She had no identification on her, though even that would not convince him. ID could so easily be faked.

"Your weapon?" he said, holding out his hand.

"If we're ambushed along the way, I'll be defenseless," she reminded him. She watched him extract the mags from the AK's, including hers, and tuck the extra ammo in his belt.

He shrugged. "And if you are not who you say you are, sweetie, and that chopper we meet is full of government troops, I'm pretty much screwed six ways from Sunday.''

She sighed, turned over the Beretta she'd taken from Humberto's desk. It would be useless to reassure Corda that she was not his enemy. Better if she did what she could to facilitate his trust. ''It pulls a fraction to the right,'' she told him.

Corda looked at her oddly, as if she'd surprised him with her compliance. She felt his dark gaze slide over her as he did a slow visual check.

Pure male appreciation gleamed right through the careful scrutiny by the agent. Martine fought her response to his obvious admiration of her body without much success. Her temperature rose automatically and she knew she probably blushed.

He was a great-looking guy and in better physical shape than anyone she knew, even her brother who obsessed with working out. There were those bronzed, finely honed muscles rippling everywhere. Jet black hair set off intoxicating eyes the color of well-aged bourbon. His sensual, mobile lips quirked way too often with a hint of sexy mischief. Yes, definitely, a killer smile. But Corda's looks weren't the main attraction for Martine. It was his humor. Show her a man who could laugh in the face of danger and she was hooked big-time. This man laughed in the face of death. Tempted though she was to start something with him and see where it led, now was definitely not the time.

''You have a backup?'' he asked.

Martine held her arms out to her side, palms up. ''Where would I put it?''

The small size man's uniform Humberto had given her hugged her body like a lover, except where the trousers bloused over her boots. Maybe he wouldn't check there. The bone knife she carried was thin and the grip of it fairly slender, making no obvious bulge as even a small pistol might.

He nodded and seemed satisfied. "Okay, let's hit the road. Which way?"

"North," she said. "I'll lead."

His smile mocked her. "Wouldn't have it any other way."

She moved quickly through the undergrowth. Every few minutes, she checked the tiny, special compass built into the back of her watch, which she had turned upside down on her wrist.

Neither of them spoke, which was fine by her. The man was entirely too savvy. She was afraid he would figure out this was her first attempt at a field assignment and decide to take over. If she could just hold it together until they got on that chopper, she was home free. Then she could pretend airsickness or something that would explain giving way to the nausea roiling inside her.

She'd killed two men today. But she couldn't think about that now. She wouldn't. Read the compass again, she told herself sternly. Look professional. Look tough.

Suddenly, he grabbed her arm and jerked her to a halt. "Smoke," he whispered.

She sniffed. He was right. Oily smoke and another stench that almost overrode it. *Oh God, the helicopter.*

Carefully, he took point and led them silently through the brush until they could view the clearing ahead. The chopper sat gutted by fire, the pilot still inside.

Within the cover of the trees just beyond that, she spied two uniformed soldiers, armed and alert, scanning the surrounding woods.

The breath she'd been holding expelled suddenly. She quickly bent double and retched into the bushes. A strong hand slid under her stomach and held her. "Steady now," he whispered. "This is not the time to lose your cool, baby."

She wiped her mouth on her sleeve and sucked in a deep breath. "I'm not a baby," she snapped, her voice almost inaudible.

He didn't argue.

Martine straightened, carefully moved back through the tangled growth of forest and headed west. "Let's go."

"Where?" he asked, but he was following her.

"Bogotá," she answered. "Plan B. We'll have to fly out commercial."

"You *are* kidding, right?"

"I might lie a little, but I never kid," she said.

Six hours later, they stopped for the night, found a little overhang in the hill to protect them from the incessant rain that had been drenching them all afternoon. Both were soaked to the skin, too exhausted to do anything but slump against the rock at their backs. She was awake now, though. Joe could tell by her breathing.

It was time they got to know one another. He kept recalling that possible glimpse into the future that consisted of nothing but her face wearing a horrified expression, abject fear. The memory replayed now when he closed his eyes, a much too up-close and personal view of Martine.

If it was a premonition, he couldn't prevent seeing it for real sometime in the near future. The best he could do was try to figure out the context of it ahead of time. Unfortunately, he'd only been able to do that a time or two in his life, a life interrupted by little snatches of what was to be.

Why such weird anomalies deviled *him,* Joe had no clue, even after exhaustive study by so-called experts on psychic phenomena. After a few months, he had dropped out of the study initiated by the university and never mentioned his "glimpses" to anyone again.

Right now all Joe wanted was to gain more information

about the woman who would eventually star in the reality version of his latest episode and prepare to deal with it ahead of time if there was any way he possibly could.

"What scares you most, Martine?" he asked her, keeping his voice soft, playing to the intimacy that had been forced on them by the elements.

"What is this? Truth or Dare?" she shot back.

"Just truth. Settle down now." He slid one arm around her and drew her close. She tensed a bit, but he knew it was only a token resistance and ignored it. "I'm chilly, aren't you? Not coming on to you here or anything, just sharing a little body heat, okay?"

"Fine," she snapped. "I'm tired, wet and hungry and not in the mood to get personal, so just behave yourself."

"I will," he promised. "I've got to tell you I have nothing but the greatest respect for you, Martine."

"Thanks. Hold that thought." She shifted her body so that she fit closer, but Joe didn't mistake it for encouragement. She was cold and trying to get more comfortable, that was all.

He stifled the urge to pull her head down to his shoulder. Instead, he carefully charged ahead with his disguised interrogation. "You're one of the bravest people I've ever met, so don't get me wrong. But tell me, does anything frighten you to the point you can't function?"

Her silence stretched on for a full minute. "Mediocrity," she declared finally.

Joe laughed and squeezed her shoulder, liking the firmness of her warmth beneath the rough wet sleeve of her uniform. Her right breast pressed firmly against his side, her hip against his leg. His body responded normally, but he wasn't uncomfortable with that. Not yet anyway. He just enjoyed it, determined to press on with his original intent to find out everything he could about her.

She wasn't giving up a thing unless he went first. Maybe not even then, but he'd try anyway.

"Dying alone scares me," he admitted, sticking strictly to fact. Somebody as savvy as she was would spot a lie in a situation like this, he figured.

"We all die alone, Joe," she said.

"I know, but I mean dying the way I would have if you hadn't come along. No one would ever have known I was dead. My family would hope, pray and search for years maybe, thinking I was a prisoner somewhere or a victim of amnesia wandering around waiting to be found. The dying part I could handle, but I'd want somebody to know where I bought it and why, you know? I'd also like to be holding a hand when I go. Somebody who would care one way or the other."

"Something to think about," she granted him, her voice thoughtful.

"Now you. What's your greatest fear?"

Again she considered his question before she answered softly, reluctantly. "Subjugating myself. Not being able to make my own decisions. Being helpless and dependent. My mother was like that. My father was…never mind. I'd rather not go into it." He thought he heard her curse under her breath.

There was a wealth of information in that revelation, one he was sure she hadn't intended to make.

But she still wasn't getting what he meant, Joe thought with a shake of his head. "No, I mean an immediate scare. What would nearly stop your heart? Make you sweat bullets?"

"Oh." She was quiet for a minute. "Being tied up, I think. Confined so I couldn't move freely. That would probably do it." She laughed quietly. "I remember once when Matt and I were small. We were playing soldiers and he took me prisoner. Bound my hands with cellophane tape."

"Ah. Well, I expect he was sorry he did that when you got free," Joe guessed.

"I beaned him with a plastic baseball bat and blacked his eye," she said with another small chuckle.

"Good for you. Bet he hasn't tied up a woman since then. See? You saved him from a life of kinky sex."

She ignored that observation. "He was a horrible brat. I suppose we both were." Joe heard the affection in her voice, recognized it as exactly what he felt for his siblings.

"Why are you doing this, Martine?" he asked, trying to stay conversational and not betray the intensity of his need to know what drove her.

"I told you the truth. My brother didn't join me when he should have. I wanted to get to Vargas and find out if he had heard from him. And to get you out of there as planned, of course."

"The other reason," Joe demanded softly, wanting to know more about what she'd revealed earlier, about the subjugation thing. About her parents and how their behavior might have led her to this point.

She sighed and leaned against his shoulder. "Could you cut the chatter now and get some sleep? We have a long walk tomorrow."

"Sure," he agreed, knowing she'd given him all the confidences he could expect for now.

He still didn't know enough about her. Considering his overpowering interest in her as a woman, maybe he never would get enough. It might be better to drop it. She wasn't what he needed, not at all what he was looking for now that he'd decided to settle down and leave this kind of work behind.

As terrific as she felt in his arms, he was going to have to bypass Martine and find somebody different.

At least he had found out one thing that could put that godawful look of horror on her face. In light of that, he ought to prepare for them to be captured. It was probably going to happen in spite of whatever he tried to do to prevent it.

Chapter 3

They had been struggling through hanging vines and palmetto fronds for hours. Joe had taken the lead, wishing like hell for a machete even if it would leave a trail a kid could follow. Though it wasn't that late in the day, the denseness of the forest blocked out most of the sunlight.

They would have to stop soon or he was going to disgrace himself and drop in a heap at her feet. Outdone by a girl. If he was a few years younger and had the energy left for any show of pride, he'd worry about that. However...

"I need a rest," he said in all candor, hoping she wouldn't kick him in the butt and tell him to keep walking.

"Thank God," she muttered, stretching her arms above her head and flexing her fingers, rolling her shoulders, generally making him sweat even more than he already was.

Joe flattened the vegetation to make a nest large enough for them to recline.

"I'll never take another steam bath as long as I live," she announced.

"Me neither." Joe stretched out and sighed with relief, thinking how nice it would be to have gills. The humidity was at least ninety-nine-point-nine percent. It was probably raining outside the canopy above them. He was as wet as if he were out there in it.

He risked a look at her to see how she was faring. Dewy was the word that came to mind. No rivulets of sweat for this chick. As Mama would say, girls didn't perspire, they *glowed.* Even in the near darkness, Martine glowed. Golden. Untouchable. Except that his leg was resting right next to hers. She raised hers just then and broke contact.

Joe grinned. "What's the matter, kid? I make you nervous?"

"Where are you really from, Corda?"

"What state?"

"No, what planet? You think every woman you meet is fair game. Catch up with the world, will you?"

Joe laughed out loud. It felt so good. Here he was in the middle of the damned jungle, half dead from exhaustion, lying next to a beautiful woman while looking about as unappealing as a guy could look and he was loving life at the moment. Just loving the hell out of it. He'd never felt quite so alive.

She turned her face to his, a look of concern clouding her features. "You're not cracking up, are you?"

He laughed again, couldn't seem to stop. Even so, he managed to shake his head. She sat up, peered down at him and slapped him. Hard!

"Damn! What'd you do that for?" he snapped, rubbing his face. She had a mean right palm.

"You needed that," she said, lying down again. "And no, you do not make me nervous. You make me tired. Now be quiet and save your energy. We have a long way to go yet."

*   *   *

Martine smiled to herself as she lay turned away from him, her face pillowed on her hands. He was keeping his distance, at least for the moment, but she didn't think he would for very long. His eyes gave it away. He wanted her. Badly.

She wanted him, too, but didn't plan to let him know yet. It had been a long time since she had wanted anyone, not since her senior year in college. Her engagement to Steven had been such a fiasco, it had almost turned her against men forever.

This time—if she decided to give in to this need of hers—she did not intend to relinquish one iota of control, not one. She suspected that Joe Corda would turn out to be a lot more demanding that Steven Prescott, engineer, had ever thought about being.

Her father's death had been a wake-up call for her. Seeing how her mother behaved after being left alone had changed Martine's life forever. Talk about totally lost!

The quiet unassuming daughter had realized she was becoming her mother all over again. Ripe for picking by a man who would rule her with an iron hand, dictate every aspect of her existence, choose her friends, even her clothes. Steven had been well on his way to achieving that until Martine suddenly and unequivocally rebelled. Thank God she had.

As for starting up something with Joe Corda, Martine knew very well that what was too easily gained would never be fully appreciated.

He was a lot like her brother. Even good men like these two thought of sex as a simple hunger. They'd hook up with whoever was handy and reasonably attractive, do the deed and never look back after the sun came up. It was the nature of the beast and she didn't blame them. However, though Martine was not looking for permanence, she at least wanted to be remembered past lunch the next day.

There would be plenty of time to explore what she was feeling for him, and also decide what course she should take, once they got out of this godforsaken country.

She wriggled out a comfier spot in the damp bed of fronds and barely managed not to jump when his arm slid around her, settling across her waist. His body rested along the length of hers, not snuggling precisely, just barely touching. Almost teasing.

Martine didn't panic. She also didn't mistake it for an attempt at seduction. She had felt his finger wrap snugly around her belt loop. He merely wanted to make certain she didn't crawl off and leave him there when he went to sleep. She was the one with the compass.

Oddly enough, his ability to reason while he was aroused gave her comfort. She really liked intelligent men, practical enough to control their impulses when it counted.

The next day passed much the same as the first. Joe could not believe the guts this woman had. It just boggled his mind. Once out of the forest, she led the way through the hills, directly to the outskirts of the city without getting lost once or encountering a single soul on the way.

Her instincts were damned near perfect. She never complained. She had never lost her cool again after that one upchuck when they had found the fried chopper. That little upset had lasted, what? Two seconds?

This morning as soon as they woke up, she had disappeared behind some bushes, giving him time to take care of his own business, then marched right back and took up the journey. Her stamina equaled and almost outstripped his.

The forest canopy had thinned enough to show that the rain had stopped, but the mud made the going rough. They'd been walking at a fast clip for hours and he could do with a rest.

She must have read his mind. "We're stopping up ahead. There's a stream."

Good as her word, she led him right to it.

"You've come this way before," he guessed.

"Yes, just this far in. I thought it wise to set up an alternate plan before I hired the driver to take me to Vargas."

While he was kneeling, scooping up water and washing his face, she was digging in the dirt. "What are you looking for, roots?" he asked, wiping his hands on his shirt.

He'd had it with snatching berries along the way. Roots would be good. Even grubs were sounding tasty at this point, his squeamish dislike of them during survival training notwithstanding.

"Candy," she informed him, continuing to scoop the earth out of the shallow hole. "Ah," she said with satisfaction, pulling a plastic bag out of the hole.

"You buried candy!" he said with a short laugh. "Sweet tooth?"

At last he got a smile from her. She hadn't smiled at him for almost twenty-four hours. He'd missed it.

She pulled a long slender knife from her boot and cut the bag open. Joe's mouth almost dropped open when he saw the blade. Didn't that prove he was losing his touch? Couldn't even disarm a woman. He ought to become a bean counter, it would serve him right.

But Martine was no ordinary woman, he reminded himself. No, she was extraordinary with a capital *E* in every respect. Some men might like helpless women they could coddle and protect, but for him, competence had always proved a large turn-on.

Of course, he had always known he'd have to change his preference when he got out of this racket, and that time was almost here. If he tried to settle down with somebody like her…well, they weren't the settling kind, now were they? Home and family would never be enough. Too bad, because Martine had him hot as a firecracker most of the time. He wasn't too sure he could ever go for help-less after having met her.

He promptly shoved aside the current wave of lust he was experiencing when he saw her stash. There were clothes in there. Civvies. Shoes. Grinning, she tossed him a passport.

Joe opened it. His photo stared back at him, an old one taken a couple of years ago. Made him look like a ter-rorist. Typical tourist picture, he thought. ''You are very resourceful, lady,'' he said, thumping the page.

She tossed him some of the clothing. ''Prepare for all contingencies whenever I can. We'll bury the uniforms. You change here, I'll go upstream. Give me about twenty minutes.''

So she was typically female after all, he thought with a laugh. He could be ready in five. She handed him a pink plastic razor. He stared down at it, turning it this way and that.

''Lose the mustache,'' she ordered, plunking a small bar of hotel soap in his hand, ''and there are some horn-rims in the bottom of the bag.''

''Gotcha,'' he replied. The girl thought of everything. ''Thanks, Martine.''

''The name is Guadalupé, José,'' she said in her perfect Spanish. ''Do not forget it.'' Then she left to do her thing.

Joe stripped, waded into the shallow water and sat down to wash. He soaped and scraped off his mustache and the couple of days' worth of beard.

Hurriedly, he dried himself on the uniform and tugged on the clothes. She'd brought nothing flashy, only muted colors. His pants were pull-ons, the shirt a dull print with a long enough tail to cover a pistol. The shoes were leather, lightweight soles, a fair fit. Not much good for walking a long way, but he suspected they were chosen because they took up little space. He stuck the passport in his shirt pocket, dug around in the bag, located a couple of Mars bars and sat down to eat one while he waited for her.

A few minutes later, she appeared. At least he thought it was her. She was wearing worn sandals and an ankle-length skirt of dark green. A long-sleeved brown pullover hung loose to her hips. He noticed a slight padding over her abdomen that made her appear a few months pregnant. But it was the rest of her that truly astounded him.

She was also checking him out and nodded her approval. "Amazing transformation, José. The bare face makes you appear quite civilized. What do you think?" She did a slow turn for his inspection.

She was brunette now and her hair was slicked severely back into a bun at her nape, the strands still wet and straight as a die. Her eyes were dark brown. Contacts, of course. And her skin had deepened several shades. A faint tint of brown lip gloss had replaced the enticing natural rose color that he knew for a fact didn't come out of a tube. He had the stupidest urge to kiss off the fake stuff.

"Wow," he said simply. "Lupé, you are a knockout!"

"Knocked-up," she corrected with a wry smile. "And let that be your last comment in English if you know what's good for us." She pulled a purse made of dark parachute cloth higher on one shoulder. "Let's get the AK and the uniforms buried."

He nodded and quickly did as she said, packing one large weapon and their clothing into the hole she'd just emptied and covering it carefully so the earth looked undisturbed. Then they headed for the road into the city.

As they walked along, she commented idly on the scenery, pointing out several wildflowers he had absolutely no interest in. He could hardly keep his eyes off her and the amazing changes she had made in herself.

She even walked differently, affecting a much more feminine sashay with a delicate little waddle thrown in.

Pregnancy became her. Her voice sounded musical, now minus its former overtone of command. Joe wasn't sure he liked it.

Had she spoken to Humberto this way? Was that how she'd grabbed the man's interest and held it to the point of letting her do damned near anything she pleased while she was supposed to be a prisoner?

He couldn't keep thinking that way, dwelling on what she might have done. It was robbing him of any good sense he might have left. Taking a deep breath and forcing a smile, Joe joined the conversation she'd been having with herself.

"So where'd you train?" he asked.

"McLean. Quantico. Local police academy and a private dojo. You?"

"Same deal, basically, plus three years with the army. Rangers," he added.

She nodded.

"How is it your Spanish is so perfect? Bet you didn't learn that in school," he observed, still digging for more facts about her.

"My mother's Andorran. Spanish was my first language."

"And your dad?" he probed.

"American. He worked for the embassy."

Joe smiled. "Totally against what you're doing for a living, I would bet."

She shook her head. "Not really."

When she didn't follow that with an explanation, Joe's curiosity overcame him. "Well? Why not?"

"He's dead."

"I'm sorry. And your mother?"

"Gone home to her family," she said simply, emphasis on the last word, her tight expression telling him in no uncertain terms that the conversation about her family was over. Obviously, she was hurt by her mother's return to Andorra, so Joe didn't pursue it.

As they walked along, she fished in the slouchy purse and handed him a cheap leather wallet. He checked the contents, finding a driver's license to match the passport she'd given him, a few photos of little Latino kids he didn't know and a fairly generous supply of pesos.

"What, no airline tickets?" he joked.

She patted the purse and smiled. "Air fare for two!"

Well, damn. Joe laughed out loud. "Talk about backup plans. You really take the cake, you know that?" His admiration knew no bounds.

"Gracias," she replied laconically as she bit down on the chocolate she'd unwrapped.

"Why didn't we simply head for the city and fly out to begin with? Why hire the chopper?"

She wrinkled her nose at him. "You really enjoyed that hike?"

Joe saw her point, but this plan was just way too easy to really work. This would be when they were captured, he knew it. Then he would see that look of horror on her face, the one he had conjured up accidentally out of her future.

But it seemed he worried for nothing. They entered the city where he hailed a cab that took them to the airport. On the way, Joe disassembled their weapons so he could ditch them in pieces. No point adding to Colombia's already significant arsenal of illegal firearms.

Martine headed for the nearest phone. In moments she was back, wearing a beaming smile, tear tracks all the way to her chin. "He's safe!"

"Your brother? Damn, that's great!" Joe exclaimed, giving her a hug that she promptly returned, holding him even longer than he would have expected. She had obviously been more worried about Duquesne than she had let on.

When he released her, she kept hold of his arm. "He had a fall and broke his leg. I don't know the details, but he's all right now. He's home."

Their mood was up. A happy couple. Joe kissed her cheek, loving the feel of her skin against his lips. She didn't resist, even a little, only smiled up at him as if he'd saved Duquesne himself.

Slick as a whistle, they grinned their way through customs, boarded a bad excuse for an airplane, endured a short, uneventful layover in Panama and flew on to Miami. Unbelievable.

Joe decided the minute they touched down that he was out of the business, as of now. He was going to turn in his resignation before he even started with Sextant, settle down in some podunk town on the Florida coast and become a couch potato slash beach bum. And if he could talk Wonder Woman into joining him, she could come, too. Maybe she was ready for a break.

Though he couldn't quite picture Martine just hanging out, boiling up crabs and watching the daily soaps, he could still dream of lazy walks in ankle-deep surf followed by hot nights in a beach shack. Did his heart good to think about it, even if there wasn't much hope that it would come to pass.

He resisted the urge to try for another vision. For one thing, it took more energy than he had at the moment, and for another, he was afraid he wouldn't like what he saw.

The last two hadn't been pleasant in the least and one of them still hadn't been realized. He and Martine had not been captured coming out of Colombia. That meant something else would happen. A chill ran up his spine.

In Miami, they stood in line for customs just like everyone else. A few of their fellow travelers were Americans returning from sojourns south, chattering about how different things were *down there*. If they only knew.

Joe kept his arm around Martine's waist, maintaining their charade as a devoted married couple who were expecting a child. No longer a critical disguise since they were safely back in the States, but he had gotten used to it really fast and hated to give it up.

No, acting the fond husband, lover and prospective father wasn't necessary at all now, but he still leaned into her, brushed a kiss over her cheek, gazed deeply into her eyes when she shot him a questioning look.

He caressed her face, trailing one finger across her forehead to brush away a strand of hair that had escaped, then closed his hand around the back of her neck in a gesture of comfort. Her skin was so soft, that nape of hers so vulnerable he wished he could kiss it.

After a while, he realized he might be overdoing the touching. It was hard to keep his hands off of her, no pretense about it.

She hadn't moved away from him the way he'd expected her to, so he leaned down and whispered in her ear, "Where are we going next, *querida?*"

"Atlanta."

"Is that where you're from?"

"That's home now," she answered in English absently just as they reached the customs agents who would plunder through her voluminous purse.

There would be so little time to talk about all that had happened. Joe wanted to talk to her openly, out loud and at length before they reported to the authorities about all that had gone on.

He worried a little that she would disappear on him before that. Nothing said she had to go with him and report anything at all. Joe just hoped she might agree to go with him to D.C. so he wouldn't have to leave her just yet.

They cleared customs in a few minutes and went to purchase tickets for the next leg of their trip.

He planned that they would go on to D.C. from Atlanta. He would, at any rate. He certainly had reports to turn in and a resignation to deliver. After that debriefing on the mission, he would be free to do as he pleased.

No longer would he have to think about every single move he made and every word he said. He wouldn't have to speak Spanish unless he was talking to his dad, and even then, he wouldn't *have* to. And, best of all, he wouldn't need to worry about not being able to fix all the world's troubles. It was somebody else's turn.

He was going to Florida and decided he'd definitely try to talk Martine into coming with him. Just for a little while. Beach life could be seductive, soothing. Maybe if she liked it enough, she'd be willing to quit what she was doing.

Damn, but he'd like to pursue what he had begun to feel about her. But not if she planned to go traipsing off every few months on some dangerous assignment.

"You look so tired," she commented with a worried look on her face.

"Yeah," he admitted with a pained sigh. "This gets to you after a while."

"Maybe you should take a vacation," she suggested.

He searched her eyes for interest and found it. "Maybe you should join me."

For a minute, Joe thought she might have been tempted to say yes. Then one of her fine, shapely brows kicked up and she smiled. "You wish."

"God knows, I do, and that's a fact."

Wouldn't it be great to lie around doing nothing but what he felt like doing, and doing it with Martine? Maybe it was for the best if he didn't do that, though. Someone who didn't talk shop, or didn't even *know* shop, would suit him a whole lot better in the long run. But a short run with Martine sure had a great appeal.

* * *

They barely had time to grab a quick burger before boarding the jet for Atlanta. Once aboard, Joe settled down to await takeoff, wishing for a drink, knowing he'd have to reconcile himself to something nonalcoholic.

He turned to Martine. "You know what? Soon as I get debriefed, I'm getting rip-roaring drunk," he informed her.

"Thanks for sharing that," she said, her tone sarcastic. "Big drinker, are you?" She smoothed the wrinkled skirt over her thighs.

Damn, but she had fine thighs. And great ankles. And nice breasts, not big enough to call her generously endowed, but quite large enough to make him sweat bullets.

"You don't strike me as the type," she commented.

The type? Oh, a drinker, not a breast man.

Joe laughed at himself, both for indulging in a galloping case of desire that was heading nowhere and for the idea of liquor settling any of his problems.

"Well, I'm no lush yet," he admitted, "but the possibility is definitely there. Yeah, I think I could adapt. Tequila. You like tequila?"

"Not much."

He watched the stewardess up front fiddling with the serving cart, stocking it with soft drinks. Bourbon would be nice, he thought with a sigh. *So* very nice.

"Until the shoot-out, you seemed to be faring well enough. You got along very well with Humberto and the others. Was this assignment really so terrible?" she asked, sounding truly interested.

"Not as bad as it could have been," he answered. That much was the truth.

She had been there almost a week herself. And surely she'd had it rougher than he had. Joe hadn't been required to share a bed with Humberto. Martine obviously had.

But then Joe reminded himself, Humberto hadn't been

48 *Down to the Wire*

ugly, despite his lack of character, and he might have been a real expert in the sack for all Joe knew.

Latin lovers got their flattering rep from somewhere, after all. He wondered if he qualified, being half-Latino himself. Probably meant he half-qualified, he thought with a laugh. She shot him a questioning look.

Joe returned it, wondering if he'd ever have a chance to find out how he qualified with present company. He'd bet she was a damn good lay. She'd done everything else with the expertise of a well-trained professional. Still it made him sick to think about her making it with Humberto.

He looked away, upbraiding himself for his silent sarcasm. No, he shouldn't judge her. He'd already decided that. She'd done what she had to do to insure a relative amount of freedom in captivity. He couldn't very well complain since that had surely saved his butt. If Humberto had locked her inside a room in the compound, she wouldn't have been where she was with that gun in her hand.

Joe felt terrible. But his conscience ragging him about being critical of her morals wasn't the only reason. Imagining what she must have done with the man was driving him crazy.

"Did I say thanks, Martine? My manners probably got lost in the shuffle down there. But I want you to know I appreciate what you did. *All* of it."

"You're welcome, Corda. Mission's accomplished and I'll get a paycheck. That's thanks enough."

God, she sounded so…well, company-oriented. "You really get off on this, don't you?" he asked.

"Your animosity is showing," she said with a smile. "And, yes, I like what I do. Otherwise, I would be doing something else. I have a pretty good head for business."

"Monkey business," he muttered under his breath while he fiddled with his seat belt.

"I beg your pardon?"

Uh-oh. Joe looked at her. Both brows were up now and she wasn't smiling at all. "I shouldn't have said that. Never mind, I know I shouldn't. It's just that I'm having a hard time getting my mind around you and Humberto, y'know? I mean, how could you just…let him?"

"Let him what?" she asked, all prim-lipped like his sixth grade teacher used to get when he'd said something off-color.

"Sex," Joe hissed through gritted teeth. "How could you have sex with somebody like him?"

For a long time, she said nothing, just trained her gaze out the window and ignored him. When they were finally in the air and the cabin noise resumed, she whispered, "I didn't."

Another of her lies, but he wanted to believe this one. Real bad. "No? Why not?"

"Humberto found out exactly who I was, so I didn't bother to lie about it. He didn't know why I was there. I told him I was looking for my brother who had disappeared on an assignment I knew nothing about."

"Truth works better in cases like that," Joe agreed. "So, since you were working for this company and not law enforcement, he figured he could persuade you to throw in with him?"

She shrugged. "That was his plan, I think. He treated me exceptionally well because he wanted me to be content to stay. Also, he enjoyed playing the Old World gallant. You know how pretentious he could be. I got a fairly good estimation of the man by assessing his traffic on the computer."

"How in the world did you manage that?" She never ceased to amaze him.

She shrugged, a small smile tickling her lips. "Let's just say I tend to wander a bit in the wee hours of the morning and Humberto was a very sound sleeper."

Joe shook his head, unable to hide his doubt. "And he let you have that free a run, given what he knew about you? How stupid was that?"

"I had a freer run than he knew I did, at least within the compound. Getting past the gate guards would have presented a problem, of course. At least before the distraction your leaving caused." She sighed and shook her head. "Maybe he knew why I had come and was waiting for me to identify you. I couldn't get a message to you without danger of your being caught. He'd been notified that DEA was in place undercover, but you could have been any one of the new people. He watched each of you like a hawk."

Joe grinned when he thought how successfully he had bypassed that scrutiny when he went to wire the truck. "Closer than he watched you?"

"Obviously." She continued the explanation. "When you took off, that as good as identified you. That's why the squad followed. And why Humberto did. He wanted to be in on the kill."

"And how did you manage to find that out?"

She grinned. "I'm a dedicated eavesdropper, Corda. Amazing how much you can learn when guys think you're just a wide-eyed female with feathers for brains." She examined her nails with a frown. "When business came up, he forgot I was around. Especially when you took off."

"So you followed. And shot him. That must have been hard for you after…" He let his words die off, wishing he'd kept his mouth shut. It was in the past now, over and done with. She'd want to forget it. Hell, *he* wanted to forget it. But he couldn't seem to. It bothered the hell out of him that she had slept with Humberto.

Martine expelled a frustrated breath. "After what?"

Joe shook his head and grimaced. "After how…close

you were. You don't owe me any explanations. I just wondered about it, that's all.''

She nodded. ''All right.''

So that was it. Joe tried to let it go and forget it.

''I take it Duquesne's your real name? Or did you and your *brother* choose that as your alias?''

''Yes, it is real. There seemed no reason to change it since neither of us is exactly famous. You see, Ames International—''

Joe interrupted ''—liberates Americans caught in embarrassing quandaries outside the boundaries. What made you go for that kind of job?''

''I think we'd better change the subject.''

Reluctantly he agreed. ''So, you coming on vacation with me?''

''Certainly not,'' she replied. A little too zealously not to have at least considered it.

''Offer stands. You could use a little R&R after shooting up Colombia, couldn't you? Just think, you could be lying on a beach down at Port St. Joe, eating oysters and watching the tide roll in this time next week. That's where I plan to be.''

''Port St. Joe?'' she asked.

''Yeah, I'm actually named for the place. Gulf Coast of Florida. My mother's a teacher at the local high school. Dad's retired. Both my sisters still live there. It's home.''

She smiled at him, a real smile that warmed his insides. ''Sounds lovely,'' she said. ''Thank you for asking me, but I can't join you. There'll be another assignment waiting when I get back.'' She sighed. ''At least, I hope there will be.''

Joe chilled around the region of his heart. ''Good grief, nobody but a newbie is that gung-ho! Tell me you're not.''

She was biting her lip, frowning, not saying squat, looking out the window instead of at him.

"You *are!* This was your first op?"

She nodded once, just a little nod.

When he got his voice back, Joe had to work hard to keep from yelling. Instead, he rasped, "You could have gotten yourself killed, Martine! Hell, you could have gotten *me* killed. What the devil was Mercier thinking about, hiring *you,* of all people?"

"Me, of all people?" she asked, definitely offended. "Why do you say that, because I'm a woman?"

"Because you're green! Damn, they don't even send green operatives down there from the Company." Joe shook his head as he ran a hand through his hair. "I gotta think Mercier didn't want me back very much if he sent somebody green."

"He sent my brother, who is very experienced!" she argued.

"Even as backup, they shouldn't send a novice." That thought alone reinforced his decision to quit the minute he got back.

"No, you shouldn't blame Mercier," Martine said vehemently. "He only contracted for my brother to go. I talked Matt into letting me go as far as Bogotá. Sort of to get my feet wet without being in on the actual operation."

Joe studied her for a minute. "So when your brother disappeared, you were the next body in line?"

"I had to make sure Matt was all right. And that you made it back, too. I'm trained to do anything Matt can do. You saw for yourself, I can shoot. No hesitation, no misses. I planned everything right down to the smallest detail and I prepared for every possible eventuality. Go ahead, tell me something I did wrong, I dare you!"

Joe couldn't. She was highly competent. No mistakes. If you didn't count sleeping with the enemy. And even that could be explained, if not condoned.

He forced himself to calm down and think rationally,

to put aside the weird swell of fury that felt a whole lot like jealousy all mixed up with a spiky wad of regret. It hurt like a sonofabitch.

"You…you did okay," he ground out. "What exactly is your job at Ames, if you don't mind my asking?"

"Technically…" She looked away, unable to meet his eyes. "Information analyst. Coordinator. That sort of thing."

He closed his eyes. His jaw clenched until his teeth ached. "A secretary?" he growled. "They sent a friggin' secretary?"

"I told you before. No one *sent* me. They sent Matt," she said with an exasperated roll of her eyes.

"Yeah, and you're the one who wound up in Humberto's bed!" Joe accused.

"He only kissed me one time! And it was just a little kiss, like a kindly old uncle's or something. We never went all the way."

Joe groaned. "*All the way?* What a quaint little old-fashioned phrase, Martine. Tell me, did you two *go steady?* Did you head him off at *second base?* God, Martine, you make my head hurt, you know that?"

"Then take a nap, Corda!" she suggested in a snippy little voice he hadn't heard her use before. "This conversation is *over.*"

"You're damned right it is! I'll take this up with your brother and your boss. You'll be lucky if they don't bury you in the bowels of the files in the basement."

"That's where I *was,*" she countered. The fire in her eyes was so bright, he thought he could see the blue burning through her brown contacts. "And if you get me demoted back there, Corda, I'll hunt you down and make you sorry. That's a promise!"

"Threatening a government agent, Martine? What're you gonna do, shoot me?"

"There's an idea." She crossed her arms over her

chest, gave him the back of her head and didn't say another word.

He was really glad right then that they'd had to ditch the weapons in order to fly.

Chapter 4

Martine hated to leave things as they stood. Neither of them had said much on the flight to Atlanta, just enough to create gross misunderstandings.

She had called her office from Miami and had left Matt a message that she was on the way. Joe had phoned his old office and stated only that his mission was complete, leaving the details for his debriefing when he arrived in D.C.

The adrenaline had ebbed along with the danger, leaving them both exhausted.

They deplaned still looking like refugees. She had ditched the padding that made her appear pregnant and her clothing hung loose on her frame. She had also removed the brown contacts that had irritated her eyes and left them red-rimmed. Corda's five-o'clock shadow had grown into a near beard. She ached for a hot shower and at least eight hours' sleep.

"Well, I'm on home turf at last," she told him when they entered the terminal, "and you soon will be."

She wondered if she would still have a job when she returned to work. Hopefully, when she admitted to her brother that she had gone to the compound after him, he and their boss, Sebastian, would see it as her taking initiative and would agree she had done as well as either of them could have under the circumstances.

They would read her the riot act, of course, and she could hardly blame them for that. But if they attempted to make her give her word she would never do anything remotely like this again, she would simply have to resign. Her days behind a desk were over.

"Is this where we part company?" Joe grinned at her, but it looked like a real effort. "I was hoping you might deliver me personally to Mercier. Plop me on his desk and demand payment for the job."

She shrugged. "Where do you go for the DEA debriefing?"

"D.C. Then on to McLean after I deliver my spiel and I'm officially released. I'll commend you to Mercier when I get there."

"Thanks." She didn't quite know what to say next. They had said so much over the course of three days. And yet so little about anything that really mattered.

The attraction they felt stood between them like a swaying rogue elephant. They both recognized it. There was no point pretending it didn't exist, but she'd been having serious second thoughts about whether they should approach and attempt to tame it. It just loomed there, promising trouble. Maybe it would be better to steal away from it in opposite directions and avoid eye contact.

Martine didn't think now that she could take a relationship with Joe as lightly as she ought to. It might mean too much to her.

He ushered her to the tram that would take them to the main terminal. Just before it reached there, he cleared his throat. She looked up at him.

"Could I buy you dinner?" he asked, then patted the folded currency they had exchanged for in Miami. "Your treat?"

She smiled. All those second thoughts she'd been having evaporated. "Sure, why not?" In the back of her mind, she knew it was a bad idea. This was leading directly to a one-night stand. They both knew it. It was there in his eyes, a promise clear as could be.

Maybe she should be offended. He thought she was promiscuous, that she had slept with Humberto as part of her cover. And that she would sleep with him for no other reason than he was there and willing. That last assumption might be a shade too close to the truth, but there was a bit more to it than that. Damn. He was looking serious and she couldn't afford to do serious.

She'd have to make certain she stayed uninvolved emotionally. And that he did, too.

"Want to hit the shops here and get you some clothes?" she asked. "I'll bill Mercier."

He laughed and plucked at his shirt. "I guess I do look a little scuzzy for a night on the town."

"Or for reporting in…tomorrow," she added, giving him the suggestion to wait until then to fly out instead of seeing him off after the dinner he promised.

His reply was nonverbal and non-tactile, but his acceptance was clear in the heated look he gave her. He would stay over.

They went to several vendors of horribly overpriced merchandise where he bought a small Swiss Army knife—he confessed it was a ritual comfort purchase he made every time he landed weaponless in an airport. He also picked up a sports bag to hold his purchases.

Next he selected a change of clothes and a few toiletries. He boldly plunked down a box of condoms with a raised eyebrow that dared her to comment.

She lifted her chin, looked him straight in the eye and said nothing. Silent consent.

No turning back now, she thought. She was committed. A frisson of excitement vibrated through her. The adrenaline was pumping again. Danger did that.

They took a cab to her apartment. On the way, he kept throwing her speculative looks that often approached the boiling point, but their conversation remained impersonal. How the weather here compared to Colombia's, the atrocious Atlanta traffic, the gold dome of the Georgia capitol, anything other than what they were both thinking about.

When they reached her place, a modest two-bedroom in LeJardin, a sprawling complex with a faintly French flavor, he hummed and nodded his approval. It wasn't terribly pricey, but it had charm and the neighborhood was nice enough. She led him up the stairs, punched in her code and opened the door.

He stood just inside for a minute, looking around. "Now, *this* is just not you. I was expecting…I don't know…not this. More sophistication, I guess. It's too homey." He looked down at her and winked. "You'll simply have to move."

"You think?" She had to laugh. Her rooms were shabby chic, so she supposed she should feel complimented.

He examined the exotic travel posters she had framed for the wall. Her globe-trotting brother had sent her souvenirs from all around the world, so her taste in accessories must seem wildly eclectic.

Nothing matched very well, but she didn't really care. One cohesive style or single identifying preference in her surroundings would be boring to live with. Her home suited her better than he knew.

"You remain an enigma," he declared, flashing that charming grin of his. "So, which way to the shower? I'll race you. Or we could share."

"How sophisticated is that? Let you watch me scrub off this disguise? I don't think so." Martine pointed to the guest bedroom. "I have two. Yours is through there. Help yourself to anything you need that you forgot to buy."

The moment he disappeared through the door, Martine hurried to her own room. The message light on her answering machine blinked like crazy. She deliberately ignored it. There would be time enough to sort things out with her brother tomorrow after Joe left for D.C.

Tonight was hers, a reward for her daring, a benefit she meant to claim. No matter what happened in the future, she would have this adventure to remember. A time when she had used all her senses, all her wiles, all her knowledge and training. A mission where she had experienced every emotion from the depth of fear right up to—she hoped—the height of passion.

When she said goodbye to Joe on Saturday morning, she would have lived to the max for once in her life.

She scrubbed away the dusky makeup easily enough. Then she shampooed out the substance she had used to temporarily darken her hair. She'd stolen that from Humberto. The man did like to cover his gray. Unfortunately, the dye left a residual shade of red in hers. She would have to bleach to get the original color back, but there wasn't time. She slathered on conditioner and hoped for the best.

At least she knew what to wear. Joe had only the black long-sleeve pullover, a pair of gray slacks and casual deck shoes, things he had purchased at the airport. Her little black dress would be perfect if she kept it simple. Gold hoops for her ears and a plain gold chain. Her black sandals with the medium heels would do.

She dried her hair, applied her makeup and dressed quickly. By the time she found her purse and went into the living room, he had already raided her fridge and found the wine. Faintly embarrassed that it was only an inexpensive bottle of Riesling, Martine blushed a little.

"Nectar of the gods," he said, handing her a glass. "Hope you don't mind. I made myself at home." His voice was a low, seductive Southern drawl. Though his dark good looks gave away his Latino heritage, his voice did not unless he spoke Spanish. She wondered which language he would use when they were intimate.

He looked very comfortable in her kitchen, very comfortable in his skin. She liked that about a man. She liked Joe. A lot.

The wine was deliciously fruity, despite the fact that it was cheap. She sipped, meeting his gaze over the rim of her glass. He looked fantastic. Very hip. Very macho. Her pulse fluttered when he smiled that way, like he knew secrets that would make her incredibly happy once he shared them.

"So, where shall we go?" he asked, rocking his wine-glass a little and glancing down into it with a thoughtful expression, then back at her.

Martine frowned at the motion, wondering if he had little cork pieces floating. She stared into her own and saw nothing but clear amber liquid. "You like Chinese?" she asked.

"Not much," he admitted and took a sip of his wine.

She watched the muscles in his throat, saw the drop of wine cling to the corner of his upper lip when he lowered the glass. Her mouth almost watered, anticipating the taste.

"You know what? I'd kill for a pizza," he told her. "You have more of this." He rocked his glass again, again watching the liquid as it swirled. "We could order out."

"It's white wine. Red goes with pizza."

"Since when do you follow rules?"

She reached to pick up the phone. It rang just before

she touched it. Her brother's number appeared on the caller ID. Reluctantly she answered.

"Hi, Matt," she said, her gaze still locked with Joe's.

"Where the *hell* have you been?" he shouted. "Never mind, I *know* where you were! What happened?"

Martine had jerked the receiver away from her ear and winced at the volume. "Glad you made it back, Matt. I'll explain everything, but not now. See you Monday," she said and hung up.

"He's a bit testy," she explained to Joe. "Must be the heat."

"Right. Temperature's definitely rising." He stepped closer so that they were almost touching. He lifted his hand and touched her face with one finger, drew a feather-light line from her brow to her chin. She shivered.

His lower body pressed hers to the wall. She could feel his breath on her cheek, his heart beat against her breasts, his leg between hers. "I thought…you were hungry," she whispered.

"Yeah. Famished," he whispered as he possessed her mouth.

Martine returned the kiss, sliding her arms around him, pulling him even closer, reveling in the pleasure of his hands. They seemed to be everywhere at once, gliding, grasping, claiming.

The growl in his throat reverberated through her, a primal demand. She pressed herself to him and undulated, an intimate, urgent age-old invitation. Her heartbeat thundered in her ears, blocking out all sound.

Suddenly he stilled. He released her and backed away as far as he could with her hands fisted in the back of his shirt. "Martine?"

"Umm?" She clung to him, her body still seeking.

"Somebody's at your door," he murmured between kisses. "I don't think they're going away."

The doorbell was buzzing, an insistent staccato as

someone punched it repeatedly. How had she not heard that?

Reluctantly, she uncurled her fingers and let him go. "Must be Matt," she said with a heavy sigh of frustration. "Sorry."

When she looked through the peephole, she saw she was right. He must have been nearby, calling from his cell phone.

"Tell me you didn't go where I think you went!" he demanded the minute she opened the door. "You were supposed to hotfoot it back here if I was even a day late returning to Bogotá! Dammit, you weren't here when I finally made it back yesterday and I was getting ready to fly back down there!"

He had pushed in past her, the cast on his foot thumping against her hardwood floor.

His hand flew to his weapon the instant he spied Joe.

Martine grabbed his arm and gave him a pinch. "Matt, behave."

Matt's assessing gaze flew back and forth between them. Joe had moved behind the kitchen counter, probably to hide his arousal, and was calmly sipping his wine.

"Hey, Duquesne," he said. "How's it going?"

"Am I...interrupting something?" Matt asked, his voice tight with disapproval.

Martine pinched him again. "Yes, you are. And I'll pay you back. Count on it."

He turned on her, ignoring Joe. "Sebastian's gonna fire your little ass, you know that? He swore if I was right and you'd gone into the middle of that mess alone, you were through at Ames. Terminated."

She smiled sweetly. "Maybe not. Corda's back in one piece. I'm okay. No problem. Want some wine? We were just about to order pizza." She closed the door and headed back to the kitchen.

She had almost reminded him that he was the one who

failed to bring Joe home. He was the one who broke his leg and was late making the rendezvous in Bogotá. But she had to hold her tongue. If anyone could talk Sebastian around to keeping her on, it would be Matt.

"Wait a minute! I want to know *exactly* what happened." He seemed to remember Joe then and stopped. "What the hell's he doing here with *you?*"

"He followed me home. Can I keep him?"

"Damn you, Martine!"

She admitted Matt had reason to be upset, but she wasn't about to apologize. Still, an explanation might be in order. "Look, you were overdue coming back. I couldn't contact you. Sebastian was…out of pocket, and Nestor was, well, you know where. There was no one else left to go looking for you. And for Joe, of course. So I went."

He looked ready to explode, speechless and fuming. Sebastian would be worse, she knew. And he would not be speechless. Better if she downplayed the whole mission.

She rubbed Matt's forearm and squeezed it gently, soothing where she had given him the sisterly pinches. "Look, Matt, I'm home now. Everything turned out fine. You don't need to worry about me. I'm sorry I upset you, okay?"

He looked over at Joe and expelled the breath he was holding. "I guess I should thank you for getting her out of there, Corda."

Joe glanced at her and smiled, took another sip of his wine and set down the glass. "Getting *her* out? Are you kidding? If she hadn't been such a great shot, I'd be rotting in the woods right now. She's a real piece of work, your sister."

Martine's breath caught in her throat. Joe must think he was helping.

Matt's mouth had dropped open. He snapped it shut, then said very quietly, "She…shot somebody?"

Joe shrugged and leaned forward, resting on the counter. "Oh yeah, I lost count how many." He shook his head as he pretended to count. "Fourteen, fifteen…can't say for sure. Then when the chopper blew up and we had to run for it, she really showed her stuff." He held up the short lock of hair he'd brushed down over the graze on his forehead. "Dazed me big-time."

Matt continued to gape.

Joe went on, picking up his wine again. "Hell, man, she carried me half the way to the airport, fed me to get my strength back and hauled our butts out of there on the first plane. Never seen anything like it. Girl's a wonder. I owe her my life." He tossed her a sappy look of gratitude over the rim of his glass.

She was going to kill him.

"Matt, he's exaggerating. I promise you…" She broke off when she saw his expression of pure disbelief. "What's the matter? Don't you think I'm capable of that? Of…of what he said?"

Matt turned without a word and slammed out of the apartment. They heard him thumping down the stairs. She rounded on Joe, throwing up her hands in sheer frustration. "What the devil did you think you were doing? You probably got me fired, you know that? I wanted him to think…"

What had she wanted Matt to think? What had she expected when she set out on this venture? That Matt and Sebastian would be so delighted when she'd proved herself, they would promote her to field work permanently? She slumped against the nearest armchair and blew out a sigh.

Joe came over and grasped her shoulders. He bent just a bit so that his face was right in front of hers. "So I beefed it up a little. They won't fire you, Martine. You really did save my life. You got me out. Maybe Matt's just ticked off because I refused to get out when he tried to get me to, and then I came back with you. What you did was well-planned and executed right down to the last detail. They can't possibly argue with your results.''

She shrugged, but she couldn't agree with him there. Matt and Sebastian would argue all right. And Sebastian Ames would probably terminate her employment immediately because she had seriously overstepped and gone way beyond her job description. But that was a worry for Monday morning. Not tonight.

She dismissed it for now. "I'll handle it. Let's forget about it for now and get that pizza. You call it in. I need to… God, I need that glass of wine."

He laughed, straightened to his full height and planted a playful kiss on top of her head. "Lighten up. Before I'm done, they'll be giving you a citation and a raise."

"Joe, please!" When he turned, eyebrow raised in question, she continued, "Please, don't do me any more favors."

He walked back over, his gait lazy, his dark eyes gleaming wickedly. She stood while his hands cradled her face and his lips met hers. The kiss had a different flavor than those Matt had interrupted. This one tasted like gratitude, something she appreciated, but not right now.

She raised on tiptoe and increased the pressure, pulling him to her, hoping to regain ground lost by Matt's unfortunate interruption.

Joe pushed away and smiled down at her. "No, Martine. Not now."

"Why not?" Her breath shuddered out, causing the words to wobble. Like her knees.

"Because I don't want to be a player in your little rebellion, that's why." He looked amused, but she sensed he meant it. "I admit I was all for this before your brother showed up, but I've changed my mind. I sense you're not

a one-night stander, Martine. To tell you the truth, neither
am I.'' He gave her a grim smile. ''At least not any
more.''

''Fine,'' she snapped, angry with herself for revealing
how much she wanted him. He obviously had more control and wasn't nearly as affected by their mutual attraction. ''Forget it.''

He slid his hands down her arms and clutched the hands
she had fisted. ''No, I'm not about to forget. But I think
I *will* postpone until I know it's *me* you really want. It
looks like you're still trying to prove something here.
Maybe show your father you're no different than your
brother, even if you are female?'' He paused and sighed.
''Dangerous work and casual sex. Not what a woman usually leaps at unless there's a reason.''

''Spare me your pop psychology. I told you my father's
dead!''

''Yeah, but he's still dictating what you do in a way,
making you feel you have to be everything your brother
is. If it means anything to you, I don't think you'd ever
have turned out a wimp, Martine. Not under any circumstances. But I don't think I want to be a party to establishing your thrill-a-minute lifestyle. Nobody likes being
used.''

''*Used?* Why, you…'' She jerked her hand free and
almost slugged him. He was waiting for it, but she stopped
just in time. Taking a deep breath, she released it slowly,
unclenched her fists and regained a little of her tattered
dignity. ''I think you had better leave.''

He nodded and stepped through the door, but turned
back to face her. ''I should. And I'm going to. It's not
that I don't want you, Martine. I want you too much.''

''It was just a few kisses, Corda. Get over yourself.''
She held his gaze, willing herself not to shake.

''I wish you had wanted more than a night's worth.''

He frowned thoughtfully as he paused again. "You know, I don't think I've ever said that to a woman before?"

She slammed the door in his face and then leaned against it.

Oh God, could he be right about her?

Joe walked to the nearest gas station and called a cab. The ride seemed long. And sad. He had met the one woman he could really go for in a big way, but he couldn't take her on the terms she offered.

He almost had, physically at least. Only seeing her as some guy's sister had made him stop and think how he would feel if it were one of his own crazy little sisters in her place and Matt Duquesne were the one doing the seducing.

He had also told Martine the absolute truth, how he felt about being used. If she wanted him for real, not just what he represented, then maybe he could handle it. Or maybe it was the excuse he had needed to let her go.

He knew Martine didn't realize she was still riding the adrenaline high. True, her heartbeat might have slowed down to almost normal. But the fever of success, the exhilaration of defeating death was clouding her judgment more than she knew. He'd been there, right where she was. As recently as a half hour ago.

Once she settled down, figured things out, she'd be relieved that he hadn't stayed tonight. His body was still humming with arousal. He would probably spend some sleepless nights between now and the time he got over her.

Forty minutes later, Joe arrived back at the airport to book his flight to D.C. He was paying the cab driver while scanning his surroundings out of habit. It was mere chance that he caught sight of the all-too-familiar profile of Carlos Humberto as he and two associates entered a taxi.

Shock at seeing a dead man walking held Joe immobile

for all of two seconds. Then he spent another few kicking himself for not climbing into that ravine and checking the body for signs of life after Martine shot the bastard. Humberto had to have been wearing a Kevlar vest.

Humberto couldn't have been right on their tail coming out of Bogotá. He would have had his hands full then arranging his own escape. But he was here now and there could only be one reason for his being here in Atlanta. He knew where to find Martine.

Joe jumped back in the cab and headed straight back to her, praying Humberto had not somehow discovered her home address.

He arrived, slung a fistful of bills at the driver as he leaped out of the cab, and tore up the steps at top speed. He had no weapons other than his hands and a stupid pocket knife. If Humberto had beat him here, he knew they had little chance of surviving.

After all he and Martine had done to the man, Humberto would have a vendetta going that no one could reason with. He would be out for blood, because there was nothing left for him to be after. Not the money, not the drugs and no possible restitution of his former life at all. Nothing but revenge.

Chapter 5

"Martine! Open up!" he called, banging on the door with his fist, punching the doorbell repeatedly.

He stopped when he heard her—at least he hoped it was her—sliding the chain off the lock. The breath he was holding huffed out when she swung the door open. "Let's go!" he ordered, grabbing her by the wrist.

"What?" She dug in her heels.

"Humberto's here. I saw him at the airport. If he knows where you are, we've got to get the hell out of here. Do you have a weapon?"

She nodded, looking dumbstruck by his news. He noticed for the first time that she was only wearing a nightshirt.

"Give me your gun. I'll stand watch while you grab some clothes. Make it snappy. And bring a cell phone."

To her credit, she grasped the urgency of the situation and flew to follow orders. He did a hurried check of the Glock she shoved into his hands. The feel of it soothed him a little.

Humberto and his friends would also have to find a way to arm themselves before coming here. They could not have brought weapons on the plane. With the spot checks of baggage, it would have been too dangerous to risk arrest. No, they would either have contacts here who could furnish weapons or they would steal them.

Several minutes crawled by as Joe stood in the shadows outside her door, peering into the night, every nerve on edge. He shuddered to think what might have happened if he'd not gone back to the airport. And with the size of that airport, he could so easily have missed seeing Humberto at all. Hell, he had thought they were home free.

"Let's roll," Martine said, handing him the sports bag he had left behind earlier and the overnight bag she had packed for herself. She pulled the door closed behind her, keys in hand. She had donned a pair of dark-brown slacks and a matching silk blouse. Her leather shoes were flat-heeled, stylish but practical. She wore a brown sweater draped over her shoulders, the sleeves tied in front. Very preppy, he thought. So not her.

He followed her to a dark Jeep Cherokee parked in the well-lit lot nearby, where she popped the locks with the remote and went straight to the driver's side.

Joe almost demanded she relinquish the keys, but told himself she knew the city better than he did. He climbed in the passenger side and took the small bag she'd brought with her into his lap. "Your cell phone in this thing?"

"Big pocket on the side."

He fished it out.

"Call Matt. Speed dial 2," she ordered.

Joe was already shaking his head and punching at the numbers on the little instrument. "If ol' Hummy knew where you'd be, he knows where your brother is. We'll give Matt a heads-up, but we aren't going there."

"Then where?" she demanded.

Joe put the phone to his ear and waited. A message

machine on the other end spat out the number of the duty agent for the local office. He tapped it in and waited some more. A woman answered. "Cunningham."

"Agent Cunningham. Joe Corda from the D.C. office here." He hesitated as she asked how she could be of help. How could she? How could he explain that he'd just come off an assignment he'd thought completed and found himself and a civilian being chased by a drug lord who had serious retribution on his agenda?

"Do you recognize the name Carlos Humberto? From Colombia?" he asked her.

"No. Do you need some information concerning this individual?"

"I have more info than I need, thanks. But look him up. He's just arrived in your city with two of his men. This is a seriously disturbed individual with murder on his mind and he has local contacts. I have reason to believe he will show up shortly at the LeJardin apartments, unit 205, loaded for bear. Get all the backup you can and take him down."

She cleared her throat. "Agent...Carter, is it?"

He spelled his name. "Listen to me, please. Humberto's entire operation in Colombia has just been shut down. He's mad as hell and about to wreak some serious havoc. Are you with me on this?"

Another small hesitation. "I have no immediate way to verify what you're saying, sir. Or even who you are. If you want to leave a number, I'll contact my superior, meet him at the office and get back to you."

Joe gritted his teeth and banged his head back against the headrest. "Look, lady, I've just delivered what amounts to the collar of the century. Can you handle this or not?"

"As soon as I have contacted and coordinated with my office and yours, of course I can," she snapped. "But I

can't very well commit agents to this without some
sort of—''

"Thanks anyway," Joe snapped and punched the Off
button. He quickly hit the speed dial for Matt Duquesne,
who answered immediately.

"Duquesne? Listen up. Humberto's here. I saw him at
the airport and have reason to believe he's after us. I'll
keep Martine out of his reach. Call in some troops, do
what you gotta do. He knew what Martine was doing in
Colombia so he'll know about Ames and its employees.
Watch yourself."

"Where are you?" Duquesne demanded.

"On the move. We'll be in touch."

"If you let him within a mile of Martine, I'll—"

"Save your breath, okay? We're not planning to make
a stand and shoot it out with him. We're headed for D.C.
She'll be safe with me."

He rang off before her brother could argue that. And
there were several arguments that would be valid. For
now, Joe intended to do precisely what he'd promised
Matt. He'd keep Martine and himself alive and reach familiar territory where he could depend on getting help
from either DEA or Sextant. Or both.

He had no clue how many contacts Humberto actually
had Stateside, but there was no point waiting around for
some of them to show up.

"I'm not going to Washington with you," Martine declared, slowing the car to an unreasonable speed for the
six-lane they were on.

He shot her a steely look. "Don't you test my determination, Martine. Put the pedal down and get us out of
this city." When she scoffed, he shouted, "Do it *now!*"

She gunned the accelerator so hard, his neck almost
snapped. "I can't believe you're running," she said.

"You damn well better believe it. Our little Humbuddy
probably knows a hell of a lot more people in Atlanta

than I do. Maybe more than *you* do. And they'll still be believing they have to depend on him for their steady supply of dope. By the time the people here get the word he's history with the cartel in Colombia, we could be dead as last week's catch.''

"Won't someone call and tell his contacts here?" she asked.

"Not likely. They won't want to admit it—not yet anyway—and besides, they're probably still looking for him there. How much gas you got?"

She glanced down. "Half a tank."

"How much money?"

"A few dollars. Fifteen, maybe. You?"

"Not enough. Get off at the next exit. Find an ATM," he ordered. "If we both withdraw the max, it should be enough to get us there. We'd better not leave a paper trail.''

"Don't be ridiculous. He couldn't trace us that way…. Could he? Why don't we just fly? We'd be there before he knew we were gone."

"Maybe. Unless he has someone watching for us at the airport. We just don't know how many people he has here. That's the problem. I've been on this guy's case for nearly a year now and his reach is incredible. You said yourself he's got contacts up the wazoo. That probably won't change unless he tries to arrange a deal involving the Colombians or until word filters through the grapevine. By that time, it would be too late for us."

Her worried gaze flashed his way briefly, then back to the road where cars were zipping past despite the fact that she was speeding big-time. "You think he's come specifically to find you?"

"To find both of us. Absolutely."

They managed to find a bank within a block of the exit and drew out the daily limit allowed from the automatic teller machine. Joe felt a bit better. They had a good vehicle, a fair head start and enough money to get them to D.C.

She filled the gas tank and then took the access road to the northernmost route that would take them to Chattanooga, Tennessee. Joe had never been there and didn't particularly want to go now, but he'd go to hell itself to keep Humberto from catching up with the woman who had shot him.

Martine checked her watch as they reached the outskirts of Chattanooga. While they had not been driving all that long, she needed to take a break. They also needed food since they had never gotten around to ordering that pizza. But they had drunk the wine. "I'm starving," she told him.

He sighed impatiently. "Pull off at the next exit and hit a drive-through. We can eat on the way. I'll take over if you're tired of driving already."

"I need to go inside," she said pointedly.

"Oh, okay."

He might sound amused, but unless he had a bladder the size of Texas, she knew he would welcome a pit stop, too. "There's a place." He pointed to the towering sign advertising a chain restaurant at the next exit.

Their meal took less than twenty minutes and when they returned to the Jeep, he asked for the keys. "You sleep a while. I'll wake you when I get too tired. We should take turns and drive straight through if we can."

"Why? There's no way Humberto can find us on the road like this. He won't know what kind of vehicle I have."

"Want to bet your life on that? I don't. He's going to come after us with every resource he's got, Martine. There's nothing left for him to lose. After we blew his operation sky-high, there's no way he could have gone back. We made him a marked man."

Martine shivered, rubbing her arms to restore warmth. "I guess he couldn't even risk going to his wife and family, could he?"

"No. His missus will surely side with her old man and he'll be out for Humberto's blood. So our boy's got nothing left now but a very temporary power here in the States and whatever funds he had access to before he left the country. That gives him a limited time in which to exact revenge on the people responsible for his downfall. Namely us."

"It could be he was only getting out of Colombia, seeking safety. Maybe you're just being paranoid," she suggested as she fastened her seat belt.

"If that's so, why would he come to Atlanta? And hey, paranoia's my friend," Joe said easily and pulled back onto the interstate. "Can't live long without it in this business."

"How long have you been doing it?"

"Too long. Way too long," he answered, his tone weary. The dash lights cast a weak glow that angled upward, exposing the planes of his features and emphasizing lines hardly noticeable in the light of day. His strong fingers flexed a few times, fitting themselves to the steering wheel as he settled his large body for the long drive ahead. He rolled his shoulders slightly. He looked exhausted.

"Joe, is something else wrong?"

"Why? That's not enough?" He smiled and tossed her a weary glance. "No, there's nothing else. You know all I know. Go to sleep, Martine."

"I meant with you. Is there something wrong with you, Joe?" she persisted.

"Nothing a few weeks on the beach wouldn't cure. When this is over, that's where I'm headed. Just me and a cooler full of Dos Equis." He glanced over again. "Offer still holds. You come, too. That is, if you want to and promise not to talk shop."

Martine laughed, leaned back and closed her eyes. "Nice dream, Joe," she said, letting exhaustion claim her. She hadn't lied. It was a nice dream.

As the purr of the motor and shimmy of slightly out-of-line tires morphed into waves rhythmically rolling onto a shore, the dream proved better than nice. It became real.

Joe, wearing only ragged remnants of the gray trousers, strolled down a sandy beach, beer in hand, grin revealing those straight white teeth as he approached. The glare of a tropical sun bounced enticingly off his heavily muscled shoulders, arms and chest. Strong, bare feet tracked through sugary white sand, bringing him ever closer.

She wore a sarong tied loosely allowing the warm ocean breeze to caress her skin as the soft garment billowed out from her body. A heady sense of anticipatory awareness created a tingle in places he had yet to touch. She quivered as she held out her arms in welcome.

He walked right into them, those amazing hands of his sliding beneath the silky fabric, creating havoc with her senses.

She breathed in his scent, a peculiar mix of cool fresh limes and hot ready man. The low timbre of his voice vibrated through her as they embraced, the landscape of his body melding perfectly with hers. She writhed in pleasure, the sun hot against her bare back, his hands even hotter against her bare flesh.

Something began tugging at her arm, calling to her, warning her to...

"Wake up!"

"No," Martine groaned in protest, even as she opened her eyes. Reality hit her like a slap in the face. Headlights from oncoming traffic flashed, causing her to squint. She gulped in a deep breath and quickly pushed herself upright in the seat, embarrassed by the fact that a dream of Joe had aroused her. She risked a glance at him and saw him frowning.

"It was just a dream," he assured her. "You groaned like you were in pain or something. Thought I'd better bring you out of it. You all right?"

Martine nodded, afraid to speak and maybe betray what she'd really been up to in that dream. What *he* had been up to. But he couldn't know. How could he? There was no way he could even guess she'd been dreaming of him. Of them together.

She released the breath she was holding and smoothed her hands over her face, raking her fingers through her hair and shaking her head to clear away every vestige of the dream. But the erotic images of them together remained, teasing her mercilessly, even as he watched.

"That bad, huh?" he asked, sounding concerned.

Not taunting her, Martine decided. He was worried. She smiled to herself, her secret safe. "I'm fine. You want me to drive now?" Her voice trembled, sounding almost as shaky as she felt.

"Not on a dare in your condition," he replied to her question about taking the wheel. "There's an exit up ahead. I think we'd better stop for a few hours. I noticed you didn't get much shut-eye on the planes. Apparently you have trouble sleeping while you ride."

Fully alert now, Martine almost laughed. The fool had no clue *he* was what disrupted her sleep. She cleared her throat and switched on the radio. "Don't worry about it. What kind of music do you like?" Anything to get his mind off that dream of hers. To get *her* mind off of it. "Oh, I remember, oldies. Right?"

He reached over and switched it off. "No music. We're finding a motel. You're too dopey to drive and I'm getting there fast."

"Let's not do that," she said, trying not to sound as if she were pleading. All she needed was to be shut up in a motel room with him, especially with that lingering vision of him half naked still clear in her head.

But Joe ignored her and slowed for the turnoff. He looked pretty determined. His jaw tight, his lips firmed, his eyes narrowed as he checked out the signs along the way advertising lodgings for the night. Vacancies everywhere. She lost the will to argue.

Surely after making it clear he wasn't interested in a brief sexual encounter with her, he would keep his distance a lot more carefully than he had before. Martine knew she wouldn't risk another rebuff like the one he'd given her after Matt left. It would be all right, she assured herself.

He bypassed the better-known chain hotels where they would need a credit card, and found a small place about two miles off the interstate. "This looks like a strictly cash establishment," he said, more or less to himself.

He was right. It certainly did. She doubted if any customers who stopped here ever gave their correct identity. Or did much sleeping, either.

Even Martine had no idea exactly where they were, which was reassuring. Humberto would never locate them here, wherever *here* was. Even if he somehow figured out they were headed for D.C., there must be thousands of motels between there and Atlanta.

"One room," Joe said pointedly, though there was no suggestiveness whatsoever in the declaration. "We need to save our cash for emergencies."

"Okay," she agreed. This wasn't a hotel where she'd like to be left in a room by herself. She could handle whatever happened, of course, but she certainly wouldn't be able to close her eyes for a minute. Then the rest of what he'd said registered. "What emergencies?"

He parked to one side of the office and unfastened his seat belt as he turned to look at her. "I saw a sign advertising a gun show at the civic center in Carnton. We might need another weapon."

"Get real. You can't buy a decent slingshot with what

we have between us now and we'll still need to eat. Plus, this," she said, shooting a dubious glance at the rundown hotel, "will cost us."

"We'll see what we can do," he said and went into the hotel office.

The room surprised her. Though the furnishings had probably been in place since the sixties, the linens actually looked clean. So did the bathroom. "Not so bad," she quipped. "The bed's king size anyway."

"Yeah," he said, eyeing the bed, then her, then the bed again.

"Don't worry," she told him, her voice a little bitter. "You're entirely safe with me."

He sighed and tossed his duffel onto the chair. "I came off a little high-handed at your apartment. Sorry."

Martine ignored him, went into the bathroom and closed the door. She stayed there for some time, until she ran out of things to do in a five-by-six tile-surfaced box with nothing but towels, T.P. and paper-wrapped soap for company.

There was a mirror, too, but she didn't really want to study her reflection for longer than it took to rake her hair back and check the circles under her eyes. The woman looking back would probably try to convince her she should go out there and make another pass at Joe and damn the consequences.

He knocked softly. "You asleep in there?"

She jumped up from the edge of the tub where she'd been sitting and unlocked the door. "Sorry," she said, brushing past him into the bedroom.

Damn, but he made her nervous now. She would have to watch every word she said and think about every gesture she made, so he wouldn't get the idea she was coming on to him again.

With that in mind, she curled up on the far side of the

bed fully clothed and closed her eyes. When he came out
of that bathroom, she meant to be sound asleep.

Of course, the very intent kept her wide-awake. That,
plus the fact that she had napped in the car. Dream-sleep
must count because she was in no way sleepy now. She'd
have to pretend, because she certainly didn't want to have
a *can-we-sleep-in-the-same-bed-and-be-nice* conversation.

Her senses went on full alert the minute he returned to
the bedroom. There was a long silence, filled only with
the overly long breaths she drew in and released.

When he did move, he wasn't particularly quiet about
it. He checked the gun. She heard it click. He sat down
heavily on the far side of the bed and toed off his shoes.
Then he stretched out full-length beside her, not touching.
"Those are some slow-moving sheep you're counting,"
he said finally.

Martine didn't respond. She crunched the pillow impatiently and snuggled deeper into the too-soft mattress.
In less than five minutes, she could tell by his breathing—
almost a soft snore—that he really had fallen asleep. Moving slowly, she carefully turned over so she could see him.

He was facing her with his eyes wide-open. And he
was smiling. "That's how you fake it."

Infuriated, she snapped, "This is the first time I've ever
had to fake it."

He laughed. "I promise you you'll never have to fake
it with me again."

Martine turned over so fast, she almost fell off the bed.
It was going to be a very long night.

Joe awoke with his hand cupped around a very shapely
butt. His chest rested comfortably against Martine's back.
It was her restlessness that had wakened him, a sinuous
backward snuggling he hated like hell to resist. But he
had to. They should have been out of the motel and on
the road hours ago.

He removed his hand, backed away a little, flicked on the lamp and gave her fanny a firm pat. "Up and at 'em, slugger." Before she could react, he had rolled off the bed, pulled on his shirt and stepped into his shoes. The pants looked as if he'd slept in them because he had. He tucked the pistol beneath his belt and fished the toothpaste and brush out of his duffel.

She bypassed him without so much as a good morning and disappeared into the bathroom with the small bag she'd brought with her. "Ah, not a morning person," he muttered. "But I knew that."

He recalled their trail to Bogotá and how silent she had been for a while after they'd awakened. Though she'd moved quickly and surely then, he had realized that it took her a while to gear up for the day.

Joe always came awake at full throttle. He could hardly help wondering then what it would be like to coax her awake slowly with touches and kisses. And now that he had the opportunity, the wondering almost became compulsion.

"No," he said to himself. "Not just yet." If he ever had Martine Duquesne—and it was looking more and more like that *if* was a *when*—he wanted all the time in the world and no distractions. He also wanted more tomorrows with her than she would promise him now. Shared danger was not enough of a connection to sustain anything more than a quick fling. Joe knew this woman was worth more than that. He'd do something about it, too, if he thought she would give up her current job.

The water turned off. "Hey, babe, get a move on, would you?" he called to her. She'd hate being called *babe,* but Joe needed the distance that little insult would throw up between them right now, or else he'd be tempted to stay right here in this dump of a motel making love to her until Humberto died of old age.

She stormed out of the bathroom looking like a sixteen-year-old who'd been stood up for her favorite concert. "If you call me that word again…!"

"Yeah, yeah, I hear you," he said and left her standing there fuming while he went in to shave. "Just what I love, sharing a bathroom with a girl. My sister spent *days* primping while I had to stand outside, waiting to pee." He quickly closed the door, grinning when something thunked against the outside of it. He felt to make sure the gun was still where he'd put it.

"You're crude, rude and…"

"Delightful to know!" he added, laughing as he heard a muffled curse through the door.

He had just lathered his face when the door flew open.

"Joe, come look! There's a dark car out there by the office. Three men just got out and went inside."

He rushed to the window and pulled the drape aside. It was impossible to see into the motel office. Though the whole front was glass, it was covered with blinds.

"Get in the Jeep," he ordered. "You drive. Pull up right behind that car and be ready to fly."

He had never seen her move so fast. She grabbed her bag, jumped into the vehicle and in seconds, she braked where he'd told her to. Joe climbed out, slashed the back tires on the black Camry and dived back in. She was peeling out of the parking lot before he had the door shut.

Shots erupted, several thunking into the back of the Jeep. Tires screeched as Martine careened onto the access road and gunned the motor.

"Turn right!" he ordered. "We'll take back roads. I hope you've got a map."

"Compass," she assured him, lifting her left wrist to remind him of the one in her watch.

"Right now any direction away from here is fine. They have us outgunned." He studied her carefully as she drove. "And you have a transmitter of some kind some-where on you or they would never have found us."

She gasped, almost veering off the road.

"On me?"

He shrugged. "Well, I've been checking *me* daily while I was there and never found anything. Besides, you were money in his pocket, remember.

"There's no chance they put it anywhere on the car because we were gone with it before they got there," he said, thinking out loud. "We've got to find and ditch it," he told her. "And we have to do it before they get those tires fixed."

Chapter 6

"Next place you see that could give any kind of cover, pull over," Joe ordered.

She chose a used car lot, fairly well lighted, and parked in between a truck and a van.

The second she cut the engine, she yanked off the watch and handed it over. "It's got to be this. Can you tell if it's in there?"

"Not without tools to open it."

"Smash it!" she insisted.

"No. We'll put it on something that's moving, preferably going south."

"Truck stop. Back to the interstate," she suggested and fired up the engine.

She drove top speed, surpassing the limit, but it seemed forever before they reached any place like what they were looking for. A Stuckey's loomed ahead and she took the exit.

Quickly, Joe jumped out when she stopped, looped the

buckled watch over the antenna of the nearest large vehicle and returned to the Jeep.

"Okay, hit it. Only go that way," he said, pointing away from the interstate.

For hours, they drove, taking turns, saying little, stopping only to refuel once. The back roads took them seriously off the nearest route to their destination in D.C., but the farther away they got, the more they relaxed.

It was nearing noon when Joe suggested they stop and rest. Food was high on his list of needs, but contact with someone who might help them came in a definite first.

When he mentioned that again, she nodded in agreement. "I guess DEA would be thrilled to get their hands on Humberto, especially if they can take him alive."

"Oh, they've had chances before. What do you think I was doing down there trying to get rid of him? They can't arrest him until he commits some crime on American soil that can be proved."

"Cold-blooded murder? Duh."

"Yeah, but if they wait until he succeeds, what good does that do us?"

"Point taken."

Joe nodded. "They can turn us over to the Marshal Service, get us in the Wit Program on the basis of what we did down there. But you know what that would mean."

She scoffed, just as he knew she would. It would mean giving up her family, her life, everything she knew. For his part, Joe knew he'd rather have a showdown in the middle of the street and be done with it. If only Martine were not involved. He couldn't stand the thought of her getting hurt, maybe even killed. She had already faced more risk than she should before they ever reached the States.

"I vote for the nearest police station, maybe call in the

State Patrol,'' she told him. ''I suggested that as we were leaving Atlanta, and now I think I have to insist.''

Joe shrugged. ''If I thought they could deal with this, I'd have already done that. But those are fully automatic weapons our boys are using, not something a small-town force would be likely to have or be able to compete with in a showdown. Also, the locals won't believe us at first— you have to admit it sounds unbelievable—and there might not be time to check our story if the transmitter wasn't in that watch.''

''Well, I don't know where else it could be,'' she argued.

Joe had a pretty good idea where it was. But he didn't want to tell Martine that it could possibly be a part of her body now. A transmitter inserted when she was sedated and unaware. The devices were so small now they could be implanted damn near anywhere. He'd made it a habit to check the surface of his skin every morning when he had showered, but who knew? She was simply the most probable carrier.

It had most likely been placed there so Humberto could track her down if she had decided to escape. Or maybe he'd been waiting for her to make contact with someone outside the compound, go out to meet whoever had sent her in to spy.

''How about the FBI?'' she questioned. ''Wouldn't they be able to do something?''

''I don't imagine they have anything more concrete on Humberto than DEA does. I told you that's why I infiltrated his organization in the first place. My job was to destroy the operation and put the head honcho out of business.''

''Well, you certainly did that,'' Martine said, shaking her head.

''Yeah, but before I left to go down there, there were only rumors he was the one running the cartel and trucking with the rebel forces to get the drugs out. He's been incredibly careful not to break any laws here. Not a one.''

''What about all the drug deals? They must have been big ones with lots of people involved.''

''He met with major dealers all over the place, but someone else made the actual arrangements. Unfortunately, none of them are in custody to testify that they were doing them on his behalf. So, we have nothing to present to any law enforcement agency except our own belief that he and his men are here specifically to get rid of us. We can't even prove he's done anything since he's been here this time.''

''I saw him about to kill you in cold blood,'' she said with a shiver.

''Even if he had committed murder there, no one could arrest him for it.''

''He put bullet holes in the back of my Jeep and would have killed us.''

Joe nodded. ''Yes, but you didn't actually see him shooting, did you?''

She sighed. ''No. Too bad he's not a terrorist, everybody would be all over him.''

Well, there it was. Joe laughed and slapped her on the shoulder. ''Out of the mouths of babes! My girl, you are something else.''

She shot him a dark look. ''Yes, I'm something else all right, not your *girl*. And definitely not a *babe!* What is it with you?''

''C'mon, Martine! You've hit on something here. Don't go all PC on me while I'm doing cartwheels!''

''What do you mean?''

''Terrorists. That's the answer.'' He kissed her soundly on the mouth and laughed again when she drew back looking stunned. ''We'll call Mercier. What would you label three foreigners using illegal weapons to shoot up a motel parking lot, endangering American citizens? That fits a terrorist in my book. You know how to reach him?''

"I certainly do.'' A smile slowly crept across her features. It was like the sun coming out after a storm. Joe dearly wanted to kiss her again. But they had a phone call to make.

Here was his chance to see what the Sextant Team was all about and whether he wanted to be a part of it. *If* he lived to be a part of it.

First off, he'd request that they stash Martine somewhere safe until all this was over. Surely they could do that much even if Mercier and his new hires turned out to be desk jockeys, simple window dressing for the new HSA organization, a show to illustrate how well agents from the different agencies could work together.

Chances were pretty good that they weren't that. After all, they had hired him, a DEA cowboy who had never been particularly photogenic. Or tactful. God help *them* if they were front men for the new outfit and expected him to deal with the press in any way. He'd wind up in Leavenworth.

"Joe?'' She glanced up into the rearview mirror again and then over at him. "There's a car trailing us about a quarter of a mile back, and it's made the last two turns I have. If it's them, I figure they're hanging back until we stop again.''

"How're you doing on gas now?'' Joe asked as he turned around to look for the tail.

"Quarter of a tank.''

He reached for the 9mm for all the good it would do against an AK-47. "We'll call in the cavalry later if we get the chance, but it looks like we'll have to handle this next skirmish by ourselves.''

Martine knew they were outgunned and outmanned. They needed a plan if they were to survive Humberto's catching up with them when they stopped for gas, which would need to be soon. She had believed that once they unloaded her watch with the transmitter, they'd be good to go. They had crossed the Virginia line about five minutes before and were traveling parallel to Highway 81.

"How do you suppose they found us?" she asked Joe.

Busy checking the weapon again, he merely shrugged.

"What aren't you telling me?"

"The transmitter," he said. "It's gotta be an implant. They make 'em about the size of a grain of rice now. Shoot it in with a hypodermic. Track you with a cell phone or global positioning system using a laptop or handheld."

A chill ran through her just imagining something foreign within her that she hadn't even known about. She racked her brain, trying to recall if she'd ever been so out of it that Humberto could have injected her with something without her knowing about it. She was a very light sleeper and as far as she knew, had not been drugged to make her sleep through such a thing.

He glanced over his shoulder again at the car following them. "If we can lose them for half an hour, maybe we can find it and get rid of it."

She was afraid to ask. "How?"

"Minor surgery," he muttered.

Martine cringed, imagining what that would involve. She promised herself it was only like removing a splinter. "Funston City's about four miles away. Maybe there's a mall there. They'd know we were there, but not exactly where. That would give us time to hide somewhere inside and look for it."

"And if we can't find it? Can you imagine the havoc if these goons open fire in a mall? Besides, I don't think there is a mall in Funston City."

"You know the place?"

"Been there to buy supplies for camping trips. An old

college buddy of mine is from Roanoke. We used to come
out this way when we were in college. Beautiful country
with pretty good fishing.''

Another idea occurred to her. ''How about the police
station there? They wouldn't follow us inside, would
they? Surely the cops could help us if they did.''

''Might work.'' He didn't sound too hopeful, however.
Humberto would still be waiting for them when they came
back outside, even if they were minus the transmitter.

''Somehow we've got to get them off our tail until we
can stop broadcasting our location,'' she said, stating the
obvious. ''Could the signal be interrupted somehow?''

''In some place where there's a lot of interference
maybe. There's no way to know how sophisticated the
little gadget is. It could be as simple as the one used to
track pets when they're lost or stolen.''

''Or not,'' Martine said, almost under her breath.

''Yeah. Or not. But I think we have to hope for that
and run on that assumption. You can bet Humberto's not
planning to trail us much longer without making another
move. I've got an idea.''

''What?'' she demanded.

He looked behind them again, then turned around to
peer into the darkness ahead. ''If we haven't passed the
turnoff already, there's a place we used to go caving once
in a while. I don't know if a ton of overhead rock will
block the signals we're putting off, but it's worth a try.
At any rate, we ought to be able to evade for a while,
even if he can track us. Caves are my thing.''

''Well, they certainly aren't *mine*,'' Martine muttered,
but she didn't elaborate. This probably wouldn't be a great
time to admit to claustrophobia.

They rode in silence for another ten minutes. Then he
pointed at a sign half overgrown with vines. ''Yeah, there
we go! Peebles Ridge. Cut the lights and hang a right.''

She swerved onto the paved, two-lane side road, blinking rapidly, trying to adjust her vision to the weak light of the half moon.

"Now watch for a break in the foliage. There's a dirt road on your right about a half mile ahead if I remember right."

It was less than that. Martine turned too sharply and almost ran into the ditch. "How far?" she gasped once the wheels were straight. "Are they back there?"

He looked. "If they are, they're running dark, too. Go left when I tell you. Good thing we've got four-wheel drive. They don't, so we're ahead of the game and should have a little lead time."

She turned when he told her and after a grueling five minutes of bumping over brush and deep ruts, he ordered her to stop. "We're here. Come on."

He brought his duffel and she grabbed her bag and they hurriedly exited the car. Brambles snagged her clothing and branches raked her hair and face as he half dragged her through the heavily wooded terrain.

She'd always been pretty good in the rough, but the last few days had taken their toll.

"Through here," he commanded, disappearing into a dark hole in the rock, about two feet wide and four feet high. Martine froze.

"Hurry up!" he added when she remained outside. Before she could protest, he reached back out and grasped her arm, yanking her inside with him. "Now stay put until I check it out. Don't venture farther in yet."

"Like there's a chance of that," she gulped.

Martine clung to the damp wall of the cave while he stepped back out. She heard him break off and drag several dead branches, she guessed to conceal the entrance. What sounded like a huff of relief whispered through the stygian darkness that had swallowed them whole. She shivered and a small whimper escaped in spite of her resolve.

Joe found her hand and gripped it. "We'll have some light in a few minutes, soon as we get deeper in. Stay stooped over so you don't bump your head."

Her head swam as if a rock had already smacked her. She felt disoriented by the total lack of light, but she placed one foot in front of the other as he pulled her along. Walls closed in, damp, fetid as bat guano and scary as hell.

She heard Joe's shoulders periodically brush the outcroppings of rock, a soft swish of fabric dragging against rough stone. She secured the shoulder strap of her bag and trailed her free hand along the wall to steady herself.

It will not collapse. We will not be crushed. The opening will get larger. There is an exit. Several exits.

She moved her lips with the made-up mantra, but allowed no sound to escape them. Joe could not know her fears. Apparently he had none, the idiot. Didn't he know they would suffocate and die in here? If the rocks didn't collapse and kill them first?

She sucked in a deep breath, more or less to prove there was enough air for that. There was nothing for it but to tough this out. If she planned to do this kind of work, she must endure whatever came along. God, even dodging bullets didn't scare her like this did.

"We'll have to crawl through here so kneel down," he told her.

Crawl? A small, hysterical laugh burst out before she could stop it. At the same time, a light came on. At last, the flashlight. Martine almost wept with relief. Then she spied the tunnel he expected her to enter.

"I'll go first," he offered.

"You'll go last, too," she gasped. "I can't, Joe. I can't do it."

"Sure you can. You have to." His voice sounded so logical, as if he weren't telling her she had to do the impossible. "On your knees for me, babe." The flashlight illuminated his grin from below, giving it a truly evil cast. "Not a phrase I'll ever repeat if you're a good girl tonight."

"You... You're trying to make me...angry...aren't you?" she panted, glancing fearfully between him and the small gaping maw that waited for them. She clung to his arm for support because her legs were quivering badly. "Angry...because you know I'm..."

"Yeah, it'll be okay, though. Is it working? You mad enough yet?" His hand came up to brush her hair back from her face and lingered to caress her cheek and ear. "Where's that kickass kid who dragged me halfway across Colombia? Is she gonna wimp out on me now?"

Martine took a deep breath and knelt. What else could she do when he put it that way?

He smiled, nodded and went ahead and crawled into the tunnel, taking the light away from the larger corridor where she waited. Through sheer force of will, Martine climbed in behind him.

The temperature must have been around fifty degrees, but she was covered with sweat. Her fingers slid on the slippery rock, wet with its own perspiration.

"This too shall pass. This too shall pass," Martine kept whispering to herself through what seemed an endless passageway.

Slivers of light dodged around Joe as he held the flashlight in front of him and low-crawled through the narrow opening cut by some ancient underground flow of water.

Several times, he grunted almost painfully while squeezing his wide shoulders past a particularly narrow point. Humberto might fit through here, Martine thought, but given the size of his two cohorts, he'd have to come in alone.

She and Joe seemed to be steadily descending since entering the tunnel. Blood must be pooling in her brain because she could hardly think now. Sensory overload, she suspected. Or oxygen deprivation. She prayed she wouldn't faint.

Suddenly Joe disappeared. An almost perfectly round exit to the tunnel loomed in front of her and his hands reached back inside to lift her out. She almost fell on top of him.

"Here we are. Careful where you step when I put you down." He had rested the flashlight on one of the stalagmites protruding from the floor of the cave room they'd entered.

The light only illuminated the immediate area of what appeared to be a very large chamber. Musical plop-plops of water echoed in the stillness as she looked around warily.

"Living cave," he explained, smiling. "Great place, isn't it?"

She frowned at his impaired mental acuity. His "great place" was her worst nightmare, second only to the narrow space she'd just experienced. "How...how deep are we?"

"You don't really want to know that, do you?"

"Maybe not." Her voice sounded very small, the way it had when she'd been a child. That would normally have made her furious with herself, but she was too wrapped up in terror at the moment to spare any other emotion. The vastness of the cave room seemed to shrink by the second. The tonnage of solid rock above and all around them, more threatening.

"Okay. Here's how I figure it," he was saying. "They'll take a while to find the entrance. Then they'll have to decide which hole we crawled into. We passed a number that are wider to enter, but will narrow too much to get through or will dead-end."

Martine took a deep breath and made herself pay attention. She could get through this. *She could. Be practical.*

Think. "We should block up this one so that it looks like it dead-ends, too, but I don't see how we could." She pointed. "Knock off some of these little tower things. We can block it with them."

Joe glanced around at the eerie formations protruding out of the ground and hanging from the ceiling. "Sorry. Against Virginia law. Can't deface anything. *Take nothing but pictures, leave nothing but footprints,* code of the caver."

"I'll pay the damn fines!" she cried in a desperate whisper.

"Not necessary," he assured her. "There are so many bends in the tunnel, the little bit of light we have won't show through to the main cave."

"You're sure?" Martine stood frozen, struggling anew to control her breathing. It wasn't so bad in here now if she didn't let herself think about having to crawl her way out again.

"Martine?"

She jumped, brushing back against a slender waist-high point that snapped under the pressure. The sound of it hitting the floor of the cave seemed to echo forever.

"It's all right, honey," Joe told her. "Just try to relax for a minute. Don't worry about that."

Yeah, getting slapped with a misdemeanor for defacing a cave was not exactly high on her worry list right now, Martine thought, catching back a sob that threatened to unleash hysteria if she let it go.

Joe was rubbing her arms, doing his best to comfort her, but it wasn't working very well. "Now comes the really fun part, I'm afraid," he said.

She was already shaking her head. "Not another crawl!"

"Nope, not yet."

"Then what?" What in the world could be worse?

"Body search," he replied, looking a little apprehensive of her stunned reaction. "We've got to find that implant."

Joe had dearly wanted to get Martine naked, but certainly not in a situation like this. She obviously wasn't that enthusiastic about it herself right now, though she was gamely unbuttoning her shirt. His gaze followed her fingers and he winced a little when he saw them tremble. "Wait."

She halted what she was doing and just looked at him, wide-eyed, awaiting further instructions.

"Let's check your neck and arms first. Maybe undressing won't be necessary." God help him, he didn't need to see her without her clothes on. Not right now. He had enough problems without arousal sapping all the blood from his brain.

When she offered one arm, he pushed up her sleeve and ran his fingertips over her skin, sliding them up to her shoulder beneath the fabric. Smooth as cream. He nodded and then began checking the other. "Any bumps you've noticed anywhere lately?" he asked, hoping for a reprieve. If not, he was in for a really uncomfortable hard-on he couldn't do anything about.

"Maybe a few bug bites, but I got those when we were hiking to Bogotá." Her voice sounded breathless.

He released her arm and slid his fingers along the sides of her neck, checked her nape, hairline, then massaged the scalp beneath that gloriously silky mane. Nothing. He sighed. "Shirt first, I guess."

She removed it. Joe held the flashlight close to her skin as he examined every visible inch, sliding her bra straps off her shoulders.

Impatiently she yanked the thing down around her waist, freeing her breasts. Joe watched her hands slide carefully over the surface of her body, her fingertips pressing against her softness, checking for any blemish that might indicate her skin had been perforated.

Breath stuck in his throat. He couldn't tear his gaze away. Her breasts were beautiful, the dusky nipples erect. Due to the cold inside the cave? He sweated as if it were ninety degrees. Or was she as turned on as he was? *Now was not the time.*

"My back?" She turned away and presented the smooth expanse of skin. Joe shut his eyes tight for a couple of seconds and flexed his fingers. Gingerly he placed his palms so that they spanned her rib cage and drew them inch by careful inch until he'd covered the area between her waist and underarms. The curve of her waist drove him crazy.

Fanning his fingers out, he caressed her shoulder blades, the indentation of her spine and on up to the smooth curve of her neck and shoulders. She shivered.

He groaned. "Lord, I wish we were doing this somewhere else," he muttered.

"And for some other reason," she added in a small voice, reminding him that she was suffering from both fear for her life and claustrophobia, not arousal.

"Pants next," he told her with a new determination to keep this businesslike. "Put your shirt back on so you won't freeze."

She tugged up her bra and put her arms through the straps, then pulled on her shirt. Without pausing, she pushed down her slacks, panties and all, so that they bunched around her ankles. Then she straightened.

Joe swallowed hard, praying for strength while he examined the enticing roundness of the nicest ass he'd seen in years. Maybe ever. She jumped a little when his fingers strayed into dangerous territory.

"I'll do that," she gasped. "Get the backs of my legs."

He crouched and did as he was told, beating back the wildest urge to kiss the backs of her knees. Though the light was too weak, he imagined he could see the faint veins there in that tender spot, the crease of thin skin, sensitive as hell. His lips tingled at the thought. He ached to taste her against his tongue.

He deliberately avoided even thinking about what she was doing to her front while he was busy at her back.

"All clear," she told him, moving a step away and hurriedly dragging her pants up. "Now for my feet. But I'd know it if it was imbedded in one of my feet. Don't you think?"

Think? Who could think? He couldn't even stand up. Instead he leaned back against the wet wall of the cave, still crouched, and patted one knee. "Balance against that stalagmite and put your foot up here."

She placed her hand against one of the sturdier-looking waist-high towers and did as she was told. Joe removed her shoe and cradled her bare foot in his hand, memorizing the shape of it right down to the length of her delicate toes. Reluctantly, he relinquished it and slid her shoe back on. "Other one," he muttered, both glad and sorry as hell he was almost done.

Near the back of her ankle was where he found it. A small, raised nodule the size of a mosquito bite. He cursed.

Chapter 7

"What? What is it?" she demanded. "You found something?"

"Looks like it," he growled. Now he was going to have to damage that beautiful skin of hers to get the transmitter out. He would have to hurt her. The thought of it made him sick, but it had to be done.

"Well, that's a relief!" she said with a protracted sigh. "That figures. It would be in the last place we looked, wouldn't it? What can you use to remove it?"

Joe placed her foot on the ground and got up. Without answering her, he pulled a clean T-shirt out of his sports bag and then found the Swiss Army knife he'd purchased at the airport gift shop when they'd bought his clothes.

He rummaged in the corner of the pocket for the cigarette lighter. Though he'd never smoked, he did possess the primitive notion that a man should carry fire wherever he went. He couldn't count the times it had been a life-saver.

He tried never to be without a lighter and a pocket

knife, two things that were very handy to have in some
situations. Every time he flew, he had to ditch a knife and
buy another when he got where he was going. Thank God
he had one now even though he was cursing what he
needed it for.

"This will have to do." He opened the smallest blade,
flicked the lighter on and ran it over the blade to kill any
bacteria. "Sit down and get as comfortable as you can.
This is going to hurt a little."

She sat, looking so pale and vulnerable against the bare
rock he could hardly stand it. He sat facing her and gently
lifted her foot to rest in his lap, her leg braced between
his knees.

"Lean forward and hold the light close. Brace your arm
on my knees," he ordered, bracing himself, trying to see
her foot as an inanimate object. "Be as still as you can."

"Just like removing a splinter, right?" she said with
blatantly fake cheer. "Go for it, doc."

Joe made a careful incision, slicing open the layers of
skin with the sharp point, regretting he had nothing to
anesthetize the area. If only they'd still been in the jungle,
he knew certain plants he could have used for that. Even
the enzyme from certain frogs, he could have used topi-
cally to deaden the tissue.

She hadn't made a sound or jerked her foot the way
he'd expected. Blood trickled out, the flow increasing the
deeper he went. He mopped at the incision with a corner
of the T-shirt he had wadded beneath her heel.

Sweat beaded his face as he worked, separating the
small wound, searching for the foreign object he was sure
would be there. *Nothing!* The tissue beneath the skin
looked totally undisturbed except for the incision he had
made.

"Damn!" he growled, grabbing the flashlight and holding it directly over the cut. Again he stanched the blood

and searched, probing with the flat of the blade until he was sure. What he was looking for simply wasn't there.

"What? What's wrong?" she asked, her voice higher pitched than usual.

Joe sighed heavily and shook his head as he looked up and met her worried gaze. "Looks like it was just a mosquito bite." But now it was a gaping little wound that was bleeding profusely and probably hurting like the devil.

"Then where could the transmitter be?" she demanded in a small voice. "Where could he have put it?"

Joe was already cutting a portion of the clean shirt to tie around her ankle as a bandage. "Looks like you might be able to pay me back for this little mistake. I guess it's my turn."

Martine watched, knowing her attention was a little too avid, as Joe sat back on his heels and hastily ripped off his shirt. Muscles rippled and gleamed in the glow of the flashlight. He wore a grim, narrow-eyed expression and she knew hers probably matched it.

"Must have slipped me a mickey one night and put it where I wouldn't notice. Dammit, I thought I'd gained his trust."

"He didn't trust anyone," Martine said with a huff.

"Start with the upper back," he ordered. "That's the most logical place to put the thing since it's the hardest to reach and the place I'd be least likely to notice a blemish." He turned as he spoke.

Martine brushed her hands over his skin, feeling the warmth and dampness against her palms.

"C'mon, you'll never find it like that. Punch around," he demanded. "Do it harder."

Do it harder. Yeah. When the lightest of touches only fueled the fire he'd started with his examination of her own body's surface.

She exhaled noisily and pressed her fingertips more

firmly into the muscles, covering every inch, wondering how much more stirred up she would get if he had to remove those pants of his and search more intimate areas of his body. Probably too physically excited to remember why she was doing this. At least it was taking her mind off where they were.

"Joe?" Just to the left of his right shoulder blade, she had felt something. She zeroed in on the spot, circling the small pea-sized lump. "This could be it."

"Dig it out," he demanded. "Don't be fussy about it. Think of cutting the eye out of a potato. And hurry up. Those batteries need to last long enough to get us out of here when you're finished."

Oh, God. The light! Crawling out with no light. She didn't want to think about that. She wouldn't.

Her hands shook when he handed her the knife and lighter and took the flashlight in his hand. He braced one palm against the wall of the cave and draped the hand holding the light over his shoulder so that it shone down on the area she was probing.

Martine shook her head to clear it, took a deep breath and concentrated on the job at hand. She had to forget about the problem of getting out of here and do what she had to do. If they didn't unload this transmitter, there was no way they'd make it to D.C. without Humberto catching them. They probably wouldn't even make it out of the cave if the transmission wasn't blocked by all this rock.

No. She couldn't think about all the rock bearing down on them from all sides. Not now.

"Do it, Martine!" he demanded. She jumped and almost dropped the knife.

To give herself a moment to focus, she wiped the knife on the knit shirt he had cut in pieces to make her bandage, and then clicked the lighter to sterilize the blade.

Joe remained steady as the rock that supported him while she gingerly drew the sharp tip of the blade over the bump she had found. Steel struck something foreign. His blood obscured whatever it was, so she patted it away with the shirt and cut a bit deeper. And there it was.

Hissing in sympathy, she pried the small cylinder free and caught it in her palm. "Got it."

"Give it to me," he said, his voice gruff, impatient.

She reached around him and he took it from her, moving the flashlight to look at what she had found. Martine quickly pressed a pad of fabric hard against the wound, though she could no longer see it. Her own incision pulsed like a bad bee sting. His must be hurting even worse.

After a few seconds, he moved away from her and rose to his feet. "We'll leave the thing here," he said, speaking in a near whisper as he placed the transmitter on a small ledge in the cave wall. "Now we need to go."

He gave her the light and pulled on his shirt. When she moved toward the tunnel they'd come through, he stopped her with a hand on her arm. "Not that way. We'd probably run right into them."

She heard his weary sigh. Something was wrong. "Joe? What is it?"

He squeezed her arm. "You trust me, don't you?"

"Like I have a choice? Yes, I do trust you." Her heartbeat had kicked up to double speed again when she'd heard the apprehension in his voice.

"Good, because I need you to do something you're not going to like." When she remained silent, he continued. "You'll have to go first this time because I'll have to lift you up."

She shivered. Quaked, really. Her nervous gaze scanned the shadows around the top half of the cave room. As if he read her thought, he directed the beam of light to an opening about six feet off the floor.

"There," he said. "It will be a longer corridor than the one we came in through and a little narrower in places. We'll have to leave the bags here, so anything you can't live without, get it if it will fit in your pockets. Your I.D. and money, maybe a comb."

She was already kneeling, digging out the things he'd listed. Fighting off her dread as best she could.

"Put your sweater on. We might have to spend the night in the woods if they've disabled the Jeep. It's not that chilly outside, but sleeves will protect your skin from the brush and bug bites."

As they moved toward the hole in the wall that he had pointed out, he kept talking steadily. Martine grasped at his every word, at his every implied reassurance that they would exit the caves and go on to other challenges she knew she could handle. But her heart was in her throat and it pounded mercilessly.

When they reached the place where he would have to lift her up, he grasped her shoulders and lowered his mouth to hers. His mouth was warm against hers, his lips parted, his tongue searching out hers. She wanted to respond, meant to. But all she could manage was mere acceptance while trying hard to lose herself in the moment. Much too soon, he pulled away, taking all the warmth with him. All the comfort.

The kiss scorched her inside and out, not dispelling her fear very much, but imbuing her with a new determination to get the hell out of this hole and see where a kiss like that could lead.

She sighed after he released her and rested against him for a couple of seconds, trying her level best to soak up some of that confidence of his.

"Up we go now," he said, shaking her firmly but gently. "You can do it, Martine. One arm over the other, push with your feet. We'll be climbing this time, so it'll take more energy. Think of surfacing, seeing that moon."

"How...how deep are we? I need to know now."

He hesitated as if remembering, measuring in his mind. "About ninety, maybe a hundred feet. Maybe not that far,'' he said. ''Piece of cake. You can do that.'' His voice was gentle, coaxing. ''Come on now, let's get it over with, okay?''

A hundred feet of rock? She caught back a moan, cleared her throat to cover it, and tried not to shiver uncontrollably when he turned her around and grasped her by her waist to lift her up. Then she remembered. ''The flashlight!'' she cried.

''Once I get up there behind you, I'll pass it to you, but we'll have to leave it off unless we run into an obstruction and need to see—''

She gasped, a horrible little sound of terror, then clamped a hand over her mouth.

He surrounded her with his arms and held her tight. His lips pressed against the side of her neck, then whispered into her ear. ''You can leave the light on. All the time, Martine. It will be okay. But you'll need to crawl in the dark far enough that I can get in there behind you. Then I'll give you the flashlight, all right? Can you do that for me?''

She nodded, a jerky movement that made her even dizzier than she had felt before. ''Let…let's go.''

The hardest thing she'd ever done was crawl into that small dark place. Fear of being confined and crushed almost overwhelmed her the second Joe's hands left her.

Suddenly she couldn't help scrambling forward just to make sure she could. *Up and out,* she huffed, hyperventilating, anything to get free, to feel open space around her, the night air, anything but all this…rock. *Faster,* the terror urged, *go faster. Get out. Get out! Now!*

Dimly, over the frantic thundering of her heart, she heard Joe call to her. But she couldn't listen, couldn't slow down. Not even for the comfort of light to lead the way. Her mind worked in fits and starts, rapidly grabbing at anything else when it touched on the thought that she wouldn't make it.

Suddenly the passageway narrowed, her hand pushed through a hole smaller than a basketball. Light bled around her body, flickering on the solid rock in front of her, on the small jagged opening. Desperately, she pushed at the obstructing wall around the aperture.

Oh, God! No room, no way through, no way out. Trapped! She screamed. And shut down.

Joe grasped Martine's ankles. She was totally limp. Probably fainted. If he dragged her backward to the right branch of the tunnel, the one she'd scrambled past, her face would be a bloody mess from scraping against the rock. Her hands were probably already ruined. This tunnel was way too narrow for him to crawl up beside her, but maybe he could turn her over and slide her back out of the dead end.

He pushed his arms up beside her as far as they would reach and gently flipped her over on her back. She didn't even moan. Joe paused to check the pulse in her ankle, terrified she might have suffered heart failure or something. The beat was fast, but steady.

He breathed a sharp sigh of relief and wiped the stinging sweat out of his eyes. Then slowly, carefully, he began to wiggle back the way they had come and pull her inch by inch to relative safety.

Though he had caved for decades and loved it, Martine's fears were insidious. He had never experienced anything like claustrophobia, but understood how debilitating fears like that could be. Now more than ever since he'd just seen it happen firsthand.

Martine was no coward. He admired the way she had bravely faced right up to the problem. Before she'd climbed into the tunnel, he had finally seen that look of abject terror on her face that had appeared to him in the premonition. But she had crawled right in to meet her worst fear head-on. Then what she dreaded most had come to pass when she'd reached that dead end. He began to feel a little antsy himself.

No use speculating what might happen if the other branch of the tunnel was blocked. It was considerably wider than this one after it branched off, but who knew what the years had brought? This was a living cave and living things changed constantly.

He almost hoped Martine would stay unconscious until he got her out, but accomplishing that would be tricky if he had to drag her all the way. They still had some forty feet or more to go.

When he reached the turnoff they had passed, Joe backed into it, relieved to have more wiggle room. Ten feet later it widened, almost large enough that they could have crawled the rest of the way on their hands and knees if she were conscious.

He might be able to bring her around and they could make it out pretty quickly. But he worried she might wake up screaming and they were now too close to the other entrance. If Humberto and his pals were already outside the caves, she could draw them right to the place where he planned to exit. That opening was not as well concealed as the one they had entered.

He continued pulling her along, wincing as the floor grew rougher and her head bumped. "Sorry, kid," he mumbled. "You're gonna have a hell of a headache, but it's better than the alternative."

Joe shifted to a sitting position and let himself collapse for a minute once they approached the opening. He could actually see it, a flattened hole about four feet across and three feet top to bottom. It was filled with blue-gray moonlight and striped with stalks of sparsely leafed weeds.

He squinted at them. They looked too evenly spaced. It gave him a little jolt, a second's worth of shock that somebody had actually installed bars. Surely not.

But he risked leaving Martine alone in the dark while he scrambled over to check, to be certain no one had put up a locked gate. He laughed silently, sheepishly when his fingers touched the stickers along the dead stalks of thistles. He and Martine weren't trapped. But he knew right then, that very second, that his days of spelunking were all behind him. Those few seconds of panic instigated by Martine's phobia had done the trick. He could not wait to get out of this cave and into wide-open spaces.

He scuttled back to her, cursing himself for leaving her there where she might wake up hysterical and get them both killed. Once she was settled in his lap, Joe rested his hand near her mouth in case he had to muffle her once she came to.

He had until then to decide whether they were safer here or out there bumbling around in the dark.

Humberto contained his rage outwardly, but inside him it roiled like lava under pressure, threatening to erupt at any second. "I would give my right arm for explosives," he muttered, shoving Thomas aside to take the lead as they exited the cave.

He kicked at the weedy ground covering of plants he did not recognize or care to. This was his first time in the wilds of this country. Aside from the major cities he flew into for business purposes—the posh hotels where he had stayed and the carefully manicured golf courses where his contacts often took him for the pleasure of a game—he had seen little of the United States. Certainly nothing this rural.

Now here he was, virtually ruined, unable to return home and left with nothing but a burning desire to punish the ones who had done this to him. And at the moment, even this final quest of his seemed doomed to failure.

"I will not give up," he muttered, looking up at the

stars that seemed to mock him, the moon that cast its bluish glow over the alien landscape.

"What do we do now, Carlos? Wait here for them to come out?" Thomas asked.

Humberto shook his head, more in frustration than to provide a negative answer. Poor Thomas, for all his bulk, possessed so little intelligence he was incapable of anything but following the most specific of orders. The other cousin, Manuelo, was little better, though he did have an imaginative flair when it came to inflicting pain. A useful talent.

What a pity these were the only two to be trusted now. Two loyal cousins with barely half a brain between them. But they were family, the only family he had left after that damned DEA agent and the bewitching Martine had destroyed his business and therefore his life.

Hatred filled his soul and fueled his determination. "There will surely be another exit to that damned hole in the ground," he explained, his voice tight with the necessity of spelling out everything. "Corda knew where this cave was, so he has obviously been here before. He would not trap himself inside without knowing there was another way out. Manuelo, go and disable the car."

"But Carlos, how will we leave this place if—"

"Disable *their* car, you imbecile!" Humberto exhaled sharply and rolled his gaze heavenward, praying for patience. "Take this pistol and give me that automatic."

"Oh, *si*," Manuelo replied, nodding. He quickly switched weapons and then lumbered off toward the vehicles.

"Thomas, you wait over there. Remain concealed and watch this entrance while I search for the other one."

"Good thinking, Carlos."

Humberto added, "Hold them at gunpoint if they emerge. Do not kill them."

"But if they try to escape, what am I to do?"

Humberto ground his teeth against a curse. "Shoot at their legs, Thomas. Disable, but do not kill them. That is for me to do? Can you understand this?"

"Of course, Carlos. You know I am a very good shot."

"Thank God for small favors," Humberto murmured as he stalked off through the weeds, his eyes scanning the rock formations for any possible openings.

Until he found and disposed of Corda and the woman in the most painful way he could devise, he would not leave this place. All he must do was wait until they emerged. Here in the wilds would be the ideal place to dispose of them.

Thank God he'd had Ramos plant a transmitter in Corda. He should have done so with Martine, but Humberto hadn't trusted the man to be in the room with her. He had similarly drugged and tagged all his men, at least all of those with full knowledge of his operations. One must always prepare for an unexpected betrayal. Corda had been the first to fool him. The only one to elicit trust and then prove to be the enemy.

The transmitter he had placed under Corda's skin obviously did not project its signal to outside the cave that concealed the couple. However, once out of there, even if they evaded capture right away, they would not be hard to follow. Unless...

Suppose Corda had deduced how he had been tracked thus far? He was a wily one. If he had somehow found and removed the transmitter, this might not be so easy after all. That possibility must be taken into account.

At any rate, the two were now trapped belowground without food or water. Sooner or later, they would have to come out. And when they did, they would pay for their treachery.

Humberto knew he could not destroy the entire force of agents who had been regularly and systematically denuding the crops in Colombia. However, this one man had reduced this to a personal battle.

Joseph Corda had successfully secured his trust. Then, not only had he destroyed the largest shipment of heroin ever attempted out of the midcountry operation, but he had somehow cracked the safe and spirited away the payment received for the last delivery. That had been earmarked for a huge purchase of weaponry slated to arrive from Jordan within the next few days.

Repercussions for these monumental losses would fall upon the head of the man in charge. Humberto would receive all the blame. A sentence of immediate death would be carried out if he allowed himself to be found.

There was no way to redeem himself, but Humberto vowed if it was the last thing he did in life, he would make Joseph Corda suffer.

And the woman. He had found out, of course, that she was the sister of the mercenary, Matthew Duquesne who worked for the Ames Company. Running a check on her identity had been child's play, accomplished in a matter of minutes on his computer. All he had needed was her prints. She hadn't even bothered to deny it.

He had treated her extremely well, offering her no insult, nothing but kindness. He had been confident that Duquesne would pay an enormous ransom to have her back, but that the soldier of fortune would also seek the ultimate revenge if she were harmed in any way.

It embarrassed him still that he had fervently hoped she would stay with him. He had so admired her cool demeanor, her class and her unearthly beauty. He had even courted her, given her his respect. He could have loved her. Unlike his wife of fifteen years, Martine would have been *his* choice.

But she had also betrayed and made a fool of him. And she would pay. The bitch would also answer for shooting him point blank without even blinking an eye.

Thank the gods he always wore a vest. He brushed a hand absently over the uncomfortable bulk of the one he wore now. Obtaining it, plus the two AKs, the SIG Sauer pistol and ammo for the three weapons had cost him dearly in terms of risk and dollars.

The money was running out, but he would conserve what he had very carefully. It only had to last until he accomplished what he had come to do. Then he would notify the general. His father-in-law must understand that he was no traitor, even if the general could not forgive Humberto's misplaced trust and the losses that resulted. It was all he could do. Then he would disappear forever.

Chapter 8

Joe held Martine in his arms. She had awakened with a tremor and one sharp little cry that he immediately silenced. Once she noticed the moonlight shining through the cave's opening, she grew calm and regained her composure. She didn't draw away from him, so he simply held her.

"You took a beating when I dragged you out. How's your head?" he whispered.

"Hard as ever," she whispered back with a scoff. "My hands are sore."

He examined them gingerly with the tips of his fingers. "The skin's not broken much, but they'll need a good soaking."

"Joe…I'm so sorry I—"

"Don't be. We made it out, didn't we?" He cradled her against him and brushed his lips over the top of her head. "That's all that counts. Will you be okay if I go take a look outside?" he said directly into her ear.

She nodded and gave him a little push of encouragement.

Joe crept to the opening and peeked between the tall stalks of the weeds. His vision was limited, but he heard the crunch of footsteps on the ground's dry vegetation. Not close by, he thought.

Carefully, he parted the weeds enough to poke his head between them and gain a panoramic view of the sparsely wooded field surrounding the outcropping of rock.

The silhouette of a man passed a good fifty yards away, headed for a much larger rock formation. Joe could clearly see the outline of an automatic weapon braced in one hand as the man crept toward his destination.

They could remain where they were, but it would not be safe for long. Humberto had obviously decided there was another opening to the cave and was looking for it. And there were not that many places for him to search. Eventually, almost surely within the next half hour, he would find this one.

He crawled back to Martine and advised her of the situation. Then he gave her their alternatives. "We could shoot him when he discovers us, but that would bring the other two down on us. Or we could wait until he rounds that rock cliff and then get out before he comes back this way."

"What about his friends?" she asked, her voice steady as his now. "Where are they?"

"That's the problem. Unless he's a total idiot, he's got one with the vehicles. The other's almost certainly at the primary entrance to the cave. We can't hope to out-shoot them with only the pistol, so we'll either have to hide, or run again while we call in help."

"I vote run," she said, squeezing his arm with her fingers. "At least we can lose them now that the transmitter's gone. How's your back?"

He felt her hand slip around him and slide lightly over

the back of his shirt. She gave a brief little hum of satisfaction. "It's dried so it must have stopped bleeding, but we need to get that looked at, get you some antibiotics or something."

"Least of our worries," he said and deliberately set out to make her angry. "Are you steady? I don't want to take off out of this cave and have to carry you all the way."

She stiffened and inhaled sharply. "I can keep up. Just because I lost it back in there—"

"Save it for later. Right now I want you to do exactly as I do, exactly what I tell you. Don't think. Don't question. Got it?"

"Got it," she huffed.

"Let's go." He crawled toward the hole in the rock and looked out again. No sign of anyone now. He bent the tall thistles aside, ignoring the prickles of the sharp spines. Silently, he wiggled through them and low-crawled along the ground until he was a few feet from the cave. A glance over his shoulder revealed a messy shock of blond hair emerging from the cave. He pivoted around on his belly and gave her a hand.

"Stay low and move slowly," he whispered, knowing he need not add that she should stay as quiet as possible.

They crawled through the brush, Joe scanning the field in all directions, until they reached the copse of trees some fifty feet distant from the rocks. He leaned close. His lips actually brushed the tender shell of her ear as he rasped, "The car is on the other side of these woods. Stay right behind me."

They waded slowly through the undergrowth, virtually soundless as they progressed. Visibility was limited, but he was glad for the leaves that gave them cover. The trees were hardwoods for the most part and if this had been late fall or winter, they would be almost as exposed as they would be on open ground. He halted when he saw moonlight glint off the chrome and the stationary glow of a flashlight.

A grunt and a foul curse in Spanish emanated from the direction of the vehicle. Joe moved closer, keeping only one large oak trunk between him and the clearing. Both vehicles were there. And one of Humberto's cronies was half hidden under the open hood of Martine's Jeep.

He reached around and patted Martine's shoulder, then pressed down on it until she sank to the ground. Then he signaled her to wait there.

Joe pulled her pistol from the back of his belt, checked the safety, then turned it around to use as a club. He couldn't afford to rouse the other two men's attention with a gunshot. He moved silently out of the trees until he was directly behind the figure beneath the hood.

Unfortunately, there was no way he could do what he had to do without giving the man time to yell out. So he waited, listening to the rasp of metal against metal, disgruntled mumbling and then a final chuckle of satisfaction.

The bulky fellow emerged from his work, a distributor cap in one hand and a wrench in the other. Joe jumped forward and struck, landing a solid blow directly behind the man's right ear.

When the big figure crumpled at his feet, Joe motioned hurriedly for Martine to join him in the clearing. Meanwhile he searched the Colombian's pockets, looking for the keys to the sedan parked about ten feet away.

"No time for repairs," he explained, keeping to a whisper as he stood with the key and the goon's pistol in one hand, Martine's Glock in the other. He handed that to her and checked the one he'd just appropriated, wishing it was one of those automatics the other two had.

Quickly they hopped into the sedan, Joe behind the wheel. With the flashlight, he checked the fuel gauge. "It's got half a tank. Enough," he said. "Ready?" All hell was going to break loose when they cranked this baby up. They'd have to tear out of here at top speed and hope the resulting hail of bullets didn't damage the tires. Or the occupants.

"Shouldn't we take that distributor cap so they can't follow us?" Martine asked, grabbing his forearm.

"Nope. They'd probably kill someone to get another car. This way, they'll think it's less trouble and probably quicker to fix the Jeep."

"And we'll also know what they're driving!" she said. The girl was no slouch in the brain department. Joe smiled, proud of her. And a little proud of himself that they had gotten this far, he admitted. It bothered him that he felt that way. He was supposed to be looking forward to giving up all this and here he was sort of enjoying it again. Adrenaline did weird things to the mind, he decided.

"Stay down," he told Martine. He shoved into neutral gear, pushed in the clutch and accelerator and twisted the key in the ignition. The sound of the engine rent the night, announcing their departure like a noisy brass band. As he gunned the motor and spun out of the clearing onto the dirt track that led to escape, the shooting began from two directions.

Five minutes of bumping over the washed-out ruts and they were home free for the moment. When they reached the highway, he floored the sedan, hoping to attract any law enforcement personnel who might be conducting speed traps. Nothing.

Finally, some ten miles down the road, they approached a crossroads community with only one gas station/convenience store, closed. But the phone booth out front was a welcome sight. He didn't want to use her unsecure cell phone for his call to D.C. Joe whipped into the parking lot. "Get on the phone and dial 911," he told her. "I want everybody in the state on this. Tell them that the three guys who shot up that hotel parking lot are on a spree, targeting civilians. I'll give you the location coordinates to repeat. Then you give a description of your Jeep complete with tag number, just in case they get it in running shape before they're surrounded.''

She did as he said, injecting just the right amount of hysteria sure to bring out the cavalry. Hopefully it would result in a convergence of forces like the 2002 shootings here in Virginia. At any rate, Humberto and his playboys would be entirely too busy to stick to their original mission. ''Well, it's over,'' he said.

''We hope,'' Martine added. She stared at the receiver in her hand as she replaced it in its hook.

Joe placed his hand over hers and stood there looking at her for a full minute. ''You okay?''

''Peachy,'' she answered. ''Shouldn't you make some calls?''

She slid her hand from beneath his and moved away to give him better access to the phone. He dialed the D.C. office and related the pertinent information to Drewbridge, the duty agent for the night. Agent Drewbridge promised to send a chopper to Roanoke first thing in the morning to pick him up.

''What will you do now?'' Joe asked Martine as he hung up.

She shrugged, eyes closed, hands clutching her arms as she hugged herself. ''I don't know. Fly home, I guess.''

''Come with me to D.C.,'' Joe insisted. ''DEA could use your input since you were there, too.'' He smiled at her. ''You were in charge of cutting Humberto's purse strings. I expect you'll get a commendation.''

She smiled back and sighed wearily. ''Maybe. But before I do anything, I want a bath.''

He took her arm and led her back to the car, opening her door for her and settling her inside. How could he expect her to make up her mind about anything when she was totally exhausted? "Tell you what. Let's go in to Roanoke, get a room and catch a few hours' sleep. I don't know about you, but I'm beat."

"Sounds like a plan," she said. Though she was nearly dead on her feet, her words didn't slur and she exhibited no signs of the weeping fit he would have expected after her harrowing ordeal. Martine was a highly unusual woman. She had shown him nothing but sheer courage, even when dealing with the claustrophobia. He was almost glad she had an Achilles' heel. Perfection would be hard to live with.

Not that he would be the one living with it, he thought with a half laugh. What had made him even think of it? Martine seemed to thrive on danger—at least as long as she could avoid closed-in spaces—and he was definitely not in the market for a girl with her proclivities. Nope. He needed a soft, willing homebody, one whose idea of a bad day was missing her favorite soap opera on TV or choosing the wrong hairdresser.

But dammit, in light of all they'd been through together, one night together would be okay, wouldn't it? One night to last him a lifetime.

Martine woke up when the car stopped. She brushed her hands over her eyes, feeling actual grit in the creases of her eyelids. Her hands stung from the prickles of those thistles they had crawled through and her ankle throbbed from the knife cut. She was such a mess, she didn't even want to face a mirror. And she didn't much want to face Joe, either, after disgracing herself in that cave. Elevators made her a little nervous, but she hadn't realized just how serious her claustrophobia was until she had to face it like that. She really owed him a profound apology for cracking up, if he would just let her say it.

"Here we are," he said. "I thought maybe we

shouldn't go for really swanky, given our current condition. I could sure stand a Jacuzzi, though.''

He had such a great smile, Martine thought. Those straight white teeth and sensuous lips were enough to drive any woman right to the edge of caution. His deep brown eyes with their long lashes and teasing glint pushed her right over. ''You're my hero.''

''Yeah,'' he said laughing. ''And you'll be mine if you swing your little hiney in there and get us registered.''

Her breath stuck in her throat. *His, if she did that?* She clicked off her seat belt and reached for the ID she'd tucked in her pocket. If that's all it took…

He followed her inside the motel office, ignoring the stares the sleepy desk clerk offered. Martine almost laughed out loud. She certainly wouldn't take any customers who looked the way they did.

''We would like a double,'' she said in her haughtiest voice, presenting her charge card with a flourish.

The clerk nodded as he took her information and scribbled it on the form in front of him. ''How long?'' he asked as if he expected her to answer in hours.

''One night,'' she confirmed, retrieving her card and tucking it away.

''Could we possibly get room service at this hour?'' Joe asked him.

''Yes, sir,'' he said hesitantly. ''Sandwiches or something like that. Breakfast isn't for…another three hours,'' he added after glancing at the clock. Then he leaned forward over the desk, looking concerned, first at Joe, then back at her. ''Are you all okay? Were you in an accident or something?''

''Yes. Something like that,'' she agreed with a nod. ''But we're fine now. Just need a little rest.''

He handed her the key card. ''Do you have any luggage?''

''Lost,'' she told him with a shake of her head.

"We have laundry facilities," he offered, "but I'm afraid the maids are not on duty yet."

"Not to worry," Martine told him with a smile. "We'll manage."

He gave directions to the room.

"Well, that went well," Joe said laughing as they got back in the car to drive it around to the room. "Think he'll call the cops on us?"

She sighed. "If he does, they'll have a devil of a time waking me up when they get here."

"Not me. I'm starved." He parked, took the key card from her and went to open the door. Martine trailed in behind him. "You take a bath. I'll order some food," he told her.

She luxuriated in the shower for a good quarter hour, using well over half the shampoo provided and scrubbing her skin until it grew bright pink. Then, wrapped in a huge white towel, she left the bathroom without even glancing in the mirror. "All yours," she said to Joe.

"God, I wish," he muttered, appraising her with his eyelids at half mast. He gave new meaning to the description *bedroom eyes*. That look jacked up her temperature several notches and made her glance at the nearest bed with anticipation.

But he obviously had his priorities a little straighter than hers at the moment. He got up and passed her, offering only a little hum of appreciation while staring at her legs, disappeared into the steamy bathroom and closed the door.

Martine sat down on the edge of the bed, ruffling her wet hair with the small hand towel she'd brought out for that purpose. Her imagination ran wild thinking about Joe.

He was in there right now, shucking that shirt, those pants, those shoes. The tap was turned on as she listened. Streaming jets of water massaging all those well-defined muscles, easing, soothing, touching what she wished to touch. His eyes would be closed, his head leaning back. Before she knew it, Martine had her hand on the door-knob, about to invade that place of dreams.

A sharp rapping sounded. Damn. Room service. She groaned, backing away from the forbidden door to go and answer the other one. But just before she unlocked it, she paused, her fingers resting on the dead bolt that remained fastened. What if it was not their early-morning snack?

What if Humberto had managed to get that distributor cap back in place and had somehow followed them without their knowing? She didn't think it was possible, but who knew? It could be that she also had one of those damned transmitters and she and Joe simply hadn't found it.

She moved toward the nightstand where Joe had left her gun. She checked to make sure her Glock was loaded, clicked off the safety and went back to the door. Looking through the peephole might get her a bullet in the eye. Instead she crouched to one side, careful to stay away from the drapery-covered window.

"Yes? Who is it?" she called, her heart racing, her body braced for whatever came next, a couple of over-priced sandwiches or an immediate hail of gunfire.

Martine swallowed hard, then called out again, louder, "Who is it?"

"Room service, ma'am," came the reply, muffled by the door. Sounded like a southern accent, she thought. Couldn't be Humberto or one of his men. She lowered the gun, shook her head sharply and tried to relax her tensed muscles, wondering if she had gone around the bend to be jumping at shadows this way. She was sup-posed to be proving herself in this business, not stacking up reasons to go back to what she had been.

"Just a second," she answered, looking down at what she was wearing. Or wasn't wearing. In her mad scramble to grab the weapon, her towel had come untucked and was now lying across the room on the floor by the night-stand. A low chuckle caused her head to snap up.

Joe stood in the doorway to the bathroom, his towel securely draped around his body just below his waist.

He walked over, scooped up her towel and tossed it to her, picked up some of the bills she had left on the night-stand, then went to answer the door. She noticed he did risk a look through the peephole before he unlocked it.

That reassured her a little that she was just being para-noid. Paranoia wasn't a bad thing. Joe once said it was his friend and had kept him alive. She laid the gun on the floor and hurriedly covered herself.

By that time he was positioning the tray on the round table in front of the window. "I ordered decaf," he explained as he turned the cups right side up to pour. He cast her a look that spent a little too long on her bare legs, then went back to what he was doing with the coffee.

Martine felt a concentrated heat wave. That was the only way to describe the sensation that began around her shaky knees and undulated right up her body, playing havoc with the torso, stopped the breath right about the region of her neck. And probably fried her brain completely because she totally forgot about the sleep she needed, the food her stomach was growling for and the fact that when this was over she probably would never see this man again.

He looked too damned good in that towel. How shallow was that? she asked herself sharply. How many times had she castigated Matt for mentioning how hot some girl or other looked? Now here she was doing the same thing. Guilty as she felt about it, she didn't even want to deny the excitement Joe generated.

"Rye or white? I got one of each," he said. She didn't miss the smile in his voice that told her he was not really thinking about bread. The body-flaunting rat knew exactly what she was feeling. He had already turned her down once. Damned if she was going to give him another chance. If he wanted her, he was going to have to make the first move. Nothing, however, said she couldn't egg him on a little.

She adopted a bold, wide-legged stance as if she were about to fire the weapon she held, then shifted her weight to one leg, causing the slit in the towel to open and grant a pretty good view of her left thigh, hipbone and the area just above it. Good, she had his attention.

Then she tilted her head a bit as she examined the nine millimeter she held out in front of her. Her two-handed grip on the pistol squeezed her breasts together enough to provide a decent line of cleavage. *There, ignore that, hotshot.*

When she raised her gaze from the gun to meet his, he had abandoned any pretense of pouring coffee. Motion arrested, mouth open, he stared.

She raised a brow in question.

He closed his mouth, swallowed hard, then set down the coffeepot. "You planning to shoot me?" he asked, his words laconic. Infuriating.

Martine stiffened. "Just maybe," she answered, then stalked over to the nightstand and plunked down the pistol. "Damn you, Joe! You make me so mad!"

"Yeah," he said, exhaling audibly. "And you scare the hell out of me."

Well, that was unexpected. "Scare you?" she repeated with a bitter laugh.

"Absolutely," he admitted. "And if you don't get away from that bed and get over here and eat, I'm about to face up to my fear. In a very large way."

"Bragging, are we?" As warnings went, Martine thought this might be the best one she'd ever had. But obviously Joe was fighting his need for her at least as hard as she was trying to stoke it. There had to be a reason for that, one even more meaningful than the one he'd given her back in Atlanta. Until she discovered what it was, she decided not to try anymore to seduce him. A girl could only take so much rejection, reluctant or not.

She huffed once, flounced over and plopped down in the straight chair next to the table. She knew her movements were not provocative. They weren't even the least bit graceful.

Bite me, Joe Corda! She thought as she grabbed up the sandwich closest to her and sank her teeth into it. She chewed furiously, hardly tasting the food.

"I guess you think we need to talk about this some more," he said, fiddling with his own food, not wolfing his down the way she was doing. "This...whatever it is between us."

Martine shook her head and took another bite.

"No? Well, you're the first woman I ever met who didn't talk a thing to death."

As if talking could change a thing. As desperately as she wanted to know the real reason he wouldn't take her up on what she offered, Martine was determined not to play the role he expected her to play here. She gulped down the bite of sandwich and slurped a swig of her coffee.

"Shut up, Joe," she ordered, and busied herself picking off the limp lettuce and flinging it down on the side of her plate. "Just shut up and eat."

"You think I don't want you, right?" he asked, sitting back in his chair, drumming the fingers of his right hand on the table where he rested his arm.

Martine shrugged and took another bite. Damn, she hated this sandwich. The bread was stale, the tomato grainy and the ham barely there. And the mayo was old. Probably tainted. She slapped the remainder of the sandwich down on top of the lettuce, choked down what she had in her mouth and leveled him with a glare. "Get

stuffed, Corda. And I mean that in the very worst sense
of the word!''

With that, she pushed out of the chair and slammed
into the bathroom to wash her clothes as best she could.
She crumpled them into the sink and turned on the hot
water.

Tonight was obviously a total bust, so she would concentrate on tomorrow. If nothing else, she had come
through this mission alive and well. Crawling home looking like a dirty ragamuffin would only lower her in Matt
and Sebastian's estimation and God only knew she felt
low enough in Joe's already.

He had seen her at her very worst. But he had seen her
at her very best, too, she reminded herself as she scrubbed
at the dirt, watching it muddy the water to a murky gray-
brown. Besides, what did looks matter?

She drained the sink and ran more water using the remainder of the shampoo as detergent, then rinsed it away.
Imagining herself wringing the neck of that mule-stubborn
man in the next room, Martine twisted the water out of
the fabric, rolled the garments in a dry towel, then hung
them over the bar that supported the shower curtain.

That done and still so angry she could spit, she wasn't
about to go back in there and make a bigger fool of herself. Instead, she washed the clothes he had left piled in
the corner of the bathroom.

"God, what am I doing?" she muttered as she flung
them on the rod beside hers. "He'll think I'm Suzy Home-
maker!"

"Actually I think you're Rambo," he said from the
doorway.

Martine whirled around, grabbing at the towel as it
shifted. When had he opened that door?

He shook his head, pushed away from the door frame
and approached her. "Okay, you win. I give up."

Chapter 9

Words just failed her. Martine knew if she could just draw a breath, she would scream invectives that would curl his hair. Instead she just stood there letting his hot gaze incinerate her good sense.

Then his arms surrounded her and enveloped the rest of her in his heat. Dimly, she was aware of moving backward, felt the coolness of the wall tiles press against her back. But, oh, the glorious warmth that encompassed her front! A wall of muscle created the most delicious friction.

His mouth devoured hers. Her palms smoothed over his wide shoulders, glided up the sides of his neck. Her fingers threaded through his hair, reveling in the crisp texture of it. His deep, visceral growl of possession reverberated through her body like a powerful current.

Strong hands gripped her hips and lifted her. Still lost in the kiss, she felt she was flying, swept away from the wall, whirled around and spirited out of the steamy bathroom to the softness of the bed. Her mouth sought his again, desperately, when he broke the kiss.

"Minute," he gasped, as she felt his hand between them, a brief break in body contact as he took care of protection. Then he renewed the welcome onslaught, covering her completely, his movements sinuous and inciting. He pressed that ridge of pulsing promise against her belly.

"Now!" she demanded, her word half lost as she struggled for breath, for surcease. Blood pounded in her ears and stars burst behind her eyes.

"Not…yet," he groaned, his weight pinning her as he stopped moving. "Too fast."

"No!" What the hell was he waiting for?

A harsh breath rushed out past her ear. His hand tightened on her hip as he slid lower and entered her in one smooth glide. Pleasure flooded her with such intensity, she felt tears push from beneath her eyelids. Joe was so right, so good, so necessary.

She moved with him, against him, her total focus on increasing the sensations he caused within her. He set the pace and held to it no matter how she pleaded with her body for him to increase it.

Suddenly, she shuddered, came apart in all directions at once until there was nothing left but pure white ecstasy of motion. All senses coalesced into an explosion that rocked the universe. Her cry, his. An indrawn breath that captured his unique scent. The slick sweet feel of his skin on hers. She forced her eyes open and looked directly into the deep brown depths of his.

What she saw there both frightened and reassured her. No wonder he had said she scared him to death. He had known before she had. Martine blinked and looked away, then closed her eyes again, unwilling to put voice or even more thought to what she had realized.

This had been a mistake. A gloriously wonderful terrifying mistake. One that she doubted could be undone. One night was all she had wanted with him. One experience, one adventure. Not a soul deep connection. So she'd thought.

"Oh, no," she whispered. This felt like love.

"Yeah," he agreed with a heavy sigh. "Yeah." Then he lowered his head, resting it on the pillow beside hers, their bodies still joined, their awareness perfectly attuned. Neither of them was ready for what they had discovered in the other.

After a few moments, he slowly disengaged and moved off of her, leaving the bed. Martine kept her eyes shut and curled away from him. She snuggled into the quilted bed-spread when he draped it over her, then retreated into herself, trying not to think, trying to obliterate the need to have him hold her and tell her that somehow they would resolve this.

Totally exhausted and her body sated, she needed to sleep. But that proved impossible with Joe lying so close. This might never happen again. She couldn't hold on, but neither could she let go.

Joe knew he couldn't love her. Didn't dare. Talk about a patently counterproductive thing to do.

"Falling for you would make me crazy," he said, his words barely audible. "I'd worry myself to death."

"I can take care of myself," she answered, her defiance evident even in the softness of her voice.

Being without her would make him crazier. He'd been this close to plenty of women without even thinking about a future with them.

He couldn't even remember the last time he had thought about that. For the last few years, he had doubted he even had a future to think about. Well, that had changed.

When Humberto was out of the picture and Joe began the new job—if he decided to take it—maybe he wouldn't be risking his neck on an hourly basis. Oh, there would almost certainly be danger involved in some of the assignments, but his days of constantly living under the scythe of the grim reaper were over. Maybe he could actually have a life.

How could he possibly hook up permanently with a woman who planned to keep doing that? He had never asked a woman to put up with that kind of worry about him, so why should he have to endure it himself?

But how could he not? Even if they shook hands right now and faked a cheery little goodbye, how could he not worry about where she was and whether she was safe?

This just wasn't like him, this asking for trouble. He might appear to be a devil-may-care risk taker, but he was secretly a planner. That's how he'd survived this long on missions that outwardly seemed suicidal. He sure hadn't intended to get this involved.

He had been in the field way too long. His brain must have been affected. This should be a simple decision, quickly made and implemented. But he kept on vacillating. One minute, figuring he'd better kiss her off for good and the next, struggling like mad to think of a way to make it work out.

"Joe?" she said softly, turning to him, her graceful hand sliding lightly over his chest, one finger threading through the hair, her nail gently scoring his skin. "Are you all right?"

He grasped her hand in his and squeezed lightly. "Poleaxed. Too confused to think straight. You?"

She sighed, a luscious sound that sent his temperature climbing, and stretched that gorgeous body like a satisfied cat. "I'm hungry again."

"That makes two of us," he muttered, giving up without a fight. He kissed her again, answering the demand she hadn't even made yet. As surrenders went, it beat any kind of victory to hell and back.

* * *

Martine awoke to his shaking her shoulder gently.

"Come on, sleepyhead. You need to get up and get dressed. I called in our location. They'll be here soon to pick us up."

She wanted to resist and kept her eyes closed.

He persisted, caressing her arm, but it felt impersonal somehow. Distant. "They'll impound the rental car and arrange a flight for you." He sounded very businesslike, she thought.

How should she respond to that? As determined as she was to present a woman-of-the-world face to him this morning, Martine didn't think she was capable of it. She certainly couldn't do flip, not after they had turned the world upside-down. About the best she could hope to do was to answer in kind.

She sat up. "All right. I'll be ready in ten." With all the dignity she could muster, she got up and walked naked into the bathroom and shut the door.

He had removed her clothes from the shower rod and folded them neatly on the counter by the sink. She wanted to cry. Instead, she turned on the shower, waited patiently for the water to run hot, then stepped under the spray.

Her body ached but not nearly so much as her heart. It was not simply sex. The connection had gone much deeper than that, just as he had known it would. It had provided the culmination of all the feelings, risks and hidden hopes they had experienced and shared since they met.

Joe had not wanted to make love to her and now she understood why. Their goals in life were so opposed.

She was only just coming into her own, realizing her potential, waking up from a slumberous life lived under a heavy cloak of male protection. First her father had kept her wrapped in batting. Expected her to stay safe, weak, dependent, like her mother. Even before he had died, Steven had stepped in, determined to guide her into teaching. Her attempt to assert herself had ended that, but had fallen flat when Sebastian hired her, then refused to let her do anything meaningful. Even Matt still tried to shelter her.

At last, with this initiative in Colombia, she finally felt alive. Capable of doing anything.

But Joe craved peace. He had lived on the edge for so long that he had earned the right to a comfortable life free of danger and worry.

His concern was very real. Flattering, but it would be stifling, too, if she let it.

What a great beach bum he would make, she thought with a wry smile. The spray of water on her face obliterated the tears and sluiced over her body to wash away the traces of their lovemaking. She only wished it could take away the memory they had made together, but nothing could ever do that. There would never be another man who could measure up to Joe Corda. She'd just have to get over him somehow.

Dressed in her wrinkled pants and shirt, her damp hair slicked back behind her ears, she took a deep breath and went out to face the music.

"Coffee?" he asked, sipping his own and pointing at the cup he had poured for her.

"Yes, please." Room service again. She could use a decent meal, but food was running a distant second to what she really needed.

"I don't recommend the pastries for taste, but they'll help to fill you up."

Martine sighed. Nothing would help do that. "Thanks, just the coffee," she said, taking the chair across from him, glad of the distraction the meager breakfast provided.

"Martine…" Oh God, he sounded apologetic. She didn't want an apology, one that she'd have to echo. What had happened was definitely her fault.

"Let it go, Joe," she advised, not meeting his eyes.

"These things happen. Hazard of the occupation, I guess."

He remained silent for a few long seconds. "We could give up the occupation and see if we still—"

"No." Not an option, she thought, shaking her head for emphasis. She could not become what she once had been. Not that clueless, plain vanilla, too-eager-to-please copy of her mother. God, she might as well move back to the old country.

"I've seen too much, Martine," he said, his voice only slightly above a whisper. He pleated a paper napkin between the fingers of one hand, worrying it, shredding it, then crushing it in his fist. "No matter how hard I try, I can't stop the evil. If I thought I could, I'd keep going, you know? But it grows like kudzu, covers everything. Kills it."

She drew in a deep breath and let it out slowly. "Yes, but if we all stop trying, where would we be?"

"I know what you're saying. I'll give the Sextant team my best shot. At least for a while. But I know I can't watch you put your life on the line every day and then die for nothing in some godforsaken jungle."

He reached over and took her hand, held it, caressed it hard with his thumb in that way he had when he grew intense. "I'll stay with it. Forever, if you'll just get out of it now. If you don't, you'll be where I am one of these days."

She reached up and brushed her fingertips over his forehead, then traced the healing scar where the ricochet had nicked him. "I'm sorry."

He nodded and leaned away, releasing her hand and breaking all contact. It wasn't an angry move, she could see that. He just seemed resigned.

For a long time, they didn't speak, didn't look at one another. Martine felt a keen sense of loss already. How much worse would it be when he was out of her life forever? "Joe? I know this sounds like the world's worst cliché, but we could stay friends."

To her relief he smiled. "Yeah, that's what they all say."

The next silence proved more than she could stand and as she struggled to find something to say to show she was holding up better than he was, she heard someone knocking on the door. She got up.

He beat her to the door to check out their visitor. "Who is it?" he called out.

"Jack Mercier," the man answered.

Joe's eyebrows rose as he cast her a glance of surprise. Then he opened the door, one of the pistols in his hand. "Identification?"

Mercier flashed a badge and picture ID. "Your office notified me after you called in."

Martine thought he looked much like he had sounded over the phone. She had taken his call to Matt about the mission to Colombia and they had talked at some length about it. Mercier was definitely on the spring side of forty, well built, deeply tanned. Early silver streaked his dark hair and his eyes were the color of polished steel.

Mercier was handsome and distinguished, but with an edge she imagined could turn menacing if he were crossed. That gray hand-tailored suit he wore fit to perfection both his body and the current image he was projecting. He wore it extremely well, but it seemed a disguise all the same.

Now he was assessing her. "Ms. Duquesne? I believe we spoke on the phone when we hired your brother."

"Martine," she affirmed and shook his hand. "Nice to meet you in person."

He smiled, transforming his face into a charming expression of determined diplomacy. "Surviving to do that must give you even greater satisfaction. It has been a near thing, so I hear."

She shrugged, risking a glance at Joe to see what he thought of Mercier. He was frowning now. She slid her hand through the crook of Joe's arm. "It was, but Mr. Corda knew precisely what to do in every instance. You'll be very lucky to have him on your team, sir."

Mercier looked from one to the other, his smile fading. "No doubt."

"What are you doing here?" Joe asked him.

"You'll be debriefed by your supervisor at our office in McLean since you're one of us now. I thought the trip back would give us a chance to get acquainted."

"I'm not one of you yet. What about Humberto? Have they got him yet?" Joe demanded.

"No. They found the Jeep abandoned five miles from the turnoff that led to the caves. He could be out of the country by now."

Joe cursed. Martine felt like it. She knew as well as Joe did that Humberto would never give up and go away forever. Unless he was found, they could expect him to turn up sooner or later to complete his vendetta. Now no one knew where he might be or what he was driving.

Mercier studied Joe for a moment. "There's a chopper waiting for us."

He continued, speaking directly to her as they left the motel room. "Martine, we have arranged for you to be interviewed separately, of course. Standard procedure. We'll part company at the airport, and you'll be flown directly to the D.C. office with an escort from the DEA. After that, they will see that you get back to Atlanta and have protection until Humberto is apprehended."

Martine looked at Joe. When he said nothing, she nodded at Mercier. "Thank you."

"We're good to go then," Mercier said. "I'll need the keys to the car you drove here. We'll see that it's returned."

Joe handed over the keys, then opened the front passenger door of the Ford that Mercier indicated was his. He waited for her to get in. Martine hesitated. "No good-byes, okay?"

He glanced at Mercier who seemed to be ignoring them. "A clean break is better."

"Clean break it is, then," she muttered as she climbed in the car. "So much for the friendship."

Joe didn't answer. He simply got into the back seat where he remained silent for the entire fifteen minutes it took them to reach the airport.

Once they met her contact, a clean-cut young agent by the name of Willowby, and were about to go their separate ways, Joe grabbed her hand and turned to her. "Look. I'll call you once in a while. Just to make sure you're all right."

"Will you?" she asked, noting that Mercier was stu-diously looking the other way and pretending hard not to listen. "You were right, Joe. Let's keep it simple. Clean break."

He released her hand, his dark eyes holding hers for two full seconds. Then he gave a decisive nod and turned away abruptly, striding for the gate to the runway where the helicopter waited for them.

Had that been anger in his eyes? Or regret? Martine supposed she would never know, but the question troubled her.

Even after a week to get over what had happened, Joe felt a large gaping hole in his chest where his heart ought to be. That part of him had gone on back to Atlanta, he guessed. The old heart, wherever it was, certainly wasn't in his work.

He liked Jack Mercier. He liked the other members of Sextant, too. But he just couldn't get worked up about throwing himself right back into the fray, even if it was a slightly different fray. Instead of insinuating himself into some drug lord's confidences or portraying a potential big-shot buyer in order to make a bust, he would be playing other roles, ferreting out terrorists. And he wouldn't be working alone anymore.

He sat in front of one of the computers in a security-cocooned inner office in the heart of McLean, pretty much up to speed now on an aspect of the world situation he had so far touched on only marginally.

For fifteen years, the drug culture had permeated his professional life. At times he'd become so immersed in the horror of it, it seemed that's all there was. Now he knew there were even worse threats.

Mercier entered, took one long assessing look at him and drew up a chair. "You're not ready yet, are you?" he said, his voice father firm.

"No," Joe admitted. "I'm not." He swiveled away from the desk and leaned forward, hands clasped between his knees, and faced his new supervisor. "I might never be."

"There's no great rush. This is a big decision for you."

"Jack, I'll be honest. I'd hoped the change of pace, the difference in focus, would make a difference." He sighed wearily. "What you've got to deal with here needs someone clicking on all cylinders. The missions are critical, more so that what I've been doing."

Mercier nodded and sat back, drumming his fingers on the arm of the chair. "You're exhausted. I still think you're the man. You just need a break, Joe. Take a couple of weeks. Go lie on a beach."

Joe laughed. "Is there anything you don't know about me?"

"I know what's good for you right now. Just go. We're pretty much in the organizational stages here and the alert level's low right now. You still have to go through a little training before taking on an assignment. The job will be here when you get back."

"You're not going to *let* me quit, are you?"

"If I thought you really wanted to do that, I wouldn't have you here right now."

Joe nodded. "I'll go down to the Gulf. See the family. I promise to give you an answer within a couple of weeks. How's that?"

Jack grinned, another stab at the camaraderie he worked hard to establish among his crew. "Think you might swing by Atlanta on the way?"

"That's not an option."

"Giving up personal relationships is not a requirement of the job, Joe."

"It's definitely a requirement as far as Martine's concerned."

"What's the matter, you don't trust her?" Mercier asked, frowning.

Joe shrugged. "Worse than that. I think I love her." He managed a wry smile. "But I'll get over it."

Mercier nodded thoughtfully. "Well, you'd know best about that, I guess. But if you do decide to see her, give her my regards."

Like hell he would, Joe thought. The relief he felt at actually being encouraged to abandon his duties for a while made him almost forget that avid perusal Martine and Mercier had given one another when the two first met. Joe had experienced an unreasonable spurt of jealousy and he knew it was unfounded, had known it even at the time. He certainly didn't need a woman who clouded his judgment that way.

But maybe he'd just layover in Atlanta for a few hours and check in with Matt Duquesne at Ames International. He didn't even have to see Martine while he was there and stir up anything.

Wasn't he sort of obligated to make sure she had adequate protection? Even if Humberto had seemed to drop off the face of the earth, Joe knew he was still out there, biding his time, waiting for defenses to drop.

"I'll finish out the day and leave tonight," he told Jack. "Thanks."

"No problem. That next weapons training session at Quantico doesn't begin until the first of the month. You'll need to be back for that." He gave Joe a friendly slap on the shoulder and left.

A few minutes later, Will Griffin appeared. "Black, right?" He set down a cup of coffee just to the right of Joe's mouse pad and didn't stick around for thanks.

Now what had precipitated that? Joe wondered. Griffin stuck his head back around the door. "Good luck. Let us know how it goes, okay?"

"How what goes?" But Griffin was gone again. Joe sipped the coffee. Last night he had joined Will for a drink at Christa's, a quiet little pub within walking distance of the office. It had become a sort of hangout when the work day was over and they had nothing else to do. But Joe couldn't recall discussing anything important there with Will. What the hell was the guy talking about?

Holly Amberson, the one female member of the team, strode in with a sheaf of papers in her hand. She flattened them against her truly admirable chest and crossed her arms over them. "I don't know you well enough yet to be giving you any advice, Joe, but don't you be stupid."

Joe sat up straight and stared at her. "Excuse me?"

Her black eyebrows climbed up to her perfect hairline and dark chocolate eyes pinned him with a warning stare. "You go see that girl, you hear?"

Joe stood, his chair rolling back and banging against a file cabinet. "Now wait just a minute—"

"No, you wait a minute," she ordered, shaking her finger with its long crimson nail very close to his nose. "You don't drag a woman through two countries, give her a quick squeeze, then cut her loose and leave her to the sharks. You go see about her. And play nice.''

Joe uttered a short cough of disbelief. Who did this woman think she was, his mother? She was younger than he was by at least four or five years. And what the hell did she know about Martine? He opened his mouth to tell her to buzz off. Instead he heard himself saying, ''I'm going. I'm going.''

She smiled and slapped the papers on the desk. ''Good boy. You'll want to check this out before you go. It's the final report on what happened after you left Colombia. Great work, Joey. Good to have you aboard.''

Joey? Nobody had called him Joey since third grade when he'd beat the hell out of Mike McCann for telling him Joey meant a baby kangaroo.

Did they all know everything about him, up to and including his sex life? Well, what did he expect working with a bunch of spies?

The whole bunch probably thrived on personal gossip since they couldn't share any secrets with anyone else in the world. Joe wasn't used to this, at least not at work. An agent's private life was just that. Private.

He picked up the report Holly had brought him, but didn't need to read it. That mission was history. So was his brief relationship with Martine. New life. New leaf.

Joe glanced around the six hundred square feet allotted to what they called The Vault. The room housed all the company's electronics and was protected from the world by lead-encased walls, scrambling devices and the latest access mechanisms.

It contained no windows and was completely secure. Even the outer offices, Joe's included, were invulnerable to intrusion of any kind except maybe a bunker buster. In the case of that, they would all be smithereens anyway.

He did like his office, never having had one all his own.

Sextant was six months old now, experimental, working better than anyone had reason to expect, so Mercier said.

Joe now knew that Jack had been with the NSA. His talent for organization and brilliant analytical ability had put him in charge. If anybody on the planet could construct a cohesive unit from alumnus of the FBI, CIA, DIA, ATF and DEA, it was Jack Mercier, the voice of reason, proponent of the big picture.

The Sextant team had become tight as a guy-wire. The five in place were already friends. Four men and one woman. One black, one Native American, and three WASPS. And now Joe, last hired, was the resident Hispanic. Holly had dubbed them the Crayola Kids and treated them all like children. *Her* children, though she wasn't even a mother for real.

Sextant was a great concept, a dream team. On one level, Joe wanted to belong. On another, he clung to his status as a loner, a real master of surface relationships. Could he fit in here?

He closed his eyes, massaging them with his thumb and forefinger.

That's when the picture appeared, clear as a well-focused photograph. One lone frame of the future behind his eyelids. Martine's face. Covered with blood.

Joe tore out of the computer vault, the vision still filling his mind. Down the corridor, passing the offices, his only thought to get to the airport as fast as possible.

Eric Vinland caught him in a headlock, effectively halting him in the hallway. "Hey, what's up?"

Joe struggled, desperate to fly to Martine, to save her. But Vinland held on, a forearm almost cutting off his air supply. It took a moment for reason to take hold. Martine was in danger, yes, but at this rate, he would kill himself getting to her.

He stopped fighting and Eric released him, even

straightened his tie. "Okay, spill it, Joe. What set you off?"

"I've gotta go. I saw…never mind." He shook his head and started to push past Vinland.

He felt a tight clamp on his arm. "A premonition?"

Joe was so stunned, he simply stood there, his mouth open.

"Yeah. We know." Eric smiled, a benign-looking expression beaming behind innocuous round-rimmed glasses. A young Brad Pitt, the picture of boyish innocence in specs and Brooks Brothers. "I have a similar…talent," Vinland admitted with a shrug.

Still Joe couldn't speak. What the hell was going on here? Was this another damned government study he was getting sucked into?

"Do all of you…?"

"No, not really. We'll talk about that later. Right now, I think you're too worried. It's the woman, right?" Eric guessed, his voice soft, cultured. Concern seemed out of place in this muscle-bound *boy* with the weird, steely eyes.

"Yes," Joe answered in spite of himself.

"We'll help," Vinland said simply.

Humberto had now relinquished all hope of regaining anything resembling the life he once led. He replaced the receiver and put the telephone back on the nightstand, handling it very gently, afraid if he gave physical manifestation to his fury, he could never regain control. Things were worse than he thought. Much, much worse.

His sweat mocked the pitiful effort of the air-conditioner cranked as high as it would go. Miami might be considerably cooler than equatorial Colombia, but a much more dangerous heat, one more difficult to escape, had been combined with that of the climate.

Other than the relatively meager amount he had managed to shift to a recently established account in the Cayman Islands, his wealth was gone. He had expected Rosa to transfer funds from their bank in Bogotá to the one he had selected in Miami. He'd thought perhaps she would even join him there once he could safely bring her out of Colombia. She was, after all, the mother of his children, the daughter of the general who had recruited him and treated him like a favored son. But no. She would not come to him. And neither would she send money. The general knew everything. Including Humberto's former fascination with the Duquesne woman.

He had lost Rosa, their life savings and all that he had invested. All of it gone. Transferred to her father's accounts for her to spend at leisure. She had laughed so bitterly.

She had been told how he had kept the woman at the compound. He wished now that Rosa had good reason to accuse him of infidelity, since he was paying the price anyway.

He should have taken the Yankee bitch instead of treating her like an honored guest. But he had enjoyed the willing company of a beautiful, cultured woman. He had been the envy of everyone in the compound. She had enthralled him, tricked him and then betrayed him.

He did not have to worry that Rosa would divorce him. She would not have to do so, he had just been informed, because he was as good as dead.

Nowhere could he find protection. The whole organization had blown sky-high. The fields were now useless, sprayed with glyphosate, a result no doubt of Corda's revealing their precise locations. Corda and the woman had ruined him more completely than he knew.

His father-in-law had put a price on his head as if Humberto were a criminal to be hunted down and shot. Miami was no longer a safe place to be now that he had phoned Rosa.

The hatred he felt for Joseph Corda and Martine Duquesne increased tenfold. Using the families of his enemies to exact revenge seemed less than honorable to Humberto, but the time had arrived when honor was no longer a luxury he could afford.

Chapter 10

Martine jumped as lightning cracked nearby, followed immediately by a jarring rumble of thunder. The weather suited her mood. Gloomy. It described her future. Unpredictable. And it made her only more eager to leave Atlanta, a place that seemed worse than inhospitable in every respect at the moment.

She couldn't believe she'd really been fired. Sebastian had been livid, much angrier than she could ever have imagined about her using her initiative. She had to admit that her reaction to his hadn't been conducive to continued employment with Ames. Tempers had flared and now she was out of a job.

Matt's loyalties were torn and he was threatening to quit, even though he agreed with Sebastian's assessment that Martine was too impulsive and foolhardy to be trusted with field work.

On top of that, she still had to worry about Humberto surfacing unexpectedly. And worst of all, she had heard nothing from Joe.

True, she had told him a clean break was best, but she had secretly hoped he would be as awed by what had happened between them as she was and his resolve would crumble. But if that had been the case, he would have called her by now.

Joe had that undefinable something that simply set her on fire. He was the kind of guy she had always admired, a real honest-to-God hero who never bragged, just did what needed doing and never took a bow. She knew that mission in Colombia was only one of many thankless assignments.

Joe's abilities and confidence in them had wowed her more than his good looks, but those sure hadn't detracted from his appeal.

He could be exasperating, but that was to be expected with a personality as forceful as his. Maybe that was part of his problem with her. He didn't want to compete for control constantly as they always seemed to do. Martine shrugged. For her, competition was a huge turn-on.

Joe might have felt the same thing she did when they'd made love. She had thought so at the time. It seemed as if they both had realized afterwards that sometimes love was just not enough.

He obviously thought she ought to give up the kind of work she was doing to prove how she felt about him. But she knew that if he couldn't love her unconditionally, then it would never work as a long-term thing. She stared out the window at the rain. Well, she wasn't changing herself for anybody, not even Joe.

It was probably just as well they had parted when they did. The longer she was with him, the stronger her feelings grew. The real problem was, now that they were apart, what she felt for him hadn't begun to subside. Not even a little.

Her life was a mess at the moment. But she had plans. It was impossible to control everything in her life, but she didn't have to settle for simply reacting to events. She had to be the one to make things happen.

Her résumé was out there making the rounds again, and even if her experience was fairly light, her credentials were nothing to sneeze at. Her grades at university had been excellent. She had maxed all the extra courses Ames had funded. She was fluent in three languages, an expert with small arms, qualified in two disciplines of martial arts and her security clearance was up-to-date for government work. Somebody was going to want to hire her.

In the meantime, she was packing to move. None of the jobs she had applied for were located here in Atlanta. It was time for a change and she meant to be ready for it when it came.

The phone rang. Probably Matt. He had been checking on her several times a day since her altercation with Sebastian. But she checked the caller ID and didn't recognize the number. *Joe?*

She snatched up the receiver. "Hello?"

"You got canned. It was my fault, wasn't it?"

Martine clamped her mouth shut on a cry of glee. Patting her chest to calm her racing heart, she inhaled and released it slowly before speaking. "Hi, Joe. What's up?"

"I just talked to Matt. I'm going to go speak with Sebastian Ames."

"No!" she cried, then lowered her voice to a reasonable level. "That's not necessary. Please don't bother."

"He needs to know just how good you are, Martine. I won't overdo it like I did with Matt. I'll just tell him how flawlessly you planned everything. How much I owe you. He'll come around."

"No, Joe. The truth is, it's high time I made a career move. Matt will never see me as anything but a kid sister and Sebastian's been like an uncle to me ever since we moved to Atlanta when I was twelve. I know they just want to keep me safe, but I have to get away and be on my own, you know?'' When he didn't answer, she changed the subject. ''So, how's the new job?''

She heard him expel a deep breath. ''Iffy. Look, I had this…sudden feeling you might be in some kind of danger or something so I called Ames to see if you were okay. You are, aren't you?''

''Sure, I'm fine. Are you calling from D.C.?''

''No, I'm in Atlanta. I just stopped by on my way to Florida.''

''Great! I'd love to,'' she said, unable to hide her excitement.

Long pause. ''Uh, Martine…''

''Sorry, Joe,'' she said with a laugh, tossing her hair back over her shoulder and wriggling out a comfy spot on the sofa, ''but you already invited me, remember? Twice, I think.''

Long silence. ''Well, that was before.''

''So this is after,'' she argued. ''I'm not after promises or commitments, Joe. Just a week on the beach.''

Another pause. Her heart fell, collapsed like a pricked balloon. She squeezed her eyes shut and tried not to cry.

''All right, bad idea,'' she said, making her voice bright, sunny as the day was dark. ''You take care now, Joe. Enjoy your vacation and—''

''Be ready in half an hour.'' *Click.*

She threw the receiver down and growled with frustration. He made her crazy. But a smile grew when she started thinking about retribution. She could make him crazy, too. She had done it once and now she knew exactly how. The red bikini would be a good start.

Joe settled into the narrow seat next to the aisle, wishing he had splurged on first class. Martine was gazing out the window, waiting for takeoff. The flight into Tallahassee would be short, fortunately, giving them little time to discuss much of anything. Joe wasn't ready for any deep discussions.

He hadn't even been ready to see her again. All he had meant to do was check with Duquesne, make sure adequate protection was still in place. What the hell was he thinking bringing her to Florida?

His mother and sisters would be planning the wedding before he set his suitcase down. Other than his girlfriends in high school, this was the first time he had ever brought a woman home with him. Well, maybe it was best this way. At least he could make sure she stayed out of trouble for a week.

He rested his elbow on the outer armrest and massaged his brow. Scrunching his eyes shut, he willed away the beginning of a headache.

Suddenly a swirl of white flashed behind his eyes, a face materialized. *Oh, God.*

"What is it?" Martine was shaking his arm. "Joe? Are you sick?"

He must have gasped or something. Joe opened his eyes and she was almost nose to nose with him. Her worried expression a direct contrast to the serene face she had worn in the vision. She'd had her eyes closed then as if waiting for a kiss.

Now her long graceful fingers grasped his forearm. Her subtle perfume threatened intoxication. He turned away.

No. That hadn't been a vision, not really. Not Martine in a wedding veil. What he had seen had been brought on by that thought just before it. The one about his mother and sisters misunderstanding his motive for having Martine with him when he arrived. That was all it was. No way in hell was he destined to marry Martine Duquesne.

Maybe it only indicated she would be a bride soon. *Someone else's bride?*

"I need a drink," Joe muttered, pressing his head back hard against the headrest of the seat, careful not to close his eyes too tightly. That's when he always got the mind pictures, when he forgot and did that. "Soon as they get this crate off the ground." He felt her fingers squeeze his and looked down. When had he taken her hand?

They hadn't even kissed or touched when he went to pick her up at her apartment. She had been on the phone with her brother when Joe arrived, telling Duquesne where she was off to and with whom.

Matt Duquesne must have been deliriously happy to have that information. Joe could just imagine his own delight if one of his sisters had called to tell him she was flying off to the beach with some guy he barely knew.

All that considered, he held on to Martine's hand through the takeoff and after, his fingers laced through hers, their ambivalent relationship remaining as up in the air as the plane in which they flew.

What would happen after they landed was anyone's guess. Maybe he should just live in the moment, enjoy the feel of her shoulder next to his, the warmth of her palm, the sound of her breathing. He turned his head to look at her, see what she was thinking.

"Excuse me, sir?" one of the hostesses said, leaning near, her voice little more than a whisper. "You're Agent Joseph Corda, right?"

Joe snapped to attention, his first thought leaped to a possible hijacking. "Yeah, what's the problem?" He was not carrying, but had registered his weapon with security and it was in his bag in the hold.

"We've had an emergency call for you, sir, from a Mr. Duquesne. He asks that you call him back immediately at the number he gave. The matter's urgent."

Apparently so. It was highly unusual for anyone to get clearance to contact a plane's cockpit directly to reach a passenger. Had to be life or death, he would imagine. He reached for the phone on the back of the seat. "The number?"

The hostess frowned at Martine, then glanced briefly to either side at the other passengers. "If you'll come with me, you might want to use the phone up front," she said, then added, "for privacy."

"Joe?" Martine started to get up when he did.

"Stay here. I'll be right back," he told her. He couldn't imagine what Matt Duquesne had to tell him, but he felt fairly sure the man wasn't calling just to warn him off Martine. It would take a damn sight more than brotherly outrage to get that kind of clearance.

"Could I get anything for you?" the attendant asked.

"Jack and Coke," Joe replied as he dialed.

The hostess remained nearby, pretending not to listen. Her face was a study in concern, so she must have been told what the problem was.

"Duquesne here," Matt answered in the middle of the first ring. "Corda?"

"Yeah, what's up?"

"It's Humberto again. I hate like hell to tell you this, man, but he's got your sister and your niece. I'm sorry, he didn't give me any names, so if you have more than one, I don't know which sister it is."

Joe almost dropped the receiver. "What? How did he...no, where? Where is he holding them?"

"He called from Panama City and asked for me here at the office. He said I'd better find a way to reach you. He's wanting to make a trade. He's demanding you and Martine for your sister and the child."

Joe felt his stomach plummet to his feet. He had no frame of reference for this. No idea what to do. His instincts were not kicking in, not where the safety of his family was concerned. His immediate urge was to find Humberto and blow him away. Not a productive idea for a rescue plan.

Matt paused for a second, then continued. "He assured me he doesn't plan to kill Martine. Not that I believed him. I told him she was with you and that it would take a while to locate you in D.C. because I wasn't sure where you worked. Since he has no idea you're almost to Florida already, that might give you some time. I'm leaving here now, getting a friend to fly me down. Where you want to hook up?''

"Stay there," Joe ordered. "Please. You're his point of contact. With that cast on your leg, you couldn't do much anyway. Martine will be safe. I'll send her back to Atlanta the minute I can get her on another plane."

Reluctantly, Matt agreed. "Anything else I can do? How about calling Mercier? Wasn't he with the FBI?"

"No," Joe answered absently, his mind shooting off in all directions, trying to form some kind of plan. "Look, I need to get off the phone and think. Call me on my cell with any further developments." He rattled off the number.

"You bet, and tell Martine—"

"You can tell her yourself. I told you I'll put her on a plane home."

"Good luck doing that," he thought he heard Matt say as he snapped the receiver back into place on the wall unit.

The hostess put a hand on his arm. "The captain said this has to do with a kidnapping in your family. Is there anything else I can do to help?"

She handed him a plastic cup filled with ice and Coke. She also offered him a miniature of Jack Daniels, which he had ordered earlier.

He downed the soft drink in a few gulps, but refused the liquor. "Ms. Duquesne and I will need to exit first when we land."

"Of course. Could I make any calls for you while we're in the air? Have the authorities meet you?"

He pulled out his credit card and handed it over. "No, but if you could please, call ahead and have a rental helicopter standing by. I'll need my bag off-loaded right away. Also Ms. Duquesne's.''

''Certainly. Describe your bags and I'll have them rushed to you. We'll be preparing to land in about twenty minutes.''

Joe told her what the bags looked like, then turned around to head back to his seat. Martine was standing directly behind him. ''Who's been kidnapped?'' she demanded.

''My sister and niece,'' he told her. ''Let's go and sit down. We'll be landing soon.'' They quickly settled in their seats and he turned to her with the rest of the story.

''Humberto didn't give names, but I think it's most likely Delores and her oldest, Nita, who is six. My other niece is just an infant and Humberto did mention a child, not a baby.'' He hurriedly explained how Matt got involved and what Humberto was demanding.

She remained quiet for a minute, thinking, then gave one succinct nod. ''Then we'll have to agree to the exchange,'' Martine said. ''Humberto will let them go once he has us. He'll want his pound of flesh before he gets rid of you and me, so that will afford us a little time to act after we turn ourselves over. We can take him.''

''Or he could kill all four of us immediately,'' Joe argued. ''We can't risk it. We'll have to locate him beforehand and get Delores and Nita safely away. Then I'll move in.''

She raised one perfect eyebrow. ''*You'll* move in, huh? All by yourself.''

''That's the plan,'' Joe said, holding her gaze with one even more determined than hers. ''I promised Matt I'd send you home.''

''I'm not going.''

''Then I'll put you somewhere safe.''

''How about a cave? Got any caves around Panama City? That's about the only place you could *put* me where

I'd be incapacitated enough to let you do this alone. You're never going to let me live down that one weakness, are you?''

"That's not fair, Martine. Did you hear me recount anything to anybody about your claustrophobia? Did you?"

"No, but you're thinking about it right now," she declared, clasping her hands in her lap and looking out the window. "You don't trust me to pull my weight."

Joe heaved out a heavy breath and shook his head. "I would trust you with my life, Martine, but I can't stand the thought of Humberto getting his hands on you. And I'll do damned near anything to prevent it."

"I can handle Humberto," she said with a huff of indignation.

Her overconfidence really worried him. "Well, we have to find him before anybody can do anything. Right now we need to decide what Matt should tell him when Humberto calls back to set up the exchange."

She shivered, chafing her arms with her palms. "We don't dare keep him waiting too long before giving him some kind of answer. He's not well known for his patience." Her gaze bored into his then. "Your eyes look a little too wild, Joe. You know you have to keep your cool."

Joe blinked, forcing himself to take a deep breath and exhale slowly, to channel his almost overpowering rage into an energy that wouldn't get everyone involved killed.

Martine slid her hand into his again. "You've got to let me help you with this. Nothing you do will work if Humberto thinks I'm out of the picture."

Damn it all, she was right. Joe just couldn't reconcile himself to putting her out there with a target on. He recalled that quick click of a vision he'd had in McLean. Martine with blood all over her face, her eyes closed.

But his visions always came in sequence. The other one he'd had more recently, right here on the plane, where she was swathed all in white was the only thing that gave him a little measure of hope. It came after the one with the blood, so didn't that mean she would survive to become a bride?

He looked at her again, that earnest expression, those beautiful features. His heart caught in his chest. Had the white been a bridal veil? Or the white satin lining of a casket?

Less than half an hour after they landed in Tallahassee, Joe boosted Martine into the chartered helicopter and they were off to Port St. Joe. He needed to make some calls, but knew there would be too much noise in the chopper.

His parents would be insane with worry if they already knew what had happened. He could only hope that they weren't aware of it yet. If they were, his dad would have immediately called the authorities and the local cops and FBI would be all over this by now.

Martine had said little and remained silent as the chopper lifted off. She appeared to be lost in thought, no doubt planning how to effect the exchange with the least risk of his family being hurt. It touched him that she would not only volunteer to surrender herself to Humberto in order to save two people she didn't even know, but that she also seemed convinced that right would prevail in the end. She just hadn't been in the business long enough to know that the good guys didn't always win.

He watched for coastline to appear on their left when they'd had time to near the Gulf. Something settled inside him when it finally came into view.

This was home, waves lapping foamy tongues at the shelly sands, shacks and quaint private cottages dotted among time-share condos and pastel hotels. Souvenir shops sporting garish signs, atmosphere provided by decrepit, peeling boats half buried in the dirt outside. There would be the ever-present gulls darting for fish and scraps from tourists. Not the most beautiful beach in the world, but it was his beach.

If not for the nightmarish circumstances that marred this homecoming, Joe knew he would be feeling an incredible rush of peace now. It's what brought him back here every chance he got. He couldn't, for the life of him, remember why he'd ever left in the first place.

This return was different, a result of his failure in Colombia, his reticence at becoming a straight-out assassin and killing Humberto with a couple of rounds to the head or a swift twist of the neck. He'd had numerous chances to do both but he hadn't.

Didn't that decision prove he should get out of the business?

Chapter 11

"It's beautiful!" Martine mouthed. Joe couldn't hear her words over the sound of the chopper. He smiled as she leaned over him to look down at the coast. He knew that up close the place wouldn't be all that impressive unless you already knew and loved it.

The sand wasn't Daytona white and the waves weren't surfer high. In the stretch fondly called the Redneck Riviera, you'd find only a few upscale amenities. But it had been a great place to grow up, a family place. He wouldn't trade it for the ritziest coast in Hawaii.

Joe directed the chopper to land on a flat section of beach near the causeway just off Highway 98. They ducked their heads against the downdraft, hefted out their two bags and Joe waved the pilot off.

They would have to hoof it for about a mile. He could call his folks to come get them, of course, but then he'd have to explain over the phone what was going on. Better to do that face-to-face.

Instead of heading for the highway where they might

have caught a ride, he took Martine's weekender from her and nodded toward the east. "That way. Kick off your shoes, but watch out for broken shells."

The whap-whap of the chopper blades had faded in the distance and left only minor traffic noise, the squawking of a couple of gulls and the swishing rhythm of the waves.

Joe drew in lungsful of the salty air as he began his trek home, welcoming the scent and humidity like old friends.

"Your family lives right on the beach?" she asked.

"Mom and Dad do. The others are farther inland. Linda lives about ten miles north. Delores has a house here near the school. I figure that must be where she and my niece were snatched. She walks over to pick up Nita at noon."

Shoes in hand, she trudged beside him, staring out at the Gulf. "We'll get them back, Joe."

"I know. Just a matter of time." He had to believe that. But he didn't have the faintest idea how to go about it. They had no clue where Humberto was. There was nothing for it but to wait until he made further contact.

Martine's cell phone chirped. She quickly snatched it out of her purse and answered. Her eyes widened as she offered it to Joe. "It's Mercier!"

Joe dropped the bags in the sand and took the phone, remembering that he had turned his off on the chopper. This must be important for Mercier to have gone to the trouble to get Martine's number. "Corda here."

"Matthew Duquesne called and told me what's going on. We're in."

"No way," Jack argued vehemently. "Humberto warned against calling in the troops. He says he'll kill my sister and her little girl."

"Hear me out. You'll be running the show. All I'm saying is that you have all our resources at your disposal, Joe. Every agency represented by Sextant. Anything you need—info, manpower, weaponry, supplies, funds—you name it.''

Joe felt overwhelmed by the offer. It was a godsend and he wasn't about to turn it down. ''Breaking rules, aren't you? This is not within Sextant's scope. National security's not threatened here.''

''Hey, you said yourself that Humberto's a foreign national, a known criminal working against his own government, who has entered our country to do deliberate harm to U.S. citizens. Four citizens targeted so far, two of them women and one, a child. Not to mention a government agent. As far as I'm concerned, that's terrorism at its most personal.''

He paused for effect, then added, ''So tell me what you need and let's take care of this.''

''We need everything. Right now we're at square one,'' Joe told him.

Martine piped in with specifics. ''Trace on the phones at Ames for the call back. Check on local rentals in the past few days. And abandoned properties. Get photos of Humberto if they can find any.''

Joe repeated what she said verbatim.

''We're on it. Turn on your phone and keep it on so we'll have two numbers to reach you. When either of you think of anything else you can use, give us a buzz. I'll get back with you soon. Oh, and give my regards to Martine,'' Mercier said.

He had used her first name. Joe wasn't sure he liked the note of familiarity.

''Yeah, sure.'' Joe thanked Mercier, signed off and returned Martine's phone. ''That's quite a deal. Sort of stunned me for a second.''

''He's wonderful, isn't he?'' she said with an encouraging grin. Then she picked up her suitcase before Joe could grab it and walked on down the beach.

He felt another stab of jealousy. Jack Mercier would

definitely appeal to a woman like Martine. To any woman, Joe suspected. Jack probably had some smooth moves. Definitely had a position of power and impressive resources. Those were resources Joe desperately needed himself at the moment, so he knew he had to squelch any personal animosity toward Mercier, deserved or not. It wasn't that Joe didn't like the guy. He did. He just didn't want Martine to keep noticing how great Jack was.

That worry was quickly supplanted by another more immediate concern. A wave of dread rippled through him as they passed the Williams' rustic little beach house and approached his parents' home.

He felt like the snake in the garden of Eden. He had brought this ugliness to paradise. If not for his damned job, this would not be happening. He should have quit sooner. Just one mission earlier and everything here would still be fine.

He stopped at the bottom of the steps leading up to the deck of the sand-colored stucco dwelling and shifted the bag in his hand.

"Well, this is it. My dad's gonna go ballistic and want to call in every law enforcement agency on the planet. Mom will probably have a heart attack."

God, he hoped not. There was no way to break this gently. How were their hearts? Had he even asked about their health lately?

She placed a palm on his back, just a comforting touch, support that he really needed right now. He looked down at her and she smiled encouragement. "I'm right behind you. If I see I'm in the way and they want privacy, I'll retreat and wait for you outside. If it goes the other way, I am trained in CPR."

Prepared for all contingencies, that was Martine. Joe wished he had time to hug her and tell her how much he appreciated her no-nonsense attitude. But that would have to wait.

* * *

Martine knew Joe was too preoccupied at the moment to focus on the investigation. She would have to pitch in until his equilibrium was restored. Thank God she had called Matt in private earlier and instructed him to get Mercier's number and tell him everything.

Any boss who would go the distance that he had to get Joe safely out of Colombia, even to paying a merc like Matt to bring him home early, would surely go all out to show Joe what the Sextant team was all about.

This kidnapping would provide a perfect opportunity to accomplish that if the rescue proved successful. It would also obligate Joe to stay with the team after everything was resolved. Mercier was no dummy. Martine had counted on that.

Once Joe got through this ordeal of telling his parents, she would question them, get the particulars on where the sister and her daughter might have been picked up and how long they had been missing. Hopefully, that information, combined with what Mercier would glean, might provide a starting point.

Joe knocked. In a couple of seconds a dark-haired little girl skipped across the glassed-in porch and unlatched the door. "Hi, Uncle Joe! Grandma, Papi, it's Uncle Joe!" She flung herself at him and clung like a little spider monkey. "What'd you bring me?"

"Nita?" His voice was a broken whisper as he clutched her with one arm. Then he cleared his throat, dropped his bag on the steps and peeled her off of him. Holding her by her slender shoulders, he crouched and looked her straight in the eye. "Where's your mama, Nita?"

The child beamed. She was a beauty except for the gap where her front teeth used to be. "She's making cookies. C'mon." She grabbed his hand with both of hers, tugged and danced backwards as she led them inside, through a living/dining area and to the doorway of a large eat-in kitchen. "Mama! Look who's here!"

Joe seemed to be having trouble assimilating the fact that his niece and sister were accounted for and safe. His other sister, the Cordas' youngest, had an infant. Martine feared she knew what was coming next, but she kept silent.

The living area, its wall of windows facing the view of the Gulf, had three other doors in addition to the kitchen, that opened off of it. There was a staircase leading up to what were probably more bedrooms. Joe's parents' home was very large, airy and comfortable. The rooms she could see were decorated with family photographs, handmade crafts and wicker furniture. She wished to heaven she'd been invited to the place under happier circumstances.

Joe embraced his sister fiercely, ignoring her laughing protest that she was sticky with cookie dough.

"Where is Linda?" he demanded, obviously having come to the same conclusion Martine had reached. If Humberto didn't have this sister, then he must have the other.

"At work, I guess. I haven't talked to her today."

"Aha, Joseph, you've come home!" A man, obviously Joe's father, rushed in, slapping him on the back and planting a kiss on either side of Joe's face. Then he noticed Martine. "And you bring pretty company. What a wonderful surprise!"

"Martine Duquesne," she said, holding out her hand. Instead of shaking it, he raised it to his lips.

"Welcome to our home. Son, you should have—"

"Where's Mama?" Joe interrupted, his impatience evident. He squeezed his sister's arm and gave her a little push. "Go and get her, Delores, while I make a phone call. I'm afraid I might have some bad news."

The happy expressions worn by Mr. Corda, Delores and the child, Nita, sobered instantly. Joe's father looked to her, his dark brows drawn together in question, probably figuring the bad news must have to do with her.

Delores returned less than a minute later with the mother. The older woman obviously had been asleep. Her short blond hair was a bit tousled and the shirt and shorts she wore looked wrinkled. She hardly looked old enough to have a son Joe's age.

"Joe, honey? What's wrong?" his mother asked, her Southern accent even more prominent than Joe's when he wasn't speaking Spanish. Her arms went around his waist as he hugged her with one arm.

He carefully replaced the receiver of the phone on the handset as his gaze met Martine's. He shook his head. No answer at his sister's house.

"Let's sit down," Joe told his mother gently, leading her over to the brightly patterned sofa that sat facing the bank of windows.

Martine looked out. You could see a panorama of surf from here and faintly hear its breathing. Even inside the house with doors closed and the air-conditioning on, the fresh scent of the ocean added its fillip to the tantalizing smell of homebaked cookies.

How the senses could lie, Martine thought sadly. All was not right with the world. And here, in this peaceful place, it should be. It really should be. She knew she felt only a trace of the awful betrayal Joe must feel at that. This was his haven. *Invaded.*

She and the rest took the chairs as Joe began. "Mama, have you spoken with Linda today?"

She shook her head. "Not since yesterday afternoon. I phoned early this morning, but... What's happened, Joe?" Her voice rose with every word.

He sighed, worrying his bottom lip for a moment before he went on. "We think Linda might have been kidnapped. Her and little Consuelo."

"Oh, my God, no!" Mrs. Corda cried. She reached out,

grasped at his shirtfront. Delores clutched Nita to her and held her protectively. They stared at Joe, speechless and wide-eyed with shock.

His father was already on his feet, fishing his keys out of his pocket. "It is that no-good man of hers! This time I will destroy that—"

"No, Papa. This has nothing to do with Paul. He's not involved in any way." He urged his father to sit back down. "Be still now and let me tell you what we know."

"Who has them and where are they?" his father demanded, still standing, his hands fisted at his sides. Martine could see where Joe got his fierce determination.

"I know the kidnapper. He's not from around here and his name is Carlos Humberto."

Joe Senior's eyes narrowed. "You know this man? From your work? This has to do with drugs?"

Martine watched Joe nod, guilt written all over his features. "We don't know where he's taken them yet. But you have to keep your head and not go off half-cocked. Agreed? We can't call in the authorities. He might panic if we do. I can handle this."

Mr. Corda exhaled harshly, finally dropped down in the chair again and pressed a hand to his face. He nodded, his conflict evident. A loving father and grandfather forced to relinquish taking an active role. His jaw clenched and his hands fisted, he narrowed his eyes at Joe. "You find them, Joseph. Today."

"I'll move heaven and earth, Papa. You know that," he promised.

Martine could see that Joe was clearly over his shock and back in control now, thinking logically, able to handle whatever came.

"But we must call the police," Mr. Corda announced.

"Joe's co-workers have offered to help, sir," Martine said. "Believe me, that's a much better alternative in this case."

All they needed was a bunch of uniforms muddying up the waters, maybe initiating tragic results if Humberto saw them as a threat. "We're advised to keep things quiet and wait for further word from the kidnapper. Then we'll know how to plan."

Joe gave her the ghost of a smile and a nod of approval as he stood up. "Martine will explain further while I go over and check at Linda's. There might be evidence there that can help me find her."

"Then go, go," his mother urged, pushing at him.

He spoke to Martine. "I'll be back as soon as I have a look around."

"I'll be here," she said, amazed when he cradled her face and brushed a quick kiss on her forehead.

"Take care, Joe," she told him as he was leaving.

When the door closed behind him, Mr. Corda pinned Martine with a worried glare. "Why did you say that to him? To have a care? Is our Joseph in danger, too?"

"A figure of speech, sir. You know Joe can look after himself. And as for your daughter and her baby, I don't believe the man who has them would harm them. I was hostage to him myself not long ago and he treated me very well, like a guest. Once he gets what he's after, he'll let them go."

"What does he want?" Delores asked. "Do you know yet?"

Martine hedged. "We're waiting on instructions."

"You were a hostage? Joe saved you?" his mother whispered, hope flaring in her wide blue eyes.

"Of course," Martine said with a wide smile to reassure the woman. "And if your son went to that much trouble for me, someone he hadn't even met before, you *know* he'll find his own sister and niece. He's the very best person to handle this."

Little Nita came over and climbed on the arm of Martine's chair, bumping one foot against the side, studying the stranger her uncle had brought home with him. "Are you going to marry my Uncle Joe? He kissed your head."

Martine noticed the others were staring at her as intently as Nita was, waiting to see what she would say. Would they be glad or upset if Joe really had brought her here with serious intentions?

A small laugh escaped. "No, no, sweetie. We're not that kind of friends. I'm only here to...well, help if I can."

"Tell us about this man, this kidnapper," Mr. Corda ordered. "What sort of person is he and what do you *think* he is after? Money?"

"Humberto's after me." She figured she could admit that much. They didn't know her so that shouldn't upset them. But Martine didn't want to be the one to tell them he was after Joe as well. "I believe he wants an exchange, and if Joe can't find and rescue Linda and little Consuelo right away, then we'll make it."

"We know something of what Joseph's job entails. This man is a drug runner," Joe's father said. "Does he also use drugs?"

Martine shook her head emphatically. "No, sir. Humberto is not your run-of-the-mill drug lord. He views himself as a very savvy Colombian businessman, not as the criminal he is. Self-delusion on his part, I know, but he behaves accordingly."

"He behaves as a gentleman?" The father of any abducted daughter would desperately hope that was true.

"Yes, sir. He always did with me," Martine said, hoping to alleviate a little of their worry.

She watched relief deflate Corda's chest. His wife and daughter looked a lot more skeptical. Did they suspect what a rosy colored picture she was painting about all of this? Of course, they must.

Martine took the little girl's hand. "Now if you would come show me where things are, Nita, we could finish baking those cookies your mother started and make some coffee or something. I don't really know anything else to tell anyone, and I'm sure your mother and grandparents will want to discuss this without little ears tuned in.''

"Or stranger ears," Nita retorted, squinting at Martine's. "We can talk to each other while they say secrets."

"You bet."

Nita gave her a look that acknowledged Martine's frankness, almost a thank-you for not inventing some phony excuse to get her out of the room. Children were so much more savvy than people gave them credit for. Martine could never understand why some people talked down to them.

Mr. Corda was already comforting his wife. Delores had set about reassuring them both about her sister's strength and how little trouble the baby was. Everything would be all right, Martine heard her say. Joe would take care of it. Linda and little Connie would be home before breakfast tomorrow. Martine prayed to God she was right about that.

All in all, they had taken the news much better than she had expected. The Cordas were a strong family who apparently bred strong children.

She smiled down at the six-year-old who exhibited a bold confidence that was pure Joe. A sudden and unfamiliar longing stirred in Martine's heart.

Her children would probably look just like this if Joe were their father. Beautiful, fearless kids with wisdom and warm humor shining out of deep brown eyes.

He would be so gentle and loving with them, but firm, she imagined. He wouldn't just demand, but would earn their respect as they grew up. He seemed to have a good example to follow. Yes, Joe would make a fine father. She would be the one lacking in the parental department, but she still had this incredible urge to give it a try.

What a rotten time for dormant maternal instincts to kick in, she thought with a sigh. This was *so* not good.

Joe hated it when his worst fears were realized. Linda's purse was on the floor in the small foyer, its contents scattered. Quickly he searched the five small rooms of the little tract house. None of the sparse furnishings were disturbed. She must have decided not to put up a fight. He was relieved about that.

In the baby's room he found the diaper bag, empty except for a crumpled paper, the daily report form from the nursery listing feedings and changes. The coverlet in the crib was wadded to one side. Joe touched it, willing his rage down to a manageable level, then hurried back to the kitchen.

There were two prepared bottles in the fridge, one lying on its side.

He propped his hands against the edge of the counter to keep from trashing the kitchen himself.

The sugar bowl was tipped over. In the spill of sugar a finger had hastily carved out the number three. Linda had left the message, probably when she'd been allowed to grab a bottle for the baby. *Three,* signifying there were three men involved, he guessed. It was all she would have known at that point.

Joe looked around more carefully. Near the sugar was an electrical outlet. And an unplugged cord which led to a cheap plastic alarm clock. Another message. The hands had stopped at six o'clock. This morning or yesterday evening?

She usually picked up Connie at the Playhouse Nursery and got home from work about five-thirty. If Humberto and his men had been waiting to take her then, the diaper bag would not have been in the nursery waiting to be packed with diapers and bottles for the next day. He would have found it with or near her purse.

Hoping against hope someone would have seen something, he went house to house and questioned her neighbors. No one had seen her leave. But the couple across the street had been outside working in their yards until long after six the day before. Her car had still been in the driveway at nine. Now it was gone. So they must have taken her this morning, at six o'clock.

He drove his dad's car back to the beach house. He had been gone for a couple of hours. It was nearly seven. They could be anywhere by now, but he felt they wouldn't be too far away. Humberto would need to have the hostages handy when it was time to make the trade.

Joe pulled out his cell phone to touch base with Mercier, knowing it was too soon for him to have found out anything significant. He was right, but at least things had been set into motion.

He pulled into the driveway and sat there for a minute wondering what in the world he could say to reassure his parents that Linda would be all right. She was their baby girl, only twenty-five. And little Consuelo was only four months old.

His father came out of the house and hurried to the car just as Joe got out and slammed the door.

"You were gone for so long! What did you find?" he asked, his dark eyes searching Joe's face.

"Linda and Connie were taken, just like I figured. Any calls?"

"None. Any sign that they were hurt?"

"No, and no indication that she resisted, which was smart." Joe quickly filled him in on his findings based on the clues Linda had provided.

"She is smart and brave, our Linda. But I worry she will anger them. Her temper is too quick."

"You know she won't endanger the baby."

His father nodded, hands on his hips as he looked off down the main drag. Traffic was fairly light, even for this late in the season, but Joe knew his dad wasn't gauging that right now. He was lost in his thoughts of what might be happening to two people he loved. "What are we to do, Joseph? How can we find them?"

"We'll find them. Let's go inside."

"This woman you brought with you, she is also working for the DEA?" He led the way back to the house, his gait weary, his head bowed.

"I'm no longer with the DEA, Papa, remember?" He didn't want to bring up anything about battling terrorists right now, but Joe wondered if the agency he *did* work now for might trigger situations every bit as bad as this one if he stayed with the job. His dad sure didn't need to hear that. "Martine is with a company out of Atlanta. A hostage rescue outfit. I met her in Colombia when I was on my last case. I thought she would have told you all that."

"She only said that you saved her from this man. That you are very good at what you do." There was more than pride in his father's voice. Joe detected profound hope that what Martine had told them was true.

"Yeah, she would say that." He tried to change the subject. "What do you think of her, Papa?"

"She knows the right things to say at times like this. And she seems willing to do what must be done. She has said that if she goes with this man, Humberto, he might release Linda and the baby. Is this true?"

"Only if he gets me, too. Did she tell you that? He plans to kill us. If I thought he would honor his word on the trade, I might try it."

"Even if it meant the death of Martine Duquesne?"

Joe looked his father straight in the eye and meant to answer, "Even then." But he couldn't form the words.

He kept seeing Martine's pale face in that vision he'd had back in McLean, her beautiful features covered with blood, her eyes closed.

Chapter 12

His father's strong hand gripped Joe's arm. "Go inside your mind and see what will happen, my son, for I can see nothing. The future hides from me."

"And it only teases me with random glimpses, Papa. None of them good. It's a curse."

"It's a gift and you must use it when it comes."

Joe shook his head and pushed open the front door, needing to see Martine alive and well and free of the gore in the vision. "It's a half-ass gift, then, one that can't be trusted."

"It is more than the gift you do not trust, Joseph," his father argued. "You would never be still long enough to search your heart." He flung out his hands. "Always moving, moving, try this, try that! The one thing I could not teach you is to have patience with yourself!"

In the open doorway, Joe turned on him. "The one thing you *did* teach me is to stand for what I believe is right, old man. I would die for any one of my family and you know it, but I do *not* think it's right to expect Martine—''

''I believe that's my call.'' Martine stood there, blue eyes spitting fire.

His father's gaze flicked back and forth between them, obviously waiting for an explosion. But Joe knew now was not the time for a battle of wills. Martine was no martyr and, even given her lack of experience in dealing with men like Humberto before Colombia, she had good instincts. Joe waited to see what else she had to say.

''I think we should try acting before we resort to reacting,'' she said. ''Time for a planning session. Tell me exactly what you found, Joe.''

Relieved to avoid a confrontation with her when he had so much else to worry about, Joe repeated what he'd told his father and elaborated a little more on the details. His objectivity kicked in while going over it. Maybe that's what she'd had in mind.

He knew one thing: in spite of his urge to protect her, he was damned glad she was here.

Martine took the chair Joe pulled out for her at the kitchen table while the others took their places.

Delores had put on a Disney video for Nita in one of the bedrooms to keep her occupied. Then she made sandwiches and opened chips and soft drinks for everyone, urging them to eat. Martine hoped Joe's youngest sister, Linda, was as practical as Delores. Linda would need all her wits to hold her own with Humberto.

By all rights, Joe should be in charge of the planning, but Martine could see he wanted to shield his mother from thinking about the worst. He would probably send her in the other room to lie down, not understanding that the woman really needed something positive to do instead of being coddled.

''All right, question,'' Martine said, jumping right in

before he had a chance to assume the lead. ''Is Linda breast-feeding the baby?''

Mrs. Corda nodded, her brow wrinkled with confusion. ''Yes. She expresses her milk for the daytime feedings while she is at work, but she is still nursing.''

''Okay, so the baby will get fed and they won't need to shop for milk,'' Martine said with a nod. ''But they left the diaper bag, which was stupid. After one stinky one, they'll realize they *need* diapers. So, Mr. and Mrs. Corda, you'll need to begin at one end of the strip and go to the other, questioning every cashier that might have checked out a man buying a generous supply today.''

''Good thinking,'' Joe said. ''They probably went for one of the convenience stores. Fewer customers and less time looking for what they wanted. What we're after is the make and model of the vehicle they're in. We can be pretty sure they will have ditched Linda's by this time.''

Martine nodded. ''Call Mercier back, Joe, and see what he has for us so far.''

''I called him on the way back from Linda's. It will be morning before he can get everything to us. He's waiting for a source to get him the photo of Humberto and will then forward it. I gave him the e-mail address here.''

''What can I do?'' Delores asked, shoving the plate of sandwiches at her father and giving him a pointed but silent order to eat.

Martine knew Delores wasn't going to like the next suggestion. ''You'll take Nita and get out of town. Humberto might just decide to up the stakes.''

Delores shook her head. ''I'll take Nita to her other grandparents right now, but I'm coming back here. I can help and so can my husband.''

Joe answered. ''Good. You two will man the phone and computer here, collect whatever Mercier sends, and call us in when you get something new. Martine and I will meet with the realtors and start checking out rental properties and get some leads on vacant buildings.''

Martine's phone rang. She looked at the display, then quickly answered, ''Matt? Did he call again?''

Martine watched Joe's face change from agent-in-charge to brother-in-pain. Delores was already standing, gripping the back of her chair with white-knuckled fingers. Mrs. Corda had paled even further, her breathing shallow, her color not good at all. Mr. Corda held his sandwich at half mast, the bite he'd just taken still unchewed. Everyone around the table was totally focused on her, waiting.

''Humberto called,'' Matt affirmed. ''He seemed nervous this time. I told him I had just located you. He said you and Joe have until tomorrow afternoon to get to Port St. Joe and be ready to make the switch. If you don't do what he says, he told me the hostages will be *sleeping with the fishes* by midnight tomorrow. Can you believe he actually said that? Guy's been watching too much American TV. We traced the number and it was a ship-to-shore phone. He's on a boat.''

''Name?''

''The *Paper Moon.* You can thank Mercier for getting with the Coastal authorities to obtain the ID. It's a forty-two-foot Flybridge, usually slipped at the Portaway Marina at Mako Beach. Captain is Harley Banks. He's a live-aboard and only hires crew when he takes her out. See if you can get a location on the boat but do it on the Q.T. The Coast Guard would go roaring in with foghorns and automatics. I wouldn't advise that. Humberto even warned me to stay where I am. Fat chance of that.''

''You'll stay, Matt. Come down here and I'll break your other leg. Any background noises on the phone?'' Martine asked, hoping for some kind of clue as to whether the boat was very far off shore. ''The motor running? Gulls or anything?''

''Too quiet except for a baby crying. Not screaming, just fussing. It was close up, so he intended me to hear it. Could have been a recording, though.''

''Let's hope not.''

''Yeah, let's. I gave Humberto your cell number so he'll be phoning you and Joe with directions for the swap.'' He paused for a second. ''But don't you go for it, Marti. He'll kill you. He said again that he wouldn't, that he just wants Corda, but that was just to get me to cooperate and get you down there. I'm coming anyway as soon as I can get a flight.''

''No, Matt. I mean it. I have a feeling he'll be checking periodically just to make sure you stay in Atlanta. There's no doubt he knows exactly what it is you do for a living and he'll see you as his biggest threat. Please, be sensible and stay where you are.''

''Only if you promise me you won't consider the exchange. Find another way.''

Martine agreed they would, but she wasn't so sure there *was* another way. She said a quick goodbye, rang off and put the phone down. It had been so deathly quiet in the room and her reception so good on the cell phone, she knew everyone had heard the entire conversation.

''We need to move tonight before Humberto realizes we're already here,'' Joe said. ''Mercier's going to have to get us a location.''

''Satellite?'' Martine asked. ''You think he has the authority for that?''

Joe sighed. ''We're about to find out. If not, he can buy the information. Anyone with enough money can. Papa, forget the convenience stores. You and Mama drive down to the marina. See what you can find out about the *Paper Moon* and how long ago she pulled out, how much her tanks hold and when she refueled. Call back here on the land line soon as you get the info. Delores, get Nita over to Terry's folks and get back here. Martine, scare up a map of the area. There should be an atlas on the book-shelf. Meanwhile, I'll call Mercier about the satellite.''

Delores went to collect Nita and her toys. Joe had barely finished giving Mercier the pertinent information about the boat and requesting his help when his sister returned to the dining room.

''Joe, a little beach bunny just appeared on the back porch insisting she's a friend of yours. I told her you were too busy but—''

''Don't mind the disguise, Joey,'' said a sultry voice from the doorway. ''I didn't know whether anybody might be watching the place or what I'd find going on, so I played the local and walked up the beach from the hotel. Y'all ready for some help around here?''

''Holly?'' Joe was too stunned to stand up. The woman was barefoot and wearing a string bikini. She had a beach towel slung over one shoulder, probably concealing her weapon. ''What the hell are you doing here?''

She rolled her eyes and grinned at Delores. ''Tell me, girl, has he always been this slow?'' Then she held out her hand. ''Name's Holly Amberson.''

Delores hesitated, then shook her hand. ''Delores Trim-ble, his sister.'' She shot Joe the same look she always had when he'd gotten himself in hot water with his girl-friends. An expression that read, ''How are you going to manage two at a time, bro?'' Then she glanced toward the other side of the living room where Martine stood with the atlas in her hands.

It was obvious Delores thought Holly and Martine shared an interest in him that had nothing to do with the kidnapping. It was also clear that she was not at all happy about the probable distraction a triangle would cause right now.

''How'd you get here so fast?'' Joe asked.

Holly grinned and did a little flourish with her well-manicured hand. ''Magic. We caught a hop down to Tyndal Air Force Base.''

''*We?*''

''Will and Eric came, too. Matt Duquesne called Jack about the trace and I just talked with him. He's pretty sure your boy's on a boat, but the guys are casing other possibilities. It can't hurt to be thorough. As for me, I'm all yours!''

Not the best declaration to make with Delores eyeing them that way. ''Holly works with me. Come on in and sit down, Holly,'' Joe said. ''Delores, scram and do what you gotta do. Martine?'' he called. ''Bring the map.''

It took less than five minutes for him to realize that Martine might have the same idea about Holly that Delores had, despite his explanation of the job situation.

Though she was polite to Holly, Joe sensed an undercurrent of wariness that could possibly be jealousy. He wondered if it was personal or professional. It would be nice if he had time to explore that a little, but he didn't.

Holly had never shown any indication of interest in him as anything other than a member of the team. He certainly had none in her, though he had not missed the fact that she was beautiful. Who wouldn't notice?

Her conduct right now was all business, but she sure was radiating sexuality in that bikini. Her skin—and she was displaying a *lot* of it—was pale caramel, only a shade darker than his. The catlike eyes were made for concealing secrets and taunting people with them. Her short cap of hair glistened like black watered silk.

Unfortunately, it was impossible not to notice her remarkable breasts straining against the triangles of electric-blue spandex, but Joe staunchly ignored them after one or two furtive glances. Martine was not quite so dismissive of Holly's most prominent features. She glared.

Joe attempted to drown the tension with a spate of information, hoping to direct their attention back to the main reason they were here. Once Holly was up to speed on everything, he turned to Martine. ''Did I tell you? Holly used to be with the FBI.''

Martine looked unimpressed. ''I'm sure her credentials are…impeccable.''

Holly just smiled, the picture of innocence. Joe knew she had a wicked sense of humor because he'd seen her ply it with the guys back in McLean. She knew exactly what she was doing. He felt like shaking her right now for putting him on the spot with Martine.

''Okay, here's the deal, you two,'' Holly said suddenly, shutting off the sensual glow around her like a light switch. ''Jack will be getting with the National Reconnaissance Office tonight. Hopefully, he'll be able to see the pictures from one of the satellites over the Gulf and try to pinpoint any forty-two-footers hanging around out there and get us some coordinates to work with.''

''There are bound to be quite a few, but I think we can be pretty sure he'll stay close. That should narrow it down a little,'' Joe said, thinking out loud.

''Timing might be a problem,'' Martine declared. ''If the pictures are even an hour or so old, the boat might not have remained stationary.''

Holly agreed. ''Yes, right. He'll compare from two sources passing over at different times if possible. The sightings that are the correct size and fairly stationary will be the suspect vehicles. The satellite views will probably be more or less straight down and boat names won't be visible.''

Joe had an idea. ''We could do a flyby early in the morning with one of the sightseeing helicopters that sell rides. They will have been flying at intervals today, so that shouldn't send up any alert that we're using them for a search.''

''We can also question other boat owners who have

been out, see if they've noticed the *Paper Moon*," Martine suggested.

"Yeah, but even if we identify the boat right away, the earliest I can get aboard is tomorrow night," Joe said. "That could be too late."

Holly raised an eyebrow. "You're to talk to Humberto by phone before then. Stall him. Then after dark, *we* do the insertion, Joe. I didn't fly all the way down here just to darken my tan."

"I'm going, too," Martine said emphatically.

"We'll see," Holly said calmly. "Right now, if you would please get on the horn and hire us a little whirlybird for the morning. Promise to double their rate if they'll have us up there first thing."

To her credit, Martine didn't argue. Joe imagined she would make up for lost time when she found out she definitely wasn't going on the boat raid, but he would deal with that when they came to it.

"I'll call around and get us some SEAL gear and an inflatable Zodiac. Joe, you'll scare us up some weapons. Get with ATF or DEA for some confiscated automatics and magazines. Throw your new weight around if you need to. Big Boss has authorized us cooperation from the top on down on every case we run. Let's see how well it works."

"Done," he assured her, already compiling a mental list of what they would need.

As it happened, his mention of Sextant worked really well. Bill Cole, an old associate working with the local DEA, promised to fix them up with a virtual arsenal.

Civilian companies obviously weren't required to cooperate quite as fully, Joe discovered. Martine hit a stumbling block.

"FlyRight wants a cash deposit up-front and an explanation of what's going on," she said. "One of us needs to go to Panama City and make the arrangements tonight if we want the helicopter tomorrow.''

As soon as Delores returned from taking Nita to the in-laws an hour later, she and Martine headed out to take care of it, which meant a forty-mile drive. Martine didn't look all that happy about leaving him there alone with Holly.

Joe decided he didn't mind Martine's little pique all that much. Payback for her deviling him about Jack Mercier and what a great guy he was. Still, he was too worried about Linda and the baby to give it much more than a passing thought.

Even so, he followed her out to Delores's car. When Martine turned, her hand on the car door, to see what he wanted, he showed her exactly what that was with a kiss.

It was over too quickly and her surprise too great for her to give much of a response. Joe had to be satisfied with her ghost of a smile and that smug little glance toward the door of the house where Holly stood observing them.

He sighed when Delores backed out of the driveway and took off. He used to be a lot more adept at managing women. But he suspected most women were a lot more manageable than Martine would ever be.

Time crawled by as the night wore on. "I can't understand why they're not back yet," Joe said, checking his watch again, then glancing at the kitchen clock to make certain the two jibed. How many times had he done that already? "It's been four hours. The cell phone is off and that worries me," he added. Surely she wouldn't have turned it off. He had swapped his for hers since Matt had given Humberto her number. Maybe his was just out of juice. He couldn't remember when he'd last charged it.

Holly poured them another cup of coffee and nodded at one of the chairs in a silent effort to get him to sit down. He couldn't seem to be still no matter how hard he tried.

"Your parents got some good info at the marina," Holly said. "We know at least two of them are out there on the boat. We should be able to find it easily enough with the chopper once Jack gets us the coordinates from the satellite pictures. How much do you figure Humberto knows about boats?"

"Not a lot, I guess, but we can't count on that," Joe warned. "He's smart. What he doesn't know, he'll find out or at least make sure he has someone around who's an expert. When I knew him, he left very little to chance. In which case, the captain might still be alive." Joe surely hoped that was so.

His parents, exhausted by worry and their trip to the marina, had gone to bed an hour before. It was after midnight already. Joe was so wired, he didn't figure he'd sleep at all tonight. Not that he'd even consider it until Martine and Delores returned and he knew everything was set for the search in the morning.

Holly looked as bright-eyed as ever. She wore one of his mother's robes over her bikini, so she wasn't quite as distracting now. He felt a little jolt of satisfaction every time he thought about Martine's reaction to Holly. He sipped his coffee and put it down again to resume pacing.

"Will you please sit?" Holly snapped, clicking one long red nail on the Formica tabletop. "You make me nervous." She shook her head and chuckled. "That girl's got you so wound up, I swear."

Joe dragged out a chair and sat. "Yeah, she does." He blew out a sigh. "You ever been nuts about somebody, Amberson?"

She nodded thoughtfully, playing with her cup, turning it around and around. "Time or two."

"How about now?" he asked, grinning at her. "I

thought I saw you looking a little cow-eyed at Will Griffin back at the office.''

She shrugged, refusing to meet his eyes. ''The boy's eye candy, what can I say?'' Then she laughed at herself, shaking her head. ''He's got a twin. Did you know that? Looks exactly like him. He's still with Alcohol, Tobacco and Firearms. Double trouble, those two.''

''So you got two shots at the gold ring?''

Again she laughed, this time more softly. ''No. No rings for me. Best I'd get out of the deal with Will would be a roll in the hay and that's not an option. Not with a co-worker. Or his brother,'' she added for good measure. ''Besides, Will's not—''

Joe jumped up as a car turned in the drive, shell gravel crunching beneath the tires. ''It's about damn time.''

He jerked open the side door and stepped out. Delores was already out of the car and running toward him, stumbling in her haste. ''He's got her, Joe!''

He caught her arms to steady her. ''Humberto?''

She nodded, catching back a sob. ''He must have been watching the house. I thought we were being followed and started to turn around. He blocked me and held a gun on us. I thought…he was going to shoot.''

''Take it easy,'' Joe told her. She was nearly hysterical. He needed a clear picture of what had happened. ''Come inside and sit down.'' He led her in, plopped her in the nearest chair and signaled Holly to get her something to drink. ''Now, step by step, sis. What happened?''

She sucked in a deep breath and plowed her hands through her hair, leaving them there as she rested her elbows on the table. ''Okay. Okay. These lights were right behind us, tailgating. I pulled over to let him pass. Before I knew what happened, he was just…there! We were blocked. He had this huge gun pointed right at Martine and ordered us out of the car. Then he hit her with it, Joe.'' She shrank into herself just thinking about it. Delores had never been subjected to violence of any kind before this, he knew.

"How hard? Did he knock her out?"

She nodded frantically and sobbed again. "Then he tied my hands with a cord of some kind and pushed me into the back seat of the car. It took me...forever to...get loose!" She rubbed her wrists which were red and raw in places.

Joe forced himself to be calm. Going berserk wouldn't help Martine. "But you did, hon. You got free. Now tell me, what did he say to you? Did he say anything?"

Again she nodded and swallowed hard. "He...he said he knew you would be looking for him and if you didn't quit, he would kill Martine." She began crying, shaking uncontrollably.

Joe had no choice but to wait until she got over it a little, then offered her the juice Holly had brought over. He wiped her eyes with a napkin.

"Here, drink this. You'll feel better," he said. Nothing, absolutely nothing could make *him* feel better at this point other than getting his hands around Humberto's throat. "Did he say anything else?"

She blinked hard and drew in a shuddery breath. "Bombs," she whispered, horror in her voice. "He said he'd planted bombs. And...and he said to be sure your phone stays turned on. He'll call." Her eyes, swimming with tears, met his. "One of those...bombs is where Linda and the baby are. Oh God, Joe, what are we gonna do?"

She collapsed again, weeping hard. Joe slammed his fist on the table and cursed. Holly quickly put her hand over his, warning him to be quiet.

She was right. If he woke up his parents, he'd have three people hysterical. Four, if he let go, too. He had to remain in control if he was to get Martine, his sister and her baby out of this.

God only knew what Humberto was up to with bombs.

Could he possibly have planned all this so far ahead? Then Joe reminded himself that Humberto had to have been doing something during the time Joe was in McLean with Sextant and Martine was back in Atlanta.

He had somehow found out about Joe's family, closely guarded information when you did undercover work. Also he had known exactly which buttons to push to get Joe to Florida, even if they hadn't already been headed there.

He wished to hell he hadn't brought Martine with him. That had not been planned, but Humberto would have found a way to get to her sooner or later. Joe just couldn't stand to think of Martine at that devil's mercy, hurt and tied up.

God, he hoped she wasn't in some confined space on top of all that. Fear tightened his chest muscles to the point of pain. He had to do something.

"Sit back down, Joe," Holly ordered. "We've got the phone number of the boat. Call the jerk and let him know we'll blow his ass out of the water if he detonates any bombs ashore."

"He'll kill them!" Delores cried, wringing her hands. "He'll kill them all!"

Holly shook her head and patted Delores's back. "No, he won't. They're his ace in the hole. Without them, how's he gonna get to Joe?"

"Linda and Connie aren't with him," Delores rasped. "He said one of the bombs was planted with Linda and the baby, and he'd make it go off if he saw anybody searching for the boat."

"All right, all right, settle down. We'll find a way," he said, speaking as much to himself as to Delores.

Holly picked up the kitchen phone. "You call the ATF, Joe. I'm calling the AIC at the Panama City FBI. Let's get everybody running checks on who's been buying boom stuff in the area. If Humberto got the materials locally, maybe we can determine how much fire power he's working with. I'm also calling in EOD teams with sniffers to check out high-traffic areas. They can bring in help and arrange a quiet sweep of the entire town.''

His call accomplished, Joe located the number for the *Paper Moon*. Holly motioned for him to wait about phoning the boat until she finished the one she was making. Joe listened.

She was talking with Mercier. ''Jack, we're officially involved now. This has escalated and there's no question that this guy's a terrorist in every sense of the word.'' She replaced the receiver on the hook and nodded once. ''It's a mission.''

Joe welcomed the help with the bomb situation. If everyone got on it, they would probably find Linda and the baby in time because there weren't that many places around Port St. Joe to hide them. But he knew in his heart that he would be going to that boat alone. It was the only way, and even at that, he had a very slim chance of saving Martine.

If Humberto had even taken her to the boat. Hell, they could be anywhere, land or sea.

Joe lifted his cell phone and dialed the number for the *Paper Moon*. The ringing went on forever, but no one answered.

Chapter 13

Martine opened her eyes, immediately aware on waking that she was on a boat. The cabin undulated, causing her stomach to lurch and her head to pound. A spot above her right temple throbbed painfully. He had hit her with the gun. A coating of dried blood pulled the skin of her face taut.

The head trauma hadn't induced any merciful bout of amnesia for her, Martine thought, catching back a groan. She remembered every detail until the split second when she lost consciousness.

Desperately, she scanned the enclosure, which consisted of wall-to-wall bed. This was the pocket cabin, she guessed, a small tuckaway space for overflow guests.

She was alone. For a few seconds, she struggled with the binding on her wrists, telling herself it was only a matter of minutes before she could work free. Don't panic, she warned herself. Stay calm.

Had Humberto killed Linda and her baby? And where was Delores? Were they onboard in another cabin?

Oh God, poor Joe. Both of his sisters and his niece were missing. And her, too. She knew he would include her in his worrying because he obviously cared. He was a caring man. Why hadn't she told him how she felt about him before it was too late?

She could hear the rhythmic slap of waves against the sides of the craft. The odor of mildew and sweat permeated the small space that seemed to close in and grow more confining by the second.

She took shallow breaths, battling the encroaching terror of having her hands bound behind her, of not being able to work free, of the sloped walls shrinking inward.

A screaming plea for release rose in her throat, but she choked it back, knowing the futility of crying out. It would only alert Humberto that she was awake. Seeing him, watching him gloat or perhaps do worse, was the last thing she needed right now.

Escape seemed impossible, but she couldn't simply give up. What had she trained for these last four years? Deliberately, she forced anger to replace the fear.

In desperation she recalled her shame at wimping out in the cave, depending solely on Joe to haul her out of that tunnel in a faint. Damned if she'd let herself get that worked up again. *Think! Plan!*

The first order of business was to get rid of the rope.

Her hands were swollen, but not to the point where she had lost feeling. *Don't struggle. Relax.* She twisted her fingers, carefully probing for the knot in the narrow nylon cord.

A soft curse escaped, but at least she was breathing more normally. Her second-worst enemy, panic, was more or less under control, at least for the moment.

Damned if she would let it end this way. Humberto had brought her here to lure Joe to the boat where he would kill them both. Knowing Humberto, they would not suffer an easy death. Then he would dump their bodies in the

Gulf and be docking in Mexico, the Islands or somewhere before they were found. If they ever were.

She remembered Joe's admission, his greatest fear. Dying alone and no one knowing. Well, at least he wouldn't be alone. She gritted her teeth and let fury flow through her.

She had no clue how long she had been unconscious. Maybe she had remained asleep for some time even after recovering from the blow to her head. The two tiny windows were covered but it wasn't completely dark. If that was daylight and not artificial light seeping through, she had to have been here at least five or six hours.

Joe might already be on his way and she had to be in a position to help him when he got here. She had absolutely no doubt that Humberto would have called to give him the location of the boat. And she knew for certain Joe would come.

"You're too hyper, Joe," Holly warned. "At this rate, you'll collapse before we get a plan in place."

She put her arm around his mother's shoulders and asked her if she had anything else in her medicine cabinet that would calm Joe down. Mama had already given Delores something and put her to bed. His father and Terry, Delores's husband, had run down to the marina again to see what else they could find out.

His mother was no sooner out of the room than the phone rang. Holly had made use of her contacts with the Bureau and theirs with the phone company. All calls dialed to the cell phone were to be rerouted to a regular land line so they could be taped for analysis and traced if necessary. All the equipment was in place.

Joe was amazed at how much she had accomplished by seven o'clock in the morning and was damned glad to have her help. He sucked in a deep breath and prayed for calm as he waited for the third ring.

"It's on speaker," Holly said. "Go ahead, Joe."

He punched the button. "Corda here," he snapped.

"Ah, you sound less than cool, amigo. Where is that charm you oozed when you secured my trust? Where is your confidence?"

"Cut the bull and get down to business," Joe ordered.

"Very well, we will dispense with amenities. My plans have changed. I have decided to let your sister, niece and Martine live if you will do precisely as I tell you."

"And the captain," Joe bargained. "Include him."

Humberto paused. "Ah, too late for the old fellow. You, of course, will have to die, too. I think you will not mind it so much. You seemed willing enough when propped against that tree and I had you in my sights. Or was that an act as well?"

"Spit it out, Humberto. Tell me what you want?"

"Two million will suffice. You owe me considerably more than that, but it is all I can reasonably expect you to gather by seven o'clock this evening."

Ransom? The demand surprised Joe, but he supposed it shouldn't. Greed was a huge part of Humberto's makeup.

Joe didn't think for a second Humberto would release Martine for any amount, but he probably would let Linda and the baby go. "Where the hell would I get two million? I can get you half that, maybe, if you give me another day."

"No room for negotiation, Corda. Get the money by seven tonight or their deaths will be on your head." His voice grew hard with the last demand. "You know I will keep my promise. Unlike some men I could mention, my word is my honor."

Honor? Joe wanted to shout. What man's honor allowed him to kidnap defenseless women and a baby? But he kept his temper in check. Years of experience had taught him much about dealing with scum like Humberto.

"How do you want it handled? Cash or transferral to an account?" Joe amazed himself with his businesslike tone. The almost overpowering urge to threaten Humberto nearly broke free, but Joe held it back. Loosing his cool wouldn't help. "Where and how do we make the exchange?"

"Cash, and you will bring it to me. I will call again at seven o'clock with instructions." His chuckle crawled through the receiver. "I know your mind must be working alive with plans to find me before that time. I warn you, do not try. And do not involve anyone else in this, Corda. I will be able to see anyone approaching and I have prepared for that."

Joe glanced at Holly as he spoke to Humberto. "I got the message. This stays between us."

Humberto made a small sound of what sounded like approval. "I hope you are not lying again, Corda. If you are and I see any sign of interference, I shall have to light up your precious Port Saint Joseph sky. There are explosive devices that will detonate at my command."

"I told you I'll be alone," Joe insisted.

Humberto continued as if Joe hadn't spoken. "One of these is planted with your sister and her child. If the deal goes well and no one follows me after our business is complete, the authorities will be notified of the locations I have wired. If not…" He paused. "Well, in either case, you have my word."

The connection broke. Joe glared at the phone and slammed his palm with his fist. "God, I need to kill that man!"

Holly placed a hand on his shoulder. "Can you raise that much money?"

Joe shrugged away, rubbing his eyes with the heels of his hands. "Hell no. But I'll think of something." He'd rob a bank if that's what it took. "I might need to show the cash to get Humberto to let me on the boat."

"I'll arrange it," she said. "We've used confiscated counterfeit sometimes in instances like this. It's not like he's going to get anywhere to spend it."

"You'd better put a tracker in with it, just in case he gets away. First, see how the bomb squad's doing finding those explosives," Joe told her. "And get the SEAL gear delivered now instead of tonight. I want their smallest Zodiac."

Holly nodded. "Will's picking up the weapons. Mac-10's with a couple of mags extra. A 9mm and a .22 apiece for backup. Enough?"

"Where is he now?"

"Should arrive in a couple of hours with the goodies."

Joe nodded approval. "I'll need a blade, too. I want to gut that sonofabitch. And I want a submersible, tanks and a wet suit in case I get a chance to go in before the deadline."

"You're not going in alone, Joe. Take Eric. He's had SEAL training and is the best at hand-to-hand you'll find anywhere."

His hackles rose. "I was a Ranger for three years and did my share of waterwork. I can handle it."

Holly threw up her hands. "Joe! What are we all about here, huh? Chuck the rivalry, will you?"

"It's not that," Joe insisted. Well, it wasn't *much* about that. But she was right. He had to think of the mission first. Logically. "Fine then. If it turns out I have to wait and go on schedule, Vinland can come. Okay? But I'm going in underwater if I can get a fix on him before rendezvous hour, and I'm going by myself. Let's get everything together so I can check out the gear."

"I'm on it," she assured him. "Meanwhile, play with that tape and see if you get any background noises. I thought I heard a car horn. He might not be on the boat right now."

Joe rewound the tape. "While you're at it, see if Jack's

got the pictures and coordinates on the forty-two-footers anchored off shore yet. If we can find the boat, I'll take the sub and go at sundown when there's glare on the surface.''

He pictured himself cutting an underwater wake, zooming toward that boat like a relentless shark with teeth bared, psyched up to tear that bastard apart.

His entire body hummed. Despite the current burst of energy, Joe knew he needed sleep, hadn't had any for over twenty-four hours. But he couldn't. Didn't dare. He had too much to do and too little time to do it.

An hour later, waiting impatiently by the computer for the satellite pictures, Joe looked up and saw Eric Vinland propped in the doorway of the downstairs bedroom his father had converted to a home office.

This was the first he'd seen of him since leaving Mc-Lean. The man moved like a ghost. Joe hadn't heard a sound when he arrived. ''What's up?''

Vinland smiled. ''We found your sister,'' he announced.

Joe jumped up so fast he almost upset the desk. ''Is she all right? And the baby?''

''Yeah, both fine. They were alone, locked in the basement of an abandoned farmhouse about fifteen miles north of here. Will's taken them to a motel down the coast for safety's sake in case Humberto's ashore somewhere. Holly's getting your folks to your sister's new location so they can go and be with her and the kid.''

''Thank God.'' As relieved as Joe was about the rescue, he couldn't help cursing the fact that Martine was still out there, still at Humberto's mercy. Not that the bastard had any mercy. ''Was there a bomb?'' Joe asked.

''Yeah, we found one, just like he said. He'd turned on the gas, too. All he'd have had to do to set that off was make a phone call. Spark from the ringer. Then the gas explosion would have set off the bomb. Too far inland for him to use a remote trigger. Guy knows his stuff."

Joe sank back into the chair, his hand to his head, thanking God for the intervention. His sister and the baby were safe. "Thanks," he whispered.

"Don't mention it," Vinland said. "All in a day's work."

"How'd you find out where he was holding them?" Joe asked.

Eric shrugged. "Oh, I zoned in. Got a feeling."

Joe hesitated. "How? Exactly?"

"Will got me one of your sister's shirts. Sometimes if I touch things belonging to a person, I'll get…notions about what they're feeling, sometimes what they're seeing. You know, just their perceptions of immediate surroundings. Worked pretty good this time, so I described the place to a local real estate agent. She identified it right away. We lucked out. I guess there aren't too many houses this close to the coast that have full basements."

"Water table's too high," Joe said, nodding. "Thanks, man. Really." He knew any gratitude he offered would never be enough. Obviously, Vinland had a much better handle on his so-called gift than Joe had ever had on his.

"Could…do you think you could do it again with something of Martine's? Just to make sure she's on a boat?" *And alive.* But he didn't add that. He wouldn't even let himself consider the alternative.

"I can try."

Joe hurried to the weekender Martine had brought with her and snapped it open. He handed Eric the item on top, a red bikini bottom, then snatched it back. The last thing he wanted was to see another guy fondling that. Instead he held up a white sleeveless pullover.

Vinland examined it as if looking for spots. Then Joe noticed he had indeed *zoned out,* as he'd described. Only his hands moved, gripping the supple fabric, moving the pads of his fingers over it, raising it to his face to breathe in Martine's essence.

Joe watched, both fascinated and apprehensive. In a few seconds, Vinland dropped the blouse back into the suitcase as if it burned his hands. "She's there." His voice sounded shaky.

"Is she all right?" Joe demanded.

He nodded. "She seemed kind of…I don't know, scattered? Her thoughts, I mean. Scared. Nothing much to see. She's in the dark or her eyes are covered. Maybe she just had them closed. But there were ocean smells, waves sloshing. Definitely on a boat." He hesitated, not meeting Joe's gaze.

"What? What's wrong?" Joe demanded.

"Does she ever, you know, panic about stuff?" Eric asked. He was rubbing his strong, pale wrists, almost clawing at them. "I sensed she was a little worse than…scared."

"Damn him to hell!" Joe cursed roundly, slamming his palm against the wall. "He's tied her up. That freaks her out. She's…claustrophobic." He winced, feeling he had betrayed Martine by admitting what she saw as her worst fault.

"Oh," Vinland said simply, nodding. "Yeah, that'd do it. Well, at least she's alive." He dropped his hands to his sides and gave a sort of shudder.

"You okay?" Joe asked.

"Yeah. It's just that the sensations are…insidious, I guess you'd call it. I'll be fine."

Then he changed the topic altogether, as if he wanted to get his own mind off Martine as quickly as he could. "Your sister was sending out signals nobody could miss. She was mad as hell." He forced a laugh.

"Yeah. Linda can be what you might call volatile." But Joe couldn't think about Linda right now. She was safe. Martine wasn't.

Vinland continued talking, hopping to yet another topic. "You know, that bomb of Humberto's was a pretty sophisticated piece of homemade ordnance. Very small in size but would have been damned effective combined with the gas. Judging by the materials we know he acquired, there's at least one more out there we haven't found yet."

"Only one?"

"Yes, and he did buy a remote garage door opener, so this second one's gonna be different. Jack tells me our perp did a stint in demolition when he was in the army down there." Vinland sighed. "Jack's got everybody on this, but a casual observer would never know it. It's an invisible op so far and it's going well."

Not nearly well enough, Joe thought. It wouldn't be *well* until Humberto and his men were dead and Martine was safe.

He leaned back against the wall and closed his eyes, pressing his thumb and forefinger against his lids for the hundredth time since all this began. But nothing came to him. Not a blessed thing.

"Relax, man, you're probably trying too hard."

Joe looked at Vinland, searching his face for truth as he asked what he had been wondering since he'd left the McLean office. "Is this why I was hired for Sextant? This…premonition thing?"

"No, but it sure didn't hurt your chances when it came to making the selection. Jack appreciates the fact that hunches play a big part in investigations and in survival. He had the records of that early study you participated in, and the results."

"Lack of results," Joe clarified. "About all we did was try to match cards and colors. I was wrong most of the time and only guessing when I got them right."

"Yeah, well, it's not as if he expects you to have any full-blown episodes on command."

"Good thing," Joe muttered, shoving away from the

wall and beginning to pace in the small confines of the bedroom/study. "'Cause I am *not* psychic."

However, he couldn't help but remember the way Martine had looked in the glow of that flashlight in the cave, terror stricken, exactly the way he had seen her in his mind not long before the reality took place.

The vision where she had blood on her face could very well have predicted what she looked like now after that blow Humberto had delivered with the gun when he abducted her last night. And that one of her surrounded by white had not yet happened.

Bride or corpse? A shiver rattled him right down to his soul. He felt dizzy and disoriented just thinking about it.

"I'm definitely *not* psychic," he repeated, arguing as much with himself as with Vinland.

Eric smiled knowingly. "Maybe. Maybe not. But you have survived missions that most agents wouldn't. Those mental snapshots you pick up occasionally are not much more than your mind's little parlor trick. More distraction than help, I expect. It's the gut instinct you run with, the one that saves you when your number should be up."

Joe frowned. "That's what Mercier was after in me?"

"Yeah. In all of us, I think. I figure you haven't realized yet how valuable a tool that can be, but you need to be aware of it. Maybe learn to trust it, and yourself, a bit more than you do."

"Strange you should say that. My father said almost the same thing." Joe studied Vinland. "You've obviously delved into all this pretty deeply."

He grinned and shrugged. "As good a hobby as any, I guess. Look, we can't do anything else for a while. You want to give it your best shot? I'll be your control. It can't hurt."

Useless effort, but why the hell not? It would at least show Vinland he ought to give up on the precognition bull where Joe was concerned. He shrugged. "Sure."

"C'mon, loosen up. Lie down over there." Eric pointed to the daybed against the wall across from the computer desk.

Joe complied, nerves skittering beneath his skin. *Loosen up? Yeah, right.* Martine was out there suffering God knew what and he was supposed to laze around playing mind games with Boy Agent?

Eric pulled a chair next to the daybed and sat down. "Fine, now close your eyes and do the muscle thing. You know, tighten and relax 'em one at a time until you're a puddle. They teach you that?"

Joe nodded. He began the exercise he had learned all those years ago. As he concentrated on that, Eric ran his mouth, yammering on and on about walking on the beach, seeing the sun go down, watching the waves roll in. The timbre of his voice melded with the actual sounds from outside the beach house. Joe focused on forcing his muscles to behave, only half listening, not even bothering to respond.

Eventually he felt the rocking motion of waves, annoyingly rhythmic, swishing over the sand, advancing, retreating, never-ending, relentless.

"Relax. Let it come at you sideways," the quiet voice droned. It was the last thing he knew until Vinland shook him awake later and Joe realized it had been a ploy to lull him into much-needed sleep. If not for his renewed energy and sharpened thought processes, Joe would have been mad as hell.

By that time six o'clock had rolled around and things were coming together. So were the principals involved in the rescue. Joe had been surprised when he woke up to see Mercier there. The entire Sextant team was, with the exception of Clay Senate who was holding down the fort in McLean.

One of the bomb squads had swept the Corda cottage last night and declared it clean. That was now headquarters. Joe's family were residing at a safe house in Panama City until the situation was resolved.

Mercier, Holly, Vinland and Joe flanked the oak table where Joe had once done his homework. He was damned glad to have partners for this project.

A map of the coast lay spread on the table now. Mercier had brought it with him with the positions of all the boats located by two satellites clearly marked. He was pointing at one in particular, one mile and ten degrees southeast off the elbow of Cape San Blas.

"This is it," Mercier announced. "One guy on deck just behind the windlass, automatic weapon within reach. One other, also armed, lounging on the aft deck." He smiled. "The EXTER-14 satellite could have read his magazine if he'd been holding it at the right angle."

An exaggeration, Joe knew, but not by much. If the angle was right, it could actually identify the numbers on a license plate.

"Big question is whether they have moved since they were spotted," Holly declared. She shot Joe a warning glance. "You know you can't go in without being sure. Suppose they aren't anchored where they were and you're out there snorkeling around looking for them when Humberto's call comes in?"

Mercier agreed. "You'll have to wait for his instructions. You'll take the Zodiac and go in above board. Eric will take the submersible, swing around and come at the boat from the opposite direction. While you create a distraction going aboard, he can slip in on the other side."

"I thought I was running this show," Joe argued.

Mercier inclined his head and gestured with one hand as if offering the lead back to him. "If you have a better plan, we're listening."

Joe felt sheepish and let it show. "No. It's sound. No alternative."

They all looked pleased. *Joe Corda played well with others.* He figured that meant he could keep his job if he wanted to. But did he? All he cared about right now was getting Martine off that boat alive.

Chapter 14

The sound of a motor sent Martine's efforts into overdrive. She almost had the knot undone. A cry of frustration slipped out as she twisted her joined wrists to unwind the bonds.

Even though they were free, her hands now felt like useless dead things at the ends of her arms. Her fingers were numb and swollen. Frantically, she rubbed and stretched them, coaxing circulation. No more time. She had to act now. If nothing else, she could divert Humberto's attention, give Joe a chance to get the upper hand.

Quietly she twisted the doorknob, opened the narrow door to her cabin and peeked out. It opened into the forward end of a main salon. To her left was the wheel, unattended now since they were at anchor.

Curtained windows lined the salon, most of them closed. Along one side was a built-in banquette and narrow trestle bolted to the floor. On the other, an efficient little kitchen. At the opposite end was the door to the aft cabin. The doorway to the deck was on her right just past the banquette seat and a storage cabinet.

She heard voices. But oddly enough, not the shouting she expected would accompany Joe's arrival. Martine dropped to her knees and crawled down the corridor of the salon. As she crept nearer the steps up to the deck the voices grew clearer.

She drew closer to the window nearest the entrance to the salon and risked moving the curtain a fraction of an inch to peek out. Humberto was climbing aboard via the swim ladder. His two men were hovering, almost obscuring her view of him. He must have been ashore in a smaller boat and just now returned. One of the guys took something from him as he boarded.

She recognized the men as two who had served Humberto as bodyguards in Colombia. They were strictly muscle and not too bright, but had seemed devoted to their leader.

When they found her free, they would tie her up again and throw her right back into that cabin. Martine thought that before she was discovered, she should simply run for it and dive over the rail. But she had no idea which way she should start swimming. They'd probably shoot her before or after she hit the water anyway. But wasn't anything better than being tied up again? An involuntary shudder shook her.

No. No way was she ready to die. And Joe would blame himself forever if she let that happen. She thought again about Joe's greatest fear.

As poor as her chances seemed right now, Martine resolved she would survive this. And if Joe came to find her, she would save him, too. Somehow.

She watched Humberto peer out over the water. He and his men were dressed like tourists or fishermen in Bermuda shorts, Hawaiian print shirts and deck shoes. His bodyguards looked ridiculous, too beefy to be anything but what they were, especially with automatic weapons worn as accessories.

Humberto looked dashing as ever, wiry and fit, his bearing only a little less soldierly in those casual clothes. She had at first thought maybe he possessed a code of honor, warped as it was. But though he had treated her well, she had soon discovered the layer of cruelty beneath that veneer in watching him deal with his men.

The man—Thomas, she thought his name was—who stood closest to Humberto wore an AK-47 on a strap slung over his left shoulder. He was holding a small box very carefully with both hands and staring at it as if it contained poisonous snakes. The other guy was hurriedly climbing down the ladder into what had to be the boat in which Humberto had arrived.

Humberto, his back to her now, was now talking on a cell phone. She could hear his voice, but couldn't make out his words. Suddenly he finished his conversation, tucked the phone into the pocket of his shorts and turned to speak to the man holding the box.

"Thomas, place that on the console just in front of the wheel. Make certain this side faces the front window." He pointed. "Understand?"

Thomas said something Martine didn't catch.

"Don't worry. It will not explode unless I give the cue." Humberto raised one hand and gingerly touched something, the top of which was just visible, in the pocket of his shirt. It appeared to be a remote control. He added, laughing, "But do be careful not to trip."

Then she heard him ask, "How is our guest?"

An engine started, obliterating anything else they might have said. She saw a small motorboat cutting through the water as it departed. Humberto and his friend with the box turned toward the salon entrance.

Martine scrambled quickly back to the door of the pocket cabin. There was no place inside the boat where she could hide for long and she'd surely be caught before she made the railing if she ran. Worse than that, she could startle Thomas and make him drop that bomb.

She closed the door quietly and climbed back into position on the bed. The cord lay taunting her. She picked it up, put both hands behind her and wound it around her wrists, knowing it wouldn't stand close inspection, but if he only looked in on her, she hoped it would fool him.

She needed time to think, time to form some kind of plan before Joe got here.

Meanwhile preparations for the rescue were under way at the Updike Marina off Port San Blas. Humberto had called promptly at seven o'clock with instructions. Joe was to leave precisely at nine from this particular place and travel due south at twenty-five knots per hour for ten minutes, then stop and await further directions. It would be pitch-dark by then. The sky was overcast and there would be no moon visible tonight.

"Humberto's obviously changed location. Eric's gonna play hell finding that boat without coordinates," Holly grumbled. "That rigged-up underwater running light on the Zodiac's not sufficient to follow with the submersible."

"It will be if he stays close behind me. We can't risk anything else. If it fails and he loses me, he can surface for a visual check. As dark as it is, he shouldn't be detected, but he'll be able to see me since I'll have lights." Joe was stating what he felt was obvious while he doggedly inspected his gear. He was trying like hell to stay as busy as possible, and not dwell on what Martine must be going through at the moment.

Humberto had ordered him to wear fitted swim trunks and nothing else so there would be no place to conceal a weapon. That also meant he wouldn't be able to wear a Kevlar vest. No protection at all.

Though the April night was warm enough, Joe felt a distinct chill.

He had been told to arrive in an open craft that would seat three, do at least 35 knots per hour and to bring extra gas. There was to be nothing else in the boat except a container bearing the money and Martine's cell phone. Humberto had the number to that and had warned Joe there might be further instructions.

Whether the extra gas was to insure that Joe had enough to reach the *Paper Moon* which might have moved any distance offshore, or to augment the motor yacht's fuel supply once the deal was done, Joe didn't know. But he would comply right down to the letter. His main objective was to get aboard the *Paper Moon* alive.

"Where's the money?" he asked.

"Will's on his way. His ETA's about ten minutes," Holly said. "Sorry to cut it so close. He had a little trouble getting a big enough case with a built-in transmitter, something that couldn't be detected and removed."

Joe checked his watch again. Twenty minutes and counting. He adjusted the flesh-colored dart pen taped to the inside of his wrist. It would need to be fired at close range and carried only one dose of paralyzing agent.

All he needed was the chance to come within three or four feet of Humberto. He had practiced with dummy darts half the afternoon and felt he was as proficient as he could get with the gadget. It was his only weapon.

The minutes crawled by. Will arrived with the money contained in a waterproof aluminum case. "Transmitter's built inside the plastic handle," Will told him as he handed it over.

Joe hefted it, then climbed into the inflatable black Zodiac. It rocked with his weight, then settled when he sat down. There were three fuel bladders secured in back, clearly visible behind the case with the money.

"Good to go," he said with a shake of his head. "God,

I wish I knew how this was going to play out.'' He looked up at Mercier, then at the others. ''Whatever happens, thanks. All of you. I owe you.''

''Buy us a drink at Christa's when we get back to Virginia,'' Mercier said. His stony expression slowly morphed into a confident smile. ''I have a feeling things will work out tonight.''

A feeling, huh? Like he was supposed to trust that. ''Right. Well, here goes nothing.''

Good thing somebody had a positive *feeling* about this, Joe thought as he switched on the running lights and cranked the motor.

The Zodiac zoomed away from the dock on an almost silent, southerly course while Joe played out every possible outcome in his mind. There was no way of knowing what kind of reception he'd get when he reached the *Paper Moon,* but short of a bullet to the head or heart the minute he got there, he meant to get rid of the threat to Martine if he had to die doing it.

''Get up. Company is on the way and we must entertain,'' Humberto said, grasping Martine's ankles and dragging her half off the bunk.

He had looked in on her shortly after he'd returned to the boat, then again later. That time he had placed his fingers to her neck and felt for her pulse. It had been racing ninety to nothing and he'd immediately realized she was awake.

Martine opened her eyes to the glare of pure hatred in his and a very lethal-looking pistol in his left hand. She had thought he might kill her right there on the bed.

Instead of showing the fear he was obviously looking for, she boldly asked to go to the bathroom. He paused to consider it, then stood back and allowed her to wriggle off the bed. Roughly he grasped her upper arm to lift her to a standing position.

She had wrapped the cord loosely enough around her wrists that she could shake it free in a second and had hoped he would put down the gun and start to untie her. That would have given her a chance to disable him with a surprise move. Instead, he backed well away from her and opened the door to the small head in the forward cabin, his nine-millimeter aimed directly at her heart.

"Some *goddess* you are now. I should humble you further, but you disgust me. You should see yourself."

She did, in the mirror over the small sink. What a mess she was and glad of it. At least he didn't seem to find her in any way tempting. Humberto was too fastidious. Blood caked one whole side of her face and neck. Her hair was matted with it and incredibly tangled. One eye was purplish and swollen.

In the cabin when she first woke up, she had noted the shorts and camp shirt she wore were a mass of dirty wrinkles and her arms and legs were streaked with dark sand and scraped raw in places. She had lost her shoes. At some point after he had taken her, he must have dragged her along the ground.

When she had finished in the bathroom—no easy task since she left the rope around her wrists—she bumped against the door. He jerked it open and waited for her to exit, then shoved her back into the pocket cabin where she fell on her side across the bunk.

"Reflect on your sins. They are about to catch up with you," he had told her then.

Well, he had come for her now and she guessed this must be the time for it. *Company coming* meant Joe, of course.

One of Humberto's men was still away. She had listened for the return of the smaller boat, but had never heard one approach. That meant only Humberto and one other guy were onboard. If Joe got in a position to take one of them out, she would rush the other.

Humberto pushed her ahead of him into the salon. She risked a glance at the wheel and saw the box with the bomb sitting just forward of it facing the window. It didn't take a genius to figure out what he planned to do with it.

He and his man would take the boat Joe came in and leave her and Joe alive on the motor yacht if he could. When he was far enough away, he planned to detonate that bomb with the remote and watch them die.

He had planned this very carefully. Nothing as simple as gunning them down would suit Humberto. Unless they forced his hand.

Martine stumbled before she reached the steps from the salon up to the deck, hoping he would run into her and she could catch him off guard. But he stopped too soon, motioning with the gun for her to continue.

There were low-level lights in the salon, the drapes drawn except for the ones in front of the wheel. She climbed the steps and exited into the breeze and total darkness. There was no moon, no stars. In the distance, she could hear the drone of a motor.

She sensed movement to her right and as her eyes became more accustomed to the dark, she could just make out the large silhouette of Humberto's man. And the automatic he held. He was standing at the rail.

Humberto switched on a deck light, blinding her in the process. The whine of the motor drew nearer. Martine willed herself to be patient and hold her hands behind her rather than drop her bonds and attack. She could take out one of the men, but the other would shoot her if she did. Then he would more than likely kill Joe before he could even board.

"Go to the swim ladder, Thomas," Humberto ordered. "When he pulls alongside, take your flashlight and check out the contents of the boat. Make certain all is as I ordered. If it is not, kill him."

Martine held her breath. Joe would be a fool to come

alone. And a damned fool to come unarmed. The running lights of the smaller craft grew closer and closer until they disappeared beneath the high railing of the motor yacht.

"Ahoy," called Joe, his voice cocky. "Permission to board?"

Thomas sat astride the break in the rail where the swim ladder attached. He held on to the raised edge beside him, leaned over and pointed the flashlight downward for a long minute.

"He has the fuel," he called back. "And he is not armed." He leaned over a little farther as if to inspect closer. When he straightened, he held a silver case aloft. "The money!"

"Drop it on the deck," Humberto ordered and Thomas did. It bounced and fell over on its side. Martine looked up just in time to see Thomas disappear over the railing headfirst. His scream of surprise ended with a loud splash. Joe climbed aboard, hands out to the side to show he held no weapon. He smiled and said, "Oops."

Thomas cried out from below, sputtering, that he couldn't swim. Then silence, another gurgling yell and then nothing. Martine thought maybe he had managed to climb in the other boat. Or maybe not.

"Thomas?" Humberto shouted when all went silent. No answer.

He cursed. But instead of running to the rail to see about his man, he grabbed Martine in a choke hold, the pistol pressed against her temple. "Stay where you are, Corda. One more wrong move and she dies," he warned. "If you do exactly as I tell you, I might spare her life."

Joe shrugged and pointed to the case lying next to his bare feet. "There's your ill-gotten gain, Carlos. Don't you want to count it?"

"Open it," Humberto demanded. Martine felt the tension in the forearm locked beneath her chin, in the strong body that pressed against her back. The cold steel of the barrel dug into her skin. She could grab him where it hurt—her hands were positioned right—but he would blow her head off and might still have time to shoot Joe.

Joe knelt on the deck and unlatched the container, raised the lid and turned it toward Humberto. ''All there. Come and get it.''

Though he wore nothing but swim briefs, Martine wondered if Joe might have a weapon. Or maybe he was merely trying to get Humberto's focus off her. She saw Joe quickly scan the part of the deck within view and the flybridge, as if he were looking for the other man.

There was no way to signal Joe that he wasn't aboard. It was all she could do to breathe with Humberto's arm threatening to cut off her air supply.

Suddenly Humberto released her and shoved her at Joe. ''Untie her!'' he ordered.

Joe reached for her hands and made a low sound of surprise when he found the ropes loose. He made a show of struggling with the knots as he asked, ''Are you hurt bad?''

''I'm fine.'' She lowered her head. ''There's only him,'' she growled in a low voice she hoped Humberto couldn't hear.

''Gotcha,'' he whispered. ''Do as he says. Help's coming.''

Humberto shouted for her to move away from Joe. She moved, hands out to her sides.

''I don't trust your fancy briefcase, Corda. I know you are not so stupid as to leave my escape to chance. You will have made provision for me to be followed. Go to the aft cabin, woman!'' he commanded Martine. ''Empty the bag on the bed and bring it to me. Do exactly as I say or I will shoot him where he stands.''

Martine scurried inside. She rushed to the right, found the dark canvas bag shaped like an army duffel bag, but only about half the size of one. She quickly pulled out everything inside it, tossing Humberto's clothes every which way.

He wanted to transfer the money to get rid of any hidden tracking device that might be hidden in the case? Well, she'd give him a device, all right, but no one would be able to follow him unless they went to hell.

When she returned to the deck with the bag, Humberto proved even more predictable than she could have hoped. "Took you long enough. Empty the money into that," he demanded.

Martine looked up at Joe as she knelt, hoping to signal him somehow, but his eyes were trained on Humberto. She began to stuff the money into the bag. Very carefully.

"I am curious, Humberto. How in the world did you find my family?" Joe asked.

Humberto scoffed. "I had your name from Vargas. He told me you were DEA. I knew how closely held your employment records would be, given your *occupation.*" He sneered at the word. "But I also knew a man with your physique naturally would have played college sports. It was child's play to discover your school, hack into the computerized records and discover your hometown. There was only one José Corda in a small town such as yours. You see, I, too, have excellent skills in the field of espionage."

"And you found Martine, too," Joe commented, acting a little impressed. Martine knew he was playing for time.

"Even simpler," Humberto bragged. "She has a passport. Her prints were on file. Her place of employment, a matter of record with your Social Security. Your country tends to underestimate the enemy. And I *am* the enemy, make no mistake. You and your people have destroyed my livelihood. My very life."

Joe heaved an audible sigh. "That's my job, Carlos."

"Destruction of drugs, I could understand. But you even tore apart my family. I am branded a traitor."

"You *are* a traitor," Joe argued, but Humberto seemed not to hear.

"My wife, my children. I have lost them because of you." He glanced at the rail where his man had disappeared. "Even poor Thomas, drowned. He is no great loss, but he was my cousin. A fair trade for that loud-mouthed sister of yours and her mewling brat, I suppose."

"Oh, I should have told you. We found them," Joe said, a smile in his voice. "Turned off the gas and dismantled your bomb."

Humberto cursed.

"We know there were two, and I expect they've found the other one by this time," Joe told him.

"I assure you, they have not." Humberto chuckled, a truly evil sound.

Martine smiled herself. He was quite right. They had not found it, but they'd know where it was soon enough.

When she had transferred the money to the bag, she stood, hands on her hips, waiting for what she knew would come next.

"Get inside, both of you," Humberto ordered and made a threatening movement with the gun. He stayed well away from Joe and kept the pistol pointed at her. "Into the aft cabin. Corda, you first, and go to the far corner, away from the door."

Joe's gaze raked the deck again, fury and desperation in his eyes. Martine noticed his near naked body tense, the muscles standing out in relief as his fists clenched, opened and clenched again. His stance screamed attack. She knew he was ready to rush Humberto if he found a chance to do it without getting her shot. "Don't do it, Joe. You know he'll shoot. Go inside."

Finally, he looked at her. She winked and tried to put a smile in her eyes to tell him everything would be all right. It would be if only Humberto didn't check the box just in front of the wheel.

"Go!" shouted Humberto. He fired one shot above their heads and retrained the gun on her.

The cabin door closed behind them and she heard the snick of the key in the lock. Joe immediately rushed to it and tried to break it down, but it was too sturdy and there was no room for him to back up and gather any force. Hardly more than a minute later they heard the muted roar of an engine catch and Martine pictured Humberto zipping away from the motor yacht, far enough away to stop and watch the fireworks. Good, he hadn't had time to go forward and check on the bomb.

Joe was already pounding on one of the two windows with his fist. He was too big to fit through it even if he managed to break out the thick tempered glass. But she wasn't. Martine smiled. He was doing everything he could to save her. There was no use trying to stop him. He was like a man gone berserk.

Suddenly he ripped a shelf off the wall above the bunk and shattered the window. "Here, crawl through. Hurry!" he said, shoving her at the window. "Dive over the rail and swim like hell. I think he's left a bomb aboard."

"No he hasn't," she argued, about to explain what she had done.

As the words left her lips, an explosion rocked the world. Joe shoved her flat on the bunk and fell on top of her, shielding her with his body.

Chapter 15

Joe lifted his head, sniffed for smoke, listened for the crackle of flames. He was amazed that the cabin was still intact, the glass unbroken except for the one he had smashed. ''Ha. We're alive! I need to get out there and assess the damage. It couldn't have been a very big bomb.''

''Yes it could.'' Martine could barely see his face. The cabin was almost dark, illuminated only by a meager amount of light coming from that on the deck. ''But he took it with him.''

Joe stared at her for a minute, then laughed, pushing up and bracing on his arms above her. ''Don't tell me. You put it in the bag with the money?''

Martine nodded. ''He must have been clicking that remote all over the place when it refused to blow us to kingdom come.''

Joe dropped a quick, gentle kiss on her lips. Her poor face was a wreck and must hurt like the devil. His rage when he had first seen it nearly had him doing a suicidal dive for Humberto. The vision of her with blood on her face had come to pass and she had survived. He felt much better about the one of her in white.

He kissed her again, drawing out the pleasure a little longer, tasting the sweetness of life. His body was super revved, still pumping adrenaline. "Have I told you how wonderful you are, Ms. Duquesne?"

"You can start showing me any time now."

He laughed again when she moved suggestively beneath him. "Not that I wouldn't love to, but we *should* try to get out of here and let everyone know we're all right." He brushed her tangled hair away from her forehead, noting how she winced. "You are all right, aren't you, *querida?*"

"Well, I could do with some bedrest. A quarter hour maybe?"

She was revved, too, apparently. "Martine..."

Her kiss shut him up nicely and he was just getting into it big-time, his heady state of arousal blocking out all the *shoulds* and *should-nots,* when he heard a sound from the broken window. The beam of a flashlight flicked over his face. Before he could react, he heard a chuckle he recognized.

"I guess you don't really need any help?" Vinland said. The light danced playfully around the bed.

"I guess not. Where the hell were you when I did?" Joe growled.

Vinland sighed, his head and shoulders backlit by the faint light from the deck. "You had another tail besides me after we left the marina. When you changed course, I surfaced, did a three-sixty and saw him. Thought I'd better take him out before you got caught in a sandwich. Had to ram him and damaged the sub. Took me a while to get it going and then I couldn't find you. That explosion scared the bejeesus out of me. Then I spotted the deck lights and came to see if there was anyone left aboard."

"Thanks," Martine said. "Now please go drive the boat, whoever you are."

"Sorry," Joe said. "Martine Duquesne, Eric Vinland, one of Sextant's finest."

"Pleased to have met you," she said, her impatience showing.

Eric took the hint and disappeared.

"Continue," she demanded when their audience left.

But Vinland's interruption had brought Joe to his senses. "When I take you again, I want hours and hours. Days, maybe." He caressed her through her wrinkled shirt and shorts, long languid strokes that did nothing to augment his decision. "I want you in something slinky and silk. I want you in…"

"I want you," she interrupted breathlessly. "Now. No promises, no conditions. Just now, like this…" she murmured against his mouth, then melded hers to it with a white-hot kiss that swept rational thought right out of his head. He devoured her, his hands acting on their own to tear away the clothes that denied him her soft skin, the feel of her pulse around him.

There was nothing on earth but Martine. His woman. His heart. He entered her in one swift stroke, desperate to reaffirm his claim, to bind her to him in any way he could. Forever if possible. For this hour, if not.

She met him thrust for thrust, gasping words he couldn't understand for the blood thundering in his veins. All the feeling he possessed had concentrated where their bodies met, where skin slid against skin, where lips scorched paths, where they became one.

On and on into a white-hot frenzy he drove her, lurching them against the slanted wall, rolling side to side, pressing her deep and deeper into the soft foam of the bunk. He felt her legs wrapped around his, the soles of her bare feet against his calves, her nails scoring the sweat-slick muscles of his back. His own palms cupped her curves, held her to a wild, savage dance with no rhythm.

The beat grew so fierce, he abandoned any semblance of control. Her cry and the tightening of her body drew him down, plummeting into euphoria, releasing all that he was.

For a long time, he lay motionless, one hand fisted in her hair, the other clutched behind her right knee, his fingers trapped and content. "Can't…move," he gasped, a half-ass apology for crushing her, he knew, but true.

She quivered around him, a final ripple of pleasure so keen he groaned. *Now,* he thought lazily, would be the time to die. *Right now.* He was already in heaven. Nothing would ever get any better than this.

The boat was moving, he realized. How long? How many minutes did he have left to own her? When must he give her up to reality and emerge from this delicious prison?

Wearily, very reluctantly, he rolled to one side, holding her close, knowing time was nearly up. Reason was creeping slowly back into his brain, adrenaline on the wane, passion spent for the moment. Martine would want to clean up and dress before they reached the marina and someone opened that door. And he really shouldn't present himself to his boss and co-workers naked except for a satisfied grin and the scent of sex.

She was first to pull away, disengage and speak normally. "Please don't say anything, Joe. We agreed, no ties."

"We do need to talk," he argued, feeling around for her clothes. He picked up a shirt and realized it was too big to be hers. It certainly wasn't his because he hadn't been wearing one. Humberto's. They were lying in a mass of garments, probably where she had emptied the bag she'd taken outside earlier for the money.

She sat up and pawed through the clothing, tossing

some of it on the floor. "Here," she said. He heard plastic rip. "New T-shirts," she explained, shaking one out and draping it over his shoulder. She pulled one over her head and began searching again, he supposed for her shorts.

Joe found his swim trunks still clinging to one ankle and put them back on. By the time he did, she was decently dressed.

"I wish I could wash my face," she muttered. "I'm a fright."

"You look beautiful," Joe argued. "Besides, everyone will be so glad to see you, they won't care. But maybe Eric will let us out now so you can find a sink and freshen up." He banged on the door with his fist.

A few seconds later, it opened. The salon was well lighted now and Vinland stood there grinning. "Humberto left the key in the lock probably so you couldn't pick it. Our ETA's about seven minutes. I was just about to give you a warning."

Martine swept by him and disappeared into the head. Joe stood staring at the closed door, unwilling to spar with Vinland just yet. His mind still felt a little too numb to come up with anything clever. Or even remotely sensible.

"What happened, Joe?" Vinland asked.

The first thought Joe had was that he was asking about what had gone on in the cabin with Martine. Then he realized Eric meant what had gone down before that with Humberto.

He shook his head to clear it. "I had to take out the bodyguard with the dart as I came aboard. Thought it would improve the odds, but it didn't. Humberto had the drop on us. He wanted the money in a different bag and sent Martine in to get one. She put the bomb inside it and the money on top."

Eric threw back his head and laughed out loud as he walked back through the salon to the wheel. "Hot damn, what a woman! I'd like to have one like that myself!"

"Yeah," Joe muttered as he plopped down on the banquette seat. So would he. The lights of the marina grew brighter as they neared San Blas.

He knew Martine, maybe even better than she knew herself. She was definitely cut out for this kind of thing. Her mind worked sharpest when she ripped into action, when the threats were greatest, when everything was at stake. She excelled in a crisis and knew it. And loved it.

No matter how much she might care about him—and he did know that she cared—he would never be able to change her. If he tried, he would lose her anyway. But he couldn't stand by and watch her risk her neck on a regular basis. He'd already decided that would drive him crazy.

Hell, he was crazy right now, ground down to raw nerves by the last two days. He needed sleep, needed rest, needed peace. But he needed her, too. She filled something inside him that had been missing all his life.

She appeared, face clean, hair wet, rivulets of water splotching the white T-shirt she had appropriated from Humberto's discarded wardrobe.

Joe stood and his arms opened without any conscious thought on his part and she walked into them, laying her damp head on his shoulder. He cradled it with one hand and held her close with the other.

"I'll never let anything like this happen to you again," he swore.

She pulled back and looked up at him, searching his eyes. But she didn't say a word. Instead, she put her head on his chest again, snuggled close and held him.

He wished to God he felt desperation in her grip, but it seemed more like comfort or maybe consolation. The desperation was all his and as useless as his wish for peace. Some things just weren't meant to be.

How could he ask her to be other than she was? Would he even love her as much as he did if she changed to suit him?

Then the boat was docking and it was too late for talk. What could they say anyway?

Not only were Holly, Will and Mercier there waiting for them, but also representatives from the FBI, the Coast Guard and Joe's old friend from the local ATF office. And the police, of course. While the anchored *Paper Moon* had not been visible from the shoreline, the explosion of the Zodiac had been and had attracted attention.

Joe sighed, thinking of the numerous debriefings that would be necessary. Separate debriefings. When they disembarked, he made a beeline for Jack Mercier who was obviously the man in charge. "Do you think Martine and I could have a few minutes alone before the circus starts?"

Jack frowned, turned away from the crowd and spoke to Joe in a low voice. "Sorry, not likely. We called them all down here. Now we have to lay it all out for them. The Navy will be jumping up and down about the loss of their equipment. The FBI's already bent out of shape because they weren't in on the plan to start with. And we don't even want to talk about the cops. That sheriff is fit to be tied, especially about the bombs, because EOD was running all over his county while he was kept totally in the dark."

Joe winced. "Not the model of agency cooperation you envisioned, is it?"

The answering chuckle was grim. "See if you can get your local buddies off our backs while I pacify the Navy rep. Holly will handle the FBI while Will takes the official statements from Martine and Eric. He can get yours later. Let's get this wrapped up, *then* you can settle things with Martine. It's not like there's a big rush on that." He paused, then frowned at Joe again. "Is there?"

Joe looked at Martine who was already engrossed in an animated conversation with Holly. "I guess not."

After relating to Sheriff Nigel all that had happened and

why local law enforcement had not been called in from the beginning, Joe excused himself to go to his family. They had arrived in force shortly after the boat had docked and he had not yet had the chance to speak with them. Surrounded by his parents, sisters and brother-in-law, Joe watched Martine disappear around the office of the marina with Mercier.

He didn't see her again. When he finally managed to break away from the family and ask where she had gone, Holly informed him that Jack had gotten a call and had to leave for McLean. Since he'd been going anyway, Martine had requested a ride to the airport with him.

Since he had half expected something like that, Joe's sudden and almost overwhelming anger surprised him. It also kept him from calling her later, after she'd had time to arrive in Atlanta. Apparently, she'd had what she wanted from him and it had been enough.

Despite Joe's exhaustion, sleep eluded him. He spent the entire first night going over everything that had happened between him and Martine. She had gone without so much as a word of goodbye. Not even a wave.

When Holly, Will and Eric stopped by the following morning, he told them he was staying in Port St. Joe and that he might not be returning to McLean at all. The three shared a look that said they were confident he would.

Joe was anything but sure of that, but he had promised himself time to think everything through. Mercier had insisted that he needed some down time and ordered him to take it. Joe knew they all expected him to return to work with Sextant. He did feel obligated because of all they had done, but he couldn't let that sway his decision.

"Put it all out of your mind for a while, Joey," his mother advised him when the others had gone. She fed him paella, fried chicken, his favorite pie, and babied him just as she always had. It felt good to be loved and indulged. But somehow it was not enough.

"Enjoy your rest," she insisted. "You'll know what to do when the time comes." She wore that knowing smile, the one that had always encouraged him to follow his heart.

Though she had been known to meddle shamelessly and ask the most personal questions a mother would dare, she carefully avoided any mention of Martine. So did his father and sisters. Joe began to think there might be a conspiracy involving reverse psychology here. Surely he was being paranoid.

For once, Joe decided he would follow orders to the letter. He wouldn't think about Martine or the job for a while. Especially Martine. If only thoughts of her were that easily dismissed. She and Joe had been so close, he missed her like he would miss an amputated limb, as if she had been a part of him he could barely function without. But he didn't talk about her.

Mercier had called the next day. "Joe? How are you?"

"I'm not coming back," Joe announced, feeling backed against a wall, forced into a hasty decision by that one simple question.

Mercier laughed. "Of course not. I don't want you to yet. I merely called to tell you the special weapons training at Quantico has been pushed back another week because they're hiring a new instructor. So you'll have three weeks down there. I'm off on assignment today and not certain when I can touch base again. Just wanted to tell you to enjoy your vacation and congratulate you on a job well done. I hear that the government forces swept over the compound not long after you left and Humberto's old outfit is pretty much as dead in the water as he is."

"Good," Joe said, uncertain what else Mercier expected him to say. That was why Joe had gone to Colombia, after all.

He remembered to give Mercier the morning's news. "They found the captain of the *Paper Moon,* by the way. Humberto's men had tossed him overboard as soon as they were out of sight of land. But the old codger was a former Navy swim instructor, swam the distance and wound up down the coast in a hospital. They say he'll be okay."

Mercier laughed. "Good for him! Bet he's mad as the devil about his boat. Eric was Navy, too. He'll get a kick out of this when I tell him."

Joe chuckled, too, his mood lightened a little. He almost wished he could be the one to tell Vinland. And the others. Would they be in the office now or getting ready to deploy on this new thing, too? He wouldn't ask. It was nothing to him anyway. "Good luck on the mission, Jack."

"Thanks. And *you* take it easy," Mercier said. "Remember, you still owe me a drink at Christa's when we get back."

The connection broke without even a goodbye. Joe suspected it was because Mercier didn't want to give him time for any further refusals.

Curiosity niggled at him. Where was Jack off to that put that undercurrent of excitement in his voice? What was this new assignment? Was it anything remotely like what Joe had been doing and what would the real day-to-day work of Sextant involve?

He tried not to think about it.

But after eight days, one thought did keep reoccurring. This vacation business was proving to be incredibly boring. Each morning Joe would wake up with a start, sit straight up in bed and throw the covers off, feeling there was something undone, something to prepare for. He soon realized he had spent so many years geared up and in a state of physical and mental readiness that he couldn't turn it off.

No amount of time spent strolling up and down the beach, watching greedy gulls, feeling the familiar pull of the waves could quite settle him down enough to enjoy this longed-for leisure.

Joe kept busy. He bought his mama roses, fixed everything that was broken around the house that his father had ignored, went fishing with his dad, baby-sat for Linda and Delores a time or two and got to know his nieces better. But at every lull in conversation, and especially every night when he was alone, Joe's mind flew North. His thoughts kept pinging back and forth between Atlanta and McLean.

After that week, his parents decided to go to Ft. Lauderdale to visit Joe's brother and his family and give Joe some time alone. The solitude only heightened his need for Martine. And, in spite of his resolve not to, he did think about the job.

To his dismay, Joe began to realize that he missed work. How could he relax knowing there was evil out there while he was simply lying around, letting it flourish, not doing one single thing to stamp out what he could of it?

And he missed Martine more than anything. What would he give to have her here beside him, dressed in that little red bikini he'd yet to see her wear? But even if she were here, she wouldn't be content simply to laze in the sun. Not with all that incredible energy of hers.

The memory of the way she felt against him would suddenly rush through him, a wave of lust drowning him in need. But he fought it as hard as he would fight to survive an actual drowning. He could not give in. He couldn't possibly live with her, so he would have to learn to live without her. God, how he missed her.

Eighteen long days into his vacation, Joe sat on the edge of a deck, the boards beneath him hot from the sun while a warm breeze warned of summer fast approaching. As much as he loved it, the urge to leave almost overpowered him with its intensity. It grew worse by the minute. And he had three whole days to go yet.

This was a place to come home to and recharge. And as long as his batteries were working even a little bit, it was no place to stay.

All this fantasizing about life on the beach with no worries had been just that. Pure fantasy, probably born of the isolation he felt when immersed undercover. Who had he been kidding? He had to *do* something or go absolutely nuts. And it ought to be something productive, something he did well. Running occasional fishing expeditions like his dad did just wouldn't cut it.

Angry at the realization, Joe stood up, dusted the sand off his shorts and went inside to call Martine. If he was destined to go full tilt at the world, he might as well admit he would never be satisfied with a woman who would do any less. He loved her. There, he'd admitted it. And he loved her in spite of what she was, most likely because of it.

His sigh of resignation made him laugh at himself. Something inside him loosened as if set free. The thought of seeing her again, holding her in his arms, laughing with her and admitting what an idiot he had been sent energy zinging through his muscles like a shot of adrenaline.

He dialed her cell phone, only to find that the number was now invalid. Her land line number was no longer in service. Matt didn't answer his.

As Joe hurriedly punched in the number for Ames International, he allowed the memory of that last vision of her to drift back to mind. *Martine in white. Surely a bride.*

He felt suddenly very anxious. He needed to talk to her, plead with her if he had to, arrange a place for them to meet halfway and see where it would take them.

The receptionist at Ames informed him that Matt was

away from the office. And, no, Ames could not give him a number where either Martine or Matt could be reached.

Joe nearly panicked. He knew the feeling wouldn't go away until he found out where she was and what she was up to. God only knew how much trouble she was in right this very minute.

Chapter 16

Martine had more to do than she had time for. The new apartment was stacked shoulder-high with boxes. Her furniture was in place but she could hardly get to her bed to sleep. The job had her in such a state she couldn't sleep much anyway.

Matt tossed her a bottle of water across the kitchen table and shoved the remainder of the pizza he had ordered to her side. "Eat, sis. You need some energy!"

She pulled out her chair and sat down, eyeing the piles of kitchen stuff that littered the counter. "Will I ever get this place straightened out?"

He laughed and sipped his beer. "It's small, but I think you'll manage to fit everything in eventually. I gotta tell you, though, living expenses up here are gonna eat you up."

She laughed. "Yes, but I'll make it. It certainly took the Bureau long enough to process my application and make a decision. What's it been, nearly a year since I applied?"

He sobered a little, tilting his bottle, staring at it. "Well, I can't say I'm sorry you got it since it's what you want. But will it be enough, Martine? The job, I mean. I know you…had feelings for Joe Corda." He looked up, his eyes narrowed. "Want me to beat him up for you?"

Martine laughed. "Like you could. It's not Joe's fault we couldn't work things out. He made it pretty clear what he wanted for the long term and I was about as far from that as I could get and still be female."

"If you had just promised to do something a little less risky than what we were doing at Ames, he would have come around," Matt argued. "He probably would, even now, if you'd just find him and talk to him about this new job. Speaking of which, will you miss the other? Instructing's not exactly a thrill a minute."

Martine shook her head as she picked a pepperoni off the pizza and nibbled at it. "No, I had about as much danger as I could stand on the Colombia thing and then Florida really capped it. I can do without that much whiplash action, thank you very much."

"You handled it, Mart. Wrapped it up like a pro." He saluted her with his beer and winked.

She sighed. "I didn't say I couldn't hack it. I could. I did. But all I wanted in the first place was a job that made a difference, you know? What I'm doing now will still do that."

Besides, she had done a lot of thinking these past few weeks. Joe had guessed right about her reasons for overcompensating.

Matt grinned back when she smiled at him. "And if you should just happen to hook up with Joe again, he'll appreciate the change in you."

She shrugged. "I don't know, Matt. I haven't really changed that much. He was pretty adamant about what kind of woman he was looking for. He wants a homebody.

I won't be any man's shadow, not like Mama was. You know what she's been like since Dad died.''

''Lost,'' he affirmed, nodding sadly and taking another sip of his beer. ''You could never be like her, though. Even when Sebastian had you safely tucked away in the file room at Ames, you had that independent streak. Sure you're not gonna miss the challenge now that you've had a taste of the action?''

''No. I'll be fine.'' She avoided Matt's questioning gaze. They had always been close and he saw too much of what she was feeling.

Would she miss Joe? Hardly a minute went by that she didn't think of him, wonder what he was doing, whether he thought of her at all.

Chances were, she'd never see him again. If their paths did cross, she wasn't altogether sure she could pretend nonchalance. *Well, hello, Joe? What have you been doing with yourself all these years? Married? Any kids yet?*

No. She just hoped if they ever wound up in the same location, she would see him first so she could run like hell and not have to hear all those answers. A clean break was best. He'd said so himself once, the first time they had parted. He'd been right.

There would be a good fifty or sixty miles between where he worked and where she was now. His job would entail a lot of travel. No real reason they should have to see one another ever again. Unless he made a dedicated effort to find her, she wouldn't be easy to locate. That was the plan. She certainly didn't want him phoning her casually, asking how she was, keeping himself in the forefront of her mind.

''If you're gonna daydream instead of finishing that and unpacking, I'm out of here. Sebastian's short-handed and needs me back in Atlanta. I'm getting this cast off next week.''

''That's too soon! What about therapy for that leg?''

Martine demanded to know. "You need to be at full strength before you tackle another assignment."

"Yes, bossy-britches. It's strong enough now to kick your little butt if you get embroiled in anything else as hair-raising as your last escapade." He stood up and tossed his bottle into the trash. "So behave yourself."

"Go unearth the box with my shoes if you can find it and quit giving me orders."

He rounded the table, cast thumping, roughly mussed her hair and went into the other room to begin unpacking. Martine felt a tear leak out the corner of one eye. She would miss him when he went home. Her aloneness would be more complete then than ever before.

But missing her brother would be nothing at all compared to how she would miss Joe. How she missed him even now. She ached for him, longed for the touch of those long, strong fingers, that buff body, that deep sexy voice breathing Spanish love words in her ear.

Maybe she had become too much like her mother after all in spite of her determination not to. No way could she ever allow a man to become her whole world, her reason for being. Especially not a man who was fully capable of enforcing his will on her. Joe would never use force, but he could be way too persuasive. She had been right on the edge of suggesting compromise when she realized if she gave an inch, he'd surely grab the proverbial mile. She had to do what she had to do and that was that.

From now on she would spend her free hours arranging this place to suit her, making it a comfortable home where she could be happy with her own company.

The rest of the time, she would dedicate to the work. The job was tailor-made for someone like her. What she would be doing was vitally important to the training of women and men who would put their lives on the line every day.

That satisfaction would have to be enough.

* * *

Three weeks of beach life had been more than Joe could stand. With two days left before he had to make a final decision, he bought himself a used Explorer, a few new suits and a couple of pairs of dress shoes and drove as straight to McLean as the highways allowed. He had to work. There was no denying it, no getting around it.

Now he was enrolled in one of the advanced weapons training classes at Quantico. It was only a three-day thing. Holly had advised him he also needed to bone up on his conversational French while he was here and had signed him up for private tutoring sessions with a contract linguist.

The French lesson had to do with the next assignment, she had said, being pretty cryptic about it. Mercier was already in place over there. Joe figured he must be slated to go over with the backup team. He certainly was eager enough to get out of the country and immerse himself in something—anything—that might take his mind off himself.

So here he was at the Academy again, same place he had completed his DEA training years ago, this time for quick brush-up.

Joe had donned the blue golf shirt and khaki pants, uniform for the weapons range. He wasn't unhappy about being relegated to student status at the ripe old age of thirty-two. Nope, he had too much misery about other things than to let this training exercise bother him even a little. He lifted his blue baseball cap, ran his fingers through his closely clipped hair and then replaced the headgear, tugging the bill down to shade his eyes.

Qualifying with anything bearing a sight and a trigger wasn't going to be a problem. What he dreaded was the crash course in French later this afternoon. His mother was the one with the facility for grasping languages. Even though English was his mother tongue, Joe knew his

Spanish was damned near perfect thanks to his dad insisting they speak it at home on alternate days for as far back as Joe could remember. But he sure wished he hadn't goofed off during his two years of high school French. And that he hadn't elected to study Russian at the University. Hell, nobody spoke Russian these days, even the Russians.

With a sigh, he got off the bus that had transported him and the rest of the eager beavers to the range. They were mostly FBI vets with a few trainees from other agencies, like himself, thrown in. None were fresh recruits. The weapons they were to play with today were not the usual issue. This was the spooky stuff, some of it not yet available either in the field or on the street.

Work was the byword in his life right now. Anything to make him forget his personal life. Or lack of one. He still hadn't been able to locate Martine.

He lined up with the others to await instruction. It felt strange to be part of a group of friendlies after going it alone for so long among the enemy. He hadn't even had time to get used to working with the other five on the Sextant team and now, here he was among twenty-odd agents he didn't know, plus the two instructors.

His gaze drifted to those two individuals wearing the darker shirts. His heart jumped when he saw the long blond ponytail threaded through the baseball cap one of the instructors was wearing. Hair like Martine's. God, he was seeing her everywhere he looked. Even now he couldn't help but imagine this woman turning around to face him, Martine's smile beaming at him, ecstatic about seeing him after nearly a month. *Ha.*

Still, wishful thinking had him moving closer to her, hungrily eyeing the curve of that fine little butt in those khaki slacks, the proud set of those shoulders, the long line of that graceful neck. *Damn. So like hers.*

She turned. No smile.

Joe's knees nearly buckled.

"If you would, form a line, please," she snapped, sounding very official as her gaze slid right over him to someone else. "We'll proceed with roll call."

Joe must have managed to comply because she didn't address him again except to say his name right after some guy's called Alex Cash. And she used the same perfunctory tone of voice.

He wanted to grab her and shake her, make her look at him, speak to him. Just to him. Explain why she'd ditched without even saying goodbye. Tell him how the hell she could have left him with a hole in his chest the size of a Florida grapefruit and a brain that wouldn't work.

By the time she had finished marking that stupid clipboard of hers, Joe had worked up the worst mad he'd had on since Roy McDonald had planted pot in his locker in the eleventh grade and almost got him arrested. Must have something to do with a person trying to wreck his entire life for no good reason.

He didn't understand a word during the entire demonstration of the new sniper rifle.

When his turn came to fire it, he missed the target completely. He was too busy shooting daggers at Martine and hitting that particular target dead-on. She ignored him. Totally.

Only when the male instructor who was running things dismissed the class and Martine started walking toward the vehicle parked near the bus did Joe have a chance to speak to her. He had to hustle to catch up. "Martine? Wait!"

She halted, did a sharp, military about-face and threw up her chin. "Yes?" The clipboard hugged her chest like Kevlar. He noticed her knuckles were white.

He gritted his teeth, took a deep breath and tilted his head to look at her. "Where the hell have you been and what are you doing *here?*"

She forced a tight little smile. "Assisting the weapons instructor, obviously. Filling in. How are you, Joe? Long time, no see. How's the family?"

"Dammit, Martine! Why did you just take off that way?"

"Excuse me. I have to leave."

"Don't you think you owe me some answers?"

"I don't believe I owe you anything at all," she said, calm as you please.

They were drawing an audience, but Joe didn't care. He started to grab her arm, but yanked his hand back and stuck it in his pocket, unsure what would happen if he touched her. He wanted to kiss her so bad he feared he might break her teeth if he did.

"How'd you get this job? You're not trained for it," he said through gritted teeth. "Are you?"

"As it happens, yes. I went through police training after college. Top graduate was sent here to the Academy. That was before Ames."

"You were a *cop?* What *else* haven't you told me?" he demanded.

"I never served as an officer. I just trained." Her lips tightened and she glanced up at the sky. Probably praying lightning would strike him. Her voice dropped to a near whisper. "What do you want from me, Joe? You know damned well I'm not going to change."

"Who the hell asked you to change?" he all but shouted.

"*You* did! We can't talk about this here. We shouldn't have to talk about it at all. I know what you want and I can't be that. It's over. End of story."

"Beginning," Joe argued, getting right in her face. "It's just beginning, Martine."

She glanced around them, her fair skin reddening. "Not here, Joe," she muttered.

"Then where?" he demanded, shaking his head. "I'm

not going away. And if you do, I won't quit until I find you this time. Count on it.''

The supervising instructor walked over, hands on his hips. He was a hulk of a guy, outweighed Joe by a good forty pounds and looked fairly lethal. Joe felt he could take the man apart in three seconds in his present mood.

The hulk glanced back and forth between them. ''Problem, Duquesne?''

''No, sir. Nothing I can't resolve, thanks.'' Her gaze flicked back to Joe. ''Don't you get me fired again!'' With that, she put the hulk between herself and Joe and stalked off to the car. Joe reluctantly entered the bus in which he had arrived. This wasn't over. Not by a long shot.

Two hours later, still grumbling to himself about the encounter, Joe paced his temporary quarters waiting for the tutor to arrive. A sudden summer storm gathered outside. Though it had grown murky in his room, he purposely left off the lights. Maybe he would pretend to be out and simply skip the little French class.

Like he wanted to sit here and listen to somebody tell him *fromage* meant cheese. He wanted to slam out of here and go find Martine, rattle some sense into her. Make her see they could work things out if she'd stop being so bullheaded and just *try*. But he had to cool off first so he wouldn't blow his chance. If he hadn't already.

Someone knocked and he strode over to the door and yanked it open. And there she was.

Martine wore a wry grimace as she shoved a book at him. ''I had nothing to do with this arrangement. I didn't know you were here until I got my schedule this morning.''

Her voice sounded raspy as if she were coming down with a cold. But it hadn't been that way earlier. Had she been crying? Over seeing him again? He tossed the book on the table.

She wore no makeup at all and had that beautiful shades-of-gold hair of hers pulled straight back, the ponytail now twisted into a bun. Downplaying her looks, he decided. Probably wise, because they would be a serious distraction for anybody trying to learn anything.

She had lost weight. A little twinge of sympathy struck when he realized Martine really had suffered, too. Joe knew she cared about him. That wasn't something she would have faked. It was just that he hadn't thought he could stand her living the way she seemed determined to live. She must have had second thoughts about it herself.

He hid his smile. Being an instructor at Quantico was probably the safest job in the world. She'd be surrounded by FBI all day long. Perfect.

But he'd changed his mind, too. She'd left him thinking he'd be spending the rest of his life bumming around Port St. Joe. Only now did it occur that she might not be nearly as pleased with *his* latest plan as he was with hers.

The laid-back lifestyle he had always thought he wanted more than anything, had bored him to death in a matter of days. Now he was itching to get right back into the thick of things. Some of his future missions might make his DEA assignments pale by comparison. What would she think of that?

"Did you mean it?" she asked carefully, her gaze straying around his room, taking in the neatly made single bed, the spotless floor, the lack of personal items.

"That I'd look for you if you disappeared again? You know it."

"Not that," she admitted. "About not asking me to change. I thought about it for the last couple of hours and realized you never did actually demand that I quit. Not quite."

"Just hinted at it about as subtly as a sledgehammer, right? Sort of begged a little, maybe? Tried to do a deal?"

Joe asked, releasing the smile he was fighting. *She was going to be a teacher. Just a teacher. Safe.*

He reached for her hand, but she stepped back. Joe sighed. He should have known it wouldn't be that easy. "I love you," he told her honestly. "Just the way you are."

Her gaze rolled upward as she sighed. "Easy for you to say now that you know what I'm doing."

"Or *not* doing," Joe agreed. He kept his distance, knowing that what he said now would make all the difference.

He began slowly, carefully. "On any mission, under any circumstance, I'd choose you above anyone else to watch my back, Martine. I admire your capabilities so much. But I love you, too. Knowing you're in danger of any kind makes me a little nuts. But if you hadn't taken this job, I could have learned to cope."

She expelled a wry little laugh as she stared out his window. Rivulets of rain were streaking the glass and the stormy sky threw her into sharp relief. Thunder rumbled in the distance as Joe waited for her to speak.

"You know you're asking me to do that, Joe. I'm well aware of what Sextant does."

"How do you feel about that? Want me to quit? I almost did. I still could."

She turned to him, searching his face. "Oh, Joe. You would never be happy on the beach or behind a desk. It's good that you realized that. But I will admit I'm glad you won't be out there working alone the way you were." She did that little one-shoulder shrug thing. "I sort of know where you were coming from. About the worry thing."

Joe approached her and held out his hand again. She took it and he felt hers tremble slightly. "I was wrong about what I thought I wanted. Except for wanting you."

She smiled up at him, her features barely visible in the semidarkness. "I guess I was, too."

Joe lifted her hands and placed them on his shoulders, felt them slide up to his neck. He closed his eyes and embraced her, holding her as if his very life depended on it. Which it did. He could never let her go again no matter what.

His lips found hers, hungry for the sweet taste of her. He tugged off her cap and pulled at the band confining her hair until the silky strands came free even as he backed her toward the single bed in the corner.

When his mouth left hers, she gasped, ''This…must be breaking every rule…in the book.''

''So they ship us out,'' he growled, nipping at the sweet curve of her neck, inhaling the scent of her subtle perfume. ''I can learn French anywhere. How do I say *Take off these damned clothes?*''

''Enlevez ces vêtements,'' she muttered breathlessly, tugging his belt loose, pushing his pants down over his hips. *''Maintenant!''*

''Yeah, *now*. I know that word.'' He already had her shirt half over her head.

They were laughing helplessly as they fell across the bunk, messing up the military precision of it. He kissed her again, this time with his entire body, glorying in the soft, sweet feel of her beneath him. How had he lived for weeks without this? He hadn't lived, he'd only existed.

''Oh, Joe,'' she sighed, opening to him in every way as he sank into her with a groan of deep relief.

Instead of rushing to completion this time, he desperately needed to prolong this, to show her how he valued her, how much he treasured this beautiful connection they shared.

He withdrew slowly, his mouth trailing down the arch of her neck to kiss those remarkable breasts, concentrating on the fascinating surface of the pebbled peaks against his tongue.

Her cry of pleasure seemed to go straight to his groin,

urging him to reenter her and assuage his greed, but he held back. Determined, he slid downward, raking his teeth gently over the curve of her waist.

She moaned something in what he thought might be French, causing him to smile against her abdomen and go lower still. His hands encompassed her breasts, alternately brushing lightly and giving her what she wanted. She tasted exotic, wildly erotic, a blend of sweetness and woman.

He hummed with the pleasure of it and felt her first tremor of completion. No way could he resist. With speed to rival the lightning in the sky outside, he moved up and over her to share it.

Thunder ripped through him, shook the building and the bed. The sky opened and torrents lashed against the window while his heart pounded just as hard. Joe thought he might never experience a storm again without climaxing no matter where he was.

They lay, replete and entwined, silently savoring the aftermath. Joe just wanted to hold on to the moment, though he knew they still had a lot to resolve. Martine might be willing to give him more than this, but he wasn't yet sure about that. Maybe all she wanted was occasional sex. She had never actually said that she loved him.

He had to know. He raised up on one elbow and looked down at her. The storm had moved on and the afternoon sun was peeking through the clouds, its weak, slanted rays gently illuminating the room with errant streaks of light. One fell across Martine.

Her eyes were closed, her long lashes like small perfect fans. Her lips looked full, a result of thorough kissing and recent arousal. The sunlight highlighted her features and the folds of white on the pillowcase, the rumpled sheet that he had drawn up to her shoulders.

"Oh, God," he murmured, his former vision of her all in white replaying itself in his mind.

Her eyes flew open. "What is it?"

Joe swallowed hard, tremendous relief all tangled up with disappointment. "At least you aren't dead."

She looked confused and also a little amused. "No. You stunned me but I'm still breathing. You were great, but let's not overestimate your effect."

"But you aren't a bride, either," he muttered.

She shrugged. "No. No, I'm not. What's all this about, Joe?"

"I had a vision of you all in white, surrounded by it. And I think this is…what I saw," he said, pointing at her swathed in the white sheet, the pillow bunched beneath her head, unwilling at the moment to go into an explanation of his so-called gift. "I didn't know what it meant at the time."

"Will you marry me, Joe?"

Elation shot through him. "You want to? Really?"

She shrugged, a slight smile playing about her mouth. "I guess we'd better."

Then he realized what she might mean. They *had* had unprotected sex on the boat. And again just now. Damn, that would screw up all her plans. At least for now. "You're pregnant?"

She laughed, wiping the frown off his face with a sweep of her finger. "No, it's not that."

"Then why?"

With one hand behind his neck, she pulled him down for a kiss. When she released him, she answered, "Because if you're going to retain a vision of me in your head, I want it to be one where my hair's combed. Why do you *think*, Joe? I love you."

"You never said," he accused.

"I'm saying now," she replied, teasing his bottom lip with her finger. "But before you make an honest woman of me, I'd like at least one more adventure as a single girl if you don't mind."

"Anything you want," he promised, grasping her to him and hugging her hard. *Adventure?* "What?"

He knew that tentative question had probably betrayed his fear that she would insist on going with him on the next mission or something equally risky. It would be just like her to demand that.

"I'd like to break some Academy rules again," she said, wriggling against him to make her intentions clear.

"Maintenant?" he asked, just to show her he'd been paying attention to her very brief but effective lesson. He was already rising to her expectations.

"Oh yeah, Corda. *Right* now."

"That would be *tout suite!* Hmm? Oh yeah, *all* my French is coming back to me now."

Her laughter was like the bright sunshine now permeating his quarters and his heart like a blessing.

Epilogue

"**D**ammit, I *knew* this would happen," Joe grumbled as they danced around the polished oak floors of Christa's. The old pub's oak and brass fittings were buffed to a high shine and gleamed with old world charm. Joe had rented the whole place for the evening and a judge friend of Clay's had performed the ceremony.

"Ah, don't tell me. You had a flash of me dressed in French couture?" The laughter in her voice was hard to resist.

He kissed her, still moving to the strains of the Righteous Brothers' "Unchained Melody," compliments of Christa's old-fashioned jukebox.

Earlier, as Martine and he had said their vows, Joe realized this, their wedding day, was only the second time he had ever seen Martine in a dress. That simple little black number back in Atlanta had been racy, but this...

She was gorgeous when barefaced, sporting jungle fatigues or that asexual getup she wore on the job. Dressed in this ultra-feminine, slinky, ivory satin number that looked like star-stuff out of a thirties movie, her hair and makeup perfect, she just blew him away. That was probably the whole idea, stunning him into compliance. Unfortunately, it might be working. He dipped her, just to get her off balance for a minute.

It wasn't that he didn't want to be with her. He sure didn't want to postpone their honeymoon. But Martine coming to France with the team on this mission seemed to be tempting fate. They had waited until just after the ceremony to tell him. "Language advisor, huh? This is a misuse of power or nepotism or something equally illegal, I bet, contracting a family member. Mercier will flip when he finds out Holly requested you for this."

"No, we weren't married when the Bureau approved it. And from what she tells me, Jack's in no position to object at the moment." She dropped her voice to a whisper. "He's in jail."

"Shh." He goosed her waist for emphasis, sliding his fingers over that special curve. "Remember where we are. And why we're here."

It was a small, private affair, owing to the speedy arrangements. Their immediate families had flown up for the ceremony and all the members of Sextant were there except for Jack, who was already in France, setting up the mission.

"So what's your role?" he asked with a resigned sigh, accepting the inevitable.

"I'm to be the cover." She pretended to preen, tossing her sunny mane and looking smug. "Wealthy author incognito and her entourage."

Joe released her long enough to twirl her around. "I'll be your bodyguard." Whether she wanted him to or not. From what he'd been told about this gig, they could be dodging worse than bullets. Joe wasn't sure that even he could protect her from what they might be facing.

"Nope," she informed him with a saucy grin. "Will's the bodyguard."

"I'm your driver?" He executed a turn expertly as his mother had taught him all those years ago when preparing him for the prom, then drew her close and slow danced like the randiest teenager.

"Sorry, Eric's the chauffeur," she said, one ice-pink nail tickling his neck just above his collar. "And Holly's my secretary. She has it all worked out."

"Then what am I, your cook?"

She giggled, a lovely throaty sound that stirred his insides. "You're my Latin lover, my boy toy! Can you handle it, Corda?"

He kissed her ear. "Typecasting if I ever heard it. Let's go buy Holly a drink."

She laughed out loud, her head back, her eyes shining up at him. The effect nearly caused him to step on her feet.

"Quit trying to lead, Mrs. Corda," Joe warned.

"Only for this dance, Joe," she promised, her laughter subsiding. "This one last dance." They both knew she was referring to the decision she had made without him.

"And after France?" he asked, praying there would *be* an after.

"The world will be a little safer for our children," she said as the music faded. She touched his brow. "Close your eyes, Joe, and tell me what you see."

He didn't need a vision. "Us. Together forever. Whatever comes."

* * * * *

Live life to the full - give in to temptation

Four new sparkling and sassy romances every month!

Be the first to read this fabulous new series from 1st December 2010 at **millsandboon.co.uk** In shops from 1st January 2011

Tell us what you think!
Facebook.com/romancehq
Twitter.com/millsandboonuk

Don't miss out!

Available at WHSmith, Tesco, ASDA, Eason and all good bookshops

www.millsandboon.co.uk

& RIVA™

With This Fling...
by Kelly Hunter
Charlotte Greenstone's convenient, fictional fiancé *inconveniently* resembles sexy stranger Greyson Tyler! Grey agrees to keep Charlotte's secret as long as they enjoy *all* the benefits of a real couple...

Girls' Guide to Flirting with Danger
by Kimberly Lang
When the media discover that marriage counsellor Megan Lowe is the ex-wife of an infamous divorce attorney, Megan has to take the plunge and face her dangerously sexy ex.

Juggling Briefcase & Baby
by Jessica Hart
A weekend working with his ex, Romy, and her baby, Freya, has corporate genius Lex confused. Opposites they may be, but Lex's attraction to happy-go-lucky Romy seems to have grown stronger with the years...

Deserted Island, Dreamy Ex
by Nicola Marsh
Starring in an island-based TV show sounded blissful, until Kristi discovered her Man Friday was her ex, Jared Malone. Of course, she doesn't feel *anything* for him, but can't help hoping he'll like her new bikini...

On sale from 7th January 2011
Don't miss out!

Available at WHSmith, Tesco, ASDA, Eason and all good bookshops

www.millsandboon.co.uk

"Did you say I won almost two million dollars?"

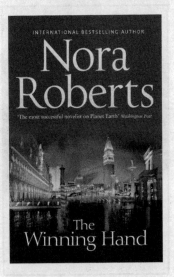

Down to her last ten dollars in a Las Vegas casino, Darcy Wallace gambled and won!

Suddenly the small-town girl was big news— and needing protection. Robert MacGregor Blade, the casino owner, was determined to make sure Darcy could enjoy her good fortune. But Darcy knew what she wanted; Mac himself. Surely her luck was in?

Available 3rd December 2010

www.millsandboon.co.uk

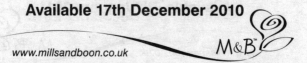

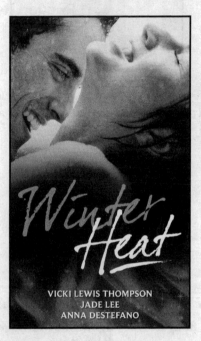
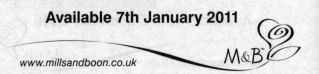